DAUGHTERS OF DARKNESS

Daughters of Darkness

LESBIAN VAMPIRE STORIES

Edited by

PAM KEESEY

CLEIS
PRESS

Published in the United States by Cleis Press Inc.,
P.O. Box 8933, Pittsburgh, Pennsylvania 15221, and
P.O. Box 14684, San Francisco, California 94114

Book design and production: Pete Ivey
Cover photograph: Phyllis Christopher
Cleis logo art: Juana Alicia

Printed in the United States of America
10 9 8 7 6 5 4 3 2

Grateful acknowledgment is made to the following for permission to reprint
previously published material: Excerpt from *Daughter of the Night* by Elaine
Bergstrom is reprinted by permission of The Berkley Publishing Group,
copyright © 1992 by Elaine Bergstrom; "Oh, Captain, My Captain" by
Katherine V. Forrest is reprinted with the kind permission of the author and
publisher from *Dreams and Swords*, Naiad Press, 1987; "Louisiana: 1850" by
Jewelle Gomez originally appeared in *The Gilda Stories*, Firebrand Books,
Ithaca, New York 14850, copyright © 1991 by Jewelle Gomez; excerpt from
Virago by Karen Marie Christa Minns, Naiad Press, 1990, is reprinted with
the kind permission of the author and publisher; excerpt from *I, Vampire* by
Jody Scott is reprinted by permission of The Berkeley Publishing Group,
copyright © 1984 by Jody Scott; excerpt from *Minimax* by Anna Livia is
reprinted with the permission of Eighth Mountain Press; "Lilith" by Robbi
Sommers is reprinted with the kind permission of the author and publisher
from *Pleasures*, Naiad Press, 1989; an earlier version of "dracula retold" by
zana first appeared in *Feminary*, Spring 1981 (under the name Marilyn
Woodsea); the current version first appeared in *Lesbian Bedtime Stories*, ed.
Terry Woodrow, Tough Dove Press 1989.

Library of Congress Cataloging in Publication Data
Daughters of Darkness : lesbian vampire stories / edited by Pam Keesey.
    p. cm.
    Includes bibliographical references.
    ISBN 0-939416-77-8 : $24.95. —
    ISBN 0-939416-78-6 (pbk.) : $9.95
    1. Vampires—Fiction. 2. Lesbians' writings, American. 3. Horror
tales, American. 4. Lesbians—Fiction. I. Keesey, Pam, 1964–
PS648.V35D38 1993
813' .0108375—dc20   93-5759
                                                  CIP

Contents

INTRODUCTION 7
Pam Keesey

DRACULA RETOLD 19
zana

I, VAMPIRE 23
Jody Scott

CARMILLA 27
J. Sheridan LeFanu

DAUGHTER OF THE NIGHT 89
Elaine Bergstrom

LOUISIANA: 1850 97
Jewelle Gomez

LILITH 137
Robbi Sommers

VIRAGO 149
Karen Marie Christa Minns

THE VAMPIRE 167
Pat Califia

O CAPTAIN, MY CAPTAIN 185
Katherine V. Forrest

MINIMAX 229
Anna Livia

Filmography/Bibliography 237

Introduction

Pam Keesey

My first contact with the world of lesbian vampires was in 1983. I went to see *The Hunger* at a local theater. I really didn't know much about the film; I knew it was a vampire movie starring David Bowie. Imagine my surprise as I watched the cool, alluring, and sophisticated Catherine Deneuve seduce Susan Sarandon there before my very eyes and on a very, very big screen. The two of them were making love in the most graphic and most erotic portrayal of lesbianism I had ever seen.

The Hunger certainly wasn't my first vampire movie. As a child, I loved watching the Saturday afternoon "Creature Feature." As a teenager, I stayed up until all hours to watch late-night vampire movies. In college, I dragged friends to out-of-the-way movie houses to see the occasional showing of old and/or foreign vampire films. By the time I saw *The Hunger*, I knew my interest in vampires was more than a passing phase. What I didn't know, sitting there in the dark with my boyfriend by my side, was that *he* was a passing phase, and that this Hollywood vampire movie would have much more of an impact on my future than I could, at that time, have possibly imagined.

My quest for lesbian vampire lore didn't occur until much, much later. I was taking a gothic literature class and decided that the topic for my final paper had to be something fun. My interest in vampires had been piqued once again by Jewelle Gomez's lesbian vampire novel *The Gilda Stories*. Like any good vampirologist (that's what they called Peter Cushing in all those great Hammer vampire movies), I began my search in earnest. What I discovered was a wealth of lesbian vampire lore much older and much more diverse than anything I had expected. The book you hold in your hands is the fruit of that research.

Female vampires have a long and varied history. Vampires have long been the favorite representation of "bad" women. Vampires are not only the supernatural creatures that haunt the night in search of blood; according to the *Random House Dictionary*, the vampire is also the woman who "unscrupulously exploits, ruins, or destroys the men she seduces." She is the "vamp."

The first vampires are equated with the destructive side of the goddess. In the best of circumstances, vampires are, like goddesses, associated with cycles of life, death, and rebirth. More often than not, however, vampires are associated with blood and death and dangerous sexuality, again aspects of the goddess. These characteristics, as interpreted from a more oppressive point of view, are the characteristics that are today most closely associated with vampires.

This representation of the goddess as vampire is, in part, tied to the rise of the Judeo-Christian influence in the West and the dichotomous vision of the world which this belief espoused. Goddesses embodied all that was evil in Judeo-Christian philosophy: they were female, sexual, pagan, and embraced death as part of the cycle of life. These women were not holy; these women were monsters.

Adam's original wife, Lilith, and his second wife, Eve, are both considered to be foremothers of today's female vampire. Like the goddesses of ancient history, Lilith and Eve were female and sexual. They defied patriarchal society, and when punished, they rebelled. They also are associated with blood, "excessive" sexuality, and at times, as in the case of Lilith, with child-eating. According to the Talmud, Lilith argued with Adam over his authority and left him. As punishment for her "sins," her children were destroyed. Lilith later returned—immortal, undead, and vengeful, according to the Biblical stories—to kill Eve's children.

In Assyrian and Babylonian traditions, the female vampire roams the night in search of the blood of young children. In Greek mythology, she is Lamia, who bore Zeus's children only to have them be killed by a jealous Hera; in revenge, Lamia wanders the earth killing as many children as possible. In India, female vampires haunt crossroads, a familiar location in vampire lore, and drink the blood of elephants. In Japan, the Vampire Cat of Nabeshima attacks people and sucks blood from their necks—an interesting association, as cats are the familiars of both witches and female vampires.

It is particularly interesting to note that when a female vampire isn't mature or sophisticated enough to rely on sexuality to lure prey, she must hunt children and/or animals for her sustenance.

Vampires of both sexes were associated with excessive sexuality. The female vampire is sexual and seductive, a creature of great appetites. She is irresistible to both men and women. She is so closely associated with women's sexual and social improprieties, it's no wonder that the female vampire came to be equated with the lesbian in the sexually repressive atmosphere of nineteenth century Europe. The female vampire is she who steps outside the realm of acceptable "feminine" behavior.

The appearance of lesbian vampires in nineteenth century English romantic literature clearly condemns homosexual love between women. Samuel Taylor Coleridge's poem "Christabel," published in 1817, relies heavily on vampire imagery. Christabel first meets Geraldine in an abandoned wood late on a dark night under a full moon. Christabel invites Geraldine to stay at her family's castle home; however, Geraldine is unable to cross the threshold until she is assisted by Christabel. The family dog is wary of the guest; the embers in the fireplace blaze as Geraldine passes. Geraldine weakens at the sight of a Christian icon, a carved cherub in Christabel's bedroom.

Of particular interest is what happens once Geraldine enters Christabel's bed chamber. Christabel decants a bottle of elderflower wine, wine that was given to her by her now dead mother to be saved for her wedding night. Geraldine undresses Christabel, and then undresses herself. Geraldine bares her breasts, a sight that Christabel describes as "one to dream of, not to tell," after which Geraldine approaches Christabel, stirring in Christabel a "desire with loathing strangely mix'd." She knows that touching Geraldine's "bosom" is somehow dangerous and forbidden, but it is a temptation she can't resist.

The next morning, Christabel awakes, feeling ashamed of what took place during the night. She doesn't know if she dreamed the act (the "act" is never described in the poem) of which she is ashamed, or if the act did indeed take place. Nowhere in the poem does any actual bloodletting happen. However, Christabel is clearly drained of her vitality by Geraldine. She becomes weak and lethargic. As Christabel weakens, Geraldine becomes stronger, brighter and more refreshed. In the end, Geraldine abandons Christabel.

The most famous and influential lesbian vampire story, "Carmilla" (1871), was an attempt by Irish writer J. Sheridan LeFanu to render Coleridge's poem into prose. LeFanu was a popular author, editor, and publisher who lived in Dublin in the middle nineteenth century. He is well known for his supernatural fiction, the most famous collection being *In a Glass Darkly*, in which "Carmilla" was first published.

"Carmilla" is the story of Millarca Karnstein, a young woman of aristocratic lineage with pale, luminous skin, dark hair, and a cat-like appearance. Using the name Carmilla, she "befriends" Laura, the young heroine of the story, proclaiming herself in love with her. Laura soon becomes ill, completely sapped of her energy and vitality by Carmilla's all-consuming "love."

Carmilla's "vamping" (the term often used to describe a vampire's hunt) of Laura is really a tale of seduction. In the novella, Laura describes her dreams, in which "there came a sensation as if a hand was drawn softly along my cheek and neck. Sometimes it was as if warm lips kissed me, and longer and more lovingly as they reached my throat." The sexual nature of these dreams becomes even more apparent as the dream goes on. Her heart beats faster, her breathing becomes heavy. She begins a sob that becomes a "sense of strangulation...turned into a dreadful convulsion," after which Laura feels her senses leave her. When Carmilla eventually enters Laura's room in physical form, she does so in the form of a cat. She then bites Laura, sucking her blood not from the throat, as in later vampire stories, but from veins in the breast. The eroticism of sucking breasts is particularly bold, especially for a Victorian audience. Not until the soft-porn vampire films of the sixties and seventies would the sexual elements of the legend be portrayed so frankly.

Our modern image of the vampire is so heavily bound to the vampire created by Bram Stoker and personified by legendary actors such as Bela Lugosi and Christopher Lee, that it is perhaps no surprise that most people have never heard of Geraldine or Carmilla. Popular mythology has it that the character of Dracula is based on a Hungarian prince by the name of Vlad Dracula who was a hero of the Hungarian wars against the Turks.

Vlad Dracula was born in 1430 or 1431. His father, also named Vlad, had been awarded the Order of the Dragon by the King of Hungary for his "valor in battle" against the Turks. *Draco* is Latin for dragon. Vlad the Elder came to be known as Vlad the Dragon, or Vlad Dracul. Dracula is the diminutive of Dracul, and Vlad's son came to be known as Vlad Dracula. He was also known as Vlad Tepes or Vlad the Impaler, as his favorite form of torture and execution was to impale people on long stakes. Vlad Dracula used his army to force the Turkish troops back from the Balkans, thereby impeding the expansion of the Ottoman Empire into Europe. After the Turkish armies retreated, Dracula continued to impale the local populace in large numbers as a way of ensuring law and order. Dracula was eventually forced from his throne by the King of Hungary. He died under mysterious circumstance in or around 1476.

Although Stoker's vampire bears the name Dracula, there is reason to believe that the activities that take place in the novel are actually based on the life of Elizabeth Bathory, a Hungarian countess of the sixteenth century brought to trial for the torture and murder of between one hundred fifty and six hundred fifty young women and girls. Bathory's castle was raided one day in December of 1610, after she came under suspicion of being connected to the disappearance of a number of young women of aristocratic lineage from neighboring villages. The raiding party found the body of one dead girl before the door of the manor house, and the bodies of two more were found inside.

Introduction

In *Dracula Was a Woman: In Search of the Blood Countess of Tran-sylvania*, Raymond McNally, Professor of Russian and East European Studies at Boston College and a specialist in the Dracula legend, outlines his reason for believing that the literary Count Dracula is based on the historical figure of the Countess Bathory:

> After having written four books revolving around the historical Dracula, the Dracula novel, and vampirism, I was reasonably certain that I had succeeded in unearthing most of the facts on the subject of Count Dracula. However, I continued to be haunted by several unanswered questions: There were no associations between the historical Vlad Dracula, know as "The Impaler" (1431–1476), and any acts of blood drinking either in the documents or in the Romanian folklore, so how did Bram Stoker, author of the novel *Dracula*, come to make Count Dracula into a drinker of human blood...? The historical Dracula, about whom Stoker knew a great deal, was actually a prince, so why did Stoker present him merely as a count? Vlad Dracula was Romanian, not a Hungarian, so in the novel, why is Count Dracula portrayed as a member of an ancient Hungarian race tracing a bloodline all the way back to Attila the Hun...? And where did Stoker get the idea of presenting the count as looking younger after he had imbibed human blood, a notion not prevalent in folklore? Furthermore, there is a great deal of eroticism in the novel, yet little in the life of the historical Vlad Dracula—from where did this eroticism come?

McNally finds the answers to these and other questions in his study of the Countess Bathory.

Elizabeth Bathory was of an aristocratic family, closely related to the kings and princes of Hungary. She was the widow of Count Ferenc Nadasdy, a powerful and influential hero of the wars against the Turks. The Count had loaned a considerable sum of money to the crown to help finance these wars. Upon his death, the Crown's debt was transferred to his widow, the Countess.

The Countess Bathory presents an interesting and horrifying historical character. Trial records confirm that the countess and her accomplices killed an extraordinary number of young women after having tortured them, and it was said that these murders gave her a certain erotic pleasure. The victims were often stripped naked, and most were bled. There were also rumors that she bathed in the blood of her victims. After the Countess's trial ended, her accomplices were executed and she was imprisoned for life in her own castle. She died, never having shown any remorse nor admitting she was guilty of any wrongdoing, in her castle cell in 1615.

There had long been rumors of the Countess's murderous activities, but it wasn't until she began to recruit her servants from the daughters of the lesser nobility that any significant action was taken to investigate her affairs. By this time, it was in the Crown's best interest to charge the Countess with criminal activity. Not only would it put the Crown in a good light for having taken action on the suspicions raised by the lesser nobility of the region. It would also mean that the Crown would be free of the debt owed the Countess if she were to be found guilty of such a felony. McNally suggests that these political considerations formed the basis for arresting and trying the Countess Bathory for the murder of her servants, not moral or ethical concerns.

Because the case was of such significance to the Crown and because the defendant was an aristocrat of such influential stature, the trial records are quite detailed and have been carefully preserved. McNally draws heavily on these records for making his case that Bram Stoker's *Dracula* is based on the life of the Countess.

The most pervasive legend concerning Bathory is that she murdered these young women in order to bathe in their blood and thereby retain her youth. Legend has it that one day a servant girl was brushing Bathory's hair and accidently yanked a snarl, pulling the Countess's hair. The Countess responded by turning around and smacking the girl across the face, causing her nose to bleed. The blood spurted from the girl's nose onto Bathory's hand. When the Countess wiped the blood away, she swore the area on her hand that had been covered by blood looked younger and healthier. From then on, she insisted upon bathing in the blood of young women to retain her youth and her beauty. Despite the tenacity of this legend, McNally finds no evidence in the trial records to indicate that such bathing took place, or that Bathory was even accused of using the blood for such a purpose. There is evidence, however, that Bathory did indeed bite the flesh of certain young women in her service. McNally describes one incident that took place while the Countess was sick and in bed:

> Elizabeth turned and twisted in her sick bed madly in convulsive contortions. She demanded that one of her female servants be brought before her. Dorothea Szentes, a burly, strong peasant woman, dragged one of Elizabeth's girls to her bedside and held her there. Elizabeth rose up on her bed, and, like a bulldog, the Countess opened her mouth and bit the girl first on the cheek. Then she went for the girl's shoulders where she ripped out a

piece of flesh with her teeth. After that, Elizabeth proceeded to bite the girl's breasts.

Years of intermarriage among European aristocratic family lines, family illness, and the indulgences allowed those born into positions of power were fairly evident within the Bathory line. McNally notes that "[o]ne of Elizabeth's uncles was reputedly addicted to rituals and worship in honor of Satan, her aunt Klara was a well-known bisexual and lesbian who enjoyed torturing servants, and Elizabeth's brother, Stephan, was a drunkard and a lecher." Widespread and recurring epilepsy, mental illness, and other physical and psychological disturbances were evident in private family letters.

The frequent references to Bathory's sexual preference and her associations with cross-dressing are particularly interesting, especially in light of the use of her character in the later development of the lesbian vampire image. Her Aunt Klara was a well-known lesbian, and Elizabeth herself liked to "dress in men's clothes and play men's games." Also, at a trial held on January 7, 1611, two witnesses testified that a chambermaid who had survived the tortures told them that "much of the bloodshedding was carried out by the Countess herself with the help of a woman dressed up as a man." Despite all of the lesbian and bisexual activity associated with Elizabeth Bathory and her counterparts, there is little suggestion in the transcripts of the trials or in the ensuing reports of her life, prosecution, and death that correlate her being lesbian or bisexual with her murderous activities.

Countess Bathory's obsession with torture, pain, and death has been transformed by Argentine poet Alejandra Pizarnik into a collection of vignettes entitled *The Bloody Countess* (1971) that leave the reader with a particularly disturbing chill. In Pizarnik's haunting prose, the Countess is a detached, often bored, observer of the torture that takes place under her order. Although *The Bloody Countess* is not a vampire tale as such, it includes many of the same themes, including an obsession with blood, lust and sexuality. Pizarnik was herself associated with lesbianism both in her personal life and in her poetry, although she never "came out" publicly. She committed suicide in 1972, and *The Bloody Countess* has since become an underground Argentine classic.

Both Carmilla and the Countess Bathory have inspired a sub-genre of their own. What might be called a Golden Age of lesbian vampire movies occurred in the early 1970s. As many as twenty different vampire movies with lesbian themes were made by a variety of independent, international film studios between 1970 and 1974 alone. The lesbian vampire characters in *Countess Dracula, Daughters of Darkness,* and *The Night of the Walpurgis* are all directly based on the Countess, while Carmilla is the basis for the Hammer Studios lesbian vampire trilogy (known as "The Karnstein Trilogy"), which includes *Vampire Lovers, Lust for a Vampire,* and *Twins of Evil.*

Daughters of Darkness, a film directed by Harry Kumel, provides another example of a lesbian vampire who has been reappropriated by a lesbian audience. The story revolves around a young couple on their honeymoon who stop at a large Belgian hotel on their way to meet the groom's "mother." There they meet the Countess Bathory, an elegant and stylish woman, and her beautiful and subservient female companion. As the story develops, the young man turns out to be a sadist whose "mother" is an aging male homosexual transvestite. The Countess, aware of the young man's sadism and the young woman's vulnerability, seduces the bride and the two women together later kill her husband. Bonnie Zimmerman, in a review of the movie appearing in *Jump Cut,* suggests that the "negative aspects of the vampire stereotype [in *Daughters of Darkness*] are mitigated...when the viewer is herself a lesbian and [a] feminist." She describes *Daughters of Darkness* as depicting lesbianism as "attractive," and heterosexuality as "abnormal and ineffectual."

Zimmerman discusses the importance of the lesbian vampire in her book, *The Safe Sea of Women: Lesbian Fiction 1969–1989:*

> Different examples [of the lesbian in fiction] written by both lesbians and nonlesbians [fix] upon the otherness of the lesbian, primarily in the shape of the glamorous and dangerous vampire....
> In self-defense, if for no other reason, we claim alienation as superiority and specialness, and glorify the status of the [lesbian] outlaw...a creature of tooth and claw, of passion and purpose: unassimilable, awesome, dangerous, outrageous, different: distinguished.

Even though lesbians have figured as central and crucial characters in these and other movies, they were presented in a less than positive light. More often than not, images of lesbian vampires reinforced anti-woman and anti-lesbian stereotypes. For a long time, however, these vampires were some of the few lesbian images available to a mainstream audience. And lesbian audiences claimed those vampires, reinterpreting the stories to reflect their own experiences. Gene Damon, describing "Carmilla" to a lesbian audience in *The Ladder,* refers to Carmilla as "no more and no less than a very clever young woman determined to run off with the girl of her choice...."

With the growing market for lesbian literature, many lesbians have taken the leap from reinterpreting traditional lesbian vampire stories to reinventing them. In her article "Writing Vampire Fiction," Jewelle Gomez comments, "I feel I can remake mythology as well as anyone...I was certain I could create a mythology to express who I am as a black lesbian feminist." Her effort to recast the myth of the vampire resulted in one of the least traditional and most innovative vampire stories to appear in recent years, *The Gilda Stories.*

Even though lesbians are writing and publishing lesbian vampire stories, it is still difficult to find those stories represented in more mainstream vampire anthologies. This is a great pity, not only because of the wealth and breadth of lesbian vampire stories, and the unique and original ways lesbians are using vampire lore to recast the myth, but also because of the crucial historical role the lesbian vampire has played in the development of vampire lore. Clearly this is another case of discovering lesbian "herstory."

Choosing the stories and movies [see the filmography at the end of this book] that would be included in this anthology created a somewhat interesting dilemma—how to distinguish between a lesbian or bisexual vampire and a vampire that simply does not differentiate between male and female prey. This proved especially difficult in regard to the movies. Although many of these movies are readily available on video, a good number of them, especially the foreign films, are still relatively difficult to find. I also found that although many of the characters in these movies are unmistakeably lesbian, the films were made by men for a predominantly straight male audience. You'll often find that scenes between women are constructed for a male "gaze" (who is that guy on the horse in *Vampire Lovers*, anyway?). Also important to note is that many of these films were made at a time when studios were directly challenging film censorship standards, creating an environment for portrayals of graphic sexual activity among and between everyone who happened to be in the film.

The filmography includes films with female vampires who actively engage in ongoing one-to-one relationships with other women—as well as films that make direct references to Countess Bathory or Carmilla. The one exception is *Dracula's Daughter*, a 1936 sequel to the classic 1932 *Dracula* starring Bela Lugosi. Countess Zaleska's female victim can only be classified as a one-night stand, but by the standards of 1936, her meeting with the young model is much more erotically charged than any of her encounters with men.

The bibliography includes all resources I was able to find that deal with lesbian vampires. There is so much available dealing with vampires and vampire lore, and a whole other sub-genre that deals with exclusively gay male vampires, that there is no way that this bibliography could ever be exhaustive.

The stories included in this anthology, like the movies, involve female vampires who have sought out one-to-one relationships with other women. Most of the stories are written by lesbians who are writing for a primarily lesbian audience, although this certainly isn't the case for all of them. Some of the stories are funny, others are highly erotic. More than a few deal openly with the most pervasive of all vampire themes, the point at which the lines between sexuality and violence become blurred.

"dracula retold" by zana is a retelling of Bram Stoker's tale. This time Lucy rather than Mina is married to Jonathan Harker. Lucy, bored with the life of a suburban housewife, chooses her vampire life, leaves her husband for lesbian land, and changes her name to "amazonclitwoman." In Jody Scott's vampire sci-fi comedy, Sterling O'Blivion is a "born that way" vampire whose family has always known that she had "it"—"the defective gene that runs through [her] family... something that terrified others, but was minor, natural, and even quite pleasant as far as [she] was concerned."

"Carmilla" is the only story in this anthology written by a man. Written during the height of the Victorian era, its underlying message is one of fear of female sexuality and warnings against affections between women. *The Ladder*, the publication of the vanguard lesbian organization The Daughters of Bilitis, referred to "Carmilla" as "a sub-basement lesbian classic." What would have happened if Laura hadn't been taught to fear her own sexuality? What then would have become of the story of Laura and Carmilla?

Elaine Bergstrom's *Daughter of the Night* is from another literary tradition. Her novel is more mainstream, directed at a general rather than a specifically lesbian or feminist audience. Bergstrom takes the gruesome history of Elizabeth Bathory and turns her into a somewhat sympathetic character, a sort of mythic half-breed in need of the love and understanding only her own kind can give.

In "Louisiana: 1850," Jewelle Gomez creates Gilda, a vampire that defies all vampire stereotypes. Gilda is black, lesbian, and feminist. She escapes the oppression of slavery after she loses the only thing of value she had left to lose: her mother. In doing so, Gilda embarks on a vampiric quest that is also a search for a family and a sense of place, and for a love that is the basis for a true sense of belonging in the world.

In Robbi Sommers's "Lilith" and Karen Marie Christa Minn's *Virago*, we see the more traditional evil vampire. "Lilith" is set in the dark streets and mythic underside of New Orleans. Lilith is the namesake of Adam's Judaic first wife, but her passions are of a decidedly different nature. Minn's vampire Darsen is truly wicked, representing a darker side of human existence. Darsen preys rather than loves, but also shows a marked preference for other females.

Pat Califia's "The Vampire" is another vampire story set in the deeper realms of human existence. Califia couples the repressed sexuality of the Bram Stoker tradition with the violence of the vampire mythos and creates a wholly new vampire whose lusts leave the reader questioning the true nature of vampirism.

Katherine V. Forrest's "Oh Captain, My Captain" is an erotic science fiction vampire tale. The enigmatic and solitary Captain Drake is the chief officer of the spacecraft *Scorpio IV* and has a preference for female military liaisons. She, like the vampires before her, must feed to survive. But she has discovered a sustenance more vital to her than blood.

Last but not least is an excerpt from Anna Livia's comic fantasy *Minimax*, a tale in which the vampires are the infamous turn-of-the-century lesbians Renée Vivien and Natalie Barney, and the vampire hunters are right–wing vampirophobes. The vampire hunters have used legislation to outlaw vampirism as an acceptable alternative lifestyle, using language that is remarkably reminiscent of the British anti-gay and lesbian legislation that outlawed the use of public funds to "promote" homosexuality as an acceptable alternative lifestyle. In *Minimax*, society is trying to force vampires back into the closet.

1996 is the centennial of the publication of Bram Stoker's *Dracula*. There will surely be some commemoration of this most famous vampire. But there is more to the vampire family tree, a family that includes sisters, mothers, aunts and other woman-identified women who have been the proverbial "skeletons in the closet." It is important to remember the crucial role of lesbian "herstory" in the development of the vampire myth.

Pulling this anthology together has really been more fun than work, more adventure than toil. And I can't tell you how many vampire fans I have met along the way. Superstition has it that you must invite a vampire to cross the threshold before the vampire can enter. I'd like to invite you to cross this threshold and meet the vampires that await you within.

Pam Keesey

Minneapolis
June 1993

Dracula Retold

ZANA

THIS TALE concerns lucy harker, a young womon of some spunk and intelligence who had nonetheless gotten herself married off to a duddy all-american-boy type named jonathan. it happens, even to the best of us. lucy was young yet, and being a wife was still a bit of an adventure. something new and different, you might say. the wedding was fun, playing house was fun, sex was...well, new and different. after a month of marriage, though, lucy was noticing that most of her days resembled each other closely, and that her adventures were limited to experimenting with recipes from her card file.

one day, while lucy was polishing the plastic fruit, a moving van pulled up next door. through lace curtains, lucy watched with some interest as muscular moving wimin unloaded a number of lavender packing crates.

that evening, when jonathan came home after a hard day of being a real estate agent, lucy inquired if he knew anything about their new neighbor. as a matter of fact, he himself had conducted the house sale and could tell his wife what an eccentric old biddy was going to live there. a foreigner, too—by the name of dracula.

the next day lucy prepared a tray of lemonade and cookies to take over to ms. dracula. she found her neighbor sitting under a shady tree reading a book called *sexual politics*. lucy was a little unnerved at the thought of a womon ms. dracula's age reading books about sex, and she didn't see what sex could have to do with politics, but she politely ignored the book and smiled brightly. ms. dracula smiled back—a slow, warm smile. her deep brown eyes riveted lucy's. the two wimin began to talk, and they talked of cookie recipes, the neighborhood, the institution of marriage, and wimin banding together to smash the patriarchy. it was quite a pleasant afternoon.

that night lucy tossed and turned. not wanting to disturb jonathan, she gathered some blankets and went downstairs to sleep on the couch.

during the wee hours she had a strange dream: a black cat came meowing to the open window...lucy invited it in, and once over the sill it changed form…into a womon…into dracula! but how different she looked! instead of a neat cotton shirt and slacks, she wore a long black velvet garment embroidered in silver with many symbols. her silver hair, which had been twisted in braids around her head, now flew loose and long. lucy was impressed.

and those eyes again—they were mesmerizing. dracula glided over to the couch and bent over lucy, maintaining eye contact the whole time. "woo-ee," thought lucy. "this sure feels real for a dream!"

in the morning jonathan grumbled and sputtered when the alarm kept ringing. lucy was always the one who quickly shut it off and hopped out of bed to fix breakfast, while jonathan grabbed a few more winks. but she was not in bed.

he stumbled downstairs. lucy was sitting on the couch writing in her journal. she didn't look up. she was wearing a light cotton nightgown, but had a wool scarf wrapped around her neck.

"where's breakfast?" jonathan demanded. "and why the hell are you wearing a muffler in the middle of july?"

lucy continued writing for a moment, then glanced up as if her attention had been caught by an interesting bug.

"breakfast? oh, i'm not really hungry so i didn't make any." she fingered the scarf, hiding a smile. "i feel a bit of a chill. maybe i'm coming down with something."

a week later, jonathan consulted a psychiatrist about his wife's continuing queer behavior.

"she wears this scarf constantly," he related. "while she was asleep i pulled it down and found two red dots on her neck. looked like a cat bite."

"*very* interesting!" cried dr. van helsing. "and you say she refuses your sexual advances? hmm-hmm!"

he produced several items from a drawer.

"we're seeing more and more cases like your wife's in this city," van helsing said, "and i think your new neighbor may be at the root of it. here are some items that such wimin find repugnant. you must invite ms. dracula over and test her with these. if she reacts badly, you must kill the evil in her by driving your, uh, stake into her. then both she and your wife will be released from their unnatural compulsions."

jonathan smiled to himself as he left van helsing's office. he'd have his lucy back again, with the good doctor's help.

at jonathan's invitation, dracula appeared at the harker home on saturday night. unfortunately, since lucy had been shunning kitchen duty, the meal consisted of jonathan's grilled cheese sandwiches. with dracula all decked out in black velvet, too.

jonathan wasn't pleased with the warm glances exchanged by his wife and his neighbor, but he hid those feelings under his thickest layer of real-estate-salesman charm.

"won't you lovely ladies come sit awhile in the living room?" he invited. "i'll put some coffee on."

while the water was boiling and as jonathan was trying to figure out the instructions on the instant coffee label, he kept one ear out for what was going on in the next room. one of the items given to him by van helsing was planted there.

"yech!" dracula cried, loud enough that jonathan dropped a coffee cup.

"oh!" lucy gasped as dracula swatted at the copy of *hustler* until it fell off the coffee table in a heap on the floor. "i'm so sorry. i can't imagine where that thing came from!"

they sipped their coffee in awkward silence—jonathan smirking, dracula and lucy looking deep into their cups.

suddenly jonathan jumped to his feet. "would you like a tour of our home, ms. dracula?"

"certainly," she replied smoothly, meeting his sharp gaze with one just as steely. lucy cringed, but dracula laid a calming hand on her arm for a brief moment.

they walked in procession up the maroon-carpeted staircase. in the bedroom, jonathan quickly flung open a closet so that dracula's image was reflected in the door-mirror. in that reflection, her plain velvet gown was covered with odd symbols, and her neatly done-up hair flew wild around her face. aha! a clear case of the hidden perversions that only a mirror could reveal. once more, dr. van helsing was proven correct!

as they left the bedroom, jonathan casually picked up a can of hairspray. dracula shrank back in horror, fleeing as he sprayed her.

"i know your secret!" he shouted, pursuing dracula from room to room. "i'm supposed to drive my stake into you and save lucy and all wimin from your perverted influence!"

just as he cornered her, dracula let out her best cat-in-heat cry. immediately the room filled with wimin wearing flowing purple gowns. as dracula greeted her sisters, jonathan gasped to see that lucy was now floating in lavender swirls instead of her patchwork hostess dress.

jonathan was easily subdued. the wimin formed a circle to decide what should be done with him.

"he knows our secret," began dracula, "and has threatened me grievously. surely we can't let him go free."

"right!" agreed a sister. "for all these centuries you—and some of us, too—have had to keep a low profile because of men like him. i'm damn sick of going around like zombies during the day with our sappy little smiles and shaved legs and bras, working at dumb jobs for peanuts."

"yes," said another sister, "but after sunset we do get to go out looking like ourselves. now we've got our wimin's bars and even a few concerts, and we can always spend a fun evening biting straight wimin and turning them on. let's be careful what we do, so we don't mess up the gains we've made."

"revisionist," grumbled another. "it's about time one of these jerks got what's coming to him, no holds barred. but the point is: we can't just off this turkey. that's male tactics. we wimin have always had a bit more finesse."

well, dear reader, you don't want a transcript of their entire meeting, since it took a good three hours to reach consensus. however, the upshot was that jonathan's karma would be accelerated a tad. through a magic incantation or two, he would find himself in the middle of his next incarnation as a more useful form of life—i.e., a ladybug.

and dracula, having finally found her love of the ages in lucy harker, decided to withdraw from the recruitment end of the political scene. she and lucy (now known as amazonclitwomon) and some of the sisters formed a wimin's community in the countryside. there they are living happily forever and ever after—discussing vegetarianism, non-monogamy, and whether converting all men to ladybugs would upset the ecology.

I, Vampire

JODY SCOTT

"GET OUT!" Papa thundered.

"And go where? And do what?" I howled.

"You are not our daughter. You are a limb of Satan," screamed my fat, pretty little mama.

The uproar went on all night. I had made the childish mistake of confessing to the crime, then retracting the confession, and on and on until they shrieked: "You swore you sucked that priest's blood!"

"I lied! I tell lies; everyone knows that."

Snow had begun to fly, and torches blazed, but my parents were adamant about not letting me back into the house. I'm sure they had been dreading this scene since the day of my birth. Maybe earlier. We all knew in our bones that I, Sterling O'Blivion, had "it," that unspeakable "it"—the defective gene that runs through our family. Something was tragically wrong with me; something that terrified others, but was minor, natural, and even quite pleasant as far as I was concerned.

My old nanny Blescu screamed The Lord's Prayer for hours, crossing herself and rolling her eyes. That nanny used to make dolls for me ("They come to life when you sleep, my little pet," she often told me), and I was her loved one, her adored favorite. But now the crass old hypocrite had gone completely barmy. She held up a crucifix and pleaded with Jesus to kill me on the spot. (Which, I am happy to say, he did not do.)

The most shocking thing was what had happened to my parents' faces. Fear had burnt away every trace of love; indeed, of everything familiar. They looked at me with such cold distaste that I could hardly believe it. They had become like the peasants, certain I was going to perform a ghoulish miracle that would destroy them.

"Papa!" I wheedled. "Please, there's nothing to worry about. You're jumping to conclusions—"

I used every bit of the charm and persuasiveness God had given me (which even then was quite something) and spoke carefully, not wanting to betray myself with the wrong words. "The superstitions are a bit misleading. It's not as bad as it sounds."

Papa's mustache trembled. He wanted to believe me, but the crime was far too disgusting—he couldn't stomach it. He made an irritated gesture with his index and little finger outstretched. It meant I was disowned, of the devil, and should go far away and die and let them forget the Gorgon monster they had spawned. Of course dying was the last thing your correspondent was planning to do.

All this took place seven hundred years ago. Nothing is left of our estate in the town of Sibiu, in Transylvania, except a ghetto which stands on the site today. Actually, one hundred thirty years later, but still bowed with grief, I was in Munich wrestling with plans for a time portal. I longed, absolutely *yearned* to go back and see my dear parents and make things come out right this time.

Yet that eruption of evil, which seems like a week ago, actually happened when I was thirteen. It was well below freezing but Papa told the servants to nail every door shut and drop rocks and boiling water if I tried to climb the bastion, which I had done all through childhood for sport.

Dozens of peasants were up there clicking rosaries and whispering, or throwing aprons over their heads when I stared a little too boldly. To keep myself from crying (because I had lost love, because I saw the handwriting on the wall, because my heart was broken) I stuck out my tongue and chanted, hair tossed back and fists on hips:

Tattletale tit,
Your tongue is going to split,
And every little dog in town
Will have a little bit.

Then, absolutely determined that Papa and Mama must believe my side of the story, I hid in the barn. I was terribly unhappy about no longer being loved, but not a bit guilty. Why should I be? My "crime" was a normal act. God had made me this way. My parents and nanny were the cruel ones, not myself. I figured out a little speech that might convince them, then cried myself to sleep between two warm, friendly cows.

The morning seemed most peaceful after that hideously tortured night. I gazed at the house, its walls rosy-tinted by the dawn, and its spires and turrets capped with fresh snow. I bowed my head and commended my soul to Saint Jude the patron saint of bloodsuckers (wherever did that idea come from? I can't imagine) and with hands clasped, while stared at by several curious ravens, I prayed: *"Omnes gurgites tui et fluctus tui super me transierunt."*

Then I washed in the pig trough, combed my tawny hair, and figured out what words to use.

As I approached the house, a rock or two whizzed past my ear.

"Summon your master, you preposterous, miserable, quivering nincompoops!" I shouted.

I had all the arrogance, all the wild humor, the enormous vitality and scornful cruelty of my race; and the servants adored me for it. Or so they had done, up to now. *Now* they thought me eerie. *Now* I was despised and rejected. But my eye flashed fire, and in a minute came a rattle of locks and squeak of hinges and out rushed Papa and Mama who both looked all puffed and haggard, as if they had slept in separate beds, unwilling to face each other.

I made a courtly bow and said: "Let me stay, and I thank you from my heart. Send me away and the pain of separation will kill me. Either way I bear no malice; indeed, I will love you forever."

It was the absolute truth.

Then…I still don't know how I pulled it off. Papa had been a knight in the last Crusade and was tough and ruthless, but with that sales pitch I had worked out so sincerely in the barn, and which would be called "hard sell" in today's jargon, I convinced him that:

1. The man who said I put him to sleep and sucked his neck was lying. Or partly lying.

2. He was a parish priest, so what? Priests have been known to lie. This one exaggerated my crime. Why? I could only guess it was because of my fine complexion, well-built body, and the certain something I possessed which charmed everyone (including Papa).

3. It was the priest's word against mine. Would they take the word of a baseborn ruffian against an O'Blivion of noble blood?

4. See for yourself, that confessor was alive and kicking. He was fit enough to bring false witness against the innocent. So what was all the screaming about?

The upshot was they let me back in; they were under the wonderful impression that a vampire drains every drop of blood and therefore I couldn't be one. Illogical, but I did not argue.

After that I learned to be sneaky enough not to get caught in the act for a whole year, although I did "it" every chance I got, being hungry—O! so ravenous—in those wild, wonderful, windy young years. And I scanned the night skies constantly from my small window under the eaves.

It was then I became absolutely certain and positive that one fine day a woman from the stars was going to land in our pasture. She'd be piloting a beautifully crafted starship. And wearing fantastic star-clothing. And we would fall deeply, passionately in love; because she, unlike everyone here in Sibiu, didn't care a rap about my "evil nature."

Then we'd zoom off in her galactic cruiser and have thrilling adventures on strange worlds, with plenty of swordplay and romance, and we would couple ourselves for love, and live happily ever after.

It's now the tail end of the twentieth century and I'm still waiting. Where are you, my light-of-wonder? This is Sterling O'Blivion sitting at her desk at the Max Arkoff Studio of Dance in Chicago. For you, soulmate and lustrous starwoman, I've kept myself alive and gorgeous (by tooth and claw! I might add, and don't you ever forget it; for after that night came a wild, savage hand-to-mouth existence that it sickens me to remember) for the better part of the millennium.

Haunted by shadows, but unbowed.

The logic of my nature tells me "something terrible is going to happen." Swift as the storm-blast, destiny comes full circle; warning signals are flashing. I'm having premonitions and the weirdest dreams. A part of me longs to break free, not only of the wheel of life and death but of my "compulsion." Not that it hasn't been a joy and a delight, after the first shock.

I'd never knock vampirism. Without it I'd be nothing, less than nothing, a bag of bones in some European crypt. My compulsion is all that sets me above the ruck of women: that scent of conquest, the noble chase, a game of wits, figuring out how I can penetrate and feast without getting my neck broken. And then the thrill of victory forever new, the ritualized ecstasy as I master the unconscious victim and at long last that slow, marvelous caress on the tongue as the Ruby slips down my throat...

Ough! Just thinking of it makes my heart pound like a triphammer.

I adore being a vampire. I love the lore, history, rich tradition and sense of fabulous majesty it confers upon an otherwise simple, sentimental, and perhaps boring older woman. The only part that wearies me is the convulsive outrage and vain lamentations, the barbed words of cruel slander, as a selfish world fights to hang onto that few lousy, crummy, measly drops of blood.

And I'm sick, too, of getting the crap beat out of me, which happens oftener than one would like to believe.

I suppose the bottom line is, I'd love to be "cured" (how I despise that vulgar, vulgar word!) without losing any of the miraculous powers and thrills that come along with the perils of my compulsion.

But...are things ever that easy?

Carmilla

J. SHERIDAN LEFANU

Prologue

Upon a paper attached to the Narrative which follows, Doctor Hesselius has written a rather elaborate note, which he accompanies with a reference to his Essay on the strange subject which the MS. illuminates.

This mysterious subject he treats, in that Essay, with his usual learning and acumen, and with remarkable directness and condensation. It will form but one volume of the series of that extraordinary man's collected papers.

As I publish the case, in this volume, simply to interest the "laity," I shall forestall the intelligent lady, who relates it, in nothing; and after due consideration, I have determined, therefore, to abstain from presenting any *precis* of the learned Doctor's reasoning, or extract from his statement on a subject which he describes as "involving, not improbably, some of the profoundest arcana of our dual existence, and its intermediates."

I was anxious on discovering this paper, to reopen the correspondence commenced by Doctor Hesselius, so many years before with a person so clever and careful as his informant seems to have been. Much to my regret, however, I found that she had died in the interval.

She, probably, could have added little to the Narrative which she communicates in the following pages, with, so far as I can pronounce, such a conscientious particularity.

Chapter One
AN EARLY FRIGHT

IN STYRIA, we, though by no means magnificent people, inhabit a castle, or schloss. A small income, in that part of the world, goes a great way. Eight or nine hundred a year does wonders. Scantily enough ours would have answered among wealthy people at home. My father is English, and I bear an English name, although I never saw England. But here, in this lonely and primitive place, where everything is so marvelously cheap, I really don't see how ever so much more money would at all materially add to our comforts, or even luxuries.

My father was in the Austrian service, and retired upon a pension and his patrimony, and purchased this feudal residence, and the small estate on which it stands, a bargain.

Nothing can be more picturesque or solitary. It stands on a slight eminence in a forest. The road, very old and narrow, passes in front of its drawbridge, never raised in my time, and its moat, stocked with perch, and sailed over by many swans, and floating on its surface white fleets of water-lilies.

Over all this the schloss shows its many-windowed front, its towers, and its Gothic chapel.

The forest opens in an irregular and very picturesque glade before its gate, and at the right a steep Gothic bridge carries the road over a stream that winds in deep shadow through the wood.

I have said that this is a very lonely place. Judge whether I say truth. Looking from the hall door towards the road, the forest in which our castle stands extends fifteen miles to the right, and twelve to the left. The nearest inhabited village is about seven of your English miles to the left. The nearest inhabited schloss of any historic associations, is that of old General Spielsdorf, nearly twenty miles away to the right.

I have said "the nearest *inhabited* village," because there is, only three miles westward, that is to say in the direction of General Spielsdorf's schloss, a ruined village, with its quaint little church, now roofless, in the aisle of which are the moldering tombs of the proud family of Karnstein, now extinct, who once owned the equally-desolate chateau which, in the thick of the forest, overlooks the silent ruins of the town.

Respecting the cause of the desertion of this striking and melancholy spot, there is a legend which I shall relate to you another time.

I must tell you now, how very small is the party who constitute the inhabitants of our castle. I don't include servants, or those dependents who occupy rooms in the buildings attached to the schloss. Listen, and wonder! My father, who is the kindest man on earth, but growing old; and I, at the date of my story, only nineteen. Eight years have passed since then. I and my father constituted the family at the schloss. My mother, a Styrian lady, died in my infancy, but I had a good-natured governess, who had been with me from, I might almost say, my infancy. I could not remember the time when her fat, benignant face was not a familiar picture in my memory. This was Madame Perrodon, a native of Bern, whose care and good nature in part supplied to me the loss of my mother, whom I do not even remember, so early I lost her. She made a third at our little dinner party. There was a fourth, Mademoiselle De Lafontaine, a lady such as you term, I believe, a "finishing governess." She spoke French and German, Madame Perrodon French and broken English, to which my father and I added English, which, partly to prevent its becoming a lost language among us, and partly from patriotic motives, we spoke every day. The consequence was a Babel, at which strangers used to laugh, and which I shall make no attempt to reproduce in this narrative. And there were two or three young lady friends besides, pretty nearly of my own age, who were occasional visitors, for longer or shorter terms; and these visits I sometimes returned.

These were our regular social resources; but of course there were chance visits from "neighbors" of only five or six leagues' distance. My life was, notwithstanding, rather a solitary one, I can assure you.

My gouvernantes had just so much control over me as you might conjecture such sage persons would have in this case of a rather spoiled girl, whose only parent allowed her pretty nearly her own way in everything.

The first occurrence in my existence, which produced a terrible impression upon my mind, which, in fact, never has been effaced, was one of the very earliest incidents of my life which I can recollect. Some people will think it so trifling that it should not be recorded here. You will see, however, by-and-by, why I mention it. The nursery, as it was called, though I had it all to myself, was a large room in the upper story of the castle, with a steep oak roof. I can't have been more than six years old, when one night I awoke, and looking round the room from my bed, failed to see the nursery-maid. Neither was my nurse there; and I thought myself alone. I was not frightened, for I was one of those happy children who are studiously kept in ignorance of ghost stories, of fairy tales, and of all such lore as makes us cover up our heads when the door creaks suddenly, or the flicker of an expiring candle makes the shadow of a bed-post dance upon the wall, nearer to our faces. I was vexed and insulted at finding myself, as I conceived, neglected, and I began to whimper, preparatory to a hearty bout of roaring; when to my surprise, I saw a solemn, but very pretty face looking at me from the side of the bed. It was that of a young lady who was kneeling, with her hands under the coverlet. I looked at her with a kind of pleased wonder, and ceased whimpering. She caressed me with her hands, and lay down beside me on the bed, and drew me towards her, smiling; I felt immediately delightfully soothed, and fell asleep again. I was wakened by a sensation as if two needles ran into my breast very deep at the same moment, and I cried loudly. The lady started back, with her eyes fixed on me, and then slipped down upon the floor, and, as I thought, hid herself under the bed.

I was now for the first time frightened, and I yelled with all my might and main. Nurse, nursery-maid, housekeeper, all came running in, and hearing my story, they made light of it, soothing me all they could meanwhile. But, child as I was, I could perceive that their faces were pale with an unwonted look of anxiety, and I saw them look under the bed, and about the room, and peep under tables and pluck open cupboards; and the housekeeper whispered to the nurse; "Lay your hand along that hollow in the bed; some one *did* lie there, so sure as you did not; the place is still warm."

I remember the nursery-maid petting me, and all three examining my chest, where I told them I felt the puncture, and pronouncing that there was no sign visible that any such thing had happened to me.

The housekeeper and the two other servants who were in charge of the nursery, remained sitting up all night; and from that time a servant always sat up in the nursery until I was about fourteen.

I was very nervous for a long time after this. A doctor was called in, he was pallid and elderly. How well I remember his long saturnine face, slightly pitted with small-pox, and his chestnut wig. For a good while, every second day, he came and gave me medicine, which of course I hated.

The morning after I saw this apparition I was in a state of terror, and could not bear to be left alone, daylight though it was, for a moment.

I remember my father coming up and standing at the bedside, and talking cheerfully, and asking the nurse a number of questions, and laughing very heartily at one of the answers; and patting me on the shoulder, and kissing me, and telling me not to be frightened, that it was nothing but a dream and could not hurt me.

But I was not comforted, for I knew the visit of the strange woman was *not* a dream; and I was *awfully* frightened.

I was a little consoled by the nursery-maid's assuring me that it was she who had come and looked at me, and lain down beside me in the bed, and that I must have been half-dreaming not to have known her face. But this, though supported by the nurse, did not quite satisfy me.

I remember, in the course of that day, a venerable old man, in a black cassock, coming into the room with the nurse and housekeeper, and talking a little to them, and very kindly to me; his face was very sweet and gentle, and he told me they were going to pray, and joined my hands together, and desired me to say, softly, while they were praying, "Lord, hear all good prayers for us, for Jesus's sake." I think these were the very words, for I often repeated them to myself, and my nurse used for years to make me say them in my prayers.

I remember so well the thoughtful sweet face of that white-haired old man, in his black cassock, as he stood in that rude, lofty, brown room, with the clumsy furniture of a fashion three hundred years old, about him, and the scanty light entering its shadowy atmosphere through the small lattice. He kneeled, and the three women with him, and he prayed aloud with an earnest quavering voice for, what appeared to me, a long time. I forget all my life preceding that event, and for some time after it is all obscure also; but the scenes I have just described stand out vivid as the isolated pictures of the phantasmagoria surrounded by darkness.

Chapter Two
A GUEST

I am now going to tell you something so strange that it will require all your faith in my veracity to believe my story. It is not only true, nevertheless, but truth of which I have been an eyewitness.

It was a sweet summer evening, and my father asked me, as he sometimes did, to take a little ramble with him along that beautiful forest vista which I have mentioned as lying in front of the schloss.

"General Spielsdorf cannot come to us so soon as I had hoped," said my father, as we pursued our walk.

He was to have paid us a visit of some weeks, and we had expected his arrival next day. He was to have brought with him a young lady, his niece and ward, Mademoiselle Rheinfeldt, whom I had never seen, but whom I had heard described as a very charming girl, and in whose society I had promised myself many happy days. I was more disappointed than a young lady living in a town, or a bustling neighborhood can possibly imagine. This visit, and the new acquaintance it promised, had furnished my day dream for many weeks.

"And how soon does he come?" I asked.

"Not till autumn. Not for two months, I dare say," he answered. "And I am very glad now, dear, that you never knew Mademoiselle Rheinfeldt."

"And why?" I asked, both mortified and curious.

"Because the poor young lady is dead," he replied. "I quite forgot I had not told you, but you were not in the room when I received the General's letter this evening."

I was very much shocked. General Spielsdorf had mentioned in his first letter, six or seven weeks before, that she was not so well as he would wish her, but there was nothing to suggest the remotest suspicion of danger.

"Here is the General's letter," he said, handing it to me. "I am afraid he is in great affliction; the letter appears to me to have been written very nearly in distraction."

We sat down on a rude bench, under a group of magnificent lime trees. The sun was setting with all its melancholy splendor behind the sylvan horizon, and the stream that flows beside our home, and passes under the steep old bridge I have mentioned, wound through many a group of noble trees, almost at our feet, reflecting in its current the fading crimson of the sky. General Spielsdorf's letter was extraordinary, so vehement, and in some places so self-contradictory, that I read it twice over—the second time aloud to my father—and was still unable to account for it, except by supposing that grief had unsettled his mind.

It said, "I have lost my darling daughter, for as such I loved her. During the last days of dear Bertha's illness I was not able to write to you. Before then I had no idea of her danger. I have lost her, and now learn *all*, too late. She died in the peace of innocence and in the glorious hope of a blessed futurity. The fiend who betrayed our infatuated hospitality has done it all. I thought I was receiving into my house innocence, gaiety, a charming companion for my lost Bertha. Heavens! what a fool I have been! I thank God my child died without a suspicion of the cause of her sufferings. She is gone without so much as conjecturing the nature of her illness, and the accursed passion of the agent of all this misery. I devote my remaining days to tracking and extinguishing a monster. I am told I may hope to accomplish my righteous and merciful purpose. At present there is scarcely a gleam of light to guide me. I curse my conceited incredulity, my despicable affectation of superiority, my blindness, my obstinacy—all—too late. I cannot write or talk collectedly now. I am distracted. So soon as I shall have a little recovered, I mean to devote myself for a time to inquiry, which may possibly lead me as far as Vienna. Some time in the autumn, two months hence, or earlier if I live, I will see you—that is, if you permit me; I will then tell you all that I scarce dare put upon paper now. Farewell. Pray for me, dear friend."

In these terms ended this strange letter. Though I had never seen Bertha Rheinfeldt, my eyes filled with tears at the sudden intelligence; I was startled, as well as profoundly disappointed.

The sun had now set, and it was twilight by the time I had returned the General's letter to my father.

It was a soft clear evening, and we loitered, speculating upon the possible meanings of the violent and incoherent sentences which I had just been reading. We had nearly a mile to walk before reaching the road that passes the schloss in front, and by that time the moon was shining brilliantly. At the drawbridge we met Madame Perrodon and

Mademoiselle De Lafontaine, who had come out, without their bonnets, to enjoy the exquisite moonlight.

We heard their voices gabbling in animated dialogue as we approached. We joined them at the drawbridge, and turned about to admire with them the beautiful scene.

The glade through which we had just walked lay before us. At our left the narrow road wound away under clumps of lordly trees, and was lost to sight amid the thickening forest. At the right the same road crosses the steep and picturesque bridge, near which stands a ruined tower, which once guarded that pass; and beyond the bridge an abrupt eminence rises, covered with trees, and showing in the shadow some gray ivy-clustered rocks.

Over the sward and low grounds, a thin film of mist was stealing, like smoke, marking the distances with a transparent veil; and here and there we could see the river faintly flashing in the moonlight. No softer, sweeter scene could be imagined. The news I had just heard made it melancholy; but nothing could disturb its character of profound serenity, and the enchanted glory and vagueness of the prospect.

My father, who enjoyed the picturesque, and I, stood looking in silence over the expanse beneath us. The two good governesses, standing a little way behind us, discoursed upon the scene, and were eloquent upon the moon.

Madame Perrodon was fat, middle-aged, and romantic, and talked and sighed poetically. Mademoiselle De Lafontaine—in right of her father, who was a German, assumed to be psychological, metaphysical, and something of a mystic—now declared that when the moon shone with a light so intense it was well known that it indicated a special spiritual activity. The effect of the full moon in such a state of brilliancy was manifold. It acted on dreams, it acted on lunacy, it acted on nervous people; it had marvelous physical influences connected with life. Mademoiselle related that her cousin, who was mate of a merchant ship, having taken a nap on deck on such a night, lying on his back, with his face full in the light of the moon, had wakened, after a dream of an old woman clawing him by the cheek, with his features horribly drawn to one side; and his countenance had never quite recovered its equilibrium.

"The moon, this night," she said, "is full of odylic and magnetic influence—and see, when you look behind you at the front of the schloss, how all its windows flash and twinkle with that silvery splendor, as if unseen hands had lighted up the rooms to receive fairy guests."

There are indolent states of the spirits in which, indisposed to talk ourselves, the talk of others is pleasant to our listless ears; and I gazed on, pleased with the tinkle of the ladies' conversation.

"I have got into one of my moping moods tonight," said my father, after a silence, and quoting Shakespeare, whom, by way of keeping up our English, he used to read aloud, he said:—

In truth I know not why I am so sad:
It wearies me; you say it wearies you;
But how I got it—came by it.

"I forget the rest. But I feel as if some great misfortune were hanging over us. I suppose the poor general's afflicted letter has had something to do with it."

At this moment the unwonted sound of carriage wheels and many hoofs upon the road, arrested our attention.

They seemed to be approaching from the high ground overlooking the bridge, and very soon the equipage emerged from that point. Two horsemen first crossed the bridge, then came a carriage drawn by four horses, and two men rode behind.

It seemed to be the traveling carriage of a person of rank; and we were all immediately absorbed in watching that very unusual spectacle. It became, in a few moments, greatly more interesting, for just as the carriage had passed the summit of the steep bridge, one of the leaders, taking fright, communicated his panic to the rest, and, after a plunge or two, the whole team broke into a wild gallop together, and dashing between the horsemen who rode in front, came thundering along the road towards us with the speed of a hurricane.

The excitement of the scene was made more painful by the clear, long-drawn screams of a female voice from the carriage window.

We all advanced in curiosity and horror; my father in silence, the rest with various ejaculations of terror.

Our suspense did not last long. Just before you reach the castle drawbridge, on the route they were coming, there stands by the roadside a magnificent lime tree, on the other side stands an ancient stone cross, at sight of which the horses, now going at a pace that was perfectly frightful, swerved so as to bring the wheel over the projecting roots of the tree.

I knew what was coming. I covered my eyes, unable to see it out, and turned my head away; at the same moment I heard a cry from my lady-friends, who had gone on a little.

Curiosity opened my eyes, and I saw a scene of utter confusion. Two of the horses were on the ground, the carriage lay upon its side, with two wheels in the air; the men were busy removing the traces, and a lady, with a commanding air and figure had got out, and stood with clasped hands, raising the handkerchief that was in them every now and then to her eyes. Through the carriage door was now lifted a young lady, who appeared to be lifeless. My dear old father was already beside the elder lady, with his hat in his hand, evidently tendering his aid and the resources of his schloss. The lady did not appear to hear him, or to have eyes for anything but the slender girl who was being placed against the slope of the bank.

I approached; the young lady was apparently stunned, but she was certainly not dead. My father, who piqued himself on being something of a physician, had just had his fingers to her wrist and assured the lady, who declared herself her mother, that her pulse, though faint and irregular, was undoubtedly still distinguishable. The lady clasped her hands and looked upward, as if in a momentary transport of gratitude; but immediately she broke out again in that theatrical way which is, I believe, natural to some people.

She was what is called a fine-looking woman for her time of life, and must have been handsome; she was tall, but not thin, and dressed in black velvet, and looked rather pale, but with a proud and commanding countenance, though now agitated strangely.

"Was ever being so born to calamity?" I heard her say, with clasped hands, as I came up. "Here am I, on a journey of life and death, in prosecuting which to lose an hour is possibly to lose all. My child will not have recovered sufficiently to resume her route for who can say how long. I must leave her; I cannot, dare not, delay. How far on, sir, can you tell, is the nearest village? I must leave her there; and shall not see my darling, or even hear of her till my return, three months hence."

I plucked my father by the coat, and whispered earnestly in his ear, "Oh! papa, pray ask her to let her stay with us—it would be so delightful. Do, pray."

"If Madame will entrust her child to the care of my daughter, and of her good gouvernante, Madame Perrodon, and permit her to remain as our guest, under my charge, until her return, it will confer a distinction and an obligation upon us, and we shall treat her with all the care and devotion which so sacred a trust deserves."

"I cannot do that, sir, it would be to task your kindness and chivalry too cruelly," said the lady, distractedly.

"It would, on the contrary, be to confer on us a very great kindness at the moment when we most need it. My daughter has just been disappointed by a cruel misfortune, in a visit from which she had long anticipated a great deal of happiness. If you confide this young lady to our care it will be her best consolation. The nearest village on your route is distant, and affords no such inn as you could think of placing your daughter at; you cannot allow her to continue her journey for any considerable distance without danger. If, as you say, you cannot suspend your journey, you must part with her to-night, and nowhere could you do so with more honest assurances of care and tenderness than here."

There was something in this lady's air and appearance so distinguished, and even imposing, and in her manner so engaging, as to impress one, quite apart from the dignity of her equipage, with a conviction that she was a person of consequence.

By this time the carriage was replaced in its upright position, and the horses, quite tractable, in the traces again.

The lady threw on her daughter a glance which I fancied was not quite so affectionate as one might have anticipated from the beginning of the scene; then she beckoned slightly to my father, and withdrew two or three steps with him out of hearing; and talked to him with a fixed and stern countenance, not at all like that with which she had hitherto spoken.

I was filled with wonder that my father did not seem to perceive the change, and also unspeakably curious to learn what it could be that she was speaking, almost in his ear, with so much earnestness and rapidity.

Two or three minutes at most, I think, she remained thus employed, then she turned, and a few steps brought her to where her daughter lay, supported by Madame Perrodon. She kneeled beside her for a moment and whispered, as Madame supposed, a little benediction in her ear; then hastily kissing her, she stepped into her carriage, the door was closed, the footmen in stately liveries jumped up behind, the outriders spurred on, the postilions cracked their whips, the horses plunged and broke suddenly into a furious canter that threatened soon again to become a gallop, and the carriage whirled away, followed at the same rapid pace by the two horsemen in the rear.

Chapter Three
WE COMPARE NOTES

We followed the *cortège* with our eyes until it was swiftly lost to sight in the misty wood; and the very sound of the hoofs and wheels died away in the silent night air.

Nothing remained to assure us that the adventure had not been an illusion of a moment but the young lady, who just at that moment opened her eyes. I could not see, for her face was turned from me, but she raised her head, evidently looking about her, and I heard a very sweet voice ask complainingly, "Where is mamma?"

Our good Madame Perrodon answered tenderly, and added some comfortable assurances.

I then heard her ask:

"Where am I? What is this place?" and after that she said, "1 don't see the carriage; and Matska, where is she?"

Madame answered all her questions in so far as she understood them; and gradually the young lady remembered how the misadventure came about, and was glad to hear that no one in, or in attendance on, the carriage was hurt; and on learning that her mamma had left her here, till her return in about three months, she wept.

I was going to add my consolations to those of Madame Perrodon when Mademoiselle de Lafontaine placed her hand upon my arm, saying:

"Don't approach, one at a time is as much as she can at present converse with; a very little excitement would possibly overpower her now."

As soon as she is comfortably in bed, I thought, I will run up to her room and see her.

My father in the meantime had sent a servant on horseback for the physician, who lived about two leagues away; and a bed room was being prepared for the young lady's reception.

The stranger now rose, and leaning on Madame's arm, walked slowly over the drawbridge and into the castle gate.

In the hall, servants waited to receive her, and she was conducted forthwith to her room.

The room we usually sat in as our drawing room is long, having four windows, that looked over the moat and drawbridge, upon the forest scene I have just described.

It is furnished in old carved oak, with large carved cabinets, and the chairs are cushioned with crimson Utrecht velvet. The walls are covered with tapestry, and surrounded with great gold frames, the figures being as large as life, in ancient and very curious costume, and the subjects represented are hunting, hawking, and generally festive. It is not too stately to be extremely comfortable; and here we had our tea, for with his usual patriotic leanings he insisted that the national beverage should make its appearance regularly with our coffee and chocolate.

We sat here this night, and with candles lighted, were talking over the adventure of the evening.

Madame Perrodon and Mademoiselle De Lafontaine were both of our party. The young stranger had hardly lain down in her bed when she sank into a deep sleep; and those ladies had left her in the care of a servant.

"How do you like our guest?" I asked, as soon as Madame entered. "Tell me all about her?"

"I like her extremely," answered Madame, "she is, I almost think, the prettiest creature I ever saw; about your age, and so gentle and nice."

"She is absolutely beautiful," threw in Mademoiselle, who had peeped for a moment into the stranger's room.

"And such a sweet voice!" added Madame Perrodon.

"Did you remark a woman in the carriage, after it was set up again, who did not get out," inquired Mademoiselle, "but only looked from the window?"

No, we had not seen her.

Then she described a hideous black woman, with a sort of colored turban on her head, who was gazing all the time from the carriage window, nodding and grinning derisively towards the ladies, with gleaming eyes and large white eye-balls, and her teeth set as if in fury.

"Did you remark what an ill-looking pack of men the servants were?" asked Madame.

"Yes," said my father, who had just come in, "ugly, hang-dog looking fellows, as ever I beheld in my life. I hope they mayn't rob the poor lady in the forest. They are clever rogues, however; they got everything to rights in a minute."

"I dare say they are worn out with too long traveling," said Madame. "Besides looking wicked, their faces were so strangely lean, and dark, and sullen. I am very curious, I own; but I dare say the young lady will tell us all about it tomorrow, if she is sufficiently recovered."

"I don't think she will," said my father, with a mysterious smile, and a little nod of his head, as if he knew more about it than he cared to tell us.

This made me all the more inquisitive as to what had passed between him and the lady in the black velvet, in the brief but earnest interview that had immediately preceded her departure.

We were scarcely alone, when I entreated him to tell me. He did not need much pressing.

"There is no particular reason why I should not tell you. She expressed a reluctance to trouble us with the care of her daughter, saying she was in delicate health, and nervous, but not subject to any kind of seizure—she volunteered that—nor to any illusion; being, in fact, perfectly sane."

"How very odd to say all that!" I interpolated. "It was so unnecessary."

"At all events it *was* said," he laughed, "and as you wish to know all that passed, which was indeed very little, I tell you. She then said, 'I am making a long journey of *vital* importance'—she emphasized the word— 'rapid and secret; I shall return for my child in three months;

in the meantime, she will be silent as to who we are, whence we come, and whither we are traveling.' That is all she said. She spoke very pure French. When she said the word 'secret,' she paused for a few seconds, looking sternly, her eyes fixed on mine. I fancy she makes a great point of that. You saw how quickly she was gone. I hope I have not done a very foolish thing, in taking charge of the young lady."

For my part, I was delighted. I was longing to see and talk to her; and only waiting till the doctor should give me leave. You, who live in towns, can have no idea how great an event the introduction of a new friend is, in such a solitude as surrounded us.

The doctor did not arrive till nearly one o'clock; but I could no more have gone to my bed and slept, than I could have overtaken, on foot, the carriage in which the princess in black velvet had driven away.

When the physician came down to the drawing room, it was to report very favorably upon his patient. She was now sitting up, her pulse quite regular, apparently perfectly well. She had sustained no injury, and the little shock to her nerves had passed away quite harmlessly. There could be no harm certainly in my seeing her, if we both wished it; and with this permission, I sent, forthwith, to know whether she would allow me to visit her for a few minutes in her room.

The servant returned immediately to say that she desired nothing more.

You may be sure I was not long in availing myself of this permission.

Our visitor lay in one of the handsomest rooms in the schloss. It was, perhaps, a little stately. There was a somber piece of tapestry opposite the foot of the bed, representing Cleopatra with the asps to her bosom; and other solemn classic scenes were displayed, a little faded, upon the other walls. But there was gold carving, and rich and varied color enough in the other decorations of the room, to more than redeem the gloom of the old tapestry.

There were candles at the bed side. She was sitting up; her slender pretty figure enveloped in the soft silk dressing-gown, embroidered with flowers, and lined with thick quilted silk, which her mother had thrown over her feet as she lay upon the ground.

What was it that, as I reached the bed side and had just begun my little greeting, struck me dumb in a moment, and made me recoil a step or two from before her? I will tell you.

I saw the very face which had visited me in my childhood at night, which remained so fixed in my memory, and on which I had for so many years so often ruminated with horror, when no one suspected of what I was thinking.

It was pretty, even beautiful; and when I first beheld it, wore the same melancholy expression.

But this almost instantly lighted into a strange fixed smile of recognition.

There was a silence of fully a minute, and then at length *she* spoke; I could not.

"How wonderful!" she exclaimed. "Twelve years ago, I saw your face in a dream, and it has haunted me ever since."

"Wonderful indeed!" I repeated, overcoming with an effort the horror that had for a time suspended my utterances. "Twelve years ago, in vision or reality, I certainly saw you. I could not forget your face. It has remained before my eyes ever since."

Her smile had softened. Whatever I had fancied strange in it, was gone, and it and her dimpling cheeks were now delightfully pretty and intelligent.

I felt reassured, and continued more in the vein which hospitality indicated, to bid her welcome, and to tell her how much pleasure her accidental arrival had given us all, and especially what a happiness it was to me.

I took her hand as I spoke. I was a little shy, as lonely people are, but the situation made me eloquent, and even bold. She pressed my hand, she laid hers upon it, and her eyes glowed, as, looking hastily into mine, she smiled again, and blushed.

She answered my welcome very prettily. I sat down beside her, still wondering; and she said:

"I must tell you my vision about you; it is so very strange that you and I should have had, each of the other, so vivid a dream, that each should have seen, I you and you me, looking as we do now, when of course we both were mere children. I was a child, about six years old, and I awoke from a confused and troubled dream, and found myself in a room, unlike my nursery, wainscoted clumsily in some dark wood, and with cupboards and bedsteads, and chairs and benches placed about it. The beds were, I thought, all empty, and the room itself without any one but myself in it; and I, after looking about me for some time, and admiring especially an iron candlestick, with two branches, which I should certainly know again, crept under one of the beds to reach the window; but as I got from under the bed, 1 heard some one crying; and looking up, while I was still upon my knees, I saw you—most assuredly you—as I see you now; a beautiful young lady, with golden hair and large blue eyes, and lips—your lips—you, as you are here. Your looks won me; I climbed on the bed and put my arms about you, and I think we both fell asleep. I was aroused by a scream; you were sitting up screaming. I was frightened, and slipped down upon the ground, and, it seemed to me, lost consciousness for a moment; and when I came to myself, I was again in my nursery at home. Your face I have never forgotten since. I could not be misled by mere resemblance. You *are* the lady whom I then saw."

It was now my turn to relate my corresponding vision, which I did, to the undisguised wonder of my new acquaintance.

"I don't know which should be most afraid of the other," she said, again smiling. "If you were less pretty I think I should be very much afraid of you, but being as you are, and you and I both so young, I feel only that I have made your acquaintance twelve years ago, and have already a right to your intimacy; at all events, it does seem as if we were destined, from our earliest childhood, to be friends. I wonder whether you feel as strangely drawn towards me as I do to you; I have never had a friend—shall I find one now?" She sighed, and her fine dark eyes gazed passionately on me.

Now the truth is, I felt rather unaccountably towards the beautiful stranger. I did feel, as she said, "drawn towards her," but there was also something of repulsion. In this ambiguous feeling, however, the sense of attraction immensely prevailed. She interested and won me; she was so beautiful and so indescribably engaging.

I perceived now something of languor and exhaustion stealing over her, and hastened to bid her good night.

"The doctor thinks," I added, "that you ought to have a maid to sit up with you to-night; one of ours is waiting, and you will find her a very useful and quiet creature."

"How kind of you, but I could not sleep, I never could with an attendant in the room. I shan't require any assistance—and, shall I confess my weakness, I am haunted with a terror of robbers. Our house was robbed once, and two servants murdered, so I always lock my door. It has become a habit—and you look so kind I know you will forgive me. I see there is a key in the lock."

She held me close in her pretty arms for a moment and whispered in my ear, "Good-night, darling, it is very hard to part with you, but good-night; tomorrow, but not early, I shall see you again."

She sank back on the pillow with a sigh, and her fine eyes followed me with a fond and melancholy gaze, and she murmured again, "Good-night, dear friend."

Young people like, and even love, on impulse. I was flattered by the evident, though as yet undeserved, fondness she showed me. I liked the confidence with which she at once received me. She was determined that we should be very dear friends.

Next day came and we met again. I was delighted with my companion; that is to say, in many respects.

Her looks lost nothing in daylight—she was certainly the most beautiful creature I had ever seen, and the unpleasant remembrance of the face presented in my early dream, had lost the effect of the first unexpected recognition.

She confessed that she had experienced a similar shock on seeing me, and precisely the same faint antipathy that had mingled with my admiration of her. We now laughed together over our momentary horrors.

Chapter Four
HER HABITS—A SAUNTER

I told you that I was charmed with her in most particulars.

There were some that did not please me so well.

She was above the middle height of women. I shall begin by describing her. She was slender, and wonderfully graceful. Except that her movements were languid—very languid—indeed, there was nothing in her appearance to indicate an invalid. Her complexion was rich and brilliant; her features were small and beautifully formed; her eyes large, dark, and lustrous; her hair was quite wonderful, I never saw hair so magnificently thick and long when it was down about her shoulders; I have often placed my hands under it, and laughed with wonder at its weight. It was exquisitely fine and soft, and in color a rich very dark brown, with something of gold. I loved to let it down, tumbling with its own weight, as, in her room, she lay back in her chair talking in her sweet low voice, I used to fold and braid it, and spread it out and play with it. Heavens! If I had but known all!

I said there were particulars which did not please me. I have told you that her confidence won me the first night I saw her; but I found that she exercised with respect to herself, her mother, her history, everything in fact connected with her life, plans, and people, an ever-wakeful reserve. I dare say I was unreasonable, perhaps I was wrong; I dare say I ought to have respected the solemn injunction laid upon my father by the stately lady in black velvet. But curiosity is a restless and unscrupulous passion, and no one girl can endure, with patience, that hers should be baffled by another. What harm could it do anyone to tell me what I so ardently desired to know? Had she no trust in my good sense or honor? Why would she not believe me when I assured her, so solemnly, that I would not divulge one syllable of what she told me to any mortal breathing?

There was a coldness, it seemed to me, beyond her years, in her smiling melancholy persistent refusal to afford me the least ray of light.

I cannot say we quarreled upon this point, for she would not quarrel upon any. It was, of course, very unfair of me to press her, very ill-bred, but I really could not help it; and I might just as well have let it alone.

What she did tell me amounted, in my unconscionable estimation—to nothing.

It was all summed up in three very vague disclosures:

First.—Her name was Carmilla.

Second.—Her family was very ancient and noble.

Third.—Her home lay in the direction of the west.

She would not tell me the name of her family, nor their armorial bearings, nor the name of their estate, nor even that of the country they lived in.

You are not to suppose that I worried her incessantly on these subjects. I watched opportunity, and rather insinuated than urged my inquiries. Once or twice, indeed, I did attack her more directly. But no matter what my tactics, utter failure was invariably the result. Reproaches and caresses were all lost upon her. But I must add this, that her evasion was conducted with so pretty a melancholy and deprecation, with so many, and even passionate declarations of her liking for me, and trust in my honor, and with so many promises that I should at last know all, that I could not find it in my heart long to be offended with her.

She used to place her pretty arms about my neck, draw me to her, and laying her cheek to mine, murmur with her lips near my ear, "Dearest, your little heart is wounded; think me not cruel because I obey the irresistible law of my strength and weakness; if your dear heart is wounded, my wild heart bleeds with yours. In the rapture of my enormous humiliation I live in your warm life, and you shall die—die, sweetly die—into mine. I cannot help it; as I draw near to you, you, in your turn, will draw near to others, and learn the rapture of that cruelty, which yet is love; so, for a while, seek to know no more of me and mine, but trust me with all your loving spirit."

And when she had spoken such a rhapsody, she would press me more closely in her trembling embrace, and her lips in soft kisses gently glow upon my cheek.

Her agitations and her language were unintelligible to me.

From these foolish embraces, which were not of very frequent occurrence, I must allow, I used to wish to extricate myself; but my energies seemed to fail me. Her murmured words sounded like a lullaby in my ear, and soothed my resistance into a trance, from which I only seemed to recover myself when she withdrew her arms.

In these mysterious moods I did not like her. I experienced a strange tumultuous excitement that was pleasurable, ever and anon, mingled with a vague sense of fear and disgust. I had no distinct thoughts about her while such scenes lasted, but I was conscious of a love growing into adoration, and also of abhorrence. This I know is paradox, but I can make no other attempt to explain the feeling.

I now write, after an interval of more than ten years, with a trembling hand, with a confused and horrible recollection of certain occurrences and situations, in the ordeal through which I was unconsciously passing; though with a vivid and very sharp remembrance of the main current of my story. But, I suspect, in all lives there are certain emotional scenes, those in which our passions have been most wildly and terribly roused, that are of all others the most vaguely and dimly remembered.

Sometimes after an hour of apathy, my strange and beautiful companion would take my hand and hold it with a fond pressure, renewed again and again; blushing softly, gazing in my face with languid and burning eyes, and breathing so fast that her dress rose and fell with the tumultuous respiration. It was like the ardor of a lover; it embarrassed me; it was hateful and yet overpowering; and with gloating eyes she drew me to her, and her hot lips traveled along my cheek in kisses; and she would whisper, almost in sobs, "You are mine, you *shall* be mine, and you and I are one for ever." Then she had thrown herself back in her chair, with her small hands over her eyes, leaving me trembling.

"Are we related," I used to ask; "what can you mean by all this? I remind you perhaps of some one whom you love; but you must not, I hate it; I don't know you—I don't know myself when you look so and talk so."

She used to sigh at my vehemence, then turn away and drop my hand.

Respecting these very extraordinary manifestations I strove in vain to form any satisfactory theory—I could not refer them to affectation or trick. It was unmistakably the momentary breaking out of suppressed instinct and emotion. Was she, notwithstanding her mother's volunteered denial, subject to brief visitations of insanity; or was there here a disguise and a romance? I had read in old story books of such things. What if a boyish lover had found his way into the house, and sought to prosecute his suit in masquerade, with the assistance of a clever old adventuress? But there were many things against this hypothesis, highly interesting as it was to my vanity.

I could boast of no little attentions such as masculine gallantry delights to offer. Between these passionate moments there were long intervals of common-place, of gaiety, of brooding melancholy, during which, except that I detected her eyes so full of melancholy fire, following me, at times I might have been as nothing to her. Except in these brief periods of mysterious excitement her ways were girlish; and there was always a languor about her, quite incompatible with a masculine system in a state of health.

In some respects her habits were odd. Perhaps not so singular in the opinion of a town lady like you, as they appeared to us rustic people. She used to come down very late, generally not till one o'clock, she would then take a cup of chocolate, but eat nothing; we then went out for a walk, which was a mere saunter, and she seemed, almost immediately, exhausted, and either returned to the schloss or sat on one of the benches that were placed, here and there, among the trees. This was a bodily languor in which her mind did not sympathize. She was always an animated talker, and very intelligent.

She sometimes alluded for a moment to her own home, or mentioned an adventure or situation, or an early recollection, which indicated a people of strange manners, and described customs of which we knew nothing. I gathered from these chance hints that her native country was much more remote than I had at first fancied.

As we sat thus one afternoon under the trees a funeral passed us by. It was that of a pretty young girl, whom I had often seen, the daughter of one of the rangers of the forest. The poor man was walking behind the coffin of his darling; she was his only child, and he looked quite heartbroken. Peasants walking two-and-two came behind, they were singing a funeral hymn.

I rose to mark my respect as they passed, and joined in the hymn they were very sweetly singing.

My companion shook me a little roughly, and I turned surprised.

She said brusquely, "Don't you perceive how discordant that is?"

"I think it very sweet, on the contrary," I answered, vexed at the interruption, and very uncomfortable, lest the people who composed the little procession should observe and resent what was passing.

I resumed, therefore, instantly, and was again interrupted. "You pierce my ears," said Carmilla, almost angrily, and stopping her ears with her tiny fingers. "Besides, how can you tell that your religion and mine are the same; your forms wound me, and I hate funerals. What a fuss! Why, you must die—*everyone* must die; and all are happier when they do. Come home."

"My father has gone on with the clergyman to the churchyard. I thought you knew she was to be buried to-day."

"*She?* I don't trouble my head about peasants. I don't know who she is," answered Carmilla, with a flash from her fine eyes.

"She is the poor girl who fancied she saw a ghost a fortnight ago, and has been dying ever since, till yesterday, when she expired."

"Tell me nothing about ghosts. I shan't sleep to-night if you do."

"I hope there is no plague or fever coming; all this looks very like it," I continued. "The swineherd's young wife died only a week ago, and she thought something seized her by the throat as she lay in her bed, and nearly strangled her. Papa says such horrible fancies do accompany some forms of fever. She was quite well the day before. She sank afterwards, and died before a week."

"Well, *her* funeral is over, I hope, and *her* hymn sung; and our ears shan't be tortured with that discord and jargon. It has made me nervous. Sit down here, beside me; sit close; hold my hand; press it hard—hard—harder."

We had moved a little back, and had come to another seat.

She sat down. Her face underwent a change that alarmed and even terrified me for a moment. It darkened, and became horribly livid; her teeth and hands were clenched, and she frowned and compressed her lips, while she stared down upon the ground at her feet, and trembled all over with a continued shudder as irrepressible as ague. All her energies seemed strained to suppress a fit, with which she was then breathlessly tugging; and at length a low convulsive cry of suffering broke from her, and gradually the hysteria subsided. "There! That comes of strangling people with hymns!" she said at last. "Hold me, hold me still. It is passing away."

And so gradually it did; and perhaps to dissipate the somber impression which the spectacle had left upon me, she became unusually animated and chatty; and so we got home.

This was the first time I had seen her exhibit any definable symptoms of that delicacy of health which her mother had spoken of. It was the first time, also, I had seen her exhibit anything like temper.

Both passed away like a summer cloud; and never but once afterwards did I witness on her part a momentary sign of anger. I will tell you how it happened.

She and I were looking out of one of the long drawing room windows, when there entered the court-yard, over the drawbridge, a figure of a wanderer whom I knew very well. He used to visit the schloss generally twice a year.

It was the figure of a hunchback, with the sharp lean features that generally accompany deformity. He wore a pointed black beard, and he was smiling from ear to ear, showing his white fangs. He was dressed in buff, black, and scarlet, and crossed with more straps and belts than I could count, from which hung all manner of things. Behind, he carried a magic-lantern, and two boxes, which I well knew, in one of which was a salamander, and in the other a mandrake. These monsters used to make my father laugh. They were compounded of parts of monkeys, parrots, squirrels, fish, and hedgehogs, dried and stitched together with great neatness and startling effect. He had a fiddle, a box of conjuring apparatus, a pair of foils and masks attached to his belt, several other mysterious cases dangling about him, and a black staff with copper ferrules in his hand. His companion was a rough spare dog, that followed at his heels, but stopped short, suspiciously at the drawbridge, and in a little while began to howl dismally.

In the meantime, the mountebank, standing in the midst of the court-yard, raised his grotesque hat, and made us a very ceremonious bow, paying his compliments very volubly in execrable French, and German not much better. Then, disengaging his fiddle, he began to scrape a lively air, to which he sang with a merry discord, dancing with ludicrous airs and activity, that made me laugh, in spite of the dog's howling.

Then he advanced to the window with many smiles and salutations, and his hat in his left hand, his fiddle under his arm, and with a fluency that never took breath, he gabbled a long advertisement of all his accomplishments, and the resources of the various arts which he placed at our service, and the curiosities and entertainments which it was in his power, at our bidding to display.

"Will your ladyships be pleased to buy an amulet against the oupire, which is going like the wolf, I hear, through these woods," he said, dropping his hat on the pavement. "They are dying of it right and left, and here is a charm that never fails; only pinned to the pillow, and you may laugh in his face."

These charms consisted of oblong slips of vellum, with cabalistic ciphers and diagrams upon them.

Carmilla instantly purchased one, and so did I.

He was looking up, and we were smiling down upon him, amused; at least, I could answer for myself. His piercing black eye, as he looked up in our faces, seemed to detect something that fixed for a moment his curiosity.

In an instant he unrolled a leather case, full of all manner of odd little steel instruments.

"See here, my lady," he said, displaying it, and addressing me, "I profess, among other things less useful, the art of dentistry. Plague take the dog!" he interpolated. "Silence, beast! He howls so that your ladyships can scarcely hear a word. Your noble friend, the young lady at your right, has the sharpest tooth—long, thin, pointed, like an awl, like a needle; ha, ha! With my sharp and long sight, as I look up, I have seen it distinctly; now if it happens to hurt the young lady, and I think it must, here am I, here are my file, my punch, my nippers; I will make it round and blunt, if her ladyship pleases; no longer the tooth of a fish, but of a beautiful young lady as she is. Hey? Is the young lady displeased? Have I been too bold? Have I offended her?"

The young lady, indeed, looked very angry as she drew back from the window.

"How dares that mountebank insult us so? Where is your father? I shall demand redress from him. My father would have had the wretch tied up to the pump, and flogged with a cart-whip, and burnt to the bones with the castle brand!"

She retired from the window a step or two, and sat down, and had hardly lost sight of the offender, when her wrath subsided as suddenly as it had risen, and she gradually recovered her usual tone, and seemed to forget the little hunchback and his follies.

My father was out of spirits that evening. On coming in he told us that there had been another case very similar to the two fatal ones which had lately occurred. The sister of a young peasant on his estate, only a mile away, was very ill, had been, as she described it, attacked very nearly in the same way, and was now slowly but steadily sinking.

"All this," said my father, "is strictly referable to natural causes. These poor people infect one another with their superstitions, and so repeat in imagination the images of terror that have infested their neighbors."

"But that very circumstance frightens one horribly," said Carmilla.

"How so?" inquired my father.

"I am so afraid of fancying I see such things; I think it would be as bad as reality."

"We are in God's hands; nothing can happen without His permission, and all will end well for those who love Him. He is our faithful creator; He has made us all, and will take care of us."

"Creator! *Nature!*" said the young lady in answer to my gentle father. "And this disease that invades the country is natural. Nature. All things proceed from Nature—don't they? All things in the heaven, in the earth, and under the earth, act and live as Nature ordains? I think so."

"The doctor said he would come here to-day," said my father, after a silence. "I want to know what he thinks about it, and what he thinks we had better do."

"Doctors never did me any good," said Carmilla.

"Then you have been ill?" I asked.

"More ill than ever you were," she answered.

"Long ago?"

"Yes, a long time. I suffered from this very illness; but I forget all but my pain and weakness, and they were not so bad as are suffered in other diseases."

"You were very young then?"

"I dare say; let us talk no more of it. You would not wound a friend?" She looked languidly in my eyes, and passed her arm round my waist lovingly, and led me out of the room. My father was busy over some papers near the window.

"Why does your papa like to frighten us?" said the pretty girl, with a sigh and a little shudder.

"He doesn't, dear Carmilla, it is the very furthest thing from his mind."

"Are you afraid, dearest?"

"I should be very much if I fancied there was any real danger of my being attacked as those poor people were."

"You are afraid to die?"

"Yes, everyone is."

"But to die as lovers may—to die together, so that they may live together. Girls are caterpillars while they live in the world, to be finally butterflies when the summer comes; but in the meantime there are grubs and larvae, don't you see—each with their peculiar propensities, necessities and structure. So says Monsieur Buffon, in his big book, in the next room."

Later in the day the doctor came, and was closeted with papa for some time. He was a skillful man, of sixty and upwards, he wore powder, and shaved his pale face smooth as a pumpkin. He and papa emerged from the room together, and I heard papa laugh, and say as they came out:

"Well, I do wonder at a wise man like you. What do you say to hippogriffs and dragons?"

The doctor was smiling, and made answer, shaking his head—

"Nevertheless, life and death are mysterious states, and we know little of the resources of either."

And so they walked on, and I heard no more. I did not then know what the doctor had been broaching, but I think I guess it now.

Chapter Five

A WONDERFUL LIKENESS

This evening there arrived from Gratz the grave, dark-faced son of the picture-cleaner, with a horse and cart laden with two large packing-cases, having many pictures in each. It was a journey of ten leagues, and whenever a messenger arrived at the schloss from our little capital of Gratz, we used to crowd about him in the hall, to hear the news.

This arrival created in our secluded quarters quite a sensation. The cases remained in the hall, and the messenger was taken charge of by the servants till he had eaten his supper. Then with assistants, and armed with hammer, ripping chisel, and turnscrew, he met us in the hall, where we had assembled to witness the unpacking of the cases.

Carmilla sat looking listlessly on, while one after the other the old pictures, nearly all portraits, which had undergone the process of renovation, were brought to light. My mother was of an old Hungarian family, and most of these pictures, which were about to be restored to their places, had come to us through her.

My father had a list in his hand, from which he read, as the artist rummaged out the corresponding numbers. I don't know that the pictures were very good, but they were, undoubtedly, very old, and some of them very curious also. They had, for the most part, the merit of being now seen by me, I may say, for the first time; for the smoke and dust of time had all but obliterated them.

"There is a picture that I have not seen yet," said my father. "In one corner, at the top of it, is the name, as well as I could read, 'Marcia Karnstein,' and the date '1698;' and I am curious to see how it has turned out."

I remembered it; it was a small picture, about a foot and a half high, and nearly square, without a frame; but it was so blackened by age that I could not make it out.

The artist now produced it, with evident pride. It was quite beautiful; it was startling; it seemed to live. It was the effigy of Carmilla.

"Carmilla, dear, here is an absolute miracle. Here you are, living, smiling, ready to speak, in this picture. Isn't it beautiful, papa? And see, even the mole on her throat."

My father laughed, and said, "Certainly it is a wonderful likeness," but he looked away, and to my surprise seemed but little struck by it, and went on talking to the picture-cleaner, who was also something of an artist, and discoursed with intelligence about the portraits or other works, which his art had just brought into light and color, while I was more and more lost in wonder the more I looked at the picture.

"Will you let me hang this picture in my room, papa?" I asked.

"Certainly, dear," said he, smiling, "I'm very glad you think it so like. It must be prettier even than I thought it, if it is."

The young lady did not acknowledge this pretty speech, did not seem to hear it. She was leaning back in her seat, her fine eyes under their long lashes gazing on me in contemplation, and she smiled in a kind of rapture.

"And now you can read quite plainly the name that is written in the corner. It is not Marcia; it looks as if it was done in gold. The name is Mircalla, Countess Karnstein, and this is a little Coronet over it, and underneath A.D. 1698. I am descended from the Karnsteins; that is, mamma was."

"Ah!" said the lady, languidly, "so am I, I think, a very long descent, very ancient. Are there any Karnsteins living now?"

"None who bear the name, I believe. The family were ruined, I believe, in some civil wars, long ago but the ruins of the castle are only about three miles away."

"How interesting!" she said, languidly. "But see what beautiful moonlight." She glanced through the hall door, which stood a little open. "Suppose you take a little ramble round the court, and look down at the road and river."

"It is so like the night you came to us," I said.

She sighed, smiling.

She rose, and each with her arm about the other's waist, we walked out upon the pavement.

In silence, slowly we walked down to the drawbridge, where the beautiful landscape opened before us.

"And so you were thinking of the night I came here?" she almost whispered. "Are you glad I came?"

"Delighted, dear Carmilla," I answered.

"And you ask for a picture you think like me, to hang in your room," she murmured with a sigh, as she drew her arm closer about my waist, and let her pretty head sink upon my shoulder.

"How romantic you are, Carmilla," I said. "Whenever you tell me your story, it will be made up chiefly of some one great romance."

She kissed me silently.

"I am sure, Carmilla, you have been in love; that there is, at this moment, an affair of the heart going on."

"I have been in love with no one, and never shall," she whispered, "unless it should be you."

How beautiful she looked in the moonlight!

Shy and strange was the look with which she quickly hid her face in my neck and hair, with tumultuous sighs, that seemed almost to sob, and pressed in mine a hand that trembled.

Her soft cheek was glowing against mine. "Darling, darling," she murmured, "I live in you; and you would die for me, I love you so."

I started from her.

She was gazing on me with eyes from which all fire, all meaning had flown, and a face colorless and apathetic.

"Is there a chill in the air, dear?" she said drowsily. "I almost shiver; have I been dreaming? Let us come in. Come, come; come in."

"You look ill, Carmilla; a little faint. You certainly must take some wine," I said.

"Yes, I will. I'm better now. I shall be quite well in a few minutes.

Yes, do give me a little wine," answered Carmilla, as we approached the door. "Let us look again for a moment; it is the last time, perhaps, I shall see the moonlight with you."

"How do you feel now, dear Carmilla? Are you really better?" I asked.

I was beginning to take alarm, lest she should have been stricken with the strange epidemic that they said had invaded the country about us.

"Papa would be grieved beyond measure," I added, "if he thought you were ever so little ill, without immediately letting us know. We have a very skillful doctor near this, the physician who was with papa to-day."

"I'm sure he is. I know how kind you all are: but, dear child, I am quite well again. There is nothing ever wrong with me, but a little weakness. People say I am languid; I am incapable of exertion; I can scarcely walk as far as a child of three years old; and every now and then the little strength I have falters, and I become as you have just seen me. But after all I am very easily set up again; in a moment I am perfectly myself. See how I have recovered."

So, indeed, she had; and she and I talked a great deal, and very animated she was; and the remainder of that evening passed without any recurrence of what I called her infatuations. I mean her crazy talk and looks, which embarrassed, and even frightened me.

But there occurred that night an event which gave my thoughts quite a new turn, and seemed to startle even Carmilla's languid nature into momentary energy.

Chapter Six
A VERY STRANGE AGONY

When we got into the drawing room, and had sat down to our coffee and chocolate, although Carmilla did not take any, she seemed quite herself again, and Madame, and Mademoiselle De Lafontaine, joined us, and made a little card party, in the course of which papa came in for what he called his "dish of tea."

When the game was over he sat down beside Carmilla on the sofa, and asked her, a little anxiously, whether she had heard from her mother since her arrival.

She answered "No."

He then asked her whether she knew where a letter would reach her at present.

"I cannot tell," she answered, ambiguously, "but I have been thinking of leaving you; you have been already too hospitable and too kind to me. I have given you an infinity of trouble, and I should wish to take a carriage tomorrow, and post in pursuit of her; I know where I shall ultimately find her, although I dare not yet tell you."

"But you must not dream of such a thing," exclaimed my father, to my great relief. "We can't afford to lose you so, and I won't consent to your leaving us, except under the care of your mother, who was so good as to consent to your remaining with us till she should herself return. I should be quite happy if I knew that you heard from her; but this evening the accounts of the progress of the mysterious disease that has invaded our neighborhood, grow even more alarming; and my beautiful guest, I do feel the responsibility, unaided by advice from your mother, very much. But I shall do my best; and one thing is certain, that you must not think of leaving us without her distinct direction to that effect. We should suffer too much in parting from you to consent to it easily."

"Thank you, sir, a thousand times for your hospitality," she answered, smiling bashfully. "You have all been too kind to me; I have seldom been so happy in all my life before, as in your beautiful chateau, under your care, and in the society of your dear daughter."

So he gallantly, in his old-fashioned way, kissed her hand, smiling, and pleased at her little speech.

I accompanied Carmilla as usual to her room, and sat and chatted with her while she was preparing for bed.

"Do you think," I said, at length, "that you will ever confide fully in me?"

She turned around smiling, but made no answer, only continued to smile on me.

"You won't answer that?" I said. "You can't answer pleasantly; I ought not to have asked you."

"You were quite right to ask me that, or anything. You do not know how dear you are to me, or you could not think any confidence too great to look for. But I am under vows, no nun half so awfully, and I dare not tell my story yet, even to you. The time is very near when you shall know everything. You will think me cruel, very selfish, but love is always selfish; the more ardent the more selfish. How jealous I am you cannot know. You must come with me, loving me, to death; or else hate me, and still come with me, and *hating* me through death and after. There is no such word as indifference in my apathetic nature."

"Now, Carmilla, you are going to talk your wild nonsense again," I said hastily. "Not I, silly little fool as I am, and full of whims and fancies; for your sake I'll talk like a sage. Were you ever at a ball?"

"No; how you do run on. What is it like? How charming it must be."

"I almost forget, it is years ago."

I laughed.

"You are not so old. Your first ball can hardly be forgotten yet."

"I remember everything about it—with an effort. I see it all, as divers see what is going on above them, through a medium, dense, rippling, but transparent. There occurred that night what has confused the picture, and made its colors faint. I was all but assassinated in my bed, wounded *here,*"she touched her breast, "and never was the same since."

"Were you near dying?"

"Yes, a very—cruel love—strange love, that would have taken my life. Love will have its sacrifices. No sacrifice without blood. Let us go to sleep now; I feel lazy. How can I get up just now and lock my door?"

She was lying with her tiny hands buried in her rich wavy hair, under her cheek, her little head upon the pillow, and her glittering eyes followed me wherever I moved, with a kind of shy smile that I could not decipher.

I bid her good-night, and crept from the room with an uncomfortable sensation.

I often wondered whether our pretty guest ever said her prayers. I certainly had never seen her upon her knees. In the morning she never came down until long after our family prayers were over, and at night she never left the drawing room to attend our brief evening prayers in the hall.

If it had not been that it had casually come out in one of our careless talks that she had been baptized, I should have doubted her being a Christian. Religion was a subject on which I had never heard her speak a word. If I had known of the world better, this particular neglect or antipathy would not have so much surprised me.

The precautions of nervous people are infectious, and persons of a like temperament are pretty sure, after a time, to imitate them. I had adopted Carmilla's habit of locking her bed room door, having taken into my head all her whimsical alarms about midnight invaders, and prowling assassins. I had also adopted her precaution of making a brief search through her room, to satisfy herself that no lurking assassin or robber was "ensconced."

These wise measures taken, I got into my bed and fell asleep. A light was burning in my room. This was an old habit, of very early date, and which nothing could have tempted me to dispense with.

Thus fortified I might take my rest in peace. But dreams come through stone walls, light up dark rooms, or darken light ones, and their persons make their exits and their entrances as they please, and laugh at locksmiths.

I had a dream that night that was the beginning of a very strange agony.

I cannot call it a nightmare, for I was quite conscious of being asleep. But I was equally conscious of being in my room, and lying in bed, precisely as I actually was. I saw, or fancied I saw, the room and its furniture just as I had seen it last, except that it was very dark, and I saw something moving round the foot of the bed, which at first I could not accurately distinguish. But I soon saw that it was a sooty-black animal that resembled a monstrous cat. It appeared to me about four or five feet long, for it measured fully the length of the hearth-rug as it passed over it; and it continued to-ing and fro-ing with the lithe sinister restlessness of a beast in a cage. I could not cry out, although as you may suppose, I was terrified. Its pace was growing faster, and the room rapidly darker and darker, and at length so dark that I could no longer see anything of it but its eyes. I felt it spring lightly on the bed. The two broad eyes approached my face, and suddenly I felt a sting-ing pain as if two large needles darted, an inch or two apart, deep into my breast. I waked with a scream. The room was lighted by the can-dle that burnt there all through the night, and I saw a female figure standing at the foot of the bed, a little at the right side. It was in a dark loose dress, and its hair was down and covered its shoulders. A block of stone could not have been more still. There was not the slightest stir of respiration. As I stared at it, the figure appeared to have changed its place, and was now nearer the door; then, close to it, the door opened, and it passed out.

I was now relieved, and able to breathe and move. My first thought was that Carmilla had been playing me a trick, and that I had forgot-ten to secure my door. I hastened to it, and found it locked as usual on the inside. I was afraid to open it—I was horrified. I sprang into my bed and covered my head up in the bedclothes, and lay there more dead than alive till morning.

Chapter Seven
DESCENDING

It would be vain my attempting to tell you the horror with which, even now, I recall the occurrence of that night. It was no such transitory ter-ror as a dream leaves behind it. It seemed to deepen by time, and com-municated itself to the room and the very furniture that had encom-passed the apparition.

I could not bear the next day to be alone for a moment. I should have told papa, but for two opposite reasons. At one time I thought he would laugh at my story, and I could not bear its being treated as a jest; and at another, I thought he might fancy that I had been attacked by the mysterious complaint which had invaded our neighborhood. I had myself no misgivings of the kind, and as he had been rather an invalid for some time, I was afraid of alarming him.

I was comfortable enough with my good-natured companions, Madame Perrodon, and the vivacious Mademoiselle Lafontaine. They both perceived that I was out of spirits and nervous, and at length I told them what lay so heavy at my heart.

Mademoiselle laughed, but I fancied that Madame Perrodon looked anxious.

"By-the-by," said Mademoiselle, laughing, "the long lime tree walk, behind Carmilla's bed room window, is haunted."

"Nonsense!" exclaimed Madame, who probably thought the theme rather inopportune, "and who tells that story, my dear?"

"Martin says that he came up twice, when the old yard-gate was being repaired before sunrise, and twice saw the same female figure walking down the lime tree avenue."

"So he well might, as long as they have cows to milk in the river fields," said Madame.

"I daresay; but Martin chooses to be frightened, and never did I see fool *more* frightened."

"You must not say a word about it to Carmilla, because she can see down that walk from her room window," I interposed, "and she is, if possible, a greater coward than I."

Carmilla came down rather later than usual that day.

"I was so frightened last night," she said, so soon as we were together, "and I am sure I should have seen something dreadful if it had not been for that charm I bought from the poor little hunchback whom I called such hard names. I had a dream of something black coming round my bed, and I awoke in a perfect horror, and I really thought, for some seconds, I saw a dark figure near the chimney piece, but I felt under my pillow for my charm, and the moment my fingers touched it, the figure disappeared, and I felt quite certain, only that I had it by me, that something frightful would have made its appearance, and, perhaps, throttled me, as it did those poor people we heard of."

"Well, listen to me," I began, and recounted my adventure, at the recital of which she appeared horrified.

"And had you the charm near you?" she asked, earnestly.

"No, I had dropped it into a china vase in the drawing room, but I shall certainly take it with me to-night, as you have so much faith in it."

At this distance of time I cannot tell you, or even understand, how I overcame my horror so effectually as to lie alone in my room that night. I remember distinctly that I pinned the charm to my pillow. I fell asleep almost immediately, and slept even more soundly than usual all night.

Next night I passed as well. My sleep was delightfully deep and dreamless. But I wakened with a sense of lassitude and melancholy, which, however, did not exceed a degree that was almost luxurious.

"Well, I told you so," said Carmilla, when I described my quiet sleep, "I had such delightful sleep myself last night; I pinned the charm to the breast of my nightdress. It was too far away the night before. I am quite sure it was all fancy, except the dreams. I used to think that evil spirits made dreams, but our doctor told me it is no such thing. Only a fever passing by, or some other malady, as they often do, he said, knocks at the door, and not being able to get in, passes on, with that alarm."

"And what do you think the charm is?" said I.

"It has been fumigated or immersed in some drug, and is an anti-dote against the malaria," she answered.

"Then it acts only on the body?"

"Certainly; you don't suppose that evil spirits are frightened by bits of ribbon, or the perfumes of a druggist's shop? No, these complaints, wandering in the air, begin by trying the nerves, and so infect the brain; but before they can seize upon you, the antidote repels them. That I am sure is what the charm has done for us. It is nothing magical, it is simply natural."

I should have been happier if I could quite have agreed with Carmilla, but I did my best, and the impression was a little losing its force.

For some nights I slept profoundly; but still every morning I felt the same lassitude, and a languor weighed upon me all day. I felt myself a changed girl. A strange melancholy was stealing over me, a melancholy that I would not have interrupted. Dim thoughts of death began to open, and an idea that I was slowly sinking took gentle, and, somehow, not unwelcome possession of me. If it was sad, the tone of mind which this induced was also sweet. Whatever it might be, my soul acquiesced in it.

I would not admit that I was ill, I would not consent to tell my papa, or to have the doctor sent for.

Carmilla became more devoted to me than ever, and her strange paroxysms of languid adoration more frequent. She used to gloat on me with increasing ardor the more my strength and spirits waned. This always shocked me like a momentary glare of insanity.

Without knowing it, I was now in a pretty advanced stage of the strangest illness under which mortal ever suffered. There was an unaccountable fascination in its earlier symptoms that more than reconciled me to the incapacitating effect of that stage of the malady. This fascination increased for a time, until it reached a certain point, when gradually a sense of the horrible mingled itself with it, deepening, as you shall hear, until it discolored and perverted the whole state of my life.

The first change I experienced was rather agreeable. It was very near the turning point from which began the descent of Avernus.

Certain vague and strange sensations visited me in my sleep. The prevailing one was of that pleasant, peculiar cold thrill which we feel in bathing, when we move against the current of a river. This was soon accompanied by dreams that seemed interminable, and were so vague that I could never recollect their scenery and persons, or any one connected portion of their action. But they left an awful impression, and a sense of exhaustion, as if I had passed through a long period of great mental exertion and danger. After all these dreams there remained on waking a remembrance of having been in a place very nearly dark, and of having spoken to people whom I could not see; and especially of one clear voice, of a female's, very deep, that spoke as if at a distance, slowly, and producing always the same sensation of indescribable solemnity and fear. Sometimes there came a sensation as if a hand was drawn softly along my cheek and neck. Sometimes it was as if warm lips kissed me, and longer and more lovingly as they reached my throat, but there the caress fixed itself. My heart beat faster, my breathing rose and fell rapidly and full drawn; a sobbing, that rose into a sense of strangulation, supervened, and turned into a dreadful convulsion, in which my senses left me, and I became unconscious.

It was now three weeks since the commencement of this unaccountable state. My sufferings had, during the last week, told upon my appearance. I had grown pale, my eyes were dilated and darkened underneath, and the languor which I had long felt began to display itself in my countenance.

My father asked me often whether I was ill; but, with an obstinacy which now seems to me unaccountable, I persisted in assuring him that I was quite well.

In a sense this was true. I had no pain, I could complain of no bodily derangement. My complaint seemed to be one of the imagination, or the nerves, and, horrible as my sufferings were, I kept them, with a morbid reserve, very nearly to myself.

It could not be that terrible complaint which the peasants call the oupire, for I had now been suffering for three weeks, and they were seldom ill for much more than three days, when death put an end to their miseries.

Carmilla complained of dreams and feverish sensations, but by no means of so alarming a kind as mine. I say that mine were extremely alarming. Had I been capable of comprehending my condition, I would have invoked aid and advice on my knees. The narcotic of an unsuspected influence was acting upon me, and my perceptions were benumbed.

I am going to tell you now of a dream that led immediately to an odd discovery.

One night, instead of the voice I was accustomed to hear in the dark, I heard one, sweet and tender, and at the same time terrible, which said, "Your mother warns you to beware of the assassin." At the same time a light unexpectedly sprang up, and I saw Carmilla, standing, near the foot of my bed, in her white nightdress, bathed, from her chin to her feet, in one great stain of blood.

I wakened with a shriek, possessed with the one idea that Carmilla was being murdered. I remember springing from my bed, and my next recollection is that of standing on the lobby, crying for help.

Madame and Mademoiselle came scurrying out of their rooms in alarm; a lamp burned always on the lobby, and seeing me, they soon learned the cause of my terror.

I insisted on our knocking at Carmilla's door. Our knocking was unanswered. It soon became a pounding and an uproar. We shrieked her name, but all was vain.

We all grew frightened, for the door was locked. We hurried back, in panic, to my room. There we rang the bell long and furiously. If my father's room had been at that side of the house, we would have called him up at once to our aid. But, alas he was quite out of hearing, and to reach him involved an excursion for which we none of us had courage.

Servants, however, soon came running up the stairs; I had got on my dressing-gown and slippers meanwhile, and my companions were already similarly furnished. Recognizing the voices of the servants on the lobby, we sallied out together; and having renewed, as fruitlessly, our summons at Carmilla's door, I ordered the men to force the lock. They did so, and we stood, holding our lights aloft, in the doorway, and so stared into the room.

We called her by name; but there was still no reply. We looked round the room. Everything was undisturbed. It was exactly in the state in which I left it on bidding her good night. But Carmilla was gone.

J. Sheridan LeFanu

Chapter Eight
SEARCH

At sight of the room, perfectly undisturbed except for our violent entrance, we began to cool a little, and soon recovered our senses sufficiently to dismiss the men. It had struck Mademoiselle that possibly Carmilla had been wakened by the uproar at her door, and in her first panic had jumped from her bed, and hid herself in a press, or behind a curtain, from which she could not, of course, emerge until the majordomo and his myrmidons had withdrawn. We now recommenced our search, and began to call her by name again.

It was all to no purpose. Our perplexity and agitation increased. We examined the windows, but they were secured. I implored of Carmilla, if she had concealed herself, to play this cruel trick no longer—to come out, and to end our anxieties. It was all useless. I was by this time convinced that she was not in the room, nor in the dressing room, the door of which was still locked on this side. She could not have passed it. I was utterly puzzled. Had Carmilla discovered one of those secret passages which the old housekeeper said were known to exist in the schloss, although the tradition of their exact situation had been lost? A little time would, no doubt, explain all—utterly perplexed as, for the present, we were.

It was past four o'clock, and I preferred passing the remaining hours of darkness in Madame's room. Daylight brought no solution of the difficulty.

The whole household, with my father at its head, was in a state of agitation next morning. Every part of the chateau was searched. The grounds were explored. Not a trace of the missing lady could be discovered. The stream was about to be dragged; my father was in distraction; what a tale to have to tell the poor girl's mother on her return. I, too, was almost beside myself, though my grief was quite of a different kind.

The morning was passed in alarm and excitement. It was now one o'clock, and still no tidings. I ran up to Carmilla's room, and found her standing at her dressing-table. I was astounded. I could not believe my eyes. She beckoned me to her with her pretty finger, in silence. Her face expressed extreme fear.

I ran to her in an ecstasy of joy; I kissed and embraced her again and again. I ran to the bell and rang it vehemently, to bring others to the spot, who might at once relieve my father's anxiety.

"Dear Carmilla, what has become of you all this time? We have been in agonies of anxiety about you," I exclaimed. "Where have you been? How did you come back?"

"Last night has been a night of wonders," she said.

"For mercy's sake, explain all you can."

"It was past two last night," she said, "when I went to sleep as usual in my bed, with my doors locked, that of the dressing room, and that opening upon the gallery. My sleep was uninterrupted, and, so far as I know, dreamless; but I awoke just now on the sofa in the dressing room there, and I found the door between the rooms open, and the other door forced. How could all this have happened without my being wakened? It must have been accompanied with a great deal of noise, and I am particularly easily wakened; and how could I have been carried out of my bed without my sleep having been interrupted, I whom the slightest stir startles?"

By this time, Madame, Mademoiselle, my father, and a number of the servants were in the room. Carmilla, was, of course, overwhelmed with inquiries, congratulations, and welcomes. She had but one story to tell, and seemed the least able of all the party to suggest any way of accounting for what had happened.

My father took a turn up and down the room, thinking. I saw Carmilla's eye follow him for a moment with a sly, dark glance.

When my father had sent the servants away, Mademoiselle having gone in search of a little bottle of valerian and sal-volatile, and there being no one in the room with Carmilla except my father, Madame, and myself, he came to her thoughtfully, took her hand very kindly, led her to the sofa, and sat down beside her.

"Will you forgive me, my dear, if I risk a conjecture, and ask a question?"

"Who can have a better right?" she said. "Ask what you please, and I will tell you everything. But my story is simply one of bewilderment and darkness. I know absolutely nothing. Put any question you please. But you know, of course, the limitations mamma has placed me under."

"Perfectly, my dear child. I need not approach the topics on which she desires our silence. Now, the marvel of last night consists in your having been removed from your bed and your room without being wakened, and this removal having occurred apparently while the windows were still secured, and the two doors locked upon the inside. I will tell you my theory, and first ask you a question."

Carmilla was leaning on her hand dejectedly; Madame and I were listening breathlessly.

"Now, my question is this. Have you ever been suspected of walking in your sleep?"

"Never since I was very young indeed."

"But you did walk in your sleep when you were very young?"

"Yes; I know I did. I have been told so often by my old nurse."

My father smiled and nodded.

"Well, what has happened is this. You got up in your sleep, unlocked the door, not leaving the key, as usual, in the lock, but taking it out and locking it on the outside; you again took the key out, and carried it away with you to some one of the five-and-twenty rooms on this floor, or perhaps upstairs or downstairs. There are so many rooms and closets, so much heavy furniture, and such accumulations of lumber, that it would require a week to search this old house thoroughly. Do you see, now, what I mean?"

"I do, but not all," she answered.

"And how, papa, do you account for her finding herself on the sofa in the dressing room, which we had searched so carefully?"

"She came there after you had searched it, still in her sleep, and at last awoke spontaneously, and was as much surprised to find herself where she was as any one else. I wish all mysteries were as easily and innocently explained as yours, Carmilla," he said, laughing. "And so we may congratulate ourselves on the certainty that the most natural explanation of the occurrence is one that involves no drugging, no tampering with locks, no burglars, or poisoners, or witches—nothing that need alarm Carmilla, or any one else, for our safety."

Carmilla was looking charmingly. Nothing could be more beautiful than her tints. Her beauty was, I think, enhanced by that graceful languor that was peculiar to her. I think my father was silently contrasting her looks with mine, for he said:—

"I wish my poor Laura was looking more like herself;" and he sighed.

So our alarms were happily ended, and Carmilla restored to her friends.

Chapter Nine
THE DOCTOR

As Carmilla would not hear of an attendant sleeping in her room, my father arranged that a servant should sleep outside her door, so that she could not attempt to make another such excursion without being arrested at her own door.

That night passed quickly; and next morning early, the doctor, whom my father had sent for without telling me a word about it, arrived to see me.

Madame accompanied me to the library; and there the grave little doctor, with white hair and spectacles, whom I mentioned before, was waiting to receive me.

I told him my story, and as I proceeded he grew graver and graver.

We were standing, he and I, in the recess of one of the windows, facing one another. When my statement was over, he leaned with his shoulders against the wall, and with his eyes fixed on me earnestly, with an interest in which was a dash of horror.

After a minute's reflection, he asked Madame if he could see my father.

He was sent for accordingly, and as he entered, smiling, he said:

"I dare say, doctor, you are going to tell me that I am an old fool for having brought you here; I hope I am."

But his smile faded into shadow as the doctor, with a very grave face, beckoned him to him.

He and the doctor talked for some time in the same recess where I had just conferred with the physician. It seemed an earnest and argumentative conversation. The room is very large, and I and Madame stood together, burning with curiosity, at the further end. Not a word could we hear, however, for they spoke in a very low tone, and the deep recess of the window quite concealed the doctor from view, and very nearly my father, whose foot, arm, and shoulder only could we see: and the voices were, I suppose, all the less audible for the sort of closet which the thick wall and window formed.

After a time my father's face looked into the room; it was pale, thoughtful, and, I fancied, agitated.

"Laura, dear, come here for a moment. Madame, we shan't trouble you, the doctor says, at present."

Accordingly I approached, for the first time a little alarmed; for, although I felt very weak, I did not feel ill; and strength, one always fancies, is a thing that may be picked up when we please.

My father held out his hand to me as I drew near, but he was looking at the doctor, and he said:

"It certainly is very odd; I don't understand it quite. Laura, come here, dear; now attend to Doctor Spielsberg, and recollect yourself."

"You mentioned a sensation like that of two needles piercing the skin, somewhere about your neck, on the night when you experienced your first horrible dream. Is there still any soreness?"

"None at all," I answered.

"Can you indicate with your finger about the point at which you think this occurred?"

"Very little below my throat—*here*," I answered.

I wore a morning dress, which covered the place I pointed to.

"Now you can satisfy yourself," said the doctor. "You won't mind your papa's lowering your dress a very little. It is necessary, to detect a symptom of the complaint under which you have been suffering."

I acquiesced. It was only an inch or two below the edge of my collar.

"God bless me—so it is," exclaimed my father, growing pale.

"You see it now with your own eyes," said the doctor, with a gloomy triumph.

"What is it?" I exclaimed, beginning to be frightened.

"Nothing, my dear young lady, but a small blue spot, about the size of the tip of your little finger; and now," he continued, turning to papa, "the question is what is the best to be done?"

"Is there any danger?" I urged, in great trepidation.

"I trust not, my dear," answered the doctor. "I don't see why you should not recover. I don't see why you should not begin *immediately* to get better. That is the point at which the sense of strangulation begins?"

"Yes," I answered.

"And—recollect as well as you can—the same point was a kind of center of that thrill which you described just now like the current of a cold stream running against you?"

"It may have been; I think it was."

"Ay, you see?" he added, turning to my father. "Shall I say a word to Madame?"

"Certainly," said my father.

He called Madame to him, and said:

"I find my young friend here far from well. It won't be of any great consequence, I hope; but it will be necessary that some steps be taken, which I will explain by-and-by; but in the meantime, Madame, you will be so good as not to let Miss Laura be alone for one moment. That is the only direction I need give for the present. It is indispensable."

"We may rely upon your kindness, Madame, I know," added my father.

Madame satisfied him eagerly.

"And you, dear Laura, I know you will observe the doctor's direction."

"I shall have to ask your opinion upon another patient, whose symptoms slightly resemble those of my daughter, that have just been detailed to you—very much milder in degree, but I believe quite of the same sort. She is a young lady—our guest; but as you say you will be passing this way again this evening, you can't do better than take your supper here, and you can then see her. She does not come down till the afternoon."

"I thank you," said the doctor. "I shall be with you, then, at about seven this evening."

And then they repeated their directions to me and to Madame, and with this parting charge my father left us, and walked out with the doctor; and I saw them pacing together up and down between the road and the moat, on the grassy platform in front of the castle, evidently absorbed in earnest conversation.

The doctor did not return. I saw him mount his horse there, take his leave, and ride away eastward through the forest. Nearly at the same time I saw the man arrive from Dranfeld with the letters, and dismount and hand the bag to my father.

In the meantime, Madame and I were both busy, lost in conjecture as to the reasons of the singular and earnest direction which the doctor and my father had concurred in imposing. Madame, as she afterwards told me, was afraid the doctor apprehended a sudden seizure, and that, without prompt assistance, I might either lose my life in a fit, or at least be seriously hurt.

This interpretation did not strike me; and I fancied, perhaps luckily for my nerves, that the arrangement was prescribed simply to secure a companion, who would prevent my taking too much exercise, or eating unripe fruit, or doing any of the fifty foolish things to which young people are supposed to be prone.

About half-an-hour after my father came in—he had a letter in his hand—and said:

"This letter has been delayed; it is from General Spielsdorf. He might have been here yesterday, he may not come till to-morrow, or he may be here to-day."

He put the open letter into my hand; but he did not look pleased, as he used when a guest, especially one so much loved as the General, was coming. On the contrary, he looked as if he wished him at the bottom of the Red Sea. There was plainly something on his mind which he did not choose to divulge.

"Papa, darling, will you tell me this?" said I, suddenly laying my hand on his arm, and looking, I am sure, imploringly in his face.

"Perhaps," he answered, smoothing my hair caressingly over my eyes.

"Does the doctor think me very ill?"

"No, dear; he thinks, if right steps are taken, you will be quite well again, at least on the high road to a complete recovery, in a day or two," he answered, a little dryly. "I wish our good friend, the General, had chosen any other time; that is, I wish you had been perfectly well to receive him."

"But do tell me papa," I insisted, *what* does he think is the matter with me?"

"Nothing; you must not plague me with questions," he answered, with more irritation than I ever remember him to have displayed before; and seeing that I looked wounded, I suppose, he kissed me, and added, "You shall know all about it in a day or two; that is, all that I know. In the meantime, you are not to trouble your head about it."

He turned and left the room, but came back before I had done wondering and puzzling over the oddity of all this; it was merely to say that he was going to Karnstein, and had ordered the carriage to be ready at twelve, and that I and Madame should accompany him; he was going to see the priest who lived near those picturesque grounds, upon business, and as Carmilla had never seen them, she could follow, when she came down, with Mademoiselle, who would bring materials for what you call a picnic, which might be laid for us in the ruined castle.

At twelve o'clock, accordingly, I was ready, and not long after, my father, Madame and I set out upon our projected drive. Passing the drawbridge we turn to the right, and follow the road over the steep Gothic bridge, westward, to reach the deserted village and ruined castle of Karnstein.

No sylvan drive can be fancied prettier. The ground breaks into gentle hills and hollows, all clothed with beautiful wood, totally destitute of the comparative formality which artificial planting and early culture and pruning impart.

The irregularities of the ground often lead the road out of its course, and cause it to wind beautifully round the sides of broken hollows and the steeper sides of the hills, among varieties of ground almost inexhaustible.

Turning one of these points, we suddenly encountered our old friend, the General, riding towards us, attended by a mounted servant. His portmanteaus were following in a hired wagon, such as we term a cart.

The General dismounted as we pulled up, and, after the usual greetings, was easily persuaded to accept the vacant seat in the carriage, and send his horse on with his servant to the schloss.

Chapter Ten
BEREAVED

It was about ten months since we had last seen him; but that time had sufficed to make an alteration of years in his appearance. He had grown thinner; something of gloom and anxiety had taken the place of that cordial serenity which used to characterize his features. His dark blue eyes, always penetrating, now gleamed with a sterner light from under his shaggy gray eyebrows. It was not such a change as grief alone usually induces, and angrier passions seemed to have had their share in bringing it about.

We had not long resumed our drive, when the General began to talk, with his usual soldierly directness, of the bereavement, as he termed it, which he had sustained in the death of his beloved niece and ward; and he then broke out in a tone of intense bitterness and fury, inveighing against the "hellish arts" to which she had fallen a victim, and expressing with more exasperation than piety, his wonder that Heaven should tolerate so monstrous an indulgence of the lusts and malignity of hell.

My father, who saw at once that something very extraordinary had befallen, asked him, if not too painful to him, to detail the circumstances which he thought justified the strong terms in which he expressed himself.

"I should tell you all with pleasure," said the General, "but you would not believe me."

"Why should I not?" he asked.

"Because," he answered testily, "you believe in nothing but what consists with your own prejudices and illusions. I remember when I was like you, but I have learned better."

"Try me," said my father; "I am not such a dogmatist as you suppose. Besides which, I very well know that you generally require proof for what you believe and am, therefore, very strongly predisposed to respect your conclusions."

"You are right in supposing that I have not been led lightly into a belief in the marvelous—for what I have experienced *is* marvelous—and I have been forced by extraordinary evidence to credit that which ran counter, diametrically, to all my theories. I have been made the dupe of a preternatural conspiracy."

Notwithstanding his profession of confidence in the General's penetration, I saw my father, at this point, glance at the General, with, as I thought, a marked suspicion of his sanity.

The General did not see it, luckily. He was looking gloomily and curiously into the glades and vistas of the woods that were opening before us.

"You are going to the Ruins of Karnstein?" he said. "Yes, it is a lucky coincidence; do you know I was going to ask you to bring me there to inspect them. I have a special object in exploring. There is a ruined chapel, ain't there, with a great many tombs of that extinct family?"

"So there are—highly interesting," said my father, "I hope you are thinking of claiming the title and estates?"

My father said this gaily, but the General did not recollect the laugh, or even smile, which courtesy exacts for a friend's joke; on the contrary, he looked grave and even fierce, ruminating on a matter that stirred his anger and horror.

"Something very different," he said, gruffly. "I mean to unearth some of those fine people. I hope by God's blessing, to accomplish a pious sacrilege here, which will relieve our earth of certain monsters, and enable honest people to sleep in their beds without being assailed by murderers. I have strange things to tell you, my dear friend, such as I myself would have scouted as incredible a few months since."

My father looked at him again, but this time not with a glance of suspicion—with an eye, rather, of keen intelligence and alarm.

"The house of Karnstein," he said, "has been long extinct: a hundred years at least. My dear wife was maternally descended from the Karnsteins. But the name and title have long ceased to exist. The castle is a ruin; the very village is deserted; it is fifty years since the smoke of a chimney was seen there; not a roof left."

"Quite true. I have heard a great deal about that since I last saw you; a great deal that will astonish you. But I had better relate everything in the order in which it occurred," said the General. "You saw my dear ward—my child, I may call her. No creature could have been more beautiful, and only three months ago none more blooming."

"Yes, poor thing! when I saw her last she certainly was quite lovely," said my father. "I was grieved and shocked more than I can tell you, my dear friend; I knew what a blow it was to you."

He took the General's hand, and they exchanged a kind pressure. Tears gathered in the old soldier's eyes. He did not seek to conceal them. He said:

"We have been very old friends; I knew you would feel for me, childless as I am. She had become an object of very dear interest to me, and repaid my care by an affection that cheered my home and made my life happy. That is all gone. The years that remain to me on earth may not be very long; but by God's mercy I hope to accomplish a service to mankind before I die, and to subserve the vengeance of Heaven upon the fiends who have murdered my poor child in the spring of her hopes and beauty."

"You said, just now, that you intended relating everything as it occurred," said my father. "Pray do; I assure you that it is not mere curiosity that prompts me."

By this time we had reached the point at which the Drunstall road, by which the General had come, diverges from the road which we were traveling to Karnstein.

"How far is it to the ruins?" inquired the General, looking anxiously forward.

"About half a league," answered my father. "Pray let us hear the story you were so good as to promise."

Chapter Eleven
THE STORY

"With all my heart," said the General, with an effort; and after a pause in which to arrange his subject, he commenced one of the strangest narratives I ever heard.

"My dear child was looking forward with great pleasure to the visit you had been so good as to arrange for her to your charming daughter." Here he made me a gallant but melancholy bow. "In the meantime we had an invitation to my old friend the Count Carlsfeld, whose schloss is about six leagues to the other side of Karnstein. It was to attend the series of fêtes which, you remember, were given by him in honor of his illustrious visitor, the Grand Duke Charles."

"Yes; and very splendid, I believe they were," said my father.

"Princely. But then his hospitalities are quite regal. He has Aladdin's lamp. The night from which my sorrow dates was devoted to a magnificent masquerade. The grounds were thrown open, the trees hung with colored lamps. There was such a display of fireworks as Paris itself had never witnessed. And such music—music, you know, is my weakness—such ravishing music! The finest instrumental band, perhaps, in the world, and the finest singers who could be collected from all the great operas in Europe. As you wandered through those fantastically illuminated grounds, the moon-lighted chateau throwing a rosy light from its long rows of windows, you would suddenly hear these ravishing voices stealing from the silence of some grove, or rising from boats upon the lake. I felt myself, as I looked and listened, carried back into the romance and poetry of my early youth.

"When the fireworks were ended, and the ball beginning, we returned to the noble suite of rooms that were thrown open to the dancers. A masked ball, you know, is a beautiful sight; but so brilliant a spectacle of the kind I never saw before.

"It was a very aristocratic assembly. I saw myself almost the only 'nobody' present.

"My dear child was looking quite beautiful. She wore no mask. Her excitement and delight added an unspeakable charm to her features, always lovely. I remarked a young lady, dressed magnificently, but wearing a mask, who appeared to me to be observing my ward with extraordinary interest. I had seen her, earlier in the evening, in the great hall, and again, for a few minutes, walking near us, on the terrace under the castle windows, similarly employed. A lady, also masked, richly and gravely dressed, and with stately air, like a person of rank, accompanied her as a chaperon. Had the young lady not worn a mask, I could of course, have been much more certain upon the question whether she was really watching my poor darling. I am now well assured that she was.

"We were in one of the *salons*. My poor dear child had been dancing, and was resting a little in one of the chairs near the door; I was standing near. The two ladies I have mentioned had approached, and the younger took the chair next my ward; while her companion stood beside me, and for a little time addressed herself, in a low tone, to her charge.

"Availing herself of the privilege of her mask, she turned to me, and in the tone of an old friend, and calling me by my name, opened a conversation with me, which piqued my curiosity a good deal. She referred to many scenes where she had met me—at Court, and at distinguished houses. She alluded to little incidents which I had long ceased to think of, but which, I found, had only lain in abeyance in my memory, for they instantly started into life at her touch.

"I became more and more curious to ascertain who she was, every moment. She parried my attempts to discover very adroitly and pleasantly. The knowledge she showed of many passages in my life seemed to me all but unaccountable; and she appeared to take a not unnatural pleasure in foiling my curiosity, and in seeing me flounder, in my eager perplexity, from one conjecture to another.

"In the meantime the young lady, whom her mother called by the odd name of Millarca, when she once or twice addressed her, had, with the same ease and grace, got into conversation with my ward.

"She introduced herself by saying that her mother was a very old acquaintance of mine. She spoke of the agreeable audacity which a mask rendered practicable; she talked like a friend; she admired her dress, and insinuated very prettily her admiration of her beauty. She amused her with laughing criticisms upon the people who crowded the ballroom, and laughed at my poor child's fun. She was very witty and lively when she pleased, and after a time they had grown very good friends, and the young stranger lowered her mask, displaying a remarkably beautiful face. I had never seen it before, neither had my dear child. But though it was new to us, the features were so engaging, as well as lovely, that it was impossible not to feel the attraction powerfully. My poor girl did so. I never saw anyone more taken with another at first sight, unless, indeed, it was the stranger herself, who seemed quite to have lost her heart to her.

"In the meantime, availing myself of the license of a masquerade, I put not a few questions to the elder lady.

"'You have puzzled me utterly,' I said, laughing. 'Is that not enough?

won't you, now, consent to stand on equal terms, and do me the kindness to remove your mask?'

"'Can any request be more unreasonable?' she replied. 'Ask a lady to yield an advantage! Beside, how do you know you should recognize me? Years make changes.'

"'As you see,' I said, with a bow, and, I suppose, a rather melancholy little laugh.

"'As philosophers tell us,' she said; 'and how do you know that a sight of my face would help you?'

"'I should take chance for that,' I answered. 'It is vain trying to make yourself out an old woman; your figure betrays you.'

"'Years, nevertheless, have passed since I saw you, rather since you saw me, for that is what I am considering. Millarca, there, is my daughter; I cannot then be young, even in the opinion of people whom time has taught to be indulgent, and I may not like to be compared with what you remember me. You have no mask to remove. You can offer me nothing in exchange.'

"'My petition is to your pity, to remove it.'

"'And mine to yours, to let it stay where it is,' she replied.

"'Well, then, at least you will tell me whether you are French or German; you speak both languages so perfectly.'

"'I don't think I shall tell you that, General; you intend a surprise, and are meditating the particular point of attack.'

"'At all events, you won't deny this,' I said, 'that being honored by your permission to converse, I ought to know how to address you. Shall I say Madame la Comtesse?'

"She laughed, and she would, no doubt, have met me with another evasion—if, indeed, I can treat any occurrence in an interview every circumstance of which was pre-arranged, as I now believe, with the profoundest cunning, as liable to be modified by accident.

"'As to that,' she began; but she was interrupted, almost as she opened her lips, by a gentleman, dressed in black, who looked particularly elegant and distinguished, with this drawback, that his face was the most deadly pale I ever saw, except in death. He was in no masquerade—in the plain evening dress of a gentleman; and he said, without a smile, but with a courtly and unusually low bow:—

"'Will Madame la Comtesse permit me to say a very few words which may interest her?'

"The lady turned quickly to him, and touched her lip in token of silence; she then said to me, 'Keep my place for me, General; I shall return when I have said a few words.'

"And with this injunction, playfully given, she walked a little aside with the gentleman in black, and talked for some minutes, apparently very earnestly. They then walked away slowly together in the crowd, and I lost them for some minutes.

"I spent the interval in cudgeling my brains for conjecture as to the identity of the lady who seemed to remember me so kindly, and I was thinking of turning about and joining in the conversation between my pretty ward and the Countess's daughter, and trying whether, by the time she returned, I might not have a surprise in store for her, by having her name, title, chateau, and estates at my fingers' ends. But at this moment she returned, accompanied by the pale man in black, who said:

"'I shall return and inform Madame la Comtesse when her carriage is at the door.'

"He withdrew with a bow."

Chapter Twelve
A Petition

"'Then we are to lose Madame la Comtesse, but I hope only for a few hours,' I said, with a low bow.

"'It may be that only, or it may be a few weeks. It was very unlucky his speaking to me just now as he did. Do you now know me?"

"I assured her I did not.

"'You shall know me,' she said, 'but not at present. We are older and better friends than, perhaps, you suspect. I cannot yet declare myself. I shall in three weeks pass your beautiful schloss about which I have been making inquiries. I shall then look in upon you for an hour or two, and renew a friendship which I never think of without a thousand pleasant recollections. This moment a piece of news has reached me like a thunderbolt. I must set out now, and travel by a devious route, nearly a hundred miles, with all the dispatch I can possibly make. My perplexities multiply. I am only deterred by the compulsory reserve I practice as to my name from making a very singular request of you. My poor child has not quite recovered her strength. Her horse fell with her, at a hunt which she had ridden out to witness, her nerves have not yet recovered the shock, and our physician says that she must on no account exert herself for some time to come. We came here, in consequence, by very easy stages—hardly six leagues a day. I must now travel day and night, on a mission of life and death—a mission the critical and momentous nature of which I shall be able to explain to you when we meet, as I hope we shall, in a few weeks, without the necessity of any concealment.'

72

"She went on to make her petition, and it was in the tone of a person from whom such a request amounted to conferring, rather than seeking a favor. This was only in manner, and, as it seemed, quite unconsciously. Than the terms in which it was expressed, nothing could be more deprecatory. It was simply that I would consent to take charge of her daughter during her absence.

"This was, all things considered, a strange, not to say, an audacious request. She in some sort disarmed me, by stating and admitting everything that could be urged against it, and throwing herself entirely upon my chivalry. At the same moment, by a fatality that seems to have predetermined all that happened, my poor child came to my side, and, in an undertone, besought me to invite her new friend, Millarca, to pay us a visit. She had just been sounding her, and thought, if her mamma would allow her, she would like it extremely.

"At another time I should have told her to wait a little, until, at least, we knew who they were. But I had not a moment to think in. The two ladies assailed me together, and I must confess the refined and beautiful face of the young lady, about which there was something extremely engaging, as well as the elegance and fire of high birth, determined me; and quite overpowered, I submitted, and undertook, too easily, the care of the young lady, whom her mother called Millarca.

"The Countess beckoned to her daughter, who listened with grave attention while she told her, in general terms, how suddenly and peremptorily she had been summoned, and also of the arrangement she had made for her under my care, adding that I was one of her earliest and most valued friends.

"I made, of course, such speeches as the case seemed to call for, and found myself, on reflection, in a position which I did not half like.

"The gentleman in black returned, and very ceremoniously conducted the lady from the room.

"The demeanor of this gentleman was such as to impress me with the conviction that the Countess was a lady of very much more importance than her modest title alone might have led me to assume.

"Her last charge to me was that no attempt was to be made to learn more about her than I might have already guessed, until her return. Our distinguished host, whose guest she was, knew her reasons.

"'But here,' she said, 'neither I nor my daughter could safely remain more than a day. I removed my mask imprudently for a moment, about an hour ago, and, too late, I fancied you saw me. So I have resolved to seek an opportunity of talking a little to you. Had I found that you *had* seen me, I should have thrown myself on your high sense of honor to keep my secret for some weeks. As it is, I am satisfied that you did not see me; but if you now *suspect*, or, on reflection, *should* suspect, who I am, I commit myself, in like manner, entirely to your honor. My daughter will observe the same secrecy, and I well know that you will, from time to time, remind her, lest she should thoughtlessly disclose it.'

"She whispered a few words to her daughter, kissed her hurriedly twice, and went away, accompanied by the pale gentleman in black, and disappeared in the crowd.

"'In the next room,' said Millarca, 'there is a window that looks upon the hall door. I should like to see the last of mamma, and to kiss my hand to her.'

"We assented, of course, and accompanied her to the window. We looked out, and saw a handsome old-fashioned carriage, with a troop of couriers and footmen. We saw the slim figure of the pale gentleman in black, as he held a thick velvet cloak, and placed it about her shoulders and threw the hood over her head. She nodded to him, and just touched his hand with hers. He bowed low repeatedly as the door closed, and the carriage began to move.

"'She is gone,' said Millarca with a sigh.

"'She is gone,' I repeated to myself, for the first time—in the hurried moments that had elapsed since my consent—reflecting upon the folly of my act.

"'She did not look up,' said the young lady, plaintively.

"'The Countess had taken off her mask, perhaps, and did not care to show her face,' I said; 'and she could not know that you were in the window.'

"She sighed and looked in my face. She was so beautiful that I relented. I was sorry I had for a moment repented of my hospitality, and I determined to make her amends for the unavowed churlishness of my reception.

"The young lady, replacing her mask, joined my ward in persuading me to return to the grounds, where the concert was soon to be renewed. We did so, and walked up and down the terrace that lies under the castle windows. Millarca became very intimate with us, and amused us with lively descriptions and stories of most of the great people whom we saw upon the terrace. I liked her more and more every minute. Her gossip, without being ill-natured, was extremely diverting to me, who had been so long out of the great world. I thought what life she would give to our sometimes lonely evenings at home.

"This ball was not over until the morning sun had almost reached the horizon. It pleased the Grand Duke to dance till then, so loyal people could not go away, or think of bed.

"We had just got through a crowded saloon, when my ward asked me what had become of Millarca. I thought she had been by her side, and she fancied she was by mine. The fact was, we had lost her.

"All my efforts to find her were in vain. I feared that she had mistaken, in the confusion of the momentary separation from us, other people for her new friends, and had, possibly, pursued and lost them in the extensive grounds which were thrown open to us.

"Now, in its full force, I recognized a new folly in my having undertaken the charge of a young lady without so much as knowing her name; and fettered as I was by promises, of the reasons for imposing which I knew nothing, I could not even point my inquiries by saying that the missing young lady was the daughter of the Countess who had taken her departure a few hours before.

"Morning broke. It was clear daylight before I gave up my search. It was not till near two o'clock next day that we heard anything of my missing charge.

"At about that time a servant knocked at my niece's door, to say that he had been earnestly requested by a young lady, who appeared to be in great distress, to make out where she could find the General Baron Spielsdorf and the young lady, his daughter, in whose charge she had been left by her mother.

"There could be no doubt, notwithstanding the slight inaccuracy, that our young friend had turned up; and so she had. Would to Heaven we had lost her.

"She told my poor child a story to account for her having failed to recover us for so long. Very late, she said, she had got into the house-keeper's bed room in despair of finding us, and had then fallen into a deep sleep which, long as it was, had hardly sufficed to recruit her strength after the fatigues of the ball.

"That day Millarca came home with us. I was only too happy, after all, to have secured so charming a companion for my dear girl."

Chapter Thirteen
THE WOODMAN

"There soon, however, appeared some drawbacks. In the first place, Millarca complained of extreme languor—the weakness that remained after her late illness—and she never emerged from her room till the afternoon was pretty far advanced. In the next place, it was accidentally discovered, although she always locked her door on the inside, and never disturbed the key from its place, till she admitted the maid to assist at her toilet, that she was undoubtedly sometimes absent from her room in the very early morning, and at various times later in the day, before she wished it to be understood that she was stirring. She was repeatedly seen from the windows of the schloss, in the first faint gray of the morning, walking through the trees, in an easterly direction, and looking like a person in a trance. This convinced me that she walked in her sleep. But this hypothesis did not solve the puzzle. How did she pass out from her room, leaving the door locked on the inside? How did she escape from the house without unbarring door or window?

"In the midst of my perplexities, an anxiety of far more urgent kind presented itself.

"My dear child began to lose her looks and health, and that in a manner so mysterious, and even horrible, that I became thoroughly frightened.

"She was at first visited by appalling dreams; then, as she fancied, by a spectre, sometimes resembling Millarca, sometimes in the shape of a beast, indistinctly seen, walking round the foot of her bed, from side to side. Lastly came sensations. One, not unpleasant, but very peculiar, she said, resembled the flow of an icy stream against her breast. At a later time, she felt something like a pair of large needles pierce her, a little below the throat, with a very sharp pain. A few nights after, followed a gradual and convulsive sense of strangulation; then came unconsciousness."

I could hear distinctly every word the kind old General was saying, because by this time we were driving upon the short grass that spreads on either side of the road as you approach the roofless village which had not shown the smoke of a chimney for more than half a century.

You may guess how strangely I felt as I heard my own symptoms so exactly described in those which had been experienced by the poor girl who, but for the catastrophe which followed, would have been at that moment a visitor at my father's chateau. You may suppose, also, how I felt as I heard him detail habits and mysterious peculiarities which were, in fact, those of our beautiful guest, Carmilla!

A vista opened in the forest; we were on a sudden under the chimneys and gables of the ruined village, and the towers and battlements of the dismantled castle, round which gigantic trees are grouped, overhung us from a slight eminence.

In a frightened dream I got down from the carriage, and in silence, for we had each abundant matter for thinking; we soon mounted the ascent, and were among the spacious chambers, winding stairs, and dark corridors of the castle.

"And this was once the palatial residence of the Karnsteins!" said the old General at length, as from a great window he looked out across the village, and saw the wide, undulating expanse of forest. "It was a bad family, and here its blood-stained annals were written," he continued. "It is hard that they should, after death, continue to plague the human race with their atrocious lusts. That is the chapel of the Karnsteins, down there."

He pointed down to the gray walls of the Gothic building, partly visible through the foliage, a little way down the steep. "And I hear the axe of a woodman," he added, "busy among the trees that surround it; he possibly may give us the information of which I am in search, and point out the grave of Mircalla, Countess of Karnstein. These rustics preserve the local traditions of great families, whose stories die out among the rich and titled so soon as the families themselves become extinct."

"We have a portrait, at home, of Mircalla, the Countess Karnstein; should you like to see it?" asked my father.

"Time enough, dear friend," replied the General. "I believe that I have seen the original; and one motive which has led me to you earlier than I at first intended, was to explore the chapel which we are now approaching."

"What! see the Countess Mircalla," exclaimed my father; "why, she has been dead more than a century!"

"Not so dead as you fancy, I am told," answered the General.

"I confess, General, you puzzle me utterly," replied my father, looking at him, I fancied, for a moment with a return of the suspicion I detected before. But although there was anger and detestation, at times, in the old General's manner, there was nothing flighty.

"There remains to me," he said, as we passed under the heavy arch of the Gothic church—for its dimensions would have justified its being so styled—"but one object which can interest me during the few years that remain to me on earth, and that is to wreak on her the vengeance which, I thank God, may still be accomplished by a mortal arm."

"What vengeance can you mean?" asked my father, in increasing amazement.

"I mean, to decapitate the monster," he answered, with a fierce flush, and a stamp that echoed mournfully through the hollow ruin, and his clenched hand was at the same moment raised, as if it grasped the handle of an axe, while he shook it ferociously in the air.

"What!" exclaimed my father, more than ever bewildered.

"To strike her head off."

"Cut her head off!"

"Aye, with a hatchet, with a spade, or with anything that can cleave through her murderous throat. You shall hear," he answered, trembling with rage. And hurrying forward he said:

"That beam will answer for a seat; your dear child is fatigued; let her be seated, and I will, in a few sentences, close my dreadful story."

The squared block of wood, which lay on the grass-grown pavement of the chapel, formed a bench on which I was very glad to seat myself, and in the meantime the General called to the woodman, who had been removing some boughs which leaned upon the old walls; and, axe in hand, the hardy old fellow stood before us.

He could not tell us anything of these monuments; but there was an old man, he said, a ranger of this forest, at present sojourning in the house of the priest, about two miles away, who could point out every monument of the old Karnstein family; and, for a trifle, he undertook to bring back with him, if we would lend him one of our horses, in little more than half-an-hour.

"Have you been long employed about this forest?" asked my father of the old man.

"I have been a woodman here," he answered in his *patois,* "under the forester, all my days; so has my father before me, and so on, as many generations as I can count up. I could show you the very house in the village here, in which my ancestors lived."

"How came the village to be deserted?" asked the General.

"It was troubled by *revenants,* sir; several were tracked to their graves, there detected by the usual tests, and extinguished in the usual way, by decapitation, by the stake, and by burning; but not until many of the villagers were killed.

"But after all these proceedings according to law," he continued—"so many graves opened, and so many vampires deprived of their horrible animation—the village was not relieved. But a Moravian nobleman, who happened to be traveling this way, heard how matters were, and being skilled—as many people are in his country—in such affairs, he offered to deliver the village from its tormentor. He did so thus: There being a bright moon that night, he ascended, shortly after sunset, the tower of the chapel here, from whence he could distinctly see the churchyard beneath him; you can see it from that window. From this point he watched until he saw the vampire come out of his grave, and place near it the linen clothes in which he had been folded, and glide away towards the village to plague its inhabitants.

"The stranger, having seen all this, came down from the steeple, took the linen wrappings of the vampire, and carried them up to the top of the tower, which he again mounted. When the vampire returned from his prowlings and missed his clothes, he cried furiously to the

Moravian, whom he saw at the summit of the tower, and who, in reply, beckoned him to ascend and take them. Whereupon the vampire, accepting his invitation, began to climb the steeple, and so soon as he had reached the battlements, the Moravian, with a stroke of his sword, clove his skull in twain, hurling him down to the churchyard, whither, descending by the winding stairs, the stranger followed and cut his head off, and next day delivered it and the body to the villagers, who duly impaled and burnt them.

"This Moravian nobleman had the authority from the then head of the family to remove the tomb of Mircalla, Countess Karnstein, which he did effectually, so that in a little while its site was quite forgotten."

"Can you point out where it stood?" asked the General, eagerly.

The forester shook his head and smiled.

"Not a living soul could tell you that now," he said; "besides, they say her body was removed; but no one is sure of that either."

Having thus spoken, as time pressed, he dropped his axe and departed, leaving us to hear the remainder of the General's strange story.

Chapter Fourteen
THE MEETING

"My beloved child," he resumed, "was now growing rapidly worse. The physician who attended her had failed to produce the slightest impression upon her disease, for such I then supposed it to be. He saw my alarm, and suggested a consultation. I called in an abler physician, from Gratz. Several days elapsed before he arrived. He was a good and pious, as well as a learned man. Having seen my poor ward together, they withdrew to my library to confer and discuss. I, from the adjoining room, where I awaited their summons, heard these two gentlemen's voices raised in something sharper than a strictly philosophical discussion. I knocked at the door and entered. I found the old physician from Gratz maintaining his theory. His rival was combating it with undisguised ridicule, accompanied with bursts of laughter. This unseemly manifestation subsided and the altercation ended on my entrance.

"'Sir,' said my first physician, 'my learned brother seems to think that you want a conjurer, and not a doctor.'

"'Pardon me,' said the old physician from Gratz, looking displeased, 'I shall state my own view of the case in my own way another time. I grieve, Monsieur le General, that by my skill and science I can be of no use. Before I go I shall do myself the honor to suggest something to you.'

"He seemed thoughtful, and sat down at a table, and began to write. Profoundly disappointed, I made my bow, and as I turned to go, the other doctor pointed over his shoulder to his companion who was writing, and then, with a shrug, significantly touched his forehead.

"This consultation, then, left me precisely where I was. I walked out into the grounds, all but distracted. The doctor from Gratz, in ten or fifteen minutes, overtook me. He apologized for having followed me, but said that he could not conscientiously take his leave without a few words more. He told me that he could not be mistaken; no natural disease exhibited the same symptoms; and that death was already very near. There remained, however, a day, or possibly two, of life. If the fatal seizure were at once arrested, with great care and skill her strength might possibly return. But all hung now upon the confines of the irrevocable. One more assault might extinguish the last spark of vitality which is, every moment, ready to die.

"'And what is the nature of the seizure you speak of?' I entreated.

"'I have stated all fully in this note, which I place in your hands, upon the distinct condition that you send for the nearest clergyman, and open my letter in his presence, and on no account read it till he is with you; you would despise it else, and it is a matter of life and death. Should the priest fail you, then, indeed, you may read it.'

"He asked me, before taking his leave finally, whether I would wish to see a man curiously learned upon the very subject, which, after I had read his letter, would probably interest me above all others, and he urged me earnestly to invite him to visit him there; and so took his leave.

"The ecclesiastic was absent, and I read the letter by myself. At another time, or in another case, it might have excited my ridicule. But into what quackeries will not people rush for a last chance, where all accustomed means have failed, and the life of a beloved object is at stake?

"Nothing, you will say, could be more absurd than the learned man's letter. It was monstrous enough to have consigned him to a madhouse. He said that the patient was suffering from the visits of a vampire! The punctures which she described as having occurred near the throat, were, he insisted, the insertion of those two long, thin, and sharp teeth which, it is well known, are peculiar to vampires; and there could be no doubt, he added, as to the well-defined presence of the small livid mark which all concurred in describing as that induced by the demon's lips, and every symptom described by the sufferer was in exact conformity with those recorded in every case of a similar visitation.

"Being myself wholly skeptical as to the existence of any such portent as the vampire, the supernatural theory of the good doctor furnished, in my opinion, but another instance of learning and intelligence oddly associated with some one hallucination. I was so miserable, however, that, rather than try nothing, I acted upon the instructions of the letter.

"I concealed myself in the dark dressing room, that opened upon the poor patient's room, in which a candle was burning, and watched there until she was fast asleep. I stood at the door, peeping through the small crevice, my sword laid on the table beside me, as my directions prescribed, until, a little after one, I saw a large black object, very ill-defined, crawl, as it seemed to me, over the foot of the bed, and swiftly spread itself up to the poor girl's throat, where it swelled, in a moment, into a great, palpitating mass.

"For a few moments I had stood petrified. I now sprang forward, with my sword in my hand. The black creature suddenly contracted toward the foot of the bed, glided over it, and, standing on the floor about a yard below the foot of the bed, with a glare of skulking ferocity and horror fixed on me, I saw Millarca. Speculating I know not what, I struck at her instantly with my sword; but I saw her standing near the door, unscathed. Horrified, I pursued, and struck again. She was gone! and my sword flew to shivers against the door.

"I can't describe to you all that passed on that horrible night. The whole house was up and stirring. The specter Millarca was gone. But her victim was sinking fast, and before the morning dawned, she died."

The old General was agitated. We did not speak to him. My father walked to some little distance, and began reading the inscriptions on the tombstones; and thus occupied, he strolled into the door of a side chapel to prosecute his researches. The General leaned against the wall, dried his eyes, and sighed heavily. I was relieved on hearing the voices of Carmilla and Madame, who were at that moment approaching. The voices died away.

In this solitude, having just listened to so strange a story, connected, as it was, with the great and titled dead, whose monuments were molding among the dust and ivy round us, and every incident of which bore so awfully upon my own mysterious case—in this haunted spot, darkened by the towering foliage that rose on every side, dense and high above its noiseless walls—a horror began to steal over me, and my heart sank as I thought that my friends were, after all, now about to enter and disturb this triste and ominous scene.

The old General's eyes were fixed on the ground, as he leaned with his hand upon the basement of a shattered monument.

Under a narrow, arched doorway, surmounted by one of those demoniacal grotesques in which the cynical and ghastly fancy of old

Gothic carving delights, I saw very gladly the beautiful face and figure of Carmilla enter the shadowy chapel.

I was just about to rise and speak, and nodded smiling, in answer to her peculiarly engaging smile; when with a cry, the old man by my side caught up the woodman's hatchet, and started forward. On seeing him a brutalized change came over her features. It was an instantaneous and horrible transformation, as she made a crouching step backwards. Before I could utter a scream, he struck at her with all his force, but she dived under his blow, and unscathed, caught him in her tiny grasp by the wrist. He struggled for a moment to release his arm, but his hand opened, the axe fell to the ground, and the girl was gone.

He staggered against the wall. His gray hair stood upon his head, and a moisture shone over his face, as if he were at the point of death.

The frightful scene had passed in a moment. The first thing I recollect after, is Madame standing before me, and impatiently repeating again and again, the question, "Where is Mademoiselle Carmilla?"

I answered at length, "I don't know—I can't tell—she went there," and I pointed to the door through which Madame had just entered; "only a minute or two since."

"But I have been standing there, in the passage, ever since Mademoiselle Carmilla entered; and she did not return."

She then began to call "Carmilla" through every door and passage and from the windows, but no answer came.

"She called herself Carmilla?" asked the General, still agitated.

"Carmilla, yes," I answered.

"Aye," he said, "that is Millarca. That is the same person who long ago was called Mircalla, Countess Karnstein. Depart from this accursed ground, my poor child, as quickly as you can. Drive to the clergyman's house, and stay there till we come. Begone! May you never behold Carmilla more; you will not find her here."

Chapter Fifteen
ORDEAL AND EXECUTION

As he spoke one of the strangest-looking men I ever beheld, entered the chapel at the door through which Carmilla had made her entrance and her exit. He was tall, narrow-chested, stooping, with high shoulders, and dressed in black. His face was brown and dried in with deep furrows; he wore an oddly-shaped hat with a broad leaf. His hair, long and grizzled, hung on his shoulders. He wore a pair of gold spectacles, and walked slowly, with an odd shambling gait, with his face sometimes turned up to the sky, and sometimes bowed down toward the ground, seemed to wear a perpetual smile; his long thin arms were swinging, and his lank hands, in old black gloves ever so much too wide for them, waving and gesticulating in utter abstraction.

"The very man!" exclaimed the General, advancing with manifest delight. "My dear Baron, how happy I am to see you, I had no hope of meeting you so soon." He signed to my father, who had by this time returned, and leading the fantastic old gentleman, whom he called the Baron, to meet him. He introduced him formally, and they at once entered into earnest conversation. The stranger took a roll of paper from his pocket, and spread it on the worn surface of a tomb that stood by. He had a pencil case in his fingers, with which he traced imaginary lines from point to point on the paper, which from their often glancing from it, together, at certain points of the building, I concluded to be a plan of the chapel. He accompanied, what I may term his lecture, with occasional readings from a dirty little book, whose yellow leaves were closely written over.

They sauntered together down the side aisle, opposite to the spot where I was standing, conversing as they went; then they begun measuring distances by paces, and finally they all stood together, facing a piece of the side-wall, which they began to examine with great minuteness; pulling off the ivy that clung over it, and rapping the plaster with the ends of their sticks, scraping here, and knocking there. At length they ascertained the existence of a broad marble tablet, with letters carved in relief upon it.

With the assistance of the woodman, who soon returned, a monumental inscription, and carved escutcheon, were disclosed. They proved to be of those of the long lost monument of Mircalla, Countess Karnstein.

The old General, though not I fear given to the praying mood, raised his hands and eyes to heaven, in mute thanksgiving for some moments.

"Tomorrow," I heard him say; "the commissioner will be here, and the Inquisition will be held according to law."

Then turning to the old man with the gold spectacles, whom I have described, he shook him warmly by both hands and said:

"Baron, how can I thank you? How can we all thank you? You will have delivered this region from a plague that has scourged its inhabitants for more than a century. The horrible enemy, thank God, is at last tracked."

My father led the stranger aside, and the General followed. I knew that he had led them out of hearing, that he might relate my case, and I saw them glance often quickly at me, as the discussion proceeded.

My father came to me, kissed me again and again, and leading me from the chapel said:

"It is time to return, but before we go home, we must add to our party the good priest, who lives but a little way from this; and persuade him to accompany us to the schloss."

In this quest we were successful: and I was glad, being unspeakably fatigued when we reached home. But my satisfaction was changed to dismay, on discovering that there were no tidings of Carmilla. Of the scene that had occurred in the ruined chapel, no explanation was offered to me, and it was clear that it was a secret which my father for the present determined to keep from me.

The sinister absence of Carmilla made the remembrance of the scene more horrible to me. The arrangements for that night were singular. Two servants and Madame were to sit up in my room that night; and the ecclesiastic with my father kept watch in the adjoining dressing room.

The priest had performed certain solemn rites that night, the purport of which I did not understand any more than I comprehended the reason of this extraordinary precaution taken for my safety during sleep.

I saw all clearly a few days later.

The disappearance of Carmilla was followed by the discontinuance of my nightly sufferings.

You have heard, no doubt, of the appalling superstition that prevails in Upper and Lower Styria, in Moravia, Silesia, in Turkish Serbia, in Poland, even in Russia; the superstition, so we must call it, of the vampire.

If human testimony, taken with every care and solemnity, judicially, before commissions innumerable, each consisting of many members, all chosen for integrity and intelligence, and constituting reports more voluminous perhaps that exist upon any one other class of cases, is worth anything, it is difficult to deny, or even to doubt the existence of such a phenomenon as the vampire.

For my part I have heard no theory by which to explain what I myself have witnessed and experienced, other than that supplied by the ancient and well-attested belief of the country.

The next day the formal proceedings took place in the Chapel of Karnstein. The grave of the Countess Mircalla was opened; and the General and my father recognized each his perfidious and beautiful guest, in the face now disclosed to view. The features, though a hundred and fifty years had passed since her funeral, were tinted with the warmth of life. Her eyes were open; no cadaverous smell exhaled from the coffin. The two medical men, one officially present, the other on the part of the promoter of the inquiry, attested the marvelous fact, that there was a faint, but appreciable respiration, and a corresponding action of the heart. The limbs were perfectly flexible, the flesh elastic; and the leaden coffin floated with blood, in which to a depth of seven inches, the body lay immersed. Here then, were all the admitted signs and proofs of vampirism. The body, therefore, in accordance with the ancient practice, was raised, and a sharp stake driven through the heart of the vampire, who uttered a piercing shriek at the moment, in all respects such as might escape from a living person in the last agony. Then the head was struck off, and a torrent of blood flowed from the severed neck. The body and head were next placed on a pile of wood, and reduced to ashes, which were thrown upon the river and borne away, and that territory has never since been plagued by the visits of a vampire.

My father has a copy of the report of the Imperial Commission, with the signatures of all who were present at these proceedings, attached in verification of the statement. It is from this official paper that I have summarized my account of this last shocking scene.

Chapter Sixteen
CONCLUSION

I write all this you suppose with composure. But far from it; I cannot think of it without agitation. Nothing but your earnest desire so repeatedly expressed, could have induced me to sit down to a task that has unstrung my nerves for months to come, and reinduced a shadow of the unspeakable horror which years after my deliverance continued to make my days and nights dreadful, and solitude insupportably terrific.

Let me add a word or two about that quaint Baron Vordenburg, to whose curious lore we were indebted for the discovery of the Countess Mircalla's grave.

He had taken up his abode in Gratz, where, living upon a mere pittance, which was all that remained to him of the once princely estates of his family, in Upper Styria, he devoted himself to the minute and laborious investigation of the marvelously authenticated tradition of vampirism. He had at his fingers' ends all the great and little works upon the subject. "Magia Posthuma," "Phlegon de Mirabilibus," "Augustinus de curâ pro Mortuis," "Philosophicae et Christianae Cogitationes de Vampiris," by John Christofer Harenberg; and a thousand others, among which I remember only a few of those which he lent to my father. He had a voluminous digest of all the judicial cases, from which he had extracted a system of principles that appear to govern— some always, and others occasionally only—the condition of the vampire. I may mention, in passing, that the deadly pallor attributed to that sort of *revenants*, is a mere melodramatic fiction. They present, in the grave, and when they show themselves in human society, the appearance of healthy life. When disclosed to light in their coffins, they exhibit all the symptoms that are enumerated as those which proved the vampire life of the long-dead Countess Karnstein.

How they escape from their graves and return to them for certain hours every day, without displacing the clay or leaving any trace of disturbance in the state of the coffin or the cerements, has always been admitted to be utterly inexplicable. The amphibious existence of the vampire is sustained by daily renewed slumber in the grave. Its horrible lust for living blood supplies the vigor of its waking existence. The vampire is prone to be fascinated with an engrossing vehemence, resembling the passion of love, by particular persons. In pursuit of these it will exercise inexhaustible patience and stratagem, for access to a particular object may be obstructed in a hundred ways. It will never desist until it has satiated its passion, and drained the very life of its coveted victim. But it will, in these cases, husband and protract its murderous enjoyment with the refinement of an epicure, and heighten it by the gradual approaches of an artful courtship. In these cases it seems to yearn for something like sympathy and consent. In ordinary ones it goes direct to its object, overpowers with violence, and strangles and exhausts often at a single feast.

The vampire is, apparently, subject, in certain situations, to special conditions. In the particular instance of which I have given you a relation, Mircalla seemed to be limited to a name which, if not her real one, should at least reproduce, without the omission or addition of a single letter, those, as we say, anagrammatically, which compose it. *Carmilla* did this; so did *Millarca*.

My father related to the Baron Vordenburg, who remained with us for two or three weeks after the expulsion of Carmilla, the story about the Moravian nobleman and the vampire at Karnstein churchyard, and then he asked the Baron how he had discovered the exact position of the long-concealed tomb of the Countess Millarca? The Baron's grotesque features puckered up into a mysterious smile; he looked down, still smiling, on his worn spectacle-case and fumbled with it. Then looking up, he said:

"I have many journals, and other papers, written by that remarkable man; the most curious among them is one treating of the visit of which you speak, to Karnstein. The tradition, of course, discolors and distorts a little. He might have been termed a Moravian nobleman, for he had changed his abode to that territory, and was, beside, a noble. But he was, in truth, a native of Upper Styria. It is enough to say that in very early youth he had been a passionate and favored lover of the beautiful Mircalla, Countess Karnstein. Her early death plunged him into inconsolable grief. It is the nature of vampires to increase and multiply, but according to an ascertained and ghostly law.

"Assume, at starting, a territory perfectly free from that pest. How does it begin, and how does it multiply itself? I will tell you. A person, more or less wicked, puts an end to himself. A suicide, under certain circumstances, becomes a vampire. That specter visits living people in their slumbers; *they* die, and almost invariably, in the grave, develop into vampires. This happened in the case of the beautiful Mircalla, who was haunted by one of those demons. My ancestor, Vordenburg, whose title I still bear, soon discovered this, and in the course of the studies to which he devoted himself, learned a great deal more.

"Among other things, he concluded that suspicion of vampirism would probably fall, sooner or later, upon the dead Countess, who in life had been his idol. He conceived a horror, be she what she might, of her remains being profaned by the outrage of a posthumous execution. He has left a curious paper to prove that the vampire, on its expulsion from its amphibious existence, is projected into a far more horrible life; and he resolved to save his once beloved Mircalla from this.

"He adopted the stratagem of a journey here, a pretended removal of her remains, and a real obliteration of her monument. When age had stolen upon him, and from the vale of years he looked back on the scenes he was leaving, he considered, in a different spirit, what he had done; and a horror took possession of him. He made the tracings and notes which have guided me to the very spot, and drew up a confession of the deception that he had practiced. If he had intended any further action in this matter, death prevented him; and the hand of a remote descendant has, too late for many, directed the pursuit to the lair of the beast."

We talked a little more, and among other things he said was this:

"One sign of the vampire is the power of the hand. The slender hand of Mircalla closed like a vice of steel on the General's wrist when he raised the hatchet to strike. But its power is not confined to its grasp; it leaves a numbness in the limb it seizes, which is slowly, if ever, recovered from."

The following Spring my father took me a tour through Italy. We remained away for more than a year. It was long before the terror of recent events subsided; and to this hour the image of Carmilla returns to memory with ambiguous alternations—sometimes the playful, languid, beautiful girl; sometimes the writhing fiend I saw in the ruined church; and often from a reverie I have started, fancying I heard the light step of Carmilla at the drawing room door.

Daughter of the Night

ELAINE BERGSTROM

$\mathcal{J}$MRE JOSIKA, eldest son of a lesser landowner whose holding bordered the Bathori estates, took advantage of the warm spring weather to organize an early fishing party on the Somes River.

The group caught far more than they expected, and Imre decided to split the catch. Sending all but a single servant home with the evening dinner, he took the remainder of the large brown trout to the Bathori house.

Though he had hoped to see his old friend, Steven Bathori, the young man had not yet arrived for the summer. Instead, Eleni Bathori came down the curving stone stairs to meet him. She gripped the decorative iron rail as well as the arm of a maid who carried her cane. The servant whispered Imre's name to Eleni as she held out her hand. As Imre bent to kiss it, she moved her face close to his for one long clear look at him. They had exchanged only a few words when she asked him to stay for dinner. Given the effort it had taken her to meet her social obligation and his father's chastisement if he did not take every opportunity to ingratiate himself to the Bathori family, Imre could hardly refuse.

A fire was lit in the large blue and gold drawing room, plain save for a huge tapestry on one wall woven with the Bathori dragon's teeth coat of arms. The simplicity of the room as well as the high stone wall surrounding the house served as a reminder that this estate, like his own, was on the frontier, subject to attack the moment the political winds shifted. But today their world was at peace and, God willing, would remain so.

A maid brought wine and pastry from the kitchen and Imre sat on a long black velvet settee with the aged countess, trying to pay attention to her words and not the bronze hunting clock clicking loudly above the carved satyrs and trees of the polished wood mantel.

The windows had been opened to let in the afternoon warmth and Imre found himself distracted from Eleni's monologue by the sound of a single horse's hooves on the stones outside. A moment later Elizabeth entered the room.

89

Though he and Elizabeth had played together when they were young, Imre had last spoken to her three years earlier in Ecsed. Since then, he had only seen the young countess at a distance, usually riding alone, dressed as she was today in loose men's clothing, her hair pinned up under a plain brown riding cap. He would have found the recklessness fetching in a servant girl. In a member of the ruling aristocracy, it seemed indecent as well as dangerous.

He noted that she had not grown much in those three years though other changes in her were nonetheless apparent. A maid rushed to hold the door for her and take her riding cape. A second brought a glass for her wine and a cup and saucer for her tea. The pair moved with frantic efficiency, never quite meeting their young mistress's eyes.

They fear her, Imre thought. He had heard rumors concerning Elizabeth's odd disappearances, the death of a servant earlier in the year, and how the household staff seemed so anxious to risk their lives by running away from the Bathori estate.

"Did you have a good ride, Countess?" he asked.

Elizabeth simply nodded as she sipped her wine and stared at him so rudely that he was convinced he had spoken his thoughts aloud.

Eleni took advantage of the silence. "I've asked Imre to stay for dinner."

"Have you?" Elizabeth's eyes never left his face as, without a pause, she added, "It's a long ride after dark. Perhaps he should stay the night as well." Without waiting for his assent, she rang for a servant and requested that the house ready a guest bedroom for his use. "I'll send one of my servants to your home with a note for your father. He'll bring you back a change of clothes."

She picked up her wineglass and left the room. Imre heard her soft voice giving the order to a servant, her light footsteps on the stone stairs.

They ate dinner in the west-facing solarium, its tall windows closed now, the black quarry tiles of the floor and dark wainscoting warming in the late-afternoon sun. Eleni, dressed in plain black, sat at the end of the table, Elizabeth across from Imre. Elizabeth's long dark hair hung loose over her shoulders and wisps of it had been curled French style around her face. The effect softened the girl's features and emphasized her deep-set eyes while the plain black dress she wore drew attention to her pale, translucent skin. The change also made her look younger than her years—a beautiful child made up to be a woman.

They discussed Elizabeth's wedding at dinner and afterward Eleni excused herself early, leaving the pair sitting in the light of the setting sun. As soon as it was polite to do so, Imre stood and began to ask a servant to show him to his room.

"I'll take you upstairs," Elizabeth said.

Carrying the candle, she went ahead of him. Then, as she paused outside his door, she confessed candidly that she desired him.

Even if he cared for her, she had manipulated him once too often today. "If you were a few years older, Elizabeth, I would be more than willing," he responded in a voice that barely remained civil. "But I do not desire children however lovely they may be."

Elizabeth's expression froze, only a flush spreading across her cheeks revealed any sign of anger or embarrassment. Nonetheless, she had the presence of mind to respond with a face-saving reply. "I'm sorry, Imre. I am not usually so direct, but I was recently betrothed and I do not approve of my father's choice. Our combined estates will be far-flung and difficult to manage. Besides, I love this country and I do not want to leave it."

Though he could hardly compete with Ferenc Nadasdy in social standing, Elizabeth was right. The Bathori and Josika estates bordered each other. Imre suggested that they take a morning ride over both their properties before he left.

Imre expected Elizabeth to slap his face. He deserved it. His remark had been rude, and if her proposition hadn't taken him by surprise, he would have thought of a better response. But either the girl was too stupid to know when she had been insulted or, more likely, she had outwitted him again when she accepted.

Either way, the result was the same, and by morning Imre had cursed his stupidity more than once. Elizabeth Bathori was already betrothed, and no matter what her opinion of her future husband, she would not be able to back out of the match. But second marriages were often less socially correct. What harm could there be in cultivating a closer friendship with the girl?

So they went for their ride though the day was gloomy and mists covered the lowlands. He and Elizabeth led, with his servant in the rear. They headed east first, then northwest into the hills. Though he had heard the warnings about the mountain roads, his household had never experienced any problem, and with two men mounted and ready for trouble, he allowed himself to relax. As to the legend of these hills, it had always struck him as ridiculous.

Then he saw Catherine standing by the side of the road, clothed in diaphanous red silks like some eastern princess. Imre reined in his horse, ready to call to Elizabeth to turn and flee, but Elizabeth had already dismounted and was running to the apparition, embracing her as a friend. Imre smiled and relaxed, thinking he had finally solved the mystery of the countess's odd disappearances and wondering how he could make the most of this strange encounter.

"Welcome to my woods," Catherine said to him softly. "Let me show you the comforts of my house."

"Would you like to ride?" Imre asked. "My servant could walk behind."

A long look passed between Elizabeth and the woman. Then the woman responded, "I will share his mount and show you the way." With no help, she jumped up behind the rider. Her long arms circled the servant's waist, and as they rode, she pressed her body against him. With her thighs over his knees, she pushed herself up so she could reach his neck and drink. As he lost consciousness, her fingers lifted the reins from his.

Imre was afraid to look at Catherine, afraid that her beauty would cause him to make a fool of himself in front of Elizabeth. So, riding in the rear of their little caravan, he kept his eyes fixed on Elizabeth's back.

They soon reached a cottage that Imre riding alone would have missed seeing altogether. The windows were shuttered, they and the walls were covered over with vines that extended across the roof as well. There was no sign of servants or stable, no sign of even a garden for food. More curious than wary, Imre helped Elizabeth dismount, then went to help Catherine. Instead of taking his hand, she dropped the servant at his feet. The man landed on his back, his lifeless open eyes staring at the sky, the side of his neck a bloody hole as if it had been gnawed at by some beast.

Imre looked up at Catherine, at her beautiful lips rouged with his servant's blood. Imre's mouth hung open but he could not say a single word. Shock and Catherine had stolen his voice. To Elizabeth, he looked most like a frightened carp on a hook.

Catherine took his hand and slipped off the horse, then without letting go of him, she led him inside, ordered him to sit and relax and forget for the moment what he had just seen.

Catherine's face was so flawless and her body so magnificent that Imre longed to be at peace here and forget the horror that had gripped him outside. Desire made control simple, and in a moment he was sitting cross-legged on the fur-covered floor with Elizabeth lounging beside him.

Catherine's attention shifted to the countess. "You could have done with this without me," she said sternly. "Why is he here?"

"I only have the rest of the week," Elizabeth explained, her cold voice hiding all the pain of the rejection. "He is my choice but he refused. He insulted me and I want you to…"

"Look at her!" Imre exploded. "She is only thirteen, hardly old enough to…"

—Silence!—Catherine ordered and Imre swallowed the rest of his words, looking so shocked that Elizabeth was certain he was about to choke on them.

Elizabeth giggled, then demanded, "Make him take off his clothes." Concerned that she may have gone too far, her voice rose to a child's plea, "Please, he is my choice. Make him love me."

Imre shuddered. Something was about to happen, something he could scarcely understand but he was certain that his will no longer had any bearing on the event. He was helpless against this woman, and if she wished it, he would do whatever she asked.

He reached out, trying to take the woman's hand and beg her to let him go. But she only pulled away and walked behind him, running her long fingers down his cheeks and neck, lifting his chin, kissing him on his closed lips.

"He does look pretty, doesn't he?" Catherine purred. "I could devour him as I did his servant and cut his fine purple shirt into ribbons for my hair. Or perhaps, if he performs as well as he thinks he is able, he might live to see the sunset."

"Live?" Imre's hands closed into tight fists. He wanted to fight or run but the woman's touch seemed to freeze his body. He could not move.

—Undress.—Catherine ordered.

"What?"

"You heard her," Elizabeth said, rubbing the back of his hand with her thin white fingers. "So did I; now do as she demands."

Imre refused. A wave of pain washed through him, so strong it left him shaking. Catherine kissed the side of his neck, and as he flinched from the touch, she tilted his head back once again and smiled. At the moment he saw her long rear teeth and tried to pull away, she moved far faster than he could ever conceive of moving. Her teeth rent the flesh of his neck and she drank.

—Undress—Catherine repeated.

The bond formed. He saw himself through her eyes, saw how much she cherished his life, and dizzy from fear and desire, he had no choice but to obey this command, knowing it was only the first of many that would follow.

When he stood naked in the center of the room, Elizabeth sat and studied him. Unlike Catherine or Klara or even Marijo who had felt so soft when Elizabeth hugged her, this man aroused nothing in her except disgust. Anxious to get her ordeal finished, Elizabeth stripped and lay across Catherine's bed, heaping pillows behind her head so that she could watch what he did.

—Go to her.—

This time, Imre recognized the source of the words. He looked at Catherine but her expression remained impassive.

—You will regret it if you do not perform as well as you are able.—

—She's a child.—Imre thought the words, wondering if Catherine could hear them.—I have no desire.—

—You will. When the time is right, I promise you that.—

Imre walked to the bed and touched Elizabeth's leg. As he did, a charge ran through him, its intensity making him shudder. Suddenly, he wanted this girl, desired her more than anyone he had ever known. Forgetting Catherine, he kissed the top of Elizabeth's foot, her ankle, then his hands began moving up the inside of her legs.

Elizabeth sensed the moment when Catherine entered Imre's mind for it was the same moment when Catherine entered hers. She and this haughty young man cared nothing for each other, so Catherine aroused the attraction each of them felt for her, playing both parts for the time it took them to complete the act. And it all seemed so perfect until, as Imre pounded his body against the girl's, Elizabeth began to claw at Imre's back, pulling him down to kiss her, sinking her teeth into his lower lip, biting it through. Imre responded with a grunt of pain but wisely did not try to pull away.

—Elizabeth, let him go!—Catherine ordered, but the girl was swooning from the blood and the passion, and if she heard, she did not obey.

Catherine rushed to the bed and, placing her hands on either side of the girl's face, repeated her order. This time the results were better and Imre was able to raise his head and stare dully, with his blood dripping down his chin, into Catherine's eyes.

Beneath him, Elizabeth was struggling, scratching at Imre's shoulders and neck, trying to pull him down and drink from him again. Catherine's mind was hardly a match for the girl's now, so she gripped Elizabeth's wrists and held them over her head, kissing her, murmuring reassuring words as she built their passion once more.

When it was over and Imre and Elizabeth, exhausted by their coupling, slept, Catherine looked down at the girl. Her face was smeared with Imre's blood. Her fingernails were caked with it as well. With horror, Catherine began to wonder what kind of a wedding night the young countess would have.

Well, Catherine would have time to dwell on that problem later. Now, she had to consider what to do with Imre Josika. For all her boasting to Elizabeth on the day they first met, Catherine knew her limits. She might have killed the girl and her female servant—at the time, there were outlaws in the hills who would have been blamed for the crimes. She often killed wealthy travelers along with area peasants who disappeared with frightening regularity without her help. However, devouring the eldest son of a local landowner was another matter.

And though Elizabeth had not given the problem any thought, she would certainly be questioned if young Josika disappeared.

However, the Josika family lived within two hours' ride of her mountains, giving Catherine an idea about how to save her and Elizabeth a great deal of difficulty. She went to the bed and kissed the young man, drinking from his wound. His eyes opened for a moment and he tried to struggle.

—Quiet, Imre. I have no need of your life. Not yet. Perhaps never.—

Calmed, Imre sighed and, as she willed, returned to a deep, silent sleep. Looking down at him, Catherine thought of the slaves, the *cows,* kept in the Austra keep. He would fit in there well with that young body, so full of beauty and passion. Yes, he was perfect. He would be her first lover-in-exile, strong enough to see her through months of use before he died. Perhaps he would even be enough to give her the courage to do what must be done today.

She and Elizabeth were alone when the girl woke that afternoon. There were tears in Elizabeth's eyes as she washed and dressed and Catherine knew that the girl wanted some reassurance that her future would be happier than this morning. Catherine could not give it. Instead, she touched the girl and showed her everything she had done to Imre, leaving Elizabeth sobbing and shaking in her arms.

"What happened need never happen again, child. I want you to leave me now and forever. I care for you as I would for my own daughter, and for that reason, I do not want you to ever return here again."

"But that won't help!" Elizabeth managed to blurt before the sobs started again. When she was able, Elizabeth told her about Klara and the servant and what little she could recall about Marijo, speaking with an odd soft focus as if she had witnessed rather than caused the wounds. "It isn't you that created this need in me, don't you see? I was like you long before we ever met and now I am so frightened of what will happen."

On her wedding night, Catherine thought again.

And when the morning after came and her bridegroom could not go out to face the well-wishers at the wedding breakfast, what would he do with his new bride?

He could lock her away in the castle, send her to a convent to live out her years, or he could have her declared a witch or a blood-drinking *mora* and the authorities would burn her. Every answer was tragic, and Catherine decided she would do anything to help this child even if it meant facing the world once again.

"Catherine," Elizabeth said, her voice soft but strained as if she were afraid that someone would hear her next words. "I know what you did last night. I want you to know that it would not make any difference if it were Imre or Ferenc or some other man in my arms. I don't desire any of them. I only desire you."

"Elizabeth, you cannot help that. You..."

"And if I had not met you, I would have loved some other woman. I am cursed like Klara. I always knew it, I think. But Klara was given to a man over twice her age, already an invalid when they married. I am being given to Ferenc and every time he touches me, I will have to struggle to keep from screaming."

"Elizabeth, can you be certain of what you are?"

"Don't tell me I am too young to know what I want or need." She held out her arms.

Catherine moved toward her, lowering her head to plant the first of many kisses on Elizabeth's bloodstained lips.

$\mathcal{L}$ouisiana: 1850

JEWELLE GOMEZ

$\mathscr{T}$HE GIRL slept restlessly, feeling the prickly straw as if it were teasing pinches from her mother. The stiff moldy odor transformed itself into her mother's starchy dough smell. The rustling of the Girl's body in the barn hay was sometimes like the sound of fatback frying in the cooking shed behind the plantation's main house. At other moments in her dream it was the crackling of the brush as her mother raked the bristles through the Girl's thicket of dark hair before beginning the intricate pattern of braided rows.

She had traveled by night for fifteen hours before daring to stop. Her body held out until a deserted farmhouse, where it surrendered to this demanding sleep hemmed by fear.

Then the sound of walking, a man moving stealthily through the dawn light toward her. In the dream it remained what it was: danger. A white man wearing the clothes of an overseer. In the dream the Girl clutched tightly at her mother's large black hand, praying the sound of the steps would stop, that she would wake up curled around her mother's body on the straw and corn husk mattress next to the big old stove, grown cold with the night. In sleep she clutched the hand of her mother, which turned into the warm wooden handle of the knife she had stolen when she ran away the day before. It pulsed beside her heart, beneath the rough shirt that hung loosely from her thin young frame. The knife, crushed into the cotton folds near her breast, was invisible to the red-faced man who stood laughing over her, pulling her by one leg from beneath the pile of hay.

The Girl did not scream but buried herself in the beating of her heart alongside the hidden knife. She refused to believe that the hours of indecision and, finally, the act of escape were over. The walking, hiding, running through the Mississippi and Louisiana woods had quickly settled into an almost enjoyable rhythm; she was not ready to give in to those whom her mother had sworn were not fully human.

The Girl tried to remember some of the stories that her mother, now dead, had pieced together from many different languages to describe the journey to this land. The legends sketched a picture of the

Fulani past—a natural rhythm of life without bondage. It was a memory that receded more with each passing year.

"Come on. Get up, gal, time now, get up!" The urgent voice of her mother was a sharp buzz in her dream. She opened her eyes to the streaking sun which slipped in through the shuttered window opening. She hopped up, rolled the pallet to the wall, then dipped her hands quickly in the warm water in the basin on the counter. Her mother poured a bit more bubbling water from the enormous kettle. The Girl watched the steam caught by the half-light of the predawn morning rise toward the low ceiling. She slowly started to wash the hard bits of moisture from her eyes as her mother turned back to the large black stove.

"I'ma put these biscuits out, girl, and you watch this cereal. I got to go out back. I didn't beg them folks to let you in from the fields to work with me to watch you sleepin' all day. So get busy."

Her mother left through the door quickly, pulling her skirts up around her legs as she went. The Girl ran to the stove, took the ladle in her hand, and moved the thick gruel around in the iron pot. She grinned proudly at her mother when she walked back in: no sign of sticking in the pot. Her mother returned the smile as she swept the ladle up in her large hand and set the Girl onto her next task—turning out the biscuits.

"If you lay the butter cross 'em while they hot, they like that. If they's not enough butter, lay on the lard, make 'em shine. They can't tell and they take it as generous."

"Mama, how it come they cain't tell butter from fat? Baby Minerva can smell butter 'fore it clears the top of the churn. She won't drink no pig fat. Why they cain't tell how butter taste?"

"They ain't been here long 'nough. They just barely human. Maybe not even. They suck up the world, don't taste it."

The Girl rubbed butter over the tray of hot bread, then dumped the thick, doughy biscuits into the basket used for morning service. She loved that smell and always thought of bread when she dreamed of better times. Whenever her mother wanted to offer comfort she promised the first biscuit with real butter. The Girl imagined the home across the water that her mother sometimes spoke of as having fresh bread baking for everyone, even for those who worked in the fields. She tried to remember what her mother had said about the world as it had lived before this time but could not. The lost empires were a dream to the Girl, like the one she was having now.

She looked up at the beast from this other land, as he dragged her by her leg from the concealing straw. His face lost the laugh that had split it and became creased with lust. He untied the length of rope holding his pants, and his smile returned as he became thick with anticipation of her submission to him, his head swelling with power at the thought of invading her. He dropped to his knees before the girl whose eyes were wide, seeing into both the past and the future. He bent forward on his knees, stiff for conquest, already counting the bounty fee and savoring the stories he would tell. He felt a warmth at the pit of his belly. The girl was young, probably a virgin he thought, and she didn't appear able to resist him. He smiled at her open, unseeing eyes, interpreting their unswerving gaze as neither resignation nor loathing but desire. The flash-fire in him became hotter.

His center was bright and blinding as he placed his arms—one on each side of the Girl's head—and lowered himself. She closed her eyes. He rubbed his body against her brown skin and imagined the closing of her eyes was a need for him and his power. He started to enter her, but before his hand finished pulling her open, while it still tingled with the softness of her insides, she entered him with her heart which was now a wood-handled knife.

He made a small sound as his last breath hurried to leave him. Then he dropped softly. Warmth spread from his center of power to his chest as the blood left his body. The Girl lay still beneath him until her breath became the only sign of life in the pile of hay. She felt the blood draining from him, comfortably warm against her now-cool skin.

It was like the first time her mother had been able to give her a real bath. She'd heated water in the cauldron for what seemed like hours on a night that the family was away, then filled a wooden barrel whose staves had been packed with sealing wax. She lowered the Girl, small and narrow, into the luxuriant warmth of the tub and lathered her with soap as she sang an unnamed tune.

The intimacy of her mother's hands and the warmth of the water lulled the Girl into a trance of sensuality she never forgot. Now the blood washing slowly down her breastbone and soaking into the floor below was like that bath—a cleansing. She lay still, letting the life flow over her, then slid gently from beneath the red-faced man whose cheeks had paled. The Girl moved quietly, as if he had really been her lover and she was afraid to wake him.

Looking down at the blood soaking her shirt and trousers she felt no disgust. It was the blood signaling the death of a beast and her continued life. The Girl held the slippery wood of the knife in her hand as her body began to shake in the dream/memory. She sobbed, trying to understand what she should do next. How to hide the blood and still move on. She was young and had never killed anyone.

She trembled, unable to tell if this was really happening to her all over again or if she was dreaming it—again. She held one dirty hand up to her broad, brown face and cried heartily.

That was how Gilda found her, huddled in the root cellar of her small farmhouse on the road outside of New Orleans in 1850. The Girl clutched the knife to her breast and struggled to escape her dream.

"Wake up, gal!" Gilda shook the thin shoulder gently, as if afraid to pull loose one of the shuddering limbs. Her voice was whiskey rough, her rouged face seemed young as she raised the smoky lantern.

The Girl woke with her heart pounding, desperate to leave the dream behind but seized with white fear. The pale face above her was a woman's, but the Girl had learned that they, too, could be as dangerous as their men.

Gilda shook the Girl whose eyes were now open but unseeing. The night was long, and Gilda did not have time for a hysterical child. The brown of her eyes darkened in impatience.

"Come on, gal, what you doin' in my root cellar?" The Girl's silence deepened. Gilda looked at the stained, torn shirt, the too-big pants tied tightly at her waist, and the wood-handled knife in the Girl's grip. Gilda saw in her eyes the impulse to use it.

"You don't have to do that. I'm not going to hurt you. Come on." With that Gilda pulled the Girl to her feet, careful not to be too rough; she could see the Girl was weak with hunger and wound tight around her fear. Gilda had seen a runaway slave only once. Before she'd recognized the look and smell of terror, the runaway had been captured and hauled off. Alone with the Girl, and that look bouncing around the low-ceilinged cellar, Gilda almost felt she should duck. She stared deeply into the Girl's dark eyes and said silently, *You needn't be afraid. I'll take care of you. The night hides many things.*

The Girl loosened her grip on the knife under the persuasive touch of Gilda's thoughts. She had heard of people who could talk without speaking but never expected a white to be able to do it. This one was a puzzlement to her: the dark eyes and pale skin. Her face was painted in colors like a mask, but she wore men's breeches and a heavy jacket.

Gilda moved in her small-boned frame like a team of horses pulling a load on a sodden road: gentle and relentless. "I could use you, gal, come on!" was all Gilda said as she lifted the Girl and carried her out to the buggy. She wrapped a thick shawl around the Girl's shoulders and held tightly to her with one hand as she drew the horse back onto the dark road.

After almost an hour they pulled up to a large building on the edge of the city—not a plantation house, but with the look of a hotel. The Girl blinked in surprise at the light which glowed in every room as if there were a great party. Several buggies stood at the side of the house with liveried men in attendance. A small open shed at the left held a few single, saddled horses that munched hay. They inclined their heads toward Gilda's horse. The swiftness of its approach was urgent, and the smell the buggy left behind was a perfumed wake of fear. The horses all shifted slightly, then snorted, unconcerned. They were eating, rested and unburdened for the moment. Gilda held the Girl's arm firmly as she moved around to the back of the house past the satisfied, sentient horses. She entered a huge kitchen in which two women—one black, one white—prepared platters of sliced ham and turkey.

Gilda spoke quietly to the cook's assistant. "Macey, please bring a tray to my room. Warm wine, too. Hot water first though." Not breaking her stride, she tugged the Girl up the back stairs to the two rooms that were hers. They entered a thickly furnished sitting room with books lining the small bookshelf on the north wall. Paintings and a few line drawings hung on the south wall. In front of them sat a deep couch, surrounded by a richly colored hanging fabric.

This room did not have the urgency of those below it. Few of the patrons who visited the Woodard place—as it was still known although that family had not owned it in years—had ever been invited into the private domain of its mistress. This was where Gilda retreated at the end of the night, where she spent most of the day reading, alone except for a few of the girls or Bird. Woodard's was the most prosperous establishment in the area and enjoyed the patronage of some of the most esteemed men and women of the county. The gambling, musical divertissements, and the private rooms were all well-attended. Gilda employed eight girls, none yet twenty, who lived in the house and worked hard hours being what others imagined women should be. After running Woodard's for fifteen years, Gilda loved her home and her girls. It had been a wonderfully comfortable and relatively tiny segment of the three hundred years she'd lived. Her private rooms held the treasures of several lifetimes.

She raised the lid of a chest and pulled out a towel and nightshirt. The Girl's open stare brushed over her, nudging at the weight of the years on her shoulders. Under that puzzled gaze the years didn't seem so grotesque. Gilda listened a moment to the throaty laughter floating up from the rooms below, where the musical entertainment had begun without her, and could just barely hear Bird introducing the evening in her deep voice. Woodard's was the only house with an "Indian girl," as her loyal patrons bragged. Although Bird now only helped to manage the house, many came just to see her, dressed in the soft cotton, sparsely adorned dress that most of the women at Woodard's wore. Thin strips of leather bearing beading or quill were sometimes braided into her hair or sewn onto her dress. Townsmen ranked her among their local curiosities.

Gilda was laying out clothes when Macey entered the room lugging two buckets of water—one warm and one hot. While stealing glances at the Girl, she poured the water into a tin tub that sat in a corner of the room next to an ornate folding screen.

Gilda said, "Take off those clothes and wash. Put those others on." She spoke slowly, deliberately, knowing she was breaking through one reality into another. The words she did not speak were more important: *Rest. Trust. Home.*

The Girl dropped her dusty, blood-encrusted clothes by the couch. Before climbing into the warm water, she looked up at Gilda, who gazed discreetly somewhere above her head. Gilda then picked up the clothes, ignoring the filth, and clasped them to her as she left the room. When the Girl emerged she dressed in the nightshirt and curled up on the settee, pulling a fringed shawl from its back down around her shoulders. She'd unbraided and washed the thickness of her hair and wrapped it tightly in the damp towel.

Curling her legs underneath her to keep off the night chill, she listened to the piano below and stared into the still shadows cast by the lamp. Soon Gilda entered, with Macey following sullenly behind holding a tray of food. Gilda pulled a large, overstuffed chair close to the settee while Macey put the tray on a small table. She lit another lamp near them, glancing backward over her shoulder at the strange, thin black girl with the African look to her. Macey made it her business to mind her own business, particularly when it came to Miss Gilda, but she knew the look in Gilda's eyes. It was something she saw too rarely: living in the present, or maybe just curiosity. Macey and the laundress, neither of whom lived in the house with the others, spoke many times of the anxious look weighing in Gilda's eyes. It was as if she saw something that existed only in her own head. But Macey, who dealt mostly with Bernice and some with Bird, left her imagination at home. Besides, she had no belief in voodoo magic and just barely held on to her Catholicism.

Of course there was talk around most dinner tables in the parish, especially after Bird had come to stay at the house. Macey was certain that if there was a faith Gilda held, it was not one she knew. The lively look that filled her employer's eyes now usually only appeared when she and Bird spent their evenings talking and writing together.

Some things were best not pondered, so Macey turned and hurried back down to her card game with Bernice, the cook. Gilda prepared a plate and poured from the decanter of red wine. The Girl looked furtively in her direction but was preoccupied with the cleanliness of the room and the spicy smell of the food. Her body relaxed while her mind still raced, filled with the unknowns: how far she was from the plantation, who this woman might be, how she could get away from her.

Gilda was barely able to draw her excitement back inside herself as she watched the girl. It was the clear purpose in the Girl's dark eyes that first caught her. A child's single-mindedness shone through. Deeper still was an adult perseverance. Gilda remembered that look many years before in Bird's eyes when she had returned from her one visit to her people, the Lakota. There was an intensity, curiosity, and vulnerability blended together behind a tight mask of resolve.

More importantly, Gilda saw herself behind those eyes—a younger self she barely remembered, one who would never be comfortable with having decisions made for her. Or with following a path she'd not laid herself. Gilda also saw a need for family that matched her own. She closed her eyes, and in her mind the musky smell of her mother's garments rose. She almost reached out to the phantom of her past there in the lamp-lit room but caught her breath and shook her head slightly. Gilda knew then she wanted the Girl to stay.

Answers to her questions slipped in among her thoughts as the Girl ate. She was startled to discover the understanding of where she was and who this woman might be. She set her glass down abruptly and stared at Gilda's narrow face which glowed with excitement even in the shadows of the lamplight. Her dark brown hair was wound low at the back of her neck leaving her tiny features exposed. Even within the tight bodice of the blue beaded dress she now wore, Gilda moved in her own deliberate way. The brown cigar she lit seemed too delicate for her broad gestures.

The Girl thought for a moment: *This is a man! A little man!*

Gilda laughed out loud at the idea in the Girl's head and said, "No, I'm a woman." Then without speaking aloud she said, *I am a woman, you know that. And you know I am a woman as no other you have known, nor has your mother known, in life or death. I am a woman as you are, and more.*

The Girl opened her mouth to speak, but her throat was too raw, her nerves too tight. She bent her mouth in recognition and puzzlement. This was a woman, and her face was not unlike her mother's despite the colors painted on it.

Its unwavering gaze was hard-edged yet full of concern. But behind the dark brown of Gilda's eyes the Girl recognized forests, ancient roots and arrows, images she had never seen before. She blinked quickly and looked again through the lamplight. There she simply saw a small woman who did not eat, who sipped slowly from a glass of wine and watched with a piercing gaze through eyes that seemed both dark and light at the same time.

When the Girl finished eating and sat back again on the settee, Gilda spoke aloud. "You don't have to tell me anything. I'll tell you. You just listen and remember when anyone asks: You're new in the house. My sister sent you over here to me as a present. You've been living in Mississippi. Now you live here and work for me. Nothing else, do you understand?" The Girl remained silent but understood the words and the reasons behind them. She didn't question. She was tired, and the more she saw of this white world, the more afraid she became that she could no longer hide from the plantation owners and the bounty hunters.

"There is linen in that chest against the wall. The chaise lounge is quite comfortable. Go to sleep. We will rise early, my girl." With that, Gilda's thin face radiated an abundant smile as youthful as the Girl's. She turned out one of the lamps and left the room quickly. The Girl unfolded a clean sheet and thick blanket and spread them out smoothly, marveling at their freshness and the comforting way they clung to the bowed and carved wood of the chaise's legs. She disturbed the placid surface almost regretfully and slipped in between the covers, trying to settle into sleep.

This woman, Gilda, could see into her mind. That was clear. The Girl was not frightened though, because it seemed she could see into Gilda's as well. That made them even.

The Girl thought a little about what she had seen when the woman opened herself to her, what had made her trust her: an expanse of road stretching narrowly into the horizon, curving gently away from her; the lulling noise of rushing wind and the rustling of leaves that sounded like the soft brush of the hem of a dress on carpet. She stared down the road with her eyes closed until she lost the dream in deep sleep.

Gilda stood outside the door, listening for a moment to the Girl's restless movement. She easily quieted the Girl's turmoil with the energy of her thoughts. The music and talking from below intruded on Gilda, but she resisted, searching out the glimmerings of her past instead. How unnerving to have stumbled upon them in that moment of recognition while watching the Girl eat her supper. The memory was vague, more like a fog than a tide after so many years in which Gilda had deliberately turned away from the past.

With her eyes closed she could slip backward to the place whose name she had long since forgotten, to when she was a girl. She saw a gathering of people with burnished skin. She was among them. The spiced scent of their bodies was an aura moving alongside them as they crossed an arid expanse of land. She couldn't see much beyond the curved backs and dust-covered sandals of those walking in front of her. She held the hand of a woman she knew was her mother, and somewhere ahead was her father. Where were they all now? Dead, of course. Less than ashes, and Gilda could not remember their faces. She couldn't remember when their eyes and mouths had slipped away from her. Where had the sound of their voices gone? All that seemed left was the memory of a scented passage that had dragged her along in its wake and the dark color of blood as it seeped into sand.

She grimaced at the sense of movement, the thing she most longed to be free of. Even there, in that mythical past she could no longer see clearly, she had moved nomadically from one home to another. Through first one war then another. Which sovereign? Whose nation? She had left those things behind sometime in the past three hundred years—perhaps even longer.

She opened her eyes and looked back toward the door to the room where the Girl slept, smiling as her own past dissolved. She no longer needed those diaphanous memories. She wanted to look only forward, to the future of the Girl and Bird, and to her own resting place where she would finally have stillness.

Again the music broke into her thoughts. For the first time in a long while she was eager to join the girls in the downstairs parlor for the evening, to watch Bird moving quickly among the rooms, and to listen to the languidly told stories the girls perfected to entertain the gentlemen and make the time pass for themselves. And when the night was edged by dawn she would gratefully lie down next to Bird, welcoming the weight of her limbs stretched across her body and the smell of her hair permeating her day of rest.

During her first few months at Woodard's the Girl barely spoke but did the chores she was directed to in the house. She began to accompany Bird or Gilda some months after, to shop for the house or buy presents for members of the household, which Gilda did quite frequently. The Girl carried the packages and straightened up Gilda's suite of rooms, carefully dusting the tiny vases and figurines, the shelves of books, and rearranging fresh flowers, which she picked from the garden once she became comfortable enough to venture outside alone.

Sometimes she would sit in the pantry while the girls were around the table in the kitchen eating, talking over previous evenings, laughing at stories, or discussing their problems.

"Don't tell me I'm ungrateful. I'm grown. I want what I want and I ain't nobody's mama!" Rachel shouted at Fanny, who always had an opinion.

"Not that we know of," was Fanny's vinegary retort. Rachel only stared at her coldly, so Fanny went on. "You always want something, Rachel, and you ain't coming to nothing with this dream stuff. Running off, leavin' everythin' just 'cause you had a dream to do something you don't know nothin' 'bout."

"It's my dream an' my life, ain't it Miss Bird? You know 'bout dreams an' such."

Bird became the center of their attention as she tried to remember what would mean the most to these girls, who were really women, who had made their home with her and Gilda.

"Dreaming is not something to be ignored."

"But going to a place like that, next to the water—ready to fall in 'cording to her dream, mind you, not mine—is just foolish," Fanny insisted.

"It's a dream, not a fact. Maybe the dream just means change, change for the better. If Rachel has a dream, she reads it. Nobody else here can do that for her," Bird said.

"Anyway, I ain't packed nothin'. I'm just tellin' you my dream, is all. Damn you, Fanny, you a stone in my soup every time!"

The women laughed because Rachel always had a way with words when they got her excited.

Occasionally Gilda sat with them, as if they did not work for her, chiming in with stories and laughter just the same as Bernice, the dark, wary cook, or Rachel, the one full of ambition. There were also Rose, kind to a fault; Minta, the youngest; and the unlikely pair who were inseparable—Fanny, the opinionated, and Sarah, the appeaser. Mostly the Girl kept apart from them. She had never seen white women such as these before, and it was frightening not to know where she fit in. She had heard of bawdy houses from her mother who had heard from the men who sipped brandy in the library after dinner. But the picture had never added up to what she saw now.

These women embodied the innocence of children the Girl had known back on the plantation, yet they were also hard, speaking of the act of sex casually, sometimes with humor. And even more puzzling was their debate of topics the Girl had heard spoken of only by men.

The women eagerly expressed their views on politics and economics: what slavery was doing to the South, who was dominating politics, and the local agitation against the Galatain Street "houses."

Located further from the center of activity, Gilda's house was run with brisk efficiency. She watched over the health of the women and protected them. But her presence was usually more presumed than actual. Most often she locked herself in her room until six in the evening. There she slept, read, and wrote in the voluminous journals she kept secured in a chest.

Bird managed the everyday affairs, supervising most of the marketing and arbitrating disputes with tradesmen or between the girls. She also directed the Girl in doing the sundry tasks assigned to her. And it was Bird who decided that she would teach the Girl to read. Every afternoon they sat down in Bird's shaded room with the Bible and a newspaper, going over letters and words relentlessly.

The Girl sat patiently as Bird told a story in her own words, then picked out each syllable on paper until they came together in the story she had just recited. At first the Girl did not see the sense of the lessons. No one she knew ever had need of reading, except the black preacher who came over on Saturday nights to deliver a sermon under the watchful gaze of the overseer. Even he was more likely to thwack the Bible with his rusty hand than read from it.

But soon the Girl began to enjoy the lessons. She liked knowing what Fanny was talking about when she exclaimed that Rachel was "as hard-headed as Lot's wife," or recognizing the name of the Louisiana governor when she heard it cursed around the kitchen table. Another reason she enjoyed the lessons was that she liked the way Bird smelled. When they sat on the soft cushions of the couch in Bird's room, bending over the books and papers, the Girl was comforted by the pungent earthiness of the Lakota woman. She did not cover herself with the cosmetics and perfumes her housemates enjoyed. The soft scent of brown soap mixed with the leather of her headband and necklace created a familiar aura. It reminded the Girl of her mother and the strong smell of her sweat dropping onto the logs under the burning cauldrons. The Girl rarely allowed herself to miss her mother or her sisters, preferring to leave the past alone for a while, at least until she felt safe in this new world.

Sitting in the room with the Girl, Bird was no longer aloof. She was tender and patient, savoring memories of herself she found within the Girl. Bird gazed into the African eyes which struggled to see a white world through words on a page. Bird wondered what creatures as invisible as she and the Girl were did with their pasts.

Was she to slip it off of her shoulders and fold it into a chest to be locked away for some unknown future? And what to do with that future, the one that Gilda had given Bird with its vast expanse of road? Where would she look to read that future? What oracle could she lay on her lap to pick out the words that would frame it?

Bird taught the Girl first from the Bible and the newspaper. Neither of them could see themselves reflected there. Then she told the Girl stories of her own childhood, using them to teach her to write. She spoke each letter aloud, then the word, her own hand drawing the Girl's across the worn paper. And soon there'd be a sentence and a legend or memory of who she was. And the African girl then read it back to her. Bird enjoyed these lessons almost as much as her evenings spent alone with Gilda. And with the restlessness that agitated Gilda more each year, those times together had grown less frequent.

Gilda and Bird sometimes retreated to the farmhouse for a day or more, spending most of the time walking in the evening, riding, or reading together silently, rarely raising questions. Sometimes Gilda went to the farmhouse alone, leaving Bird anxious and irritable. This afternoon Bird prolonged the lesson with the Girl a bit. Uncertainty hung in the air around her, and she was reluctant to leave the security of the Girl's eagerness to learn. She asked her to read aloud again from the sheets of paper on which they'd just printed words. The halting sound of the Girl's voice opened a space inside of Bird. She stood quickly, walking to the curtained window.

"Go on if you understand the words, stop if you do not," Bird said with her back to the room.

She pulled the curtain aside and tied it with a sash, then fingered the small bits of pearlized quill stitched onto the leather band around her neck. Outside, the stableman was raking out hay for the horses of the evening visitors. Bird was pleased with the comfort she felt at the normal movements around the house and at the sound of the Girl's voice, which in the past year had lightened to seem more like a child's than when she'd first come. Bird turned when she heard a question.

"Tell me again of this *pox* please?" the Girl asked, pointing at the word on the paper.

"It came with the traders. They stole many things and breathed the disease into my people and sold it to us in their cloth. It makes the body feverish and causes spots over the body and many deaths."

"Why did you not die?" the Girl asked, carefully matching her words to the rhythm she had heard in Gilda's voice, just as she often imitated her walk when no one watched. She wondered if Bird's escape from the pox was connected to the rumors that she and Gilda were conjure women. She had seen many oddities since coming to the house, but none of them seemed near to conjuring to the Girl so she generally dismissed the talk.

Bird stared at her silently, startled for a moment to hear the familiar inflections from the Girl. "When the deaths came, some members of my clan moved away from the others. My mother and her brothers thought we could escape the air that was killing us. We came south to the warmth to burn away the disease from our spirits. I was sick for a time as we traveled, but we left it on the trail behind us." Bird ached as she spoke, remembering the brothers who'd become fearful of her when she'd fallen ill with the disease and then suspicious when she recovered.

In the end they were convinced she was a witch because she had survived. They chased her away from their small band into the night that had become her friend.

"Do you still have the spots?"

Bird laughed, and the small scar that lanced her eyebrow rose slightly. "Yes, there are some on my back. There is no more infection, simply the mark. Did you not have this disease before..." Bird's voice trailed off. She did not want to remind the Girl of past sadness.

"No disease with spots. Some fevers came, through the waters my mother said. Can I see your spots?"

Bird undid the tiny buttons at her wrists and down the front of her shirtwaist, shrugged her shoulders from the cotton dress, then turned her back toward the lamp. The Girl's eyes widened at the small raised circles that sprayed across the brown skin. She let her fingers brush the places where disease had come and placed a small finger gently atop one spot, fitting it into the indentation at its center.

"Your skin is smooth like a baby's," she said.

"Gilda has a lotion she used to rub into my back when I first came here. It makes the skin soft."

"Can I have some for my hands?"

Bird reached down and took the Girl's two hands in her own. Their fingertips were calloused in a way that Bird knew was not the result of the light cleaning and washing done at the house. She nodded and pressed the small hard hands to her face quickly, then let them go.

"Why white people feel they got to mark us?" the Girl asked, slipping back into her own vocal rhythm. Bird pushed her arms back into her sleeves as she thought for a moment.

"Maybe they're afraid they'll be forgotten." She gathered the papers from the table, then added, "They don't know that we easily forget them, who they might be. All we ever remember is their scars."

The Girl saw the deeply etched whip marks that had striped her mother's legs as she looked down at her own thin, hardened fingers. She remained silent as Bird put the papers into the wooden box holding all their lessons.

Bird wanted to tell just one more story, a happy one, but saw that the Girl, a meticulous worker, was becoming anxious. Her chores for the evening still lay ahead of her, and guests would be arriving in several hours. Or, Bird thought, anxiety might be her natural state.

The Girl left and Bird followed, locking her door behind her. Upstairs at Gilda's door she used the same key to enter. She opened the drapes slightly once inside its blackness, to let the twilight seep in, and then lay down beside the still figure. Even at its cool temperature Gilda's body had warmed the satin that lay over the soft earth. Bird didn't sleep. She watched the shadows, enjoying the familiar quiet of the room, thinking about the Girl and Gilda.

Bird enjoyed the days more since the Girl's arrival. She was grateful for her earnest curiosity and she saw Gilda responding similarly. Yet Bird was uneasy with the new way of things. Gilda was, indeed, more open and relaxed, but she was also less fully present, as if her mind were in a future none of them would know. When she tried to draw her back, Gilda only talked of the true death, how soon her time might come. Then they argued.

Even after their new routine had become old and their futures seemed secure, Bird was certain Gilda still held thoughts of true death but would speak of them to her only obliquely. When Bird asked her about the Girl and what might become of her should they decide to leave Woodard's, Gilda remained cryptic.

"She will always be with us, just as I'll always be with you," Gilda answered with a smile.

"How can that be so?" Bird asked, certain Gilda was making a joke.

"She is as strong as either of us and knows our ways."

"She's a child; she can't make the decision you'd ask of her!" Bird said with alarm when she realized it was no jest.

"We were all children at one time. And time passes. I expect she will be ready when I am."

"Ready?" Bird responded, still not able to grasp the idea of the Girl becoming one of them.

Gilda understood Bird's reluctance and lightened her voice. "Yes, ready to challenge you, my dear one. She'll be the best student you've ever had, perhaps even a scholar. We will then turn Woodard's into a college for girls!" Gilda laughed loudly, steering the conversation away from anything Bird might pursue.

In remembering that talk, Bird decided not to broach the questions now, even with herself. She simply wanted to feel Gilda near, listen to the sound of her heart as she awakened. They would go out to find their share of the blood later, perhaps together, when there was darkness.

After her second year at Woodard's the Girl began to look upon it as a home. She had grown three inches by the end of her third year and had the rounded calves and breasts of a woman. Each morning she scrubbed herself clean with cool water before coming down to the kitchen and to Bernice, who had become accustomed to her solemn, shining face. She watched the Girl closely until it seemed to her that she had gained enough weight. And the women of the house teased her gently and asked her about her lessons. Most of them were, in spite of their paint, simple farm girls and sometimes liked having a younger one to look after.

When the Girl was not doing chores or studying with Bird she stayed to herself, working in the garden. Minta sometimes joined her there, her thin, pale skin hidden under a large hat. She was only two years older than the Girl, although she had been at Woodard's for several years and carried herself as if she had always lived in a brothel.

On Minta's twentieth birthday Gilda took her into town to buy her a new dress. Not an unusual event, but the party Gilda and Bird planned was. Everyone at Woodard's dressed for dinner that evening. The kitchen was filled with teasing laughter which continued in the salon late that evening. A few of the clients who came brought Minta flowers or small trinkets, but Minta was most pleased by the simple cotton blouse the Girl had sewn especially for her.

Pride suffused Gilda's smile as she watched the girls, all of whom were women now. Even her young foundling had become Bird's assistant in the management of the house. They all had the manners of ladies, could read, write, and shoot. Rachel, to whom Minta had been closest, left for California just before Minta's birthday, hoping to start a fresh life and find a husband. The talk heard most often in the salon now was about abolition and the rising temperatures of the North and South. Even at Minta's party the passion of politics couldn't be resisted.

An older Creole man, a frequent visitor to the house, was pounding the piano ineptly but with enthusiasm as a circle of women cheered him on. The Girl served a tray of champagne and stood by the settee near the door in order to listen for Bernice calling her to the kitchen. She placed herself so she would be able to overhear the many conversations in the salon.

But it was Gilda's voice, raised slightly at the other side of the room, that came to her. "I'll say this just once tonight. The years of bartering in human flesh are near their end. And any civilized man will be grateful for it." She peered sternly at a pinched-faced man standing against the window. "You may discuss Lincoln's election in your own parlors, but I will listen to no talk of war in my house tonight."

Fanny tried to turn the conversation to horses, a subject she was most familiar with, but two men cut her off. "Horses! Nigras! It's the same damn thing, more trouble than they're worth. I say we just ship..."

The man at the piano stopped playing.

"As I've said gentlemen, the only name on the deed to this place is mine." After a beat of deep silence, the piano music started again and the Girl began to gather empty glasses. She backed out of the room with a full tray.

In the kitchen Bernice asked, "What that ruckus 'bout in there?"

"War talk."

"Umph, men got nothin' but war talk. Like it more'n they like hoppin' on top 'a these girls." She sucked the air through her teeth as she poured more wine into the glasses. She passed one to the Girl, and they both drank quickly.

Bernice looked more like her mother than anyone the Girl had met since running away, but she seemed like a sister too.

"What you think...if they get freedom?" Bernice asked as she slid her tongue around the rim of the champagne glass.

"We free already, Bernice. Won't mean so much over here, you think?"

"Gal, they's whole lot of us ain't free, just down the road!"

"Think they gonna come here?" the Girl asked, having a difficult time making the full picture of the world take shape in her head. The memory of the women and men, her sisters still at the plantation, made her feel slightly faint.

"Who know what they do. If they got no work, who know. With nobody to take care 'bout and nobody to pay them like Miss Gilda do us. Who know." Bernice poured more champagne into their glittering crystal.

A surge of fear welled up in the Girl. "We gotta keep this place safe, Bernice, no matter how the war goes. They'll be people needin' to come here I 'spect," the Girl said, remembering the smell of the dark earth of the root cellar where she'd taken refuge.

"Umph," Bernice said, letting her voice drop slightly, "we keep our eye out, maybe some folks need to take to root, if you knows what I mean. Me an' you can do that. I been figurin' on something like that. It's not the war, it's the freedom we got to keep our eye on."

"I remember how to do that," the Girl said, taking the last sip from her glass.

As the Girl hurried back into the salon Minta stopped her at the door, taking two glasses from the tray and setting one behind her on the mantel. She whispered in the Girl's ear conspiratorially, "You'd think these gents would give up arguin' with Miss Gilda. She's stubborner than a crow. I can't says I blame her."

"Why you say that? Don't you think there's gonna be war?"

"Sure, for certain sure. Just ain't no need talkin' it up. Be here soon enough. They always got to spoil somethin'. I'll be goddamned if one of 'em is gonna spoil my birthday!"

The Girl was full of questions but was afraid to ask them here. Sarah and Fanny came over to them, Fanny saying, "You gonna drink 'em all just cause it's your birthday?"

"If that's my desire," Minta said, draining her glass with a flourish.

She turned on her heel, picked up her other drink from the mantel, and strode to the far side of the room.

"She's a terrible slut. I can't understand why Miss Gilda keeps her here," Fanny said.

"Oh, she's alright," Sarah responded, tickling Fanny under her breast. "You jes' jealous 'cause she got a special handmade blouse for her birthday." Fanny refused to smile as she took a glass from the tray.

The Girl smiled shyly. "Aw, Miss Fanny ain't got nothin' to worry 'bout. She gets presents every day." Fanny tried to look remote and superior, but a tiny smile turned up the corners of her mouth.

Sarah threw her arm around Fanny's waist and pulled her away saying, "Yes, and if she's lucky I'll get to wear her new brooch this Saturday." The two women, who seemed to the Girl not much more than girls themselves, made their way to the piano. Gilda and Bird stood apart at the far end of the room.

The Girl approached them with the last two glasses on her tray. "Miss Gilda?" she said in a low voice.

Gilda took a glass and gave it to Bird. Then she said, "You have that one, child."

Bird tapped the rim of the Girl's glass with her own before sipping. She turned to Gilda. "I think we're ready to move on to French."

"So soon!" Gilda was surprised and pleased.

"If we're learning one grammar, it might as well be two."

The Girl's head buzzed with excitement. She was still shocked that she could put letters and words together and make sense of them in

English and that Bird had been able to teach her to understand the words of her nation. Sometimes when they were shopping in town she and Bird confused the shopkeepers along Rue Bourbon by switching back and forth between languages.

Their arrival was inevitably met by either bold, disdainful smirks or surreptitious glances. Everyone knew of the Indian from Woodard's place and now found the addition of the "dark one" a further curiosity they couldn't resist. Bird and the Girl were self-consciously erect as they meandered from one shop to the next, making their way easily among the creamy-colored quadroons who, with mighty effort, pretended they did not see them. It was some time before the Girl understood that these graceful, cold women shared her African blood. She had been so confused and upset by it that she cried as Bird tried to explain the social system of New Orleans, the levels of deceit and manners that afforded the fairer-skinned their privileges and banished the darker ones from society.

For many weeks the Girl could not bring herself to return to town to shop with Bird. First she feigned illness, then begged off because of duties with Bernice. She didn't understand her own fear of these people who tried to look through Bird as if she were glass and simply dismissed her as a slave. Only after an afternoon of making an effort to help Bernice in exchange for being excused from the shopping trip did the Girl find it possible to resume her routine. Bernice had asked her, directly, to explain herself. The Girl found the words for the shame she felt in front of those women, although she could not say why she thought this was so.

"I'll tell you what the problem is…you shamed alright," Bernice said in her now familiarly blunt manner, "but it's them you shamed of. Know how I knows? 'Cause long as you been here you ain't never looked shamed about nothin'. Even that first night when she dragged you in here like a sack. You was your mama's daughter and that was that. What you shamed about is them folks thinkin' they white and they ain't. Thinkin' being nasty to dark folks is gonna help make them white. That's a shame alright. Not yours…theirs, so just go on 'bout your business."

The Girl resumed her shopping with Bird from that afternoon on. Soon they started to speak the languages as often as they could and watched the shopkeepers' and customers' discomfort. Then they would leave the store choking back their giggles. Now to add French! She would be able to understand what she'd been certain were remarks being made about her and speak as well as they did, for Bird had said her facility with languages was excellent. The Girl was even happier than when she'd constructed her first sentence on paper. Gilda was pleased that she'd been correct; the Girl was the one who would give Bird her connection to life. Bird had opened herself to her as she had with no one else at the house except Gilda.

"So Français it is, *ma chère.*"

Gilda's unwavering gaze both excited and discomfited the Girl.

She sensed some question being answered in Gilda's mind.

"Can I take that, Miss Bird?" the Girl said, lifting her tray. She was relieved to have a reason to leave the room for a moment. She needed to think about what had been raised this evening: war, French, as well as the look of satisfaction in Gilda's eyes. She had tried to read Gilda's thoughts as she had been able to do on occasions in the past but was not completely successful now. She perceived a sense of completion that was certainly focused on her, but the pictures that sometimes formed in her mind when she had questions did not appear this time. She left the glasses and tray in the kitchen and stepped into the small den that was used for coats, wanting to sit quietly for a moment. The bubbling wine and excitement had given her a slight headache, and she waited for it to recede so she could rejoin the others when Minta played the piano. She rose as a gentleman entered looking for his coat.

"May I help you, sir?" she inquired.

"You sure can, little gal," he said, smiling blandly. "I've been over here to New Orleans more than a couple of times now. And I got to say this is the best house west of Chicago."

His look appraised her although he was speaking of Woodard's. She continued to meet his almost-translucent eyes, as if she might hold his gaze and keep it from traveling over her body.

"Thank you, sir. I'll be sure and tell Miss Gilda you said so." The Girl waited for the man to point toward his coat, but he stood silently with his eyes on her. The Girl had not known the auction block. She had never stood upon one and had never had any occasion to see the one used regularly in the center of the city. His look, however, made her know it intimately. The gaze from his hazel eyes seared her skin, but her face remained impassive as she spoke.

"Your coat, sir?"

"Not just yet. How old would you say you were, little gal?" The Girl's eyes were almost on a level with his.

"About seventeen. Miss Gilda gave me a birthday party last year. She said she figured I was about seventeen."

"How's it come you don't remember how old you are?" Even after the uneventful years that had passed since her arrival at the house, the Girl was still wary of white men asking questions. The talk of abolition and maybe a war meant little to her. Any of these men could capture her and take her back to the plantation.

"I was really sick for a while when I was little. My mistress, Miss Gilda's sister, died before she could tell Miss Gilda the exact information."

"Well, you don't look more'n fourteen to me."

She wondered why he told such a foolish lie. "Could be, sir, but I don't think so."

"Come over here and let me get a closer look at you." The Girl took two steps nearer, not sure what to expect. He reached out and rubbed her breast. The Girl jumped back, startled. "Aw come on, little gal, let me just get a little somethin' here."

"No, sir!"

"Then we'll go up to your room. I'll pay the regular price."

"No, sir! I just do housekeeping for Miss Gilda. If you want I'll call one of the other girls in."

"I don't want one of the other gals. I'm looking to get to you right now. Come on upstairs."

The Girl recognized the look in his eye. It came back to her from a place far away. She had the dream only rarely now, but whenever she did she awoke crying in terror. Here, not sleeping, the nightmare stood before her, and instead of fear she felt an icy anger. Her hands clenched and unclenched fitfully, as she thought how she would distract his attention and run from the room. She did not want to cause a fuss and spoil Minta's birthday. She closed her eyes, and her mother's face was pictured clearly. Often it had been hard to remember what her mother looked like, but now here was the African face that had comforted her so often. The Girl was awash with tears.

The girls talked often of the gentlemen, usually with a tinge of indulgence as if they were children being kept busily playing while the women did important things. Never had they indicated any fear of the men who visited Woodard's. Whatever gossip she had heard about violence seemed to come from town, frequently about the haughty, fair-skinned ones and their white lovers. Mistreatment was something she knew Gilda would never tolerate, and the Girl realized just then that neither could she.

When she opened her eyes the moisture spilled out and she said, "Please sir, Miss Gilda will be looking for me in the kitchen. I got chores now."

"This won't take long," he said and took her wrist.

"Sir, I've explained—"

She stopped short as Gilda opened the door.

"May I help you, sir?" Gilda's voice was sweet, her anger concealed under the syrup of manners. He loosened his grip on the Girl and gave a deep bow in Gilda's direction.

"Just thought I'd have a little entertainment here."

"I'm sorry, sir. The Girl works only in the kitchen. I'm sure there are others you'd like to meet."

"Don't you think it's about time you broke this one in?"

"No, sir. I don't. If you'll leave the management of my girls to me, you just go about having a good time. Why don't we rejoin the party?" She turned toward the Girl. "Go to Bernice, I'm sure she could use your help. They're about to bring out the cake." The Girl squeezed past Bird who had appeared silently in the doorway.

"I bet you could do a lot of business with that nigra gal, Miss Gilda. You don't know what kind of opportunity you lettin' pass by."

"As I said, let me do the managing. You just enjoy yourself."

"I was kinda hopin' to enjoy myself with her," he said insistently.

"Well, that's not possible," Gilda said. The syrup froze around the sentence, and her back stiffened. Without turning she felt Bird enter the room and said, "Will you see that this gentleman gets a fresh glass of champagne? I have to go out for a while." Gilda left through the kitchen.

Bernice started to speak but stopped herself when she saw the jerky movement and aura of rage that swept along beside Gilda.

Gilda welcomed the coolness of the night air against her cheeks. They were flushed with anger. She was surprised by the rage she had felt when she sensed the Girl was in trouble.

In her lifetime, Gilda had killed reluctantly and infrequently. When she took the blood there was no need to take life. But she knew that there were those like her who gained power as much from the terror of their prey as from the life substance itself. She had learned many lessons in her time. The most important had been from Sorel and were summed up in a very few words: The source of power will tell in how long-lived that power is. He had pointed her and all of his children toward an enduring power that did not feed on death. Gilda was sustained by sharing the blood and by maintaining the vital connections to life. Her love for her family of friends had fed her for three hundred years. When Bird chose to join her in this life, Gilda was filled with both joy and dread. The weight of the years she had known subsided temporarily; at last there would be someone beside her to experience the passage of time. Bird's first years at Woodard's were remote now— Bird moving silently through their lives, subtly taking control of management, finding her place closer and closer to Gilda without having to speak of it.

Before she had even considered bringing Bird into her life she had wanted to feel her sleeping beside her. She had not been willing to risk their friendship, though, until she was certain. And Bird had opened to her, deliberately, to let her know her desires were the same as Gilda's. When they first lay together, Gilda sensed that Bird already knew what world it was Gilda would ask her to enter. She had teased Gilda later with sly smiles, about time and rushing through life, until Gilda had finally been certain Bird was asking to join her.

Despite the years of joy they had known together, tonight, walking along the dark road, Gilda felt she had lived much too long. Only now was it clear to her why. The talk of war, the anger and brutality that was revealed daily in the townspeople, was a bitter taste in her mouth. She had seen enough war and hatred in her lifetime. And although her abolitionist sentiments had never been hidden, she didn't know if she had the heart to withstand the rending effects of another war.

And as always, when Gilda reflected on these things she came back to Bird: Bird, who had chosen to be a part of this life, a choice she seemed to have made effortlessly. Gilda had never said the word *vampire*. She had only asked if Bird would join her as partner in the business and in life. In the years since she'd come to the house she always knew as much as was needed and challenged Gilda any time she tried to hide information from her. Bird listened inside of Gilda's words, hearing the years of isolation and discovery. There was in Gilda an unfathomable hunger—a dark, dry chasm that Bird thought she could help fill.

But now it was the touch of the sun and the ocean Gilda hungered for, and little else. She ached to rest, free from the intemperate demands of time. Often she'd tried to explain this burden to Bird, the need to let go. And Bird saw it only as an escape from *her*—rather than a final embrace of freedom.

Thoughts jostled inside her as she moved—so quickly she was invisible—through the night. She slowed a few miles west of the Louisiana state line, then turned back toward her township. When she came to a road leading to a familiar horse ranch within miles of her farmhouse, she slackened her pace and walked to the rear of the wood-frame building.

All of the windows were black as she slipped around to the small bunkhouse at the back where the hands slept. She stood in the shadows listening. Once inside she approached the nearest man, the larger of the two she could see in the darkness. She began to probe his dreams, then sensed an uncleanness in his blood and recoiled. His sleeping face did not bear the mark of the disease that coursed through his body, but it was there. She was certain. Gilda was saddened as she moved to the smaller man who slept at the other end of the room.

He had fallen asleep in his clothes on top of the blankets and smelled of whiskey and horses. She slipped inside his thoughts as he dreamed of a chestnut-colored bay. Under his excitement lay anxiety, his fear of the challenge of this horse. Gilda held him in sleep while she sliced through the flesh of his neck, the line of her nail leaving a red trail. She extended his dream, making him king of the riders as she took her share of the blood. He smiled with triumph at his horsemanship, the warmth of the whiskey in him thundering through her. She caught her breath, and the other ranch hand tossed restlessly in his sleep. Although she no longer feared death she backed away, her instincts readying her hands to quiet the restless worker if he awoke. Her touch on the other sleeper sealed his wound cleanly. Soon his pulse was steady and he continued to explore the dreams she had left with him. As their breathing settled into a calm rhythm, Gilda ran from the bunkhouse, flushed with the fullness of blood and whiskey.

The road back felt particularly dark to Gilda as she moved eastward. The clouds left little moonlight visible, but she was swift. Blood pounded in her head, and she imagined that was what she would feel once she finally lay down in the sea and gave up her life. Her heart beat with excitement, full of the need to match its rhythm with that of an ocean. There, Gilda would find her tears again and be free of the sounds of battles and the burden of days and nights piled upon each other endlessly. The dust from the road flew up around her as she made her way toward home. She remembered the dusty trek that was the one clear image of her childhood. They had been going toward water, perhaps the sea. The future had lain near that sea, somehow. It was survival for her mother, father, and the others who had moved relentlessly toward it. Now it was that again for Gilda—now and more. The sea would be the place to rest her spirit.

Once back in her room she changed her dusty jacket and breeches and sat quietly alone in the dark. As dawn appeared on the horizon behind the house, Gilda let down her dark hair and was peaceful in her earthen bed. She was relieved to finally see the end of the road.

In the soft light of a fall afternoon the Girl worked in the garden as she had done for so many years. By now she knew the small plot well, picking the legumes and uprooting the weeds without much thought, enjoying the sun and air. When she looked up at the house Bird waved to her, then pulled the curtain tight across the window of Gilda's room.

The Girl's reverie was lazy and undirected. She started at Minta's shadow when it crept over her.

They both sat quietly for some time before the Girl asked Minta, "How long you been here at Woodard's?"

"I was younger than you was when you come," she answered proudly, "but I think I'm gonna move on soon, though. Been savin' my money and thinkin' about goin' west where Rachel is. Look around for a while."

"How long Bird...has Bird been here?" the Girl asked, picking her way through the rules of grammar.

"I don't know. Long as any of us can remember. She left once, that's what I heard Bernice say, but she come back quick. Them Indian folks she come from didn't want her back."

Both girls were quiet for a moment, each feeling younger than either had since going out into the world on her own. Minta spoke with hard resolve as if to cover her vulnerability. "When I leave, I'm gone. Gonna make me a fortune in California, get away from this war talk."

"You think Rachel let you stay with her?"

"Well, she sent me a letter with her address and everything. She went to that man Miss Gilda said would give her a hand if she need it. And he put her up in a place 'til she got her own and said he'd help her find a little shop." Minta could feel the Girl's unspoken doubt. She pushed ahead with assurance as much for herself as for the Girl. "She right there on the water and got lotsa business. And she say there not enough women for anybody." A smirk opened her mouth then, but she tried to continue in a businesslike way. "She want to move if she save the money. Get in a quiet district with the swells." Simply talking about Rachel and her new life seemed to make Minta breathless. "She said the women and men there wear the prettiest clothes she ever seen. She want to get a place nearer to the rich people and leave them sailors behind."

The Girl looked aghast, trying to picture Rachel alone in a western city, owning a shop, mixing with rich people who weren't trying to get in her bed. But the image was too distant to get it into focus.

"Say, you think you want to come too? I bet we could get us a little business goin' out there the way you can sew and all."

Leave Gilda and Bird? The thought was a shock to the Girl who had never considered such a possibility; it seemed ludicrous as she knelt under the warm sun feeling the softness of the earth's comfort beneath her. And even with the war coming and talk of emancipation and hardship, the Girl had little in mind she would run away to. "Naw, this is my home now, I guess."

"Well, you just be careful."

"What do you mean?"

"Watch yourself, is all." Minta said it softly and would speak no more. The Girl was puzzled and made anxious by the edge in Minta's voice as well as the silence that followed. Her look of frustration tugged at Minta. "There's lots of folks down this way believe in haunts and such like. Spirits. Creoles, like Miss Gilda, and Indians, they follow all that stuff." Minta spoke low, bending at the waist as if to make the words come out softer. "I like her fine, even though some folks don't. Just watch, is all." She skittered through the garden to the kitchen door.

The Girl finished her weeding, then went to the kitchen steps to rinse her hands at the pump and dust her clothes. Bernice watched from the back porch.

"What you say to Minta, she run upstairs?"

"I ain't certain. She's so nervous I can't get hold to what she sayin' half a while. I know she wants me to go out there with her to stay with Rachel."

"What else?"

"She afraid of something here. Sometimes I think maybe it's Miss Gilda. What you think?"

Bernice's face closed as if a door had been locked. "You ain't goin' is you?"

"I'm here for the war no matter what, if there's gonna be one."

"Listen gal, you been lucky so far. You got a life, so don't toss it in the air just to stay 'round here." Behind Bernice's voice the Girl could sense her conflict, her words both pushing the Girl away and needing her to stay.

"My life's here with you and Miss Gilda and Bird. What would I do in California—wear a hat and play lady?" she said, laughing loudly, nervously. She saw the same wary look on Bernice's face that had filtered through Minta's voice.

"What is it? Why you questioning me with that look?" the Girl asked with a tinge of anger in her voice.

"Nothin'. They just different. Not like regular people. Maybe that's good. Who gonna know 'til they know?"

"You sayin' they bad or somethin'?" The challenge wavered in the Girl's throat as her own questions about Gilda and Bird slipped into her mind.

"No." The solid response reminded the Girl of how long Bernice had been at Woodard's. "I'm just saying I don't know who they are. After all the time I been here I still don't know who Miss Gilda is. Inside I don't really know what she thinkin' like you do with most white folks. I don't know who her people is. White folks is dyin' to tell each other that. Not her. Now Bird, I got more an idea what she's up to. She watch over Miss Gilda like…like…" Bernice's voice trailed off as she struggled for words that spoke to this child who was now almost a woman.

"That ain't hurt you none, now has it?" The Girl's response was hard with loyalty to the women who'd drawn her into their family.

"Not me. I'm just waitin' for the river to rise." Bernice didn't really worry about who Gilda and Bird were. Her concern was what would become of this Girl on her own.

On a day soon after Gilda took the Girl and Bird with her to the farmhouse, Minta stood by the empty horse stall nearest the road. Her face was placid, yet she was again bent at the waist as if still whispering. The Girl caught a glimpse of her when the buggy rounded the bend in the road, and she leaned over looking back. She was excited about this journey away from the house, but Minta's warnings itched her like the crinoline one of the girls had given her last Christmas.

The evening sky was rolling with clouds as they drove the buggy south to the farm, yet the Girl could feel Gilda's confidence that there would be no storm. They talked of many things but not the weather. Still, from simply looking into Gilda's eyes and touching Bird's hand she knew there was a storm somewhere. She felt a struggle brewing and longed to speak out, to warn them of how much everyone in town would need them when the war came. She knew that would not be the thing to say—Gilda liked to circle her point until she came to a place she thought would be right for speaking. It didn't come on the road to the farmhouse.

When the three arrived at the farmhouse, the Girl stored her small traveling box under the eaves in the tiny room she slept in whenever they visited here. She wondered if Minta knew Gilda spoke without speaking. That might be the reason she had cautioned her. But the Girl had no fear. Gilda, more often aloof than familiar, touched the Girl somehow. Words were only one of many ways of stepping inside of someone. The Girl smiled, recollecting her childish notion that Gilda was a man. Perhaps, she thought, living among the whites had given her a secret passage, but knowledge of Gilda came from a deeper place. It was a place kept hidden except from Bird.

The fields to the north and west of the farmhouse lay fallow, trimmed but unworked. It was land much like the rest in the Delta sphere, warm and moist, almost blue in its richness—blood soil, some said. The not-tall house over the shallow root cellar seemed odd with its distinct aura of life set in the emptiness of the field. Gilda stood at the window looking out to the evening dark as Bird moved around her placing clothes in chests. Gilda tried to pull the strands together, to make a pattern of her life that was recognizable, therefore reinforceable. The farmhouse offered her peace but no answers. It was simply privacy away from the dissembling of the city and relief from the tides, which each noon and night pulled her energy, sucking her breath and leaving her lighter than air. The quietness of the house and its eagerness to hold her safe were like a firm hand on her shoulder. Here Gilda could relax enough to think. She had hardly come through the door before she let go of the world of Woodard's. Still her thoughts always turned back toward the open sea and the burning sun.

The final tie was Bird. Bird, the gentle, stern one who rarely flinched yet held on to her as if she were drowning in life. Too few of their own kind had passed through Woodard's, and none had stayed very long. On their one trip west to visit Sorel, neither could tolerate the dust and noise of his town for more than several weeks. And until the Girl's arrival, Gilda had met no one she sensed was the right one. To leave Bird alone in this world without others like herself would be more cruel than Gilda could ever be. The Girl must stay. She pushed back all doubts: Was the Girl too young? Would she grow to hate the life she'd be given? Would she abandon Bird? The answer was there in the child's eyes. The decision loosened the tight muscles of Gilda's back as if the deed were already done.

The Girl did not know why they had included her in the trip to the farmhouse this time. They rarely brought her along at midseason. The thought that they might want her to leave them made her more anxious than Minta's soft voice. Yet each day Bird and she sat down for their lessons, and in the evening, when Gilda and Bird talked quietly together, they sought her out to join them. She would curl up in the corner, not speaking, only listening to the words that poured from them as they talked of the women back at the house, the politics in town, the war, and told adventurous stories. The Girl thought, at first, that they were made up, but she soon heard in the passion of their voices the truth of the stories Gilda and Bird had lived.

Sometimes one of them would say, "Listen here, this is something you should know." But there was no need for that. The Girl, now tall and lean with adulthood, clung to their words. She enjoyed the contrasting rhythms of their voices and the worlds of mystery they revealed.

She sensed an urgency in Gilda—the stories had to be told, let free from her. And Bird, who also felt the urgency, did not become preoccupied with it but was happy that she and Gilda were spending time together again as it had been before. She unfolded her own history like soft deerskin. Bird gazed at the Girl, wrapped in a cotton shirt, her legs tucked under her on the floor, and felt that her presence gave them an unspoken completeness.

She spoke before she thought. "This is like many times before the fire in my village."

"Ah, and who's to play the part of your toothless elders, me or the Girl?" Gilda asked, smiling widely.

The Girl laughed softly as Bird replied, "Both."

Gilda rose from the dark velvet couch. Her face disappeared out of the low lamplight into the shadow. She stooped, lifted the Girl in her arms, and lay her on the couch. She sat down again and rested the Girl's head in her lap. She stroked the Girl's thick braids as Bird and she continued talking.

In the next silence she asked the Girl, "What do you remember of your mother and sisters?" The Girl did not think of them except at night, just before sleeping, their memory her nightly prayers. She'd never spoken of them to Gilda, only to Bird when they exchanged stories during their reading lessons. Now the litany of names served as memory: Minerva, small, full of energy and questions; Florine, two years older than the Girl, unable to ever meet anyone's eyes; and Martha, the oldest, broad-shouldered like their mother but more solemn. She described the feel of the pallet where she slept with her mother, rising early for breakfast duties—stirring porridge and setting out the rolls. She described the smell of bread, shiny with butter, and the snow-white raw cotton tinged with blood from her fingers.

Of the home their mother spoke about, the Girl was less certain. It was always a dream place—distant, unreal. Except the talk of dancing. The Girl could close her eyes and almost hear the rhythmic shuffling of feet, the bells and gourds. All kept beat inside her body, and the feel of heat from an open fire made the dream place real. Talking of it now, her body rocked slightly as if she had been rewoven into that old circle of dancers. She poured out the images and names, proud of her own ability to weave a story. Bird smiled at her pupil who claimed her past, reassuring her silently.

Each of the days at the farmhouse was much like the others. The Girl rose a bit later than when they were in the city, for there was little work to be done here. She dusted or read, walked in the field watching birds and rabbits. In the late afternoon she would hear Bird and Gilda stirring. They came out to speak to her from the shadows of the porch, but then they returned to their room, where the Girl heard the steady sound of their voices or the quiet scratching of pen on paper.

The special quality of their life did not escape the Girl; it seemed more pronounced at the farmhouse, away from the activity of Woodard's. She had found the large feed bags filled with dirt in the root cellar where she hid so long ago. She had felt the thin depth of soil beneath the carpets and weighted in their cloaks. Although they kept the dinner hour as a gathering time, they had never eaten in front of her. The Girl cooked her own meals, often eating alone, except when Bird prepared a corn pudding or a rabbit she had killed. Then they sat together as the Girl ate and Bird sipped tea. She had seen Gilda and Bird go out late in the night, both wearing breeches and woolen shirts. Sometimes they went together, other times separately. And both spoke to her without voices.

The warning from Minta and the whispers of the secret religion, vodun, still did not frighten her. She had known deep fear and knew she could protect herself when she must. But there was no cause for fear of these two who slept so soundly in each other's arms and treated her with such tenderness.

On the afternoon of the eighth day at the farmhouse the Girl returned from a walk through the fields to get a drink of water from the back pump. She was surprised to hear, through the kitchen window, Gilda's voice drawn tight in argument with Bird. There was silence from the rest of the room, then a burst of laughter from Gilda.

"Do you see that we're fighting only because we love each other? I insist we stop right this minute. I won't have it on such a glorious evening."

The Girl could hear her moving around the small wooden table, pulling back a chair. Gilda did not sit in the chair, instead lowering herself onto Bird's lap. Bird's expression of surprise turned into a laugh, but the tension beneath it was not totally dispelled.

"I'm sick of this talk. You go on about this leaving as if there is somewhere in the world you could go without me."

Her next words were cut short by Gilda's hand on her mouth. And then Gilda's soft, thin lips pressed her back in the chair.

"Please, my love, let's go to our room so I can feel the weight of your body on mine. Let's compare the tones of our skin as we did when we were young."

Bird laughed just as she was expected to do. The little joking references to time and age were their private game. Even knowing there was more to the kisses and games right now, she longed to feel Gilda's skin pressed tightly to her own. She stood up, still clasping Gilda to her breasts, and walked up the stairs with her as if she were a child.

The Girl remained on the porch looking out into the field as the sun dropped quickly behind the trees. She loved the sound of Gilda and Bird laughing, but it seemed they did so only when they thought no others were listening. When it was fully dark she went into the kitchen to make supper for herself. She put on the kettle for tea, certain that Bird and Gilda would want some when they came down. She rooted through the clay jars until she had pulled together a collection of sweet-smelling herbs she thought worthy. She was eager to hear their laughter again.

That evening Bird took the buggy out and called to the Girl to help load the laundry bags inside. The Girl was silent as she lifted the bags up to the buckboard platform to Bird, who kept glancing up at the windows.

"Tell Minta I said hello." The Girl spoke tentatively when the quiet seemed too large. "Tell her not to leave without me." She figured that was a good enough joke since Minta had been deviling everybody with her dreamtalk of going west.

Bird stood straight, dropping the final bundle on the floor of the buckboard, and looked down at the Girl. "What does that mean?"

"I'm teasin'. She keep talkin' about movin' out there with Rachel like I goin' with her."

Bird turned silent, sat, and grasped the reins of the restless horse. The Girl felt more compelled to fill the air. "I'm not goin'."

"You could, you might want to. Eventually you'll want to start your own life, your own family somewhere." Bird's voice was even, but the Girl recognized a false quiet in it from the times she had heard her arguing with Gilda or talking to drunken clients.

"Any family startin' to do will be done right here." The Girl felt safe having finally said what she wanted out loud. She looked up at Bird's face shyly and was pleased to see the flash of Bird's teeth sparking her grin.

Bird climbed up to the seat and spoke casually, the voice of the woman who always kept the house. "I'll stay in town tonight and return tomorrow evening for tea. If there is any danger, you have only to call out to me."

Bird drew the horse out onto the road, leaving the Girl on the porch wondering what danger there might be. Her warning not to have concern was more frightening to her than Minta's cautionary words.

Upstairs, Gilda was silent in her room. She did not join the Girl after Bird was gone but came down later in the evening. She moved about the parlor, making a circle before resting on the arm of the sofa across from the Girl who sat in Bird's favored chair. The Girl's dark face was smooth, her brow wide and square under the braided rows that drew her thick, springy hair to the nape of her neck. Gilda wore pants and a shirt cinched tightly at her waist by soft leather studded with small white beads. She spoke to the Girl in silence. *Do you know how many years I have lived?*

"Many more years than anyone."

Gilda rose and stood over the Girl. "I have Bird's love and yours, I think?" The end of the sentence curled upward in a question.

The Girl had not thought of love until the word was spoken. Yes, she loved them both. The remembered face of her mother was all she had loved until now. Tears slipped down her cheeks. Gilda's sadness washed over her, and she felt the loss of her mother, new and cutting.

"We can talk when I return." Gilda closed the door and was lost in the darkness.

The Girl walked through the house looking at their belongings as if it were the first time she had seen them—their dresses folded smoothly and the delicate linens, the chest that held small tailored breeches and flannel shirts that smelled of earth and lavender water.

She touched the leather spines of the books which she longed to read; some were in languages she did not recognize. Sitting on the edge of the bed that Gilda and Bird shared, she looked patiently at each item in the room, inhaling their scent. The brushes, combs, and jars sat neatly aligned on the dressing table. The coverlet, rugs, and draperies felt thick, luxurious, yet the room was plain. Without Gilda and Bird in the house the rooms seemed incomplete. The Girl walked slowly through each one as if it were new to her, crossing back and forth, searching for something to soothe the unease that crept up into her. Everything appeared just as it had during all the days she had been with Gilda and Bird, except that she felt someone had gone before her as she did now, examining objects, replacing them, pulling out memories, laying them aside.

When the house became cold, the Girl built a fire and curled up on the sofa under her cotton sheet. She fingered the small wooden frame with its rows of beads that Bird had been using to teach her accounting. The clicking of wood on wood was comforting. When Gilda returned she found the Girl asleep, clutching the abacus to her breast as she might a doll. The Girl woke up feeling Gilda's eyes on her and knew it was late by the chill of the air. The fire glowed faintly under fresh logs.

"We can talk now," Gilda said as if she'd never gone out. She sat beside the Girl and held her hand.

"There's a war coming. It's here already, truth be told..." She stopped. The effort of getting out those few words left her weary.

"Do you understand when I tell you I can live through no more?"

The Girl did not speak but thought of the night she decided to escape from the plantation.

Gilda continued. "I've been afraid of living too long, and now is the end of my time. The night I found you in the cellar seems only a minute ago. But you were such a child, so full of terror, your journey had been more than the miles of road. When I picked you up your body relaxed into mine, knowing part of your fight was done. I sensed in you a spirit and understanding of the world, that you were the voice lacking among us. Seeing this world with you has given me wonderful years of pleasure. Now my only fear is leaving Bird alone. It's you she needs here with her."

The Girl looked at Gilda's face, the skin drawn tightly across the tiny bones, her eyes glistening with flecks of orange. She wanted to comfort this woman who'd lifted her out of her nightmares.

"You must want to stay. You must need to live. Will you trust me?"

"I never thought to leave you or the house. My home is here as long as you'll have me," the Girl said in a clear voice.

"What I ask is not an easy thing. You may feel you have nothing to go back to, but sooner or later we all want to go back to something. Usually some inconsequential thing to which we've never given much thought before. But it will loom there in our past entreating us cruelly because there is no way to ever go back. In asking this of you, and in the future should you ask it of others, you must be certain that you—that others—are strong enough to withstand the complete loss of those intangibles that make the past so alluring."

The Girl said nothing, not really certain what Gilda meant. She felt a change in the room—the air was taut with energy.

"There are only inadequate words to speak for who we are. The language is crude, the history false. You must look to me and know who I am and if the life I offer is the life you choose. In choosing you must pledge yourself to pursue only life, never bitterness or cruelty."

The Girl peered deeply into the swirling brown and flickering orange of Gilda's eyes, feeling herself opening to ideas and sensations she had never fully admitted before. She drew back, startled at the weight of time she saw behind those eyes.

"Don't be frightened by the idea of death; it is part of life in all things. It will only become worrisome when you decide that its time has come. Power is the frightening thing, not death. And the blood, it is a shared thing. Something we must all learn to share or simply spill onto battlefields." Gilda stopped, feeling the weight of all she wanted to say, knowing it would be too much at once. She would leave the rest to Bird.

The Girl listened to the words. She tried to look again into the world behind Gilda's eyes and understand what was being asked of her. What she saw was open space, no barriers. She saw a dusty road and heard the silence of determination as she felt the tribe close around her as it had closed around Gilda, the child. She saw forests spanning a distance of green too remote for even Gilda to remember.

"My dream was to see the world, over time. The real dream is to make a world—to see the people and still want to make a world."

"I haven't seen much, but what I've seen doesn't give me much appetite," the Girl said, remembering the chill she felt from Bernice's words about the war's aftermath.

"But what of the people?" Gilda's voice rose slightly. "Put aside the faces of those who've hunted you, who've hurt you. What of the people you've loved? Those you could love tomorrow?"

The Girl drew back from the fire in Gilda's voice. Her mother's hands reaching down to pull the cloth up to her chin as she lay on the mattress filled her vision. Her mother's darkened knuckles had loomed large and solid, something she had not articulated her love for. She remembered hearing Bird's voice for the first time below her in the house announcing the entertainment. The deep resonance sent a thrill through her body. Minta's soft warning was all but forgotten, but her tender concern, which showed in the bend of her body, filled the Girl with joy. The wary, protective way Bernice had watched her grow, their evenings alone in the kitchen talking about the ways of the world—these were things of value. She opened her eyes and looked into Gilda's. She found love there, too. And exhaustion beyond exploration. She could see no future in them although this was what Gilda wanted to promise her.

Reading the thoughts that Gilda tried to communicate, the Girl picked her way through. "You're offerin' me time that's not really time? Time that's gonna leave me by myself?"

"I've seen this world moving on many different paths. I've walked each road with curiosity, anxious to see what we would make of our world. In Europe and to the south of us here have been much the same. When I came here the world was much larger, and the trip I had to make into the new world was as fearful as the one you've made. I was a girl, too, much too young to even be afraid.

"Each time I thought taking a stand, fighting a war would bring the solution to the demons that haunted us. Each time I thought slavery or fanaticism could be banished from the earth with a law or a battle. Each time I've been wrong. I've run out of that youthful caring, and I know we must believe in possibilities in order to go on. I no longer believe. At least for myself."

"But the war is important. People have got to be free to live."

"Yes, and that will no doubt be accomplished. But for men to need war to make freedom…I have never understood. Now I am tired of trying to understand. There are those of our kind who kill every time they go out into the night. They say they need this exhilaration in order to live this life. They are simply murderers. They have no special need; they are rabid children. In our life, we who live by sharing the life blood of others have no need to kill. It is through our connection with life, not death, that we live."

Both women were silent. The Girl was uncertain what questions she might even ask. It was like learning a new language. When she looked again into Gilda's eyes she felt the pulsing of blood beneath the skin. She also sensed a rising excitement that was unfamiliar to her.

"There is a joy to the exchange we make. We draw life into ourselves, yet we give life as well. We give what's needed—energy, dreams, ideas. It's a fair exchange in a world full of cheaters. And when we feel it is right, when the need is great on both sides, we can re-create others like ourselves to share life with us. It is not a bad life," Gilda said.

The Girl heard the edge in Gilda's voice but was fascinated by the pulsing blood and the swirling colors in Gilda's eyes.

"I am on the road I've chosen, the one that is right for me. You must choose your path again just as you did when you ran from the plantation in Mississippi. Death or worse might have met you on that road, but you knew it was the one you had to take. Will you trust me?" Gilda closed her eyes and drew back a little, freeing the Girl from her hypnotic gaze.

The Girl felt a chill, as if Gilda's lowered lids had shut off the sun, and for a moment she was afraid. The room was all shadows and unnatural silence as Gilda disappeared behind her closed eyes. Finally, confusion lifted from the Girl who was intent on listening to more than the words: the highs and lows, the pitch, the rhythm were all molded by a kind of faith the Girl hoped she would reach. It was larger than simply a long life. It was a grand adventure for which her flight into freedom had only begun to prepare her.

"Yes," the Girl whispered.

Gilda opened her eyes, and the Girl felt herself drawn into the flowing energy. Her arms and legs became weak. She heard a soft humming that sounded like her mother. She couldn't look away from Gilda's gaze which held her motionless. Yet she felt free and would have laughed if she had the strength to open her mouth. She sensed rather than felt Gilda pull her into her arms. She closed her eyes, her muscles softened under the touch of Gilda's hand on her arm. She curled her long body in Gilda's lap like a child safe in her mother's arms.

She felt a sharpness at her neck and heard the soothing song. Gilda kissed her on the forehead and neck where the pain had been, catching her in a powerful undertow. She clung to Gilda, sinking deeper into a dream, barely hearing Gilda as she said, "Now you must drink." She held the Girl's head to her breast and in a quick gesture opened the skin of her chest. She pressed the Girl's mouth to the red life that seeped from her.

Soon the flow was a tide that left Gilda weak. She pulled the suckling girl away and closed the wound. Gilda sat with the Girl curled in her lap until the fire died. As the sun crept into the dark room she carried the Girl upstairs to the bedroom, where they slept the day through. Gilda awoke at dusk, the Girl still tight in her arms. She slipped from the bed and went downstairs to put a tub of water to boil. When she returned to finish dressing, the Girl watched her silently.

"I'm not well," the Girl said, feeling the gorge rising in her throat.

"Yes, you'll be fine soon," Gilda said, taking her into her arms and carrying her downstairs and outside. The evening air made the Girl tremble in her thin shirt. Gilda held the Girl's head down over the dirt, then left her sitting alone on the back stairs. She returned with a wet cloth and wiped her mouth and face, then led her inside again. She helped her remove her clothes and lifted her into the large tub standing beside the kitchen table. Then she soaped, rinsed, and massaged the Girl into restfulness, drawing out the fear and pain with her strong, thin hands as she hummed the tune from the Girl's childhood. She dressed her in a fresh gown, one of her own bordered with eyelet lace, smelling of lavender, then put her back to bed.

"Bird will return soon. You mustn't be afraid. You will ask her to complete the circle. It is she who will make you our daughter. Will you remember that?"

"Yes," the Girl said weakly.

"You must also remember, later, when time weighs on you like hard earthenware strapped to your back, it is for love that we do this." Gilda's eyes were fiery and unfocused. The power of them lulled the Girl into sleep, although she felt a pang of unease and hunger inside of her. Gilda's lips again brushed her forehead. Then she slept without dreaming.

She awoke abruptly to find Bird standing over her in darkness shadowed even further by a look of destructive anger, her eyes unblinking and dry.

"When did she leave you?" Bird's voice was tight with control although her hands shook as they clutched several crumpled sheets of paper.

Gilda had said don't be afraid and she wasn't, only anxious to understand what would happen now. "It seems long ago, before dark. She wore her walking clothes and said you would complete the circle. I was to be sure and tell you that."

Bird stalked from the room. Downstairs she stood on the porch, turning east and west as if listening to thoughts on the wind. She ran to the west, through the field, and disappeared for three hours. Her clothes were full of brambles when she returned. She went to the cellar and climbed part way through the door. She could see the new sacks of fresh soil stacked beside the ones she and Gilda had prepared so long ago. She stepped back outside and let the cellar door drop with a resounding thud, then came into the house where the Girl lay weak, unmoving except for her eyes, now dark brown flecked with pale yellow.

Bird looked down at her as if she were a stranger, turned away, and lit a lantern. Again she read the crumpled pages she'd dropped to the floor, then paced, trying not to listen to the Girl's shallow breathing. The darkest part of night passed. Bird stood on the porch again and peered at the stars as if one might signal her.

When the sun began its rise Bird retreated to the shadows of the house, moving anxiously from corner to corner, listening. She was uncertain what to expect, perhaps a ripping sound or scream of pain inside her head. She felt only the Girl weakening upstairs and a cloying uneasiness. In her head she replayed recent conversations with Gilda. Each one came closer and closer to the core.

Gilda had needed Bird to step away so she could end this long life with the peace she sought. And each time Bird had resisted, afraid of losing the love of a woman who was the center of her world. Upstairs was the Girl, now in her charge, the one who'd given that permission for which Gilda had yearned.

Full daylight came behind the closed drapes. Bird stood tense, her body a bronze rod, dull and aching, her full length of flesh and hair calling out for hours. The answer came like the sunlight it was. She felt Gilda lying naked in the water, marveling at its coolness and silence. Then she dove into the darkness of the tide. Without the power of her native soil woven into her breeches, she surrendered easily. The air was squeezed from her lungs and she eagerly embraced her rest. Bird felt a moment of the sun's warmth, her head filled with Gilda's scent. In her ear was the soft sigh of pleasure she recognized from many mornings of their past together, the low whisper of her name, then silence. She knew the knife-edged sun rays stripped the flesh from Gilda's bones. The heat seared through Bird, lightning on her skin and in her marrow. Then, like the gradual receding of menstrual pain, Bird's muscles slackened and her breathing slowed. The crackling was silenced. It was over. Gilda was in the air no more.

Bird went upstairs to the Girl whose face was ashen, her dark eyes now flecked with orange. A frost of perspiration covered her body, and tears ran down the sides of her face. She opened her mouth but no sounds came out. Bird sat against the pillows and pulled the Girl into her arms. She was relieved by the cool tears washing over her brown arm as if she were weeping herself. Bird pulled aside her woolen shirt and bared her breasts.

She made a small incision beneath the right one and pressed the Girl's mouth to it. The throbbing in her chest became synchronous with the Girl's breathing. Soon the strength returned to the Girl's body; she no longer looked so small.

Bird repeated the exchange, taking from her as Gilda had done and returning the blood to complete the process. She finally lay her head back on the pillows, holding the Girl in her arms, and rested.

Their breathing and heartbeats sounded as one for an hour or more before their bodies again found their own rhythms. Even then, Bird remained silent.

"She's gone then?" Bird heard her ask. She only nodded and eased her arms from around the Girl's body.

"I'll build a fire," she said and rose quickly from the bed. Alone in the room Bird found the crumpled letter and returned it to the box Gilda had left on the dressing table. She heard the sound of a robe brushing the carpet below as the Girl moved about laying wood on the fire, then settling the kettle atop the stove in the kitchen. She called to Bird to come down. Her voice, now strong and vibrant, was a shock in the late afternoon quiet without Gilda.

They sat in the twilight in front of the low flames, not speaking for some time. Then Bird said, "She wanted you to be called Gilda."

"I know."

"Will you?"

"I don't know."

"It will be dark soon—we must go out. Are you afraid?"

"She said there's little to fear and you'll teach me, as always." They were quiet again. "She loved you very much, Bird."

"Loved me so much that she traded her life for yours?" Bird almost shouted. In all else there'd been some reasoning, but she could find none in this. Here in the place of the woman to whom she'd given her life sat a child.

"I'm not a child, Bird. If I can hear her words and understand her need, why can't you? I didn't steal her life. She took her road to freedom—just like I did, just like you did. She made a fair exchange. For your sake."

"Fair exchange?" Bird was unnerved by the words she had heard so often in the past when she had been learning the manner of taking the blood and leaving something in return—how to partake of life and be certain not to take life. She chafed under the familiar words and inflection. "You for her?" Bird spit it out. "Hundreds of years of knowledge and wit in exchange for a girl who hasn't lived one lifetime yet."

"It's not just me, it's you. Her life, her freedom for our future. You are as much a part of the bargain as I am. She brought me to this place for your need as well as for mine. It's us seeing the future together that satisfies her needs."

Bird heard the past speaking to her, words she had chosen to ignore. Tonight she stood face to face with their meaning: Gilda's power over her own death was sacred, a decision all others were honor bound to respect. Bird had denied Gilda's right to her quietus and refused to even acknowledge that decision. It was a failure she could not wear easily.

Darkness seeped through the drawn curtains of the parlor. The glow of the almost-steady flame burned orange in the room, creating movement where there was none. The two women sat together as if they were still at their reading lessons. Finally Bird spoke.

"Gilda?"

"Yes."

"It's time now."

They dressed in the warm breeches and dark shirts. Bird took Gilda's hand and looked into the face of the woman who had been her pupil and saw the childlike roundness of her had melted away. Hunger filled her eyes.

"It is done much as it was done here. Your body will speak to you. Do not return to take from anyone too soon again: it can create the hunger in them. They will recover though, if it is not fed. And as you take from them you must reach inside. Feel what they are needing, not what you are hungering for. You leave them with something new and fresh, something wanted. Let their joy fill you. This is the only way to share and not to rob. It will also keep you on your guard so you don't drain life away."

"Yes, these are things she wanted me to know."

"I will teach you how to move about in indirect sunlight, as you've seen us do, and how to take your rest. Already your body sheds its mortal softness. You'll move faster than anyone, have the strength of many. It's that strength that you must learn to control. But we will talk more of these things later. It is better to begin before there is pain."

Gilda and Bird turned west. Their path through the flat field was invisible. Bird pushed aside all thoughts for the moment, remembering only her need to instruct, to insure that the girl gained enough knowledge for her survival. Gilda allowed the feeling of loss to drift through her as they sped into the darkness. Along with it came a sense of completion, too. There was certain knowledge of the world around her, excitement about the unknown that lay ahead, and comfort with her new life. She looked back over her shoulder, but they had moved so quickly that the farmhouse was all but invisible. Inside, the fire was banked low, waiting for their return.

Lilith

Robbi Sommers

Tⱻ**HEY HAD BEEN** exploring New Orleans the entire day, and as dusk began to blanket this humid city, they finally reached their destination, the French Quarter.

This was the first trip Francine and Kay had taken together and, as both had agreed over lunch, New Orleans was the perfect choice. Francine had originally pushed for New York City—for the plays, the lights, the shopping—but Kay, who was more prone to get her way most of the time anyway, had done an intense amount of research on the city of New Orleans. After presenting a pile of pamphlets to Francine, Kay had gone on to describe the remarkable flavor of this city—the tours of the majestic old plantations full of histories and memories, the ride down the Mississippi on the Delta Queen, the musicians and tap dancers on street corners, the spicy and mysterious Cajun people. There were rumors of dark women who could read the future, hints of voodoo and of shadows that walked the night—and of course, the shopping, the restaurants, the clubs. Nevertheless, New Orleans was turning out to be even more than either of them had anticipated.

Climbing out of the back of a rather beat-up taxi, Francine handed the old black driver a ten-dollar bill. Kay, right behind her, carried the two shopping bags.

"Good evening, ladies," the wrinkled old man said with a wry smile on his face. "Keep your eyes open for Mis' Mattie. She'd be showing you the real New Orleans." He tipped his frayed straw hat and pulled the taxi away from the curb, leaving Francine and Kay deep in the heart of the French Quarter.

The sun had set, and yet the city still was hot, demanding in its heat, not even a slight breeze to offer relief from the humidity. Wiping a small bead of sweat from her brow, Kay turned to Francine and said in a curious tone, "Who do you think this Miss Mattie is?"

Francine, turning to look up and down the deserted street where the driver had left them, said quickly, "I don't know, but I have a weird feeling this isn't Bourbon Street. I did tell him Bourbon, didn't I? Where are we anyway? Damn!"

For some inexplicable reason, Francine had felt a little on edge since they had gotten out of the taxi. Distracted by this feeling, she had let the cab driver leave without paying much attention to where they were. She walked over to the street sign. Burton Street.

"Shit!" Francine complained. "He let us off at Burton Street. Not Bourbon."

"Oh, well," Kay answered with her usual optimistic perspective on things. "Bourbon Street can't be far. The French Quarter's not that big, is it? Let's walk up to the first main street that we reach and ask directions, or catch a cab there. No big deal."

"Okay," Francine responded, still feeling a little uneasy.

Where in the hell are we? she thought, glancing down the dark street. Up at the far end was a light, perhaps a small market, beckoning to them.

"Let's walk up to that store and get directions from there."

As they began their journey up the dark empty street, Francine couldn't help but think about the article she had read describing the hidden city of New Orleans—the one that most visitors don't see: the weaving of mysteries, voodoo, the eyes that watch from darkened alleys, the shadowless entities that allegedly call New Orleans their home.

Only their footsteps echoed—heels against concrete, click-clack...Around another corner, the light closer, a small sign below a welcoming halo read, "Miss Mattie Tarot Card Readings."

"Look!" Kay said excitedly. "This is what the cab driver was telling us about. Let's go in! Wouldn't it be fun!"

"I don't know..." Francine hesitated.

"Oh, come on!" Kay insisted, pulling Francine by the hand up to the door. A large brass lion's head served as the knocker. Kay lifted the ring in the lion's mouth, rapping several times on the old wooden door.

Within seconds, the door opened. A dark old woman—hair hidden under a deep blue bandanna shawl wrapped around her thin frame—stood before them.

"Reading?" she questioned, staring directly into Francine's eyes. Not blinking, not smiling, just staring, as if she had been waiting for Francine.

The door creaked as it opened. Miss Mattie let the women into a small candle-lit room.

"You first," Francine whispered, nudging her friend in front of her.

Kay, sensing Francine's reluctance, walked over to the tapestry-covered table and sat directly across from where Miss Mattie had seated herself.

"Twenty," Miss Mattie said. "Two readings twenty dollars."

Francine reached into her pocket, pulled out two tens, and placed the bills in Miss Mattie's dark palm.

"Now," Miss Mattie said, directing her gaze to Kay after quickly pushing the money into a small leather pouch. She removed a small black and gold scarf from the table to reveal a tattered deck of Tarot cards. She turned one, then two, then three cards onto the table.

"Lucky in love, aren't you?" she said in a deep monotone. "But she walks away only to return an altered woman." And with that Miss Mattie picked the cards up from the table.

"Does that mean that my relationship will—"

"Lucky in love," Miss Mattie interrupted sternly. "But she walks away only to return an altered woman!" Quickly Miss Mattie reached over to a basket and handed Kay a small brown and black bead on a leather cord. "Wear this. Please. You must not look her in the eyes when she returns. You must send her away."

Kay opened her hand, allowing Miss Mattie to drop the necklace into her palm.

Miss Mattie looked over at Francine. "Next," she said, once again staring fervently into Francine's eyes.

Francine walked over to the table and sat down. Miss Mattie began to shuffle the cards, carefully, not turning her deep dark eyes from Francine. She flipped over one, two, three, four, five cards.

"She watches you. The mistress of the night. The labyrinth awaits you. Let this be a warning. You must leave New Orleans at once!"

Miss Mattie broke her stare and hurriedly picked up the five cards.

"I—" Francine began to ask.

"At once!" Miss Mattie said even more harshly, rising from the table, leaving the room, disappearing down the darkened hallway.

Francine, quite stunned, turned to Kay. "Well, what the hell do you suppose that means?"

"Oh, Francine," Kay said, trying to let the whole incident be more of a fun experiment than anything else. "Don't take things so seriously. That's what these people are supposed to do for the tourist. You know—mystery, voodoo…Come on, let's go find Bourbon Street."

With Miss Mattie not returning, Kay and Francine let themselves out. And there, in front of Miss Mattie's brick house, sat the old man in the beat-up taxi.

"Mis' Mattie said you might be needing a ride," he said wearily, shaking his head. "That woman, she keeps me a-comin' an' a-goin'."

"Bourbon Street, please," Kay said cheerfully, trying to pull Francine out of her sudden silence and into the taxi. They climbed back into the cab and within minutes were on Bourbon Street, an extreme contrast to the dark streets they had just left. Bourbon street was alive—full of music, lights, people, saloons.

Let it go, Francine thought, as she tried to rid herself of a shadowy after-chill. *Leave New Orleans at once!* What foolishness! The heartbeat of Bourbon Street was beginning to lift the chill, to warm her. She felt light again, free of that earlier darkness.

And once again, Kay and Francine began to explore the city: in and out of clubs, dancing, drinking, listening to saxophones, jazz. Another club, another drink—they were dizzy, lightheaded. They spent the evening laughing, joking, flirting and talking at tables for two, at bars. Finally, they ended up in the quiet lounge off the lobby of the hotel they were staying in, ten minutes from the French Quarter.

They were sitting at a small table in the almost empty cocktail lounge. Francine, slightly intoxicated, leaning back against a mirrored wall, slowly scanned the room: the piano player in the corner playing a sultry tune; the dim lighting—a candle in a red glass holder on each table; the bartender engrossed in conversation with a large-bosomed woman in a tight, red-sequined dress; a man and woman at another table, his arms around her, leaning into each other kissing slowly, erotically. As Francine's focus began to drift back towards Kay, she happened to notice a woman, alone, a few tables away, just sitting, looking directly at Francine.

Francine tried to look away, to see past the other tables back to lovely Kay. But no, it was as if her eyes had their own will...and they were choosing to stay fixed on the image of the auburn-haired woman.

She was rather striking—that glossy hair pulled away from her face into some sort of a twist. Francine couldn't see much of the woman's face, hidden as it was beneath a mesh net draped from a black velvet hat. A small gem—a diamond?—seemed to hold the net to the hat. The woman's black silk dress plunged rather low, exposing cream-colored skin, strong shoulders, the ample cleavage of her voluptuous breasts. A thin string of pearls was clasped tightly against her marvelous long neck. Francine felt hypnotized.

It was almost as if the woman had been waiting—waiting for Francine's eyes to finally find her—patiently sitting alone, sipping her drink and waiting for that very moment. And although Francine could vaguely see her eyes through the net, it seemed as if they were imploring Francine to meet her gaze. Francine felt somewhat dizzy. She could hear a faint humming somewhere, perhaps in the very heart of her soul. A tingling, a warmth, an excitement overcame her. Without turning away, the woman carefully lifted the veil—exposing first the full lips, then the chiseled nose, and finally, those burning, deep eyes.

Bringing her drink to her lips—almost in a toast—she took a sip and then placed the glass back on the table.

"Francine? Francine! What in heaven's name are you staring at?" Kay demanded, turning to see exactly what Francine was so taken with.

Kay scanned the room quickly—the musician still at the piano, the bartender still in conversation with the woman in red, the man and woman, still embracing.

"Francine, I think you're drunk. Let's go up to the room, honey. You're in a stupor."

"No, please," Francine said distractedly. "You go ahead. I just think I need to relax. Be alone for a while."

"Well, I don't know what your problem is. Fine! You sit there by yourself! I'm going up to the room!"

Kay got up, looked around the bar one more time trying to see what could have mesmerized Francine. But there was nothing. Probably too much alcohol, Kay mused. Fine. Let her see what it was like to be alone!

Kay, annoyed, left the lounge, leaving Francine by herself, still entranced.

Only seconds after Kay left, the woman in black rose from the table. Graceful and fluid, as if she rode the very air itself, she walked, rather floated, over to Francine's table.

Francine could barely breathe, so taken was she by this raven-like enchantress who approached, the air around her fragrant with an exotic scent. Her eyes were green, like the forest, piercing, aware. Her cheekbones, high, regal, highlighted a face even more extraordinary than Francine had anticipated.

As she reached the table, to the very place where Kay had been sitting just moments before, she placed her long smooth fingers on the back of Francine's hand. Francine glanced down to the table, to her hand, to the long fingers. A large ruby in an antique setting adorned the middle finger of this remarkable hand. The deep fire of the stone was almost as spellbinding as the woman's jade green eyes.

"Francine," the woman said softly, her voice soothing, almost magical. "I have been waiting for you." She shifted her fingers ever so slightly, the light from the candle catching in the ruby's facets—sending a glint of red sparkle into Francine's eyes.

"But I..." Francine tried to respond, trying so hard to pull her eyes away from the ruby ring, yet unable to do so.

"But you do, my lovely Francine. You know me, in your soul you do. Yes. You may look at me now."

Francine felt a sudden jerk, almost as if her focus had been forced to that ruby and now it was released. Slowly, she lifted her face toward the woman. Eyes meeting eyes.

Francine felt an overwhelming rush of heat throughout her body as she stared, then fell into the woman's gaze. Once again that silent humming began—only now the sound was curiously in time with her heartbeat, in time with the blood that was pushing, surging, rushing through her now stimulated body.

"I am Lilith. How very forward of me, how very rude, approaching you without so, without so much as even a name. I want to show you the rest of New Orleans. The part you haven't seen yet...the hidden New Orleans."

Francine listened to the rhythmical sound of Lilith's voice. She had an accent of some sort, unrecognizable yet so seductive and engaging.

"Yes. The hidden city," Francine heard herself saying. Those words seemed familiar—but from where, she could not say. She felt herself rising, her hand still in Lilith's almost as if they had always been connected in this way.

"Perhaps I should..." Francine couldn't seem to remember exactly what it was she should be doing. Something about this place...Was there someone waiting for her somewhere? Upstairs? She could feel an odd sensation of someone thinking, calling, crying. An image of a woman on a bed, face in her hands, weeping; she had short brown hair, lovely small breasts. She was wondering, awaiting her arrival. The image turned into small light particles that swirled and twisted like tiny fireworks and then disappeared. It was too difficult to remember.

Lilith was leading her out of the lounge, through the lobby, to the elevator. And slowly up and up in the small elevator car, they climbed to the center of the tall building. Francine huddled in the corner as Lilith, in front of her, leaned into her, pressing against her—speaking to her, coaxing her.

"I watched you outside Miss Mattie's today. Getting out of the taxi. Your lovely blond hair, that air of uncertainty. Edginess. I felt you so strongly. I was in the darkness. No, of course you didn't see me, but you felt me, didn't you?"

She was whispering in Francine's ear as she spoke—that intoxicating perfume creating a haze in Francine's mind as Lilith's tongue darted quickly in and out of her ear between sentences.

"I wanted to have you then, to claim you, but Miss Mattie can be so difficult at times—with her potions and charms—and all that. Tell me she wasn't." Still she whispered, circling that hot tongue around the outside of Francine's ear, down her cheek, down her neck.

Suddenly, the elevator car stopped and the doors opened wide.

Francine had no idea which floor they were on. She could see the last number lit up above the elevator door. They must be many levels up from the lobby.

Lilith clasped Francine's hand and glided down the hall to a door. Again, numbers—Francine's brain was having trouble registering what the symbols on the door actually meant.

Lilith unlocked the door with a touch of that ruby-laden finger and moved lightly into the shadowy room. Francine, behind her, seemed to float along with her. Somehow the door closed. Somehow she heard it lock—once, maybe twice. The room danced in the flicker of candlelight. The scent of that unusual perfume was overwhelming in the room. Francine felt dizzy again.

A hurricane of images began twirling in her mind: the smile on the cab driver's face; Miss Mattie's strong, insistent gaze. Let this be a warning, Miss Mattie seemed to be saying over and over as she pointed at Francine. Kay, her palm open, held something in her hand. The bead—the thought of it stung in Francine's mind. The idea of the bead hurt. The images revolved, twisting. Let this be a warning. *Let this be a warning!*

"Enough, Francine," Lilith was saying rather firmly. "Let it go. That's a dream. Let it go." Francine looked up to Lilith who was now a few feet away, surrounded by a halo of candlelight. She was moving provocatively in some sort of dance. Francine was again mesmerized. The storm of images evaporated. All that mattered was Lilith—lovely, lovely Lilith—pulling the silk straps from her shoulders, removing the black velvet hat, stepping out of the high black shoes, letting the dress float to the floor.

Francine felt overcome with desire. Lilith, undressed, was so exciting, her body so erotic—the shoulders strong, the breasts round and ripe with small pert nipples pointing slightly towards the ceiling. Her slim waist budding into full petal-like hips. Between her firm, full thighs, the triangular patch of dark red hair covering her secret.

Francine felt a surge of electricity shudder through her. Every part of her was alive. Her own nipples felt as though someone was rolling them, squeezing them. Her clitoris began to throb.

"Francine," Lilith murmured, a narcotic summoning the broken-down addict. "Come to me. Please. Come to me."

Francine felt compelled to walk over to Lilith. She drew Francine into her arms, circling her in a fog of intense sexuality.

"You. You are so lovely," Lilith was saying breathlessly. "I must have you." Circling, including Francine in her movement, she stopped to lift Francine's blouse, to remove Francine's pants. She stepped away from her to enjoy the beauty of Francine's body, then pulled her back in. Arms wrapped around her, Lilith's full breasts pushed into Francine's small, soft breasts. Rocking, swaying, Lilith kissed every inch of Francine's face and neck—little kisses, hot kisses, then her tongue, just her tongue licking over and over. Every bit of Francine's neck was damp with Lilith's saliva.

Lilith moved Francine onto the bed, then pulled herself down on top of Francine. Still licking, she lightly nipped her neck, shoulders, breasts.

Francine had never felt anything so overpowering. With just kisses, little bites, she was beside herself with pleasure.

Lilith propped herself directly above Francine, her face perhaps ten inches away. She was saying something, but Francine had trouble hearing or understanding the words. She looked into Lilith's face—searching for her lips, hoping somehow to see the words as they fell out of Lilith's mouth.

There was something about "forever," "everlasting," "deathless." Lilith's skin looked surprisingly pale in this light. The whites of her eyes were almost blue. What was she saying? What did she mean?

"And it will feel so sweet. So very sweet. Letting go is the secret. Giving it up to me is the deepest pleasure of all…"

Lilith was pulling on Francine's large square nipples, still whispering over and over. The words, like the numbers on the door, were not making much sense.

"You are such a jewel. Such a beauty. When you first arrived in New Orleans, I could feel your presence. I have been waiting, forever it seems, for you to come to me." Lilith's words were so soft as they passed from her full lips into Francine's small available ear.

Still unable to interpret, exactly, the words—the meaning behind Lilith's murmuring—she was able to hear the rhythm, the musical cadence of Lilith's voice—suggesting, enticing, luring Francine into a deeper trance.

"And when you finally returned to the hotel, I was beyond myself in desire for you. Seeing you across the room—talking, laughing. Hearing the intake of air as you'd inhale, feeling the warm breath of you as you exhaled. But of course, you do not know how finely honed my senses of sound, touch, sight. You could be miles away from me and I could smell your scent, feel your presence."

Francine's thought process no longer seemed to be functioning properly. She could barely hear at all, yet she could feel what Lilith was thinking. Francine's body, quite heavy, tingling as if asleep, was on the bed as if weighted down and yet at the very same moment it felt light, almost floating.

But the kisses, Lilith's tiny electric kisses on Francine's neck were starting to sting a little. Lilith continued to dart her tongue back and forth across a small area on Francine's soft peach-like neck while her fingers gently squeezed Francine's nipples. She pushed her firm belly down on Francine's.

Francine felt hot, very hot. Those little kisses hurt as if a snake were striking at her neck. Slashing, attempting to sear, to puncture, to poison, her tongue lashed back and forth.

"You want me, my love, don't you?" Lilith said. Still propelling her tongue, she moved her fingers between the blond curls that protected Francine's delicate sex.

Francine could feel Lilith's finger between her swollen lips; it slid up the side of her clitoris, across the shaft and down the other side. She was slippery, slick. Lilith's repeated touch was light, yet very direct. Francine felt herself arch ever so slightly to encourage Lilith's finger to press even a little harder.

Lilith, her lips flush against Francine's neck, her tongue flicking quickly, could sense Francine's readiness for more. Immediately Lilith's fingers began to search for the hard jewel between Francine's lips, and as hot as Francine was, Lilith had no difficulty finding it. Within seconds, Lilith had her at her peak—moaning, writhing in pleasure, wildly jerking in a frenzy. Lilith still rubbing her, still licking, nipping at her neck.

As Francine reached the height of her climax, Lilith let her sharp teeth pierce the soft skin on Francine's neck. In her pleasure, Francine did not immediately realize what was happening, but suddenly, the fiery ache in her neck drew her out of orgasm.

She began to struggle, to push violently at Lilith. The pain was becoming excruciating, unbearable. Lilith overpowered her with brute strength. Pinning her to the bed, she forced Francine's head to the side and clamped her lips to Francine's neck. She sucked lightly at first and then feverishly while she jerked her own clitoris up against Francine's hipbone.

Rocking back and forth, she felt the pleasure in her own clitoris as she continued to drink from Francine.

The fire began to spread throughout Francine's body—burning, searing, raging. Every part of her ignited in scalding, relentless pain. And yet something was beginning to change. Along with the pain, an intense feeling of bliss, of gratification, of surrender began to emerge.

Her mind was starting to let go of the pain, starting to embrace oneness with Lilith. Lilith, still sucking, was moaning and purring, almost growling. Her body was hot; the sweat sizzled on her skin. Grasping

Francine harder and harder, she jerked her mouth away and let out a guttural scream.

Francine—dazed and tense from pushing and gripping Lilith—looked up. Lilith was looking straight ahead, her eyes rolled back in their sockets. Dark blood was smeared around her full lips, he chin, her cheeks.

"Mine!" she screeched in fury. "*Mine!*"

Kay was startled by the light scraping on her hotel room door. A chill ran through her tired body. She had been waiting hours for Francine's return—alternating between crying, pacing, calling the lobby the lounge—swearing angrily, praying desperately. She was exhausted, depleted.

"Francine?" Kay whispered as she turned toward the door.

Nothing.

"Francine?" Kay asked, raising her voice. "Is that you?"

Kay placed her ear against the cool wooden door frame. "Is that you?" she repeated, feeling a sudden sense of vulnerability. *You must send her away. You must send her away.* Miss Mattie words suddenly came into her mind.

"Francine?"

"Yes," Francine responded. "Yes, dear Kay, please let me in."

Kay quickly unlocked the door and pulled it open.

Without warning, Kay was stunned by the striking scent of oranges and anise that seemed to surround Francine. Kay felt faint, dazed. She stepped back, shaking her head, as if trying to force away this sudden lightheadedness.

Dizzy, she attempted to center herself, trying to focus on Francine who, in the dim light, looked pale and worn, almost limp. Kay opened her eyes wider, as if trying to let more light in, to see more clearly. Dark circles were under Francine's once-vibrant blue eyes. There was a certain vacantness to her gaze. Kay looked slowly from Francine's face down to her bruised, swollen neck.

"What in God's name?" Kay cried out, pulling Francine into the room.

"I came to take you with me," Francine whispered as she staggered into the room, her eyes glazed. The energy she emitted was a mixture of hot and cold, light and dark.

"What are you talking about?" Kay demanded, forcing herself to look at the floor, for some reason not wanting to meet Francine's eyes.

"You must come with me. I've seen the hidden city of New Orleans, dear Kay. It awaits you…us." Francine seemed more on edge now, a little frantic. As she grasped Kay's hand, she pleaded, "Come. Come with me. To a place where it is so warm and so…"

Kay was enticed by that unusual fragrance Francine was wearing. Unable to make sense of things, she tried to step back, to appraise. Slowly, she allowed her eyes to drift back up toward Francine's neck. The bruise, deep purple in color was framed by two small tears in the slightly swollen flesh. A silver chain brushed the bruised area. Kay's eyes followed the necklace to an antique ruby pendant that rested right in the hollow of Francine's neck. The light from the room seemed to hit the stone's facets just so, sending a glimmer of red fire from the ruby into Kay's eye. The effect was compelling. It was difficult to turn away from that entrancing sparkle.

Suddenly, Francine's grip became stronger, more forceful. She was forcing Kay into her arms, grabbing her, pinning her against the wall—kissing, nipping, almost biting her neck.

Francine's sudden shift from frailness to intense strength took Kay by surprise. She was stunned, taken off guard.

Francine was struggling, forcing Kay's head to the side, trying to bite into Kay's vulnerable neck. Suddenly Kay had a clear understanding— beautiful, wonderful Francine was no longer Francine at all.

"No!" she screamed, panicked. "No! Francine, no. No!" She was punching, kicking, flailing her arms—anything to push Francine away. She fought with all her strength.

Kay ran to the bed and grabbed a pillow, a hanger, a paperback book—as if any of these things could protect her. Could stop Francine!

She backed into a corner, between the bed and the bureau, and at that moment, arms full of useless weapons, she remembered the bead on the leather necklace. Words began to twirl in her mind: *Send her away. Do not look her in the eye!* She dropped the hanger, book and pillow and grabbed the necklace, quickly putting it over her head.

"Look at me, Kay. Please." Francine said softly, her voice suddenly filled with the love and compassion it used to have.

Kay, still in the corner, lifted the bead between her thumb and forefinger. She was confused. She knew that she absolutely must send Francine away immediately! And yet, she could not help but remember the depth of the love they had shared. She wanted so much to look, one last time, into her lover's eyes—to connect, just once more, before sending her away forever.

Francine, as if sensing Kay's thoughts, slowly moved across the room. Tenderly, she reached out her long, pale fingers and gently cupped Kay's face. Using the subtlest pressure, she began to lift Kay's chin.

Eyes to meet eyes, Francine thought, hungrily summoning all the power within her to appear loving. *Just one look and she's mine.*

Virago

◆

KAREN MARIE CHRISTA MINNS

"THE AMAZON—a living emerald broken only by a sapphire ribbon as we hurtled down toward the landing strip, and I was only a few years older than you, Manilla, a new Ph.D. trying to make my mark and about to be changed forever, about to step into my own lush Hell." Slater suddenly shot Manilla into the plane—so real this power that Manilla could feel the worn seats flex as she leaned forward.

The probe would take them both back. Slater hadn't done this as completely ever before—but this night it was imperative. Simple words, images, none could convey the power that was Darsen...

"We packed light for the trip—my first into the bush, only for surveillance. If the tribe I was looking for could be approached, or was even known by the surrounding people, I planned to come back later, better equipped and better funded for a complete study. This time there was only the guide, myself and what could fit into the plane's cargo rack.

"That first moment...Look, Manilla...out the window, see for yourself..."

Manilla smelled the airplane fuel, the old leather of the seats, the sweat of the guide, Slater's perfume. Gasping at the sudden altitude, Manilla leaned forward and touched the edge of the pilot's seat, feeling its solidity. No dream, no story, she was here, with Slater—above the jungle—and below was the Amazon River!

"Tighten your seatbelts, folks, landing's gonna be rugged," the pilot coughed back at them.

The guide put a hand around Slater's shoulder. She brushed it off, glaring at him. Manilla started to say something and noticed that he paid not a glance to her. It was real, for her, each smell, each snarling sound, everything—and yet they did not see her there; she couldn't communicate except to Slater. A strategic ghost—but one with feelings—Manilla felt very vulnerable.

Slater sensed the shifting fear rising inside the young woman. She pulled the probe back gently. Manilla experienced a warming sensation and then a blurring of everything in the cockpit. More dreamlike now...Yes, easier this way...She could handle it if it was a dream...Slater allowed the probe to settle Manilla's mind and then went back...

The landing was rough. The wings of the plane clipped the edges of the rain forest as it descended onto the pitted road. Perhaps not even a road, only a wash now used as a path through the bush. The plane coasted over the bumps, knocking them about, spilling the contents of Slater's pack into the aisle. A camera, some film canisters, a few lenses, pencils and a bush knife bumped and banged around their ankles. Slater reached for the camera. The guide's huge paw grabbed her wrist and held it.

"Wait till we stop...want to break a finger or your wrist?" He attempted a smile. His teeth were long, white, dangerous.

Slater shook him off. She slammed back into her seat as the plane drop-dead stopped.

"We're here!" The pilot grinned.

"Where's the village?" Slater unlatched her seatbelt and sprang for the camera.

"No village around here, lady. Who told you there was a village?" The pilot pushed his cap over his bald spot.

"Johnston—you said..." Slater was trying not to sputter, trying to hold the rage in check.

Fear crawled over Manilla like a spider. The airplane prop was cooling and little pings and pops of contracting metal punctuated the jungle sounds.

"Look *professor,* you wrote and said you wanted a guide to show you possible sites of the Maneatos Indians. There ain't nothing close to anywhere you're going to find Maneatos—that is the point isn't it?" He stooped to avoid bashing his head against the cabin ceiling. He grabbed two khaki packs and moved toward the door.

"Closest town is Tefe, lady, and that's uh, maybe two hundred fifty, three hundred miles, right on the Amazon proper..." The pilot has softened his tone.

"The Amazon proper—aren't we supposed to be on the Amazon now?" Slater slammed her fist into a seat cushion.

"Well, you are, sort of. The river to your immediate right is the River Branco and it forks into the River Negro about seven miles down." The pilot checked the instruments. "God, Prof., they're all the same, you know? This is it—the real Amazon—just like the travel brochure says. Wild and wet—uncivilized, isn't that what you wanted? Lots of woolly bully geeks dancing in voodoo masks?" The guide banged the door open and jumped out.

The gush of air was almost iridescent with oxygen. Screaming macaws broke from the trees. The heat hit Manilla like a wet tongue.

"Johnston, I know where the River Branco is—these are tributaries. I wanted the actual main river. If I'm going to test my theory I need—" Her voice was tinny, desperate.

"Oh, I know what you need, Prof.—now let's just haul ass out of here—or don't. I get paid either way. No refunds—it's in the contract. I ain't going to lose my license just because some damned Yanque cunuo goes soft." Johnston's eyes were brilliant blue-green, matching the jungle behind him. He looked absolutely huge in the full daylight. His hair spiked out, red-gold around his crown.

Manilla wanted to grab Slater by the belt, haul her back into the seat, tell the pilot to hit it, leaving the bastard Johnston behind to rot in the reddish mud. She tried to call out but nothing, nothing. All she could do in this place was observe, listen, follow. No voice. No touch. Simply a receiver.

"Ma'am, we all get a little bushy out here. Between the fucking revolutionaries, the Indians, scorpions and giant cats—it's bit of a hell, you know what I'm saying? You professors come out here, flash a lot of cash, make men greedy, come out with your film crews to do your *National Geographics* and such, well, you leave here and leave nothing—so, no disrespect intended, but fuck you, ma'am and your damned University! Just listen to the guide and I'll be back for you both in three days."

Slater tried not to shiver. The air felt very cold. These two were in it together. What had been promised, to the University, through the government—all ashes. These stupid, sad men—why had she thought it would be different here? She could go back, yes, raise Cain about the trip, admit she couldn't handle these people—get someone to come back with her, arrange it all for her, or she could bite her lip and go on.

"Unload the rest of it, Johnston. You be back here when you say you will, same strip, or I swear the Embassy and whoever else bloody needs to know about it will have your ass! I mean it! People know where I am, when I'm due and who I'm with, so, have a nice day." Slater climbed out.

"Well ma'am, looks like Johnston's got your ass now so you have a nice day, too." The pilot spat out at them and waved as Johnston slammed the door shut.

The plane didn't wait for them to get off the path before it revved. Wings nearly hit them as it moved.

Just when Slater thought it would smash into a bank of trees, it rose.
"That's it, we're home." Johnston shouldered his pack and grabbed a smaller bundle.
"Right." Slater slid into her own pack.

It was past noon when they broke through the last creepers and over-sized fronds. Before them was the mud-colored water of the River Negro. Slater pulled her boots off, leaving her socks neatly tucked into the tops—against scorpions and spiders. She'd read her bush books. Johnston grunted, dropping his pack to the earth.

Slater left him to slog down to the water. The air was buzzing with insects, some of them hundreds of feet overhead in the rain forest canopy. The birds were mostly silent in deference to the white invaders.

Slater's feet were scalded. She'd been toughening them for weeks, stalking through the salt marshes by the college, running five miles a day—but the dampness, the already mildewing material of her socks, the blistering heat, all had softened her feet to mush. Hot spots had rubbed into blisters and then popped—no blood yet but her toes looked as promising as raw hamburger. As she stepped close to the water she counted the number of large bubbles on the sluggish surface. She knew it wasn't piranha, too little action. Nothing moved as she threw in a stick. Carefully she chose her footing, knowing that a mis-step could land her in the mud smack on top of an electric eel—six hundred and forty volts right up through the scum and into her foot. Fried. Upside down lightning storm, really. If she wanted to swim, best to hop over the shallows and float at the top. Alligators and kaman were either downstream scoping out otters for lunch or snoozing. If she didn't touch down in the water she would be safe from the giant cat-fish, too. Yes, risky business, but a kind of joy in it—she felt alive. If not for Johnston's onerous presence all would be perfect. She let the fil-ter of light pass over her and felt as if she were already swimming.

"Best watch for cuts." Johnston stood behind her, picking his teeth with his fingernail. "First thing you know you'll get botflies taking a chunk out of you and leaving eggs—course then they eat their way out. You wake up and find some of your arm gone and your skin covered with the little darlings. Black flies are bad too, they cause river blind-ness—but then, you know that, don't you? Sand flies are the worst in my book, they bring on the leishmaniasis, you know, a dingy kind of leprosy, all your best parts drying up and falling off…"

"You just love it, don't you? Just get the hell away from me, John-ston, I'm no White Princess. Do your job and leave me alone." Slater turned away, the scene no longer inviting, only filled with the ominous buzzing and high whine of enemies.

"Well, since you're so prepared, I'll just take a quick forty winks till the air cools. We'll travel till nightfall, pitch camp. Can't travel in the dark, now, can we? Even with a good moon, it's the fastest way to somebody's dinner, no matter what we think we know, eh?"

Manilla stood off, near a cassava plant. She watched Slater dry off her feet and move to her pack, a few yards away from the bivouacked Johnston.

Slater took out a first-aid kit and slathered dun colored cream over the tops of her toes, then neatly covered them with gauze and tape. The jungle sizzled around her.

She pulled netting out of the pack, tussled with the fine fabric, ensnaring as well as covering herself. The rest of the scene slowly bled away...the film fast-forwarded to night camp—Manilla finding herself seated on a log at the edge of a raging fire. The heat scorched her face. It seemed too much for the two explorers.

*　*　*

The night felt alive around them. Johnston was propped up against a tree with pistol, machete and bourbon around him, hoping to "stand guard."

"You're the one who told me there wasn't anyone or anything around for two hundred miles, right? You're going to burn us down with that forest fire you made." Slater moved her sleeping bag and netting farther back from the roar.

"Look, I've been hearing things all day; someone's following us. Didn't want to spook you, but it's most likely a damned Indian wanting some booze or my gun—so I'm just letting them know I know and we don't need any trouble, all right?"

"Jesus, I'm beginning to think I'd be safer with *them*. Don't lose it on me, okay Johnston? I don't know my way back there, not totally anyway; please try to keep it together." Slater's voice was a bit softer.

Braced by her tone, the man seemed to settle down. He would be all right. He could handle it, handle anything. Right.

Slater fell into an exhausted sleep. They had traveled non-stop for hours, the last of it through almost solid vegetation. The night was long, hot and alive with things moving just beyond Johnston and the fire. Manilla tried to watch with him, but the dreamy mist held her and things moved slowly out of focus.

It was the silence which awoke Slater and snapped Manilla from the dreamspace.

"Johnston?" There was no answering swear, no snoring reply.

"Johnston?" Slater's whisper was as loud as a scream in the jungled bush.

A third attempt. Again, nothing.

Slater fumbled with the zipper of her netting, sure that whatever had taken her guide would pounce before she could release herself from the bag. Finally, she was free.

"JOHNSTOOOOOONNNNNNNNN!'

A monkey screeched back at her, rudely shaken from its own dark sleep by her call. She had crawled into her bag fully booted so now she didn't have to spend time fumbling in the dark for clothes. She stepped out and down. She felt a nauseating crunch and slide. Her flashlight revealed a spider the size of a baseball, mashed almost flat. Slater shuddered.

Moving toward the dead fire, she kicked at the ashes, trying to fan a bit of a flame. Carefully she nurtured a small tongue out of the face of the fire pit. She fed it carefully until a decent flame lit up the campsite.

Footprints, booted and not, surrounded them. No sign of struggle, no stolen pack, and not even an empty whiskey bottle. Slater knew Johnston wouldn't be foolish enough to ditch her in the middle of the night without his pack. And she hadn't slept so soundly as to be oblivious of a fight. But there was no evidence—not so much as a string— to show signs of struggle. She took a few steps into the bush. The howl of a nocturnal monkey sent her running back to the fire. She would sit tight. She would wait for daylight. She would wait for Johnston...The bastard...

The sun was broiling. Toucans yammered directly above her, whether playfully or maliciously, she couldn't decide, tearing twigs and dropping them on her head. She must have slept. When? Her body felt as if it had stood guard, mindlessly, the entire night. A ringed kingfisher darted out of the jungle and headed for the water. Water—she was becoming dehydrated. The splitting headache was less from tension and more from lack of moisture. Picking up her water filter and her now-dented canteen she cautiously made her way to the edge of the river.

Macaws, parrots, giant herons, all blasted up and away from her as she grew nearer to the muddy edge. The brilliance of the green almost blinded her. So much saturated color—even the air was hued. She stretched out her arms, almost touching the rainbowed air. Johnston was missing, yes, and she was ill-equipped to be alone in this rain forest; still, the absolute energy of this paradise filled her. She was not afraid...

The water was drinkable, the filter was guaranteed—any parasites getting through would be commended. She wondered if First Alert Company would award a full refund posthumously. Slater struggled into her pack. Johnston wasn't coming back. It would do no good to just sit here. She wrote a hasty note and stuck it to his sleeping bag. She would travel southeast...eventually she would have to hit Manaos or at least some outlying villages. There was no possibility of finding the airstrip on her own. She'd report McGilly and Johnston to the authorities upon her return—demand that they refinance this botched expedition. She'd go with female guides next time and check their packs for drugs before they left.

Slater checked her compass, repacked it, and headed out.

It was late. The sun set like a deflating balloon in the forest. She had to make camp soon. She pulled out the compass. The cracked crystal showed spidery points in all directions. Dammit—it must have struck her knife handle or the camera when she hurriedly packed it earlier. Slater slung it into the woods. Something scurried away as she stepped out again. Hopefully it was an armadillo. She tried following the river for a while. Wasps and hornets molested her as she stepped into a muddy patch by the water. Swatting in desperation, she stopped long enough to realize that the forest seemed oddly familiar.

Slater walked along the fallen trunk of a giant tree—and came upon the deserted pack of Johnston. The footprints were still there and the dead fire untouched. A damned circled hike! She stripped off her pack and angrily collected wood. Well, at least if the guide stumbled back he'd know where to find her. By this time perhaps he would have sobered up.

The night was hotter than the evening before. Slater would not sleep. The moon rose, almost full, lighting the woods around her as brilliantly as the fire. It struck her that perhaps what was held back by the fire during the darker nights would not be so intimidated this night...

The moon went behind a cloud and with it the blinding light that obscured her vision. And then...the figure stood out darkly just beyond the fire's ring.

Slater gasped—tried to call out Johnston's name even as she realized it was not the missing guide. Reaching behind her for her knife, she tried not to breathe, not to betray her intent to whatever was watching her.

The moon slammed out from behind the cloud bank and the figure was gone...

All night Slater was on her feet, pacing, yelling, her knife in one hand, a burning stick in the other—taunting whomever to face her, angry at the insidious torture.

When the moon descended, sending the sun up after, she was still adrenalated. Stopping only for some beef jerky and a sip of water, she grabbed her pack, stuffing whatever food was salvageable from Johnston's pack. His compass, pistol, knife—all missing. Even his flares were gone. She was on her own. He was not going to find her.

The bush seemed to reach out and attempt to strangle her with each footstep. Four times she went down in the rotting vegetation, sending small armies of termites and ants scurrying out from beneath her. She felt nothing, not the stings nor bruises, not even the slashes from branches and undergrowth that had whipped across her face—nothing but blind panic as she crashed through the forest, trying to find safety in speed.

A few times she had felt "it"—knew something or someone was trailing her—pacing her—measuring her resilience. She would not give it the satisfaction, did not even stop for water when the canteen went dry, but pushed on, hotly, madly, fear overriding all.

She realized that often, in the past, what had seemed frightening was little more than problematic. She had never been truly hungry nor cold enough to fear death, had never been threatened with anything that would seriously thwart her life, had never been pursued in such a hideous manner—the enemy concealed—the danger a taste in her mouth but invisible, a poison gas about to choke her.

For hours she ran, trying to keep the river to her right—sure of only that—realizing that the river would wind back and forth and might actually have branched down. But it was her only direction. Finally the night caught her. There was sun and then there was no sun.

Day animals had retreated, the night stalkers were stretching. Somewhere, perhaps all around her, it was watching. It had kept pace with her and now was its hour. She stopped but there was no clearing to build a fire—her pack had torn open and all was lost except what was in her pockets: damp matches, a pen-knife, I.D. So, she would fight, then. Without fire, without real weapons, she would scratch and claw and not give in until it killed her. She would try to take it with her, if she could. The cold fury that came with the realization that this thing, this trailing monster, could beat her into exhaustion and now attack, unfairly, attack and take all that was her away, fueled her, gave her a second wind, new strength.

When the moon rose, fully round, awesome witness to her face-off, she screamed. It was not the scream of the victim. A final irony: she who had come there to find the Amazons had become one in her last stand. And then, Slater screamed again.

A tall, lean figure moved from behind the wall of green. Ruby eyes glittered madly, and then, a trick of light, went dark.

"I am here," a voice said.

At first Slater thought she was going mad. But the voice came again, quiet, intense, but not frightening.

"I am here. Come to me." It was the voice of a woman.

Slater dropped her knife. Tears crawled down her cheeks. English, civilized, a woman in the bush—not jaguar nor head-hunter—not even a jungle-crazed Johnston—simply, beautifully, another woman.

Slater stepped closer. The figure emerged to meet her, slender arms extended, ruby nails like so many tiny flames in the moonlight.

"Thank Goddess." Slater ran toward those arms and collapsed, heat exhaustion, dehydration and relieved shock coming to a head.

The tall stranger did not crumple under the expected weight, merely lowered Slater gently down. Carefully, almost tenderly, she raised a canteen to Slater's chapped lips. She bathed a dark cloth with more water and wiped the grime from Slater's cheeks. Then strangely, she touched the filthy thing to her lips.

Manilla felt immediate revulsion as she watched—felt, too, the movement of the woman as she turned and stared—not quite seeing but sensing Manilla's presence. In that second there was immediate recognition.

Darsen.

* * *

Darsen.

Slater pulled back from the probe, felt Manilla recoil, then clench. Gently Slater softened the picture, filming over it, misting it. She allowed Manilla's own memory to take over. Reading the remembered encounter in Collegetown between Darsen and Manilla, Slater silently rejoiced that this risk with Manilla was worthwhile. True, yes, yes. There was a dark and deadly connection in what she had felt—even in her attraction to Manilla. Some great power was pulling them to a final confrontation, and even in the midst of this probing, Manilla knew it too.

Slater moved her fingertips off Manilla's pulse. It was crucial to time this perfectly; too easy to get caught up in the telling too much.

Manilla's mind would implode at the reality. No, she would truncate it, but still she must expose Darsen's insidious power. Just a bit more...back, back...The probe gently in place...Their pulsepound becoming one...Her voice, her mind...her will...now taking over Manilla's...misting in...drawing Manilla back, back to the jungle...to Darsen's arms...back.

There was a house—two stories, brilliantly lit from inside; a porch swing moved gently in the humid night air. Darsen held her close as they climbed the stairs.

The screen door swung open. A toucan on an ironwood perch hollered at the stranger. Darsen silenced it with a glare. The room seemed golden, unreal. Orchids and incense hung in the air, adding to her drugged exhaustion.

Darsen lowered her onto a soft couch. She brought a basin of cool water, some bandages vaguely smelling of peppermint.

Slater started to protest when Darsen began to loosen her blouse; the dark blue of the stranger's eyes stopped her. She could trust those eyes in this land of emerald and Mardi Gras palettes. The ice within that look cooled her fever, gave her delicate shivers. Quietly, she settled back, allowing the intense woman to undress her. Occasionally, a single nail would brush over nipple or navel, touch gently on inner thigh; yet there was no fear in her, no revulsion at this alien touch. Only ease, coolness, safety. She was like a baby once terrified, lost, but now found, returned home; home.

Months of struggle, of scraping money and letters together to fund her expedition, of dancing around old men and young men all peeking down her blouse or reaching up her skirt and secretly begrudging her every academic victory, the loneliness of her divorce—all melted now at the touch of this strange woman. Slater began to drift off, never questioning that this night, in absolute safety, she would sleep.

* * *

Days later, weeks? Slater seemed always tired, coming back from odd dreams, dreams where she ran light-footed through the jungle, laughing, always safe, with Darsen...

Darsen...whenever Slater would wake, the tall woman would be there, bringing her food, drink, re-bandaging her wounds, stroking her—a touch like that of the enormous blue butterflies she saw often in the air on the front porch—a touch she never believed she would find in this life. Darsen of the perfect teeth, the unmarked skin, the ebony hair. And then, when she woke, Darsen would take her for walks…so often at night, when the moon was new…the paths lit only by occasional light…Darsen began to teach her how to see with new eyes, and it was as if she had a different sense. She could see into the darkness…penetrate the bush with a glance. Had she ever been afraid of this paradise? When? Why?

Finally, she woke in a lazy afternoon, the sound of rain beating on the wooden roof, like the sound of tiny hands clapping.

Darsen was not with her. Slater got to her feet, smiling at the soft dress Darsen had put on her—the color of the orchids which surrounded the room.

"Darsen?" Slater called. There was no answer save for the rain.

Slater moved through the wooden kitchen, then down a small hallway to the bedroom. The shutters had been pulled against the rain. A candle burned, attracting moths, lacing the humid air with the scent of beeswax. Briefly she watched the insects dive-bomb the flame. She blew it out. A single moth fluttered against her cheek, carrying the smell of burning upon its wings. Slater brushed it away.

"Darsen?"

At the end of the hall was a door she had not noticed before. The wood was dark, mahogany most likely, stronger-looking than anything else in the house. There was no lock. Hesitating only a moment, Slater knocked.

"Yes." Darsen was in front of her.

"I didn't see the door open, I mean," Slater stumbled in her surprise.

"I think it's the malaria—you've been through a lot these past few weeks. It will never totally be out of your system—you must always be careful, Katherine. Come in, please, I've been wanting to show you…my work…for some time. Come in." Darsen held out her hand.

Slater noticed a small silver ring on the left little finger. The silver was hammered, like moonlight, it shone softly on the elegant hand. In its center, like a perfect drop of blood, a ruby was cradled.

Slater took the hand into her own.

The room was half again the size of the original cabin. As Slater's eyes adjusted to the light she recoiled. Around the edges of the ɔom were dozens of cages, and in each cage, bats.

"We've never really had a chance to talk about why I'm here or what you're doing out here—I think it's time." Darsen sat on a high-backed stool.

Slater sat next to her, in a lower chair. The bats were beginning to awaken, the day's early darkness triggering their response.

"You know," Darsen said, "the Finnish believe, at least old land Finns, that our solid bodies let go of souls at night and those souls turn into bats flying around until morning when they return. Egyptians used different parts of bats for medicinal purposes. Their Indian counterparts still use bat skin for the occasional poultice. But the real draw for me are the South American and Central American stories—did you know that two thousand years ago in the Mayan culture their god Zotzilaha had a human body but the head and wings of a bat? He demanded human sacrifice—which was no mystery for the Mayans—he often appeared holding a human heart in one hand and a knife in the other. What is more amazing is that in Guatemala, in Zotzil, there is, to this day, a bat-worshipping tribe. The bat was long admired, the fear and bastardization only coming in later years through fiction and unnamable fear of the twentieth century—your culture, my culture. I'm studying these mammals. I'm an artist, a painter—working my way through the Amazon kingdom, as it were. I like to do field studies usually, but with the bats it's a bit difficult, as you can well imagine. I was attempting a night study when I came upon you, actually. It seems sometimes the bats do not want to soar with my soul." Darsen smiled, her ruby lips parting slightly, her hand touching the edges of Slater's hair.

Slater allowed the touch. The bats were only slightly unnerving. She trusted Darsen so completely that the explanation seemed more than plausible.

"Would you like to see my work?" Darsen was off the stool and across the room before Slater could answer. Perhaps Darsen was right about the malaria—Slater's sense of sight and timing was more than a bit awry...

Darsen pulled back the cloth sheet covering a huge canvas panel. It was as if she had simply revealed a window to the jungle beyond the house. So perfectly detailed was the painting that Slater was momentarily puzzled that there was no sound...

"So, you like it?" Darsen was again beside her.

Slater shrugged, "Don't know what to tell you; I've never seen paintings like these before." Slater stared at the canvas jungle. Her heart was filling up with sudden pain, as if a fist were gently squeezing it, changing its rhythm. "Darsen, I have to lie down...I'm not feeling very well." The tears came in huge, wracking sobs. Not understanding what was making her feel or behave in this way, Slater ran from the studio, out into the hallway, feeling the walls of the house reeling...

When she awoke, Darsen was beside her. A fire was quietly sputtering in the fireplace. She was drenched in sweat.

"Katherine, don't try to sit up. It was another spell. I've radioed for help, it will be another week before bearers can reach us, maybe more. The only way in is up river and the rains have come early this year. I'm afraid it was too much, your stumbling on my studio, the animals—it must all seem so strange to you." Darsen knelt next to her, stroking her hair, running her slender fingers along Slater's cheek and neck. Occasionally the ruby ring would catch the firelight and gleam, like a silent animal, between them.

"Darsen, your work is so magnificent—I don't know what to say. You've been wonderful to me—but I have to get back to my work. There must be people looking for me. And Johnston, my guide—never any sign of him…I'm confused…it all started poorly, this trip, so hard to get it started; I had to fight with so many of them to trust me…The dead-ends, so little belief in the Amazon reality, laughing, always laughing at me…"

"I know. When you were delirious, you spoke of the expedition. The radio confirmed who you are, don't worry. Please, my sweet woman, it seems we are closest to what is truth when it seems most difficult. Maybe, if you let me, maybe I can help. There are certain things I've stumbled upon while I've been out here, but later, later for all of this." Darsen moved closer.

Slater closed her eyes. She could feel Darsen's cool, clean breath. With each soft exhalation there was the scent of orchid. Darsen…She felt her heart beat strangely—and then the momentary fear was lessened. Darsen…The lips touched her own gently, moved toward her throat. Slater arched her neck. Yes—surprisingly, yes—she wanted this. So close now, so human…It had been such a long, long time…Yes…

Weeks passed. They were rained in, the river swollen with the season. Slater kept careful notes. Darsen had small artifacts to show her—had, indeed, made contact with the Manteos.

One night, as they lay together in front of the fireplace, Slater stroked Darsen's ring. It seemed to wink at her, causing her to chuckle softly.

"There's a reason why you're drawn to it, you know." Darsen propped herself up on one elbow, stroking Slater's thigh with the other hand.

"Oh?" Slater purred.

"The myth of the Amazons turning men to stone—then dropping the stones into the river? A medicine man, a Hekura, gave me this stone when I first came out here. I took care of his daughter before she died of some kind of poisoning. He had never seen a white woman before—and never a woman as tall as I. He called me a name that translated to Amazon—or close to it. Before I left them he took me to his hut. He had a basket there with a clay bottom. He shook it. This stone fell out into his palm. He said it was great magic; it once had been the soul of a man. A woman warrior had turned it into a stone and threw it into the river. His grandfather had found it spear-fishing. The story had been in the tribe for generations, so grandfather recognized the stone immediately. The chief, I think, thought I was the woman warrior come back for my stone." Darsen kissed Slater long and full, her tongue caressing the inside of Slater's lower lip.

Still kissing her deeply, Darsen reached down for Slater's hand and slipped the ring onto her finger. It fit.

"Darsen," Slater whispered into the darker woman's ear, "oh darling, I can't accept it—truly." Slater pulled her hands through Darsen's ebony hair.

"You already have." Darsen silenced her weak protest with a slow penetrating kiss.

*   *   *

"Bad news, wake up, come with me." Darsen shook Slater to consciousness.

"What, what's wrong? My God, have you been out in the rain?"

"Just get your boots on and follow me, please." Darsen handed Slater a poncho.

It was pouring outside, the rain coming down from the tree-topped canopy as if the leaves were alien clouds.

Slater slipped through the rotting creepers and red mud, trying to keep up with the nimble Darsen. Finally, pulling up behind the taller woman, she stopped on the path.

"My Goddess—oh." Slater took one look and vomited to the side of the trail.

In front of them was an anaconda, its belly split wide and spilling out the partially digested form of a man—enough remaining to be identified as the missing Johnston.

"But it's been almost eight weeks—how—" Slater didn't look again, simply shook the words out.

"He must have been living in the bush—not a great feat for someone with a bit of experience. Maybe he made it to a village and came back looking for you after a little guilt soaked in. Whatever the reason, he got what he deserved. I saw the snake this morning, figured it was a small deer or a villager. After I got a good look—he falls out. Sorry, I'm really, for you, Katherine." Darsen put her arm around her.

"Don't leave him like that, please, Darsen." Slater turned briefly away.

"What else can I do? You've identified him—I'll radio it back. Do you want to paw through the slime for some I.D.? Anyway, the jungle will take care of it—it's too wet to burn. We'll come back in a week, set a marker. A man like that doesn't usually leave a lot of loving relatives. Don't worry, Katherine, trust me." Darsen started down the trail.

Slater never questioned Darsen. Here, with the rain insulating them, in the heart of the emerald bush, this was reality. Darsen was her angel. When Slater got back she could begin to decipher things. For now it was easier to live day to day. Her book outline was filling out enough to receive further funding. Darsen could illustrate it or it could become a collaborative effort. She was beginning to incorporate Darsen in everything, beginning to think of their life outside of the jungle...

"Do you love me?" Darsen was across the room, standing in front of the fire. Her outline seemed etched in gold. The rest of the cabin was blue-black. Outside, night owls screeched through hunting calls.

"Do you love me?" Darsen's voice was low, velvety as the dark.

"Yes." There could be no other answer.

"What about when we leave here—what then?"

"Darsen, I will always love you—there doesn't have to be any what-ifs. come back with me. I can't imagine being back there without you—you must know that."

"It isn't the jungle, then?" Still, Darsen did not approach her.

Slater opened her arms. Her heart was pounding. Images flooded her—lovers, her husband, all those who had ever attempted closeness—all melting and reforming, reforming back into the quiet, beautiful woman across the room. No doubt, none, yes, she wanted Darsen...

Darsen came across the wide-board floor.

In the dream-probe, even now in its lessened state, Manilla tried to pull away. She did not want to see this—too much, too close...Her heart began to match the hearts of the women—but there was no looking away...

The candle was lit—it moved toward her. Slater closed her eyes. She had made a choice—the only choice. Her angel moved closer, carrying the candle.

The bed was soft, the fresh linen pulled tight. The white was almost...sacramental. Slater smiled, stretching out fully, the sheets luxurious against her hot skin. She could feel the flames. She was unafraid...

The candle was placed on the nightstand. Then swiftly, so swiftly that it took her breath away, she felt Darsen's light touch upon her brow. So light, light as the candle's glow, light as the night air wafting in closely. Jungle flowers, night-blooming luscious scents dripping fragrance on the air, caressed them both.

Darsen's hand traced a perfect line across her brow, the hard nails gentle. Slater wanted to laugh softly; she wanted to moan. The knowledge of the sacrament of these moments made her relax; there was no fear.

The dark woman was very close now, her long ebony hair trailing over her shoulders like black lace. Her eyes were as cold and blue as the precious stones they so resembled. Her lips were pale and fine, paler than at any time before that Slater could remember—pale and slightly drawn back.

Slater let Darsen hover over her, fingers like hummingbirds tracing nectar trails across her flesh. She felt her nipples hardening, growing stiff as Darsen traced the aureoles. Eager, so eager now, she could feel the dense and hollow pounding between her thighs, could feel the great vein carrying its fire inside the ruby-tide, the beat of her hunger, echoed.

Darsen...She called the woman to her. Burning with the want of her.

She arched her back, pressing her belly upwards. She felt the quick, hot tongue begin its descent. Her hands caressed and tangled themselves in Darsen's dark mane. No sound now, nothing but the pounding drum of heart and pulse. Sweat bathed her, made her mad with its salt tickle and burn; she could wait no longer.

She cupped Darsen's head and brought it down, down. Her moisture rose, her vulva heavy with the ache that would not be still; her heart seemed to have lowered itself and now throbbed there, the need making her open.

With a single movement that was all pain and pleasure, she felt those pale, soft-petalled lips part her own. They sank down, down into that most secret cave...

And then she knew the terror of Darsen's final secret.

Manilla pulled back hard, fighting for air, her own heart a drum. Slater kept her there, increasing the pressure at her wrist, changing the girl's pulse to her own. Almost finished. The final scene absolutely necessary.

In the morning Darsen remained with her—brought her her first drink. And she had refused the blood of the young tapir, retching at the truth.

For two weeks she had tried to starve herself even as Darsen explained the transformation, the story unraveling, crossing lines, giving new light to histories only hinted at in ancient texts. Finally, in desperation, Darsen brought a child, from some village down the river, already half-dead from Darsen's own deadly feasting. Slater could not finish the act. She slammed it out of the hated one's bloody hands and lay on the bed, sobbing, huge choking sounds all that was left of her human side.

Darsen screamed in rage, finished the child in front of her. And then left, moved away from her in a flash of light and horror, stripped of all human form—unmasked. Gone.

And once again, Slater was alone. Nights passed, days…until finally, the sound of flames woke her from her dreamless sleep.

The heat had caused the bedclothes to burst into flames. The entire house was on fire.

Screaming, she fled the room, only to find the shutters nailed from outside, the door bolted. Her strength gone from so long without nourishment, she could not break the door apart. There was no praying now, not after what she had become. Who would listen? And what would become of her after the burning? Darsen had never revealed it.

She knew pain. Her skin began to blister, redden. All about her hissed and sputtered. Spiders and scorpions scrambled from hidden cracks, dropped from the ceiling onto her. Batting them off, she rushed about. And then saw the fireplace. Laughing in hysteria, she kicked out the flaming logs and began her hellish ascent.

Smoke choked her lungs. Her skin was peeled back by the rough stone, her eyelashes and hair singed. She tasted the burning of her own flesh. Tighter and tighter the chimney grew—the top narrowing to keep out unwanted animals. She bent bones and sinew, realizing, in the middle of her own death, that she did not want to die. These weeks of horror, of absolute knowledge, the promise of power, of unending youth—realization of the monstrous choice she had made—in all of it she had prayed for death. Now, with the prayer about to be answered, there was some last act that must be attended to. A last evil to be put away. She must make it out of there to finish the greatest demon that had ever come to Earth. The death of Darsen gave her the strength of life.

Manilla watched in fascinated horror as Slater finally emerged. So much flesh had been burned or scraped off that her skin seemed to be black and red. Hairless, bent over like some hag, the woman fell from the flaming roof of the house, crashing through jungle to the sodden ground…

Slater let go of Manilla's wrist. Scanning, she felt the story inside the young woman's mind. Pushed back, beyond her dreams, it would remain there. Only the understanding that would allow trust would remain, a shadowed feeling to be called up when the time was right. Slater knew she could count on Manilla.

It had taken much out of her. Not in years had she been so drained. Slater rubbed her eyes, waiting for the young woman to come back, back into the home on the lakeshore, back to New York, Weston, the present.

The fire was low, coals sputtering half-heartedly. Manilla opened her eyes. The room was dark, cold. Manilla watched the professor switch on lights.

"God, how late is it? Have we been talking all this time? It feels like I just got here, Professor. Must be the wine—I didn't pass out, did I? Jesus, I'm really sorry, you must think—"

"You didn't pass out, Manilla—you're just a bit drowsy. It's very late, we've had a nice evening, I think. We'll do it again if you would be so inclined." Slater smiled, walking to Manilla's chair, pulling it gently away from the table.

The student smiled back, sleepily. She stood, and then, totally on impulse, turned and embraced the older woman. Slater hugged her back, hard.

The night was blazing, cold. Geese honked warnings at the edge of the lake. They were keeping watch, keeping guard.

Manilla turned, hearing the sound on the wind, then wondering if maybe it was Slater she heard, but the door to the Professor's house was shut, lights out. She felt slightly stupid. She turned back to the road again, heading for her dorm. As she moved she no longer was tired, but felt almost easy, light. Somehow, in the muddle of everything she recognized that she wasn't alone, not alone anymore.

The Vampire

ᗢ

Pat Califia

PURGATORY was fairly crowded that night. About sixty men and a score of women had assembled in the tiny club by one o'clock in the morning. Most of the women (other than one who was naked and being led around on a leash) were clad in the high fashion of the bizarre—leather skirts, spike heels, PVC corsets, thigh-high boots, studded wristbands or belts, black latex evening gowns. A handful of scruffy lesbians, dressed like destitute bikers, kept to themselves around a low set of stairs along one wall, covered with carpet and meant to be sat upon. The men (other than a few slumming, well-built leathermen) were in casual, even sloppy street clothes. The mistresses stood by the bar, under track lights, impassive and unapproachable, each one giving out some ominous signal—perhaps toying with a whip around her waist or keeping time to the music with a riding crop in her gloved hand. No one but Teddy, the bartender, spoke to the few ex-pensively attired tourist couples who walked around clinging to one another, wearing fixed, exaggerated smiles which were belied by the tight grip they kept on each other.

Solitary male submissives prowled around the dance floor and the two large bondage frames in the corner, up the stairs to the bathroom, down the stairs, toward the back and down the hall which opened into half a dozen tiny cubicles with plywood walls, back to the dance floor and up to the bar, to the well-lit women, and then stood humbly, wist-fully, heads down, for long minutes until hope ran out and they moved off again to make another restless circuit of the premises. Occasionally a dominatrix would focus her gaze on a particular man and beckon him forward to kneel, get her a drink, light her cigarette, answer some insulting question, and kneel again.

A young man, perhaps more confident because he was better look-ing than the older, slack-bellied submissives, accosted a dark-haired, dignified mistress and asked if he might give her a foot massage. She acquiesced, and they adjourned to the carpeted stairs, where he sat on the floor, lovingly removed one of her high heels and kissed it. He cra-dled her stockinged foot in his lap and polished the sole with his thumbs. The leather dykes had made room for them, and one leaned over to offer the dominatrix a joint. She shook her head, but held it down for the submissive man to take a toke. He smiled and said, "Thank you, Mistress," and wondered why the act he was performing gave him so much pleasure. Would she, he wondered, let him remove her stockings and actually kiss her feet, lick them? She took the joint away from him and passed it up the stairs, then rested the foot that was still shod upon his crotch. "Do you like my shoes?" she asked. He nearly fainted as the spike pressed between his balls, and the sole threatened to flatten the shaft of his hardening penis. This was a very lucky night.

Back at the bar, someone noticed this spontaneous interaction and felt jealousy gnaw at his heart. He was one of a gaggle of submissives dancing attendance upon a very lovely, very young professional who styled herself The Goddess Domina. For a moment, he stopped competing for her attention and watched the mistress seated on the stairs grind her heel into the boy's crotch while he leaned back, yielding to her, suffering written all over his face. She was older and plainer than Domina, but she was calm and self-assured, handling her young man with such understanding, easily claiming him for her service. Domina, on the other hand, was already drunk, a criminal waste of the small fortune in cocaine she had snorted before coming to Purgatory. Her jealous submissive knew exactly how much coke there had been because that was the price of being brought to this club with her. Why did he always have to pay? He told himself that Domina was the best-looking woman in the club. The other submissives must surely be jealous of him because he belonged to such a gorgeous bitch-goddess. Why, then, did he want to keep watching the foot-slave and his newly found mistress instead of keeping track of Domina's tiresome antics and pretending it was a privilege to light her cigarettes?

His Goddess was uncoiling a short bullwhip, only four feet long, and ordering one of her submissives to crawl away from her.

She tried to hit him as he scuttled away and wound up tangling the end of her whip in the taps behind the bar. Before anything could get broken, Teddy plucked it from her hands. "Domina," he said sharply, "you know we don't allow bullwhips in here. The club just isn't large enough." The rebuke was administered in a way intended to save her face. After all, he had not told her what he really thought, which was that she was an incompetent alcoholic who ought not to be allowed to hit anyone with so much as a feather duster. She gave him an evil look anyway, the ungrateful, spoiled twit. Let her sulk, Teddy told himself.

"Let's go to the Mine Shaft," one of the leathermen urged his partner, slapping his gloves against one palm. He was wearing a shiny, custom-made leather jacket and chaps that were so new, they creaked. His cover was an American attempt to imitate the Muir motorcycle cap. It was decorated with cheap chain and a badly cast American eagle. He wore his keys on the left, and they jangled as he rocked from one boot to the other.

"Mmm, we will," said the other man absently. His head (as was fitting) was bare, and he kept his hair short, to make the small bald spot look like a tonsure. He wore his keys on the right, where they had, over time, left an impression, an indent in the chaps that cushioned them, kept them quiet. His leathers were not as fancy or as shiny as his companion's. The completely broken-in latigo hugged his burly body. "Who just came in?" he said, lifting his head to stare toward the door. "Oh, this is a treat, Howard."

Howard couldn't see what the fuss was about. "Huh?" he said. It was just a skinny little boy, wearing *brown* leather, no less, with a Muir, which of course was black. The tight pants were tucked into knee-high boots, the sleeves on the leather shirt were rolled up in concession to the summer night, and the peaked cap was ornamented with a silver skull and crossbones on the front. The leather was the color of dried blood. The boy had short, black hair and an olive complexion. A cat-o'-nine-tails and two flails were threaded through the large key ring on his left hip. There was a dagger stuck in his belt behind his right hip and another, smaller, tucked in his right boot. "I didn't know you were into chicken, Gil."

Gil sighed. "That's Kerry," he explained. "Have you ever seen her work?"

Her? This became even less exciting. Why had they left all the hot men at the Spike to come to this weird hangout?

"We should stick around, Howard."

Now it was Howard's turn to sigh. There was usually no arguing with Gil when he used that tone of voice. "Get me another beer, boy," he ordered sharply.

"Yes, sir," Gil said courteously, and went at his own pace to obey.

Iduna overheard this interaction (her hearing was very sharp) and chuckled. She was in her usual place at one end of the bar, where she could play dice with Teddy. For most of the night, she stood, but Teddy kept a stool there in case she wanted to sit down. None of the regulars sat there, even if she was not in that night. Teddy would warn away tourists who made the mistake of trying to occupy her spot if he thought they had potential to become members of the scene. If he wanted to get rid of them, he let nature take its course. Helping people to see themselves as others saw them was Iduna's greatest gift.

Tonight, she was wearing a long black dress with spaghetti straps. It was very low-cut, but a short jacket with long sleeves was worn over the dress, and concealed everything except a white diamond of cleavage. A brilliant red stone carved in the shape of a skull glittered between her breasts. Beneath the jacket, the waist of the dress was reinforced with whalebone stays, giving her a wasp waist and a very straight back. It also shaped her ample ass and made it swell out invitingly, but her imperious manner made it quite clear that you would lose your hand if you touched her. She had long blond hair, and she was drinking a glass of red wine.

None of the submissive men approached this lady, but they kept track of her out of the corner of their eyes. So did the leather dykes and the dominatrices. This was easy to do, because her complexion was so pale it was luminous. In the dark, she almost seemed to glow. Anyone who had gotten close enough would have seen that there was something odd about her skin. It seemed to lack pores or wrinkles. The few people who did get that close to her were usually too busy with their own troubles to make note of her peculiarities. But they did notice that it was difficult to tell how old she was. No one would have mistaken her for a youngster, but she was not middle-aged, either. It was as if her biological clock was not set to the human year.

"Teddy," Domina said breathily, "here's my riding crop."

"What?" For one glad moment, he thought she was asking to be thrashed with it. Then she deigned to explain.

"Keep it behind the bar," she snapped, and tried to stalk away.

"Domina!"

She came back, piqued. Teddy held out her crop. "I don't have room back here for this," he said brusquely, and began to lift glasses and swab underneath them.

Iduna smiled. Her cane, with its red and black leather handle, was neatly racked above Teddy's bottles, along with a handful of implements that belonged to other mistresses he had honored. Teddy would have been glad to provide a similar service for Kerry, but she never let any of her whips out of her hands.

Then Iduna realized that the show Gil had promised Howard was about to happen. Kerry had ordered a bottle of beer and stood with her back to the rest of the room, one foot up on the bar rail. She drank with intense concentration, like a thirsty animal. It looked as if she were oblivious to everything except the beer gurgling down her throat. But when a largish, clumsy-looking man lumbered toward her, she turned around and snarled at him before he could touch her. The noise was uncanny. There were no words, but you would have to be crazy not to understand that it meant, "Keep away—or pay the price." No wonder he jumped away from her. But Domina snickered at him, and Iduna thought, oh dear, now he'll have to get angry and prove something.

"The name's Bill," he said heartily, shoving his hand at Kerry. She looked at it as if it were leprous. There was a long silence. She regarded him from behind her mirrored shades. No telling what she thought. Iduna looked lovingly at that full mouth and the two tiny puckers in it over the prominent canine teeth. She was sure no one else could have spotted these minute irregularities, or known why there were two places where Kerry's lips could not quite meet.

Finally, the leatherwoman spoke. "Can I help you?" she said softly, speaking each word slowly and precisely. It was not a question. Ooh, Iduna squealed to herself, massacre alert, massacre alert!

"Wall, Ah don't know what a little bitty thang like yew could do fer me," he drawled. An out-of-towner, Iduna thought. But that was no excuse. She was an out-of-towner herself, and she knew better.

Kerry smiled. On her face, this expression signified the opposite of its usual meaning.

The fool kept on talking. "Why Ah don't reckon yew could even make a dent in my hide," he chuckled. "Probably be a waste of time. Ah kin take quite a lot, yew know. Wouldn't want ta embarrass a lil gal like yew—yew are a gal, ain'tcha?"

Then the fatuous ass pronounced his own sentence: "Ah kin take anythin' yew kin dish out, sister."

It took one well-placed kick to take him down. Iduna was the only one who could follow the swiftness of that booted foot. Once down, he stayed down, and Kerry kicked him in the direction she wanted him to go. The pointed toe of her boot made a crunching noise when it hit his buttocks and ribs. She hustled him to the foot of a large ladder that stood in one corner of the dance floor. Then she put her boot on the back of his neck and pushed him flat. She bent down to speak to him. What she told him made him keep very still, then shudder and hide his head beneath his arms. Eventually, she lifted him up off the floor— literally lifted him, with one hand—and hauled him up to face the whipping ladder.

A revolving ball with mirrored facets spun a dizzy procession of colored lights over the scene. The ball was part of the special effects for the disco music played on other nights of the week. This club had a different name then, and catered to vanilla swingers. But Kerry, a master of her craft, was not distracted. She knew you must practice this despised art where you can, and disregard what is tawdry or unclean—

or learn to love the dirt, the sleaze, because it represents your membership in the elite.

Now she had him remove his shirt and grab a rung far above his head. He was stretched on his tiptoes in front of her. She asked him a question that only Iduna could hear. "Ah don't want no bondage," he said loudly. Iduna and Teddy shared a brief, unpleasant laugh. Even planarians can learn.

Even Howard sat up and took notice when Kerry began to work on Bill's naked back with a short, suede flail. Hanging from her belt, it looked homemade, innocuous. In her hand, it was a weapon. She whirled it so quickly that there was no apparent difference between the sound it made swinging through the air and the sound it made striking skin. It was one continuous, ominous tone, a single voice that became a duet when the man began to scream. However, he did not let go. Gil leaned toward Howard and whispered that he had seen some people cut and run at this stage. Howard was still skeptical, but now he was keeping an open mind.

Everyone watched. It was what you did at the club when someone hung by their cold and sweating palms and took a beating. Granted, not all of them approved. By tomorrow night, rumor would have it that Kerry had half-killed someone. Heavy s/m is not popular with most of the adherents of light bondage and discipline. Unless you love pure pain, for its own sake, it is difficult to see that deliberately administered, controlled agony retains its own severe sensuality. Iduna rocked on her bar stool, separating her legs enough to let the edge of it press across the middle of her cunt. Teddy spared a glance for her and smiled at her flushed cheeks, then ran a hand along his own erection. It had been a long time since he had played with Kerry. She hadn't been in for a while. Maybe Iduna would take a quick stint behind the bar.

The leatherwoman had switched to a longer flail. It was not suede, and the tails had knots in them. Bill's broad back was now an evenly raised mass of bruises. Kerry danced behind him, side to side, quick as a cat, cruel and exact. He was crying out continuously, twisting from side to side. He seemed to have forgotten he could let go of the ladder. Iduna swallowed a mouthful of wine and thought, how delicious, it would take only one good stroke to split that wide open. And of course this is what Kerry (wielding the braided cat now) did. Nine narrow tails whistled through the air, and the skin divided, rent, bled. She shifted her weight to the other hip and reversed the motion, criss-crossing the previously inflicted lashes.

Bill let go of the ladder and turned around as soon as the first stroke drew blood, but the woman behind him was so fast, she inflicted a

dozen times nine crimson and overflowing welts, each bleeding bouquet placed an even distance from its mates, before he could get out of
her way. As he turned to face her, she continued to flog him overhand,
catching his shoulders, then changed direction and came down hard
across both of his tits. The welts were instantly visible, even in the club
twilight.

"Jesus," Iduna heard Howard say, "this is a bit sick." Gil sighed
again.

"I'm sorry!" Bill screamed, falling to the filthy concrete floor.

"Please stop, please stop, please stop!" She jerked her arm back, and
the incomplete stroke came back into her own stomach. He was
crawling back now, reaching for her hand. Despite being an out-of-
towner, he must have heard enough of Kerry's legend to know that she
allowed select victims to kiss her ring. But Iduna knew he would never
receive that boon, even after taking all that punishment. He had
promised her he could take *anything,* and then he had tried to get away.
Kerry didn't like it when they moved, let alone tried to get away.

Indeed, a boot in the face stopped his progress, and its owner removed her silver shades to give him one hard stare that shut his whin-
ing mouth. There was something funny about this, since she wasn't
even looking into his face. She was looking at the blood that ran in thin
but eager trickles to the floor. In the middle of his renewed and tear-
ful apologies, she spun on her heel and made for the door, tucking the
blood-stained cat beside its fellows. "Shit!" Teddy said, and slammed
his beer down on the bar. He turned to complain to Iduna, but she was
not there.

Kerry was not pleased to be intercepted between the coatcheck and
the door by her personal, self-appointed voyeur, wine glass in hand.
She made quite a provocative picture, this full-bosomed, very pale
woman in her black dress, but she was in the way and a nuisance. Then
she became impertinent. She tilted the glass to her lips and let a half-
swallow of wine run out of the corner of her mouth. It was just a little too purple to be blood, that tiny rivulet, the few drops clinging to
her lips.

Kerry snarled and went sideways to get by, angry, almost pushing
the woman who had arranged this strange tableau for her. A man who
had behaved that way might have gotten a broken jaw for his bad manners. But she was known for her chivalry. It was part of a code she
thought all true leathermen (regardless of gender) should obey. Let
women make do with their feminine wiles and plots and foibles. She
did not want to become entangled in them. This creed of Kerry's took
a form that dismayed many of the heavier masochists in the scene: she

could rarely be persuaded to treat women like sides of beef. Only men were usually that stupid or lucky. In her lofty unconcern with women's untidy minds and manipulative ways, Kerry had somehow omitted to learn who this impudent blonde (whom she had certainly seen many times before) was. Ignorance is bliss, but we are rarely allowed to remain in that happy state.

There was another club, Roissy, just three blocks away, closer to the docks. That was where Kerry headed now, whips swinging at her hip, the knife scabbard bumping the small of her back, her boot heels making a satisfying tempo on the pavement, a rhythm that confirmed that she was in motion, making progress, getting away from those thin scarlet streams, the smell of life that made her mouth water and her jaws ache.

She knew immediately that she was being followed. She also had no trouble detecting that the person behind her was wearing spike-heeled shoes, and so she knew who was following her. The why of it bothered her, and the notion that anybody in spikes could keep up with (let alone catch or combat) someone in boots amused her.

She cut through an alley, thinking, 'Let's see if the bitch will come into the darkness and teeter around in the trash and rubble for the sake of a closer look at me.' Besides, it was a shortcut to Roissy.

Surprise! There at the mouth of the alley was her pursuer, somehow ahead of her and once again blocking her way. She was wearing a satin cloak with a red lining, and a sudden gust of wind (uncharacteristic for the season) lifted it and spread it out until it fluttered about her like wings. Her breasts gleamed like alabaster, even in the absence of street lights and moonlight.

Kerry had reached for her boot and belt and unhitched her blades the second she realized she was being followed, despite her contempt for the mettle of her opponent. She did not consciously plan to use them on the other woman. She was sure she could take her with her bare hands, if a physical contest was necessary. But that seemed unlikely. No, the blades were for others, stronger and more dangerous, who might come upon them and interrupt their tête-à-tête.

Silence poured into the space between them, filled it up, then spilled over into speech.

"Why are you running away?" purred the woman in the black dress, red flames playing all around her. She was very sure of herself.

Startled, Kerry blurted, "What the hell are you talking about?" then bit her lip and repented not keeping silent. She knew she was about to be laughed at.

She was. The laugh was rich, full of private enjoyment and secret knowledge. It was not mocking, but it was too intimate, and it made her hate the intrusive blonde whose name she wished she could re-member, so she could chew her out properly.

"You haven't fed for months now. You still draw blood, but you don't allow yourself to taste it."

This time, Kerry held her tongue, put her hand onto her dagger, and watched to make sure the other did not come any closer. If she had spoken, she wondered if she would be able to hear herself talking over the noise that her blood was making, roaring in her ears. This was start-ing to feel like her worst-case scenario, hardly a fair price to pay for a little mayhem at a braggart's expense.

"I think I'm the only one who's noticed. It's so much a part of your legend, this penchant you have for flaying someone with your cat-o'-nine-tails until the walls and innocent bystanders are spattered with blood, or using your knife to release the hot, sticky, salty fuel that feeds the heart, the lungs and the brain. It appalls everyone so much that they don't realize you've ceased to put your lips to the wound, to swal-low what you've set free, or clean your blade with your tongue. But I do. I do. And I wonder why. Would you like to tell me why?"

The leatherwoman shook her head so hard that the gesture looked painful. The nerve! What could they possibly have to talk about? She owed no one any explanations. When she spoke, it was not to the point: "Stay right where you are."

"I'm not here to assault you!" The tone was hurt surprise. "I'm not going to approach you without permission. I just want to have a little chat. I may want you to come to me, later, when we understand one another better. But I promise I won't move one step from this spot, no matter what happens."

Was this some crazy kind of come-on, then, from a dominant who wanted to bottom for her? Kerry had received many invitations like these. Perhaps she was being paranoid. But if that was the case, her rule was that the other must make an explicit request. It would be insult-ing to anticipate such needs in a colleague. So they watched each other in renewed silence, taking measurements, making calculations.

Like most women, the blonde did not seem to be able to hold her tongue. Kerry braced herself when she saw that whorishly lipsticked mouth, with its bee-stung lower lip, open. But the woman only said, "I was in such a hurry to catch up with you that I left my cigarettes at the bar. Would you happen to have one?"

A pack was extracted from a leather shirt pocket and went flying to-ward Iduna, closely followed by a silver lighter. She caught them both in the same hand, took a cigarette, lit it, and tossed both pack and lighter back. They were caught and returned to the breast pocket.

Kerry waited two heartbeats, then relented and fished them out again and lit a cigarette for herself. Iduna smiled. It was a minor triumph, a small victory, to have them share even this much common ground—a quiet smoke together in a dark alley, with rats just out of eyeshot, telling each other their tribal stories about eating garbage and tormenting human babies, fucking their mothers and devouring their own succulent children.

Smoke curled around her fingers as she resumed talking. "I have been an archivist of your legend ever since I came to the city. In fact, your legend is what brought me here." Kerry gave her a brief nod, accepting this as her due. "I've been collecting all the stories about you, verifying what I can, making observations of my own. I'm always interested in legends even if the people who inspire them are not really of mythic proportions. But when I realized just how legendary you truly are, I began to keep very close track of you. As far as I know, James was your last...shall we say, completely satisfying experience? It's a little less cold than calling him a meal. He says you tied him down, took a scalpel, exposed an artery in his thigh and partially sutured it, slit it between the sutures and drank nearly a pint of his blood before you pulled the stitches tight and closed the incision with butterflies of surgical tape. All with his permission, of course, and he says it made you quite sick to have that much at once. He was close to passing out, so he may have been hallucinating. But I don't think so. Was his blood bad? Is that what stops you now? A fear of tainted blood? Disease, perhaps? Or did you get enough from him to last you all this while?"

Now they both knew the game, her question and the answer, and Iduna saw the mirrored shades removed for her benefit, saw herself regarded by cold eyes, eyes surrounded by darkness, eyes that already saw her dead in six different positions. "James," said Kerry hoarsely, "talks too much."

"Don't be hasty," Iduna cautioned, smiling and blowing smoke up at the moonless sky. "Surely you haven't lived this long by being rash and impulsive."

Now it was her turn to be laughed at. After all her casual conversation about other people's blood, it was horrid to feel her own turn to cold sludge, stop running through her veins, then freeze solid, liable to break like glass and cut her to pieces inside if she moved.

Well, but...Iduna had been in some very dangerous places, and she always spoke to the people she met there. Otherwise, life would turn into an ordeal instead of an adventure. Now, she spoke as if to her lover, which of course is the most dangerous audience of all.

"Wouldn't you like to know how I figured it out?" The question was a caress. She made herself wait for the curt, reluctant nod before she continued. "To begin with, there is your name. It means 'son of the dark one.'" She paused for that to sink in, then said politely, "You have not asked, but my name is Iduna. In ancient Norse mythology, Iduna guarded the golden apples of immortality." 'But in our case, my love, the apples are the brightest, truest red imaginable,' she thought, but did not say.

Kerry twitched. But Iduna felt like being a little ruthless. It was rude, forcing someone to make their own introduction. "You have trouble remembering your age and your birthday. You've told some people you're twenty-two and other people you're thirty-five. There are certain historic periods you are very fond of, and when you speak about them, you occasionally lapse into the first person and the present tense. You speak several languages; however, none of them (with the exception of your American English) is contemporary. I am enough of a linguist to recognize nineteenth-century French when I hear it, and your German is full of colloquialisms from the 1930s. You say you were born here, but there is no birth certificate on file for you in any of the five boroughs of New York City." In the process of investigating Kerry, Iduna had figured out how to dummy up this basic I.D. for herself. 'You need some help,' she thought. 'It's dangerous to fall behind the times.'

"You are photophobic. You don't even like the brightly lit area of the bar where all the other s/m dominants stand and model. You wait for your prey in shadows. You have unusual strength, you are preternaturally quick, and you have an ability to see in the dark and hear things no one else can hear. Your sense of smell is also very keen. I've traced some of your employment, and much of it is at places where you can handle blood or blood products. All of these jobs have been abruptly terminated for mysterious reasons, and you have not had one for quite some time. You do not have sex, ever, with anyone that I've been able to locate and, given your reputation, I would imagine that someone who had come close enough to even lie about it would have claimed they had made love with you by now."

Kerry shuddered delicately. "Sex with a victim," she said with great distaste, "is out of the question."

Iduna ignored this aside. "All of this could simply mean you are an adventurer, a liar, a psychopath, a soldier of fortune, or a celibate, amateur hematologist, but I don't think any of these explanations are logical. So many of the stories about...your people are idle fantasy or vicious gossip motivated by religious bigotry, but I know enough not to expect you to run away from crosses. Your kind is far older than Christianity. You love garlic, and you have a perfectly good reflection in a mirror. But I don't need evidence as crude as that to recognize you for what you are. You are a predator, and human beings are your natural prey. Humans like to believe that they are the ultimate predators, at the top of the food chain. They sleep secure in the belief that nobody stalks them. It is only their deep need for this illusion that keeps people from recognizing you, running away from you, and screaming their fool heads off."

A grin matched the skull on Kerry's cap. "Ah, but people do run from me, screaming."

"When you are partially unveiled, yes. During the epiphany, then they scream and escape if they can."

"But you have not screamed. Or tried to run. You came after me, Iduna."

Her own name spoken in Kerry's cold voice made her shiver. "Perhaps it's because, despite all my circumstantial evidence, I'm still not sure just who or what you are. And there is only one way for me to be sure, isn't there?" She put her hands to her bodice and touched the ruby skull. "This dress has a built-in corset, a very old-fashioned one, of a seventeenth-century pattern," she said. "The jacket covers the laces so most people don't notice. It has a busk in the front. That was the earliest form of stay, you know. Only my busk is rather special." From between her breasts she pulled a very slim blade. The grinning jewel was its pommel.

Before it was fully exposed, Kerry had a knife in her hand, poised for use. Iduna ignored this, put the thin steel between her teeth, and removed her black jacket. The long sleeves were quite tight, and she had to turn the damn thing inside out to get it off.

"Have you ever noticed my veins? Probably not. You haven't been watching me the way I've been watching you, and anyway, I don't expose a lot of skin in the clubs. I like to show cleavage and nothing else, not even my forearms or my calves." Kerry was staring at her décolletage. Iduna knew that her breasts were very prominent and was always amused by men and women who were so attracted to them that they talked to her tits rather than to her face. It was appropriate, in a way, because breasts were symbolic of nurturance. 'But the nourishment I provide,' she thought, 'is not milk, but a different humor.'

She continued her pedantic, distracting speech. "My skin is very pale, almost transparent. It looks fragile, but I heal very quickly. My veins are close to the surface, easy to get to. See how thick and blue they are? I never have any trouble giving blood. The needle just pops right in, and out it spurts. Easy as sin."

She was picking at her wrist with the point of the blade, then caressing the inside of her elbow. "All it would take is a little more pressure, and we'd have a fountain here. A scarlet fountain, pouring onto the dirty ground, completely wasted, unless…unless someone had a use for it. Unless someone caught it in their mouth before it hit the ground. Caught it and drank it, took life from it, rolled it around their tongue and palate and described the vintage to me, swallowed and swallowed as if they would never get enough. Look, my pulse is beating right here."

The arm held out was steady, not shaking. A glinting edge pressed against old scars along the vein, hard enough to make an indentation but not to break the skin. The sight made Kerry's leather-clad hips jerk, just once, but Iduna saw it and was immediately excited. How interesting, to see a reflexive response there, in the crotch, instead of just the jaws and hands. What possibilities it opened up…but the words the leatherwoman spoke next shattered her erotic fantasies.

"You will bleed to death if you cut yourself there, that way," said she. It might have been a report on the temperature and time of day.

"Don't you want it? Need it? Wouldn't you like to smell it, falling through the air? The wind is behind me. It would bring the scent to you at once, fresh and abundant."

The other shook her head. "No."

"No?"

"No. Why are you surprised? Even if this mad story you've concocted is true, you yourself said I've already gone without it for months."

Iduna made the mistake of arguing. "Then the need must be intense right now. You must be hungry. I don't think you'll die without blood, but it must make you feel a little sick to be deprived. A little less powerful than usual, a little less energetic. Distracted. Frustrated. Off."

Iduna had never had someone pay so much attention to her with such a look of utter indifference on their face. She had not anticipated this much resistance. This was even more difficult than locating her quarry in the first place. Clearly, the offer of her wrist was not enough. Perhaps scars annoyed them. She thought they had a heat-seeking sense, like rattlesnakes. She imagined that scars would be like cold streaks in the hot aura that radiated through the skin, making the marked person less appealing than someone with a smooth body. Perhaps this one was just fastidious about unzipping an old scar, thought of it as drinking from a glass someone else had already used.

She probed again, looking for the weak spot, the turning point, the breaking point. "Do you prefer men, is that it? Is it because women are weaker, smaller, and too quickly drained? But then, I've never heard of you leaving anyone bloodless and dead. So why should it matter? I know most of you don't need as much blood as the stories say you do. Too many of those legends are about the stupid and greedy ones, the ones so unrelentingly selfish they get caught. Or the ones who unfortunately can't live on anything other than human blood. Why are you denying yourself this pleasure?" She dared to allow compassion to creep into her voice. "You must have had to develop an enormous amount of self-control and get awfully good at living in a constant state of deprivation. Is that why you stopped after James, to prove that you could do without it if you had to? But it's not necessary now. I want you to have me."

The stony face of the other said, 'Don't try to cozen me. In a thousand years, you could never understand what I am, where I have been, what living has done to me.'

Iduna despaired. Her head drooped, and Kerry almost felt sorry for her. Then inspiration struck. "Or could it be that you would rather drink your life from a woman, hold her in your arms, slit her throat with your teeth, then eagerly gulp down what wells up around your mouth—yet you refuse to let yourself have me because you would enjoy it too much and then want it and need it again? Are you afraid you would lose control if you got what you really want?"

There was no change in the other's fighting stance and icy expression. The air between them simply became busier, hummed like a high-voltage wire, stank of ozone, seemed to turn an even darker shade of midnight blue.

Now or never. It was the moment that would decide the outcome of the hunt. Iduna stared into Kerry's eyes, covered with the reflecting aviators, and used the tiny portrait in them to guide her hand while she made two slashes at the place where her breasts came together, a little 'v' that fit into her cleavage. The blood immediately started to rill, and she cupped her hands under her breasts to help her corset push them close enough together to gather it and keep it in a pool.

She knew that she was as beautiful then as she ever would be—her head tossed back, her mass of curly blond hair being rearranged by a breeze, her white throat, shoulders and breasts exposed, and the red color of the thread of blood just barely distinguishable from the ebony of her dress in the darkness.

She thought for a moment that her adversary had disappeared, because she suddenly was not where she had been. But then muscular hands dug into her back, claws bent and held her. There was a tongue lapping between her breasts, but what was there was quickly consumed, and then there were sharp teeth biting, and warm, soft, strong lips pressing around them, sucking. The pain disappeared as soon as her blood mingled with the fluids in the other's mouth. Of course there's no pain while they're feeding, she thought sleepily. It's an adaptive trait, evolutionarily speaking...The hands moved to her breasts and began to knead them, like nursing kittens, and she writhed from the sudden pleasure it brought her. Apparently she moved too much, because one of the hands left her breast and took her by the hair. Steel fingers kept her bent back in a perfect bow, the bleeding part of her uppermost, taut, an available feast.

She could smell her own blood. It was sickening and yet very satisfying, familiar, comforting. The scent of fresh blood was nicer than menstrual fluid, though it was always pleasant to bleed. The body over her moved convulsively, paying heed only to what it was drawing in from her, taking care only that she would not escape until she had given satisfaction, satiation, quieted all hunger. She was painfully aware of her heart beating in her left bosom, and realized that was the breast that the brutal hand kept milking and bruising, as if to keep the heart pumping, as if to squeeze its contents directly into the waiting mouth full of razors.

Iduna slipped on the gravel, and immediately the hand left her breast and a strong arm was wedged between her legs, the hand grasping the small of her back, holding her the way a mother holds an infant. She realized by the mushy feel of her panties against Kerry's leather sleeve that she was wet down there, as wet as the mouth that fed on her. Her assailant realized it, too, because she ripped at her panties, literally clawed them to pieces, and then she was being crammed full, opened terribly, spread far too wide, almost lifted off her feet by the force of the fucking, and it hurt so much for so long that she came, came even as the canines sank another notch into her cuts and drank fresh blood from the deepened wound. Which penetration made her come? She did not know.

Then she was being picked up, cradled. Adults are usually not lucky enough to re-experience this infantile pleasure. Even she had not guessed just how strong Kerry really was. A face was close to hers, familiar for its wolfish features, unfamiliar for its look of peace. The teeth in that smile were stained, and the tongue was cupped. The mouth came toward hers, and she opened her mouth, and the tongue slid into her and fed her a mouthful of her own blood. They kissed around it, neither one swallowing, keeping the blood between them to taste, play with, and savor for as long as possible, until their mouths were so full of saliva they had to swallow or let it run down their chins. Then Kerry bent down and took more, and offered it to her again, and this time Iduna leaped for it, bit at it, then worried the mouth that spit blood into hers. Now there were words being spoken in between the kisses, words that said, "Be careful. Are you really sure you want some of my blood?"

Iduna almost wept with gladness. So there was love here, or at least need—a need to keep her available for another feeding. It is only when they become indifferent or vengeful that the undead make their victims like themselves, immortal predators and thus useless and untouchable. When passion returned, she was careful not to bite the other's lips or tongue.

"Take me with you," she whispered, and her bearer did not ask her where or when, just carried her away in a rush of black and silent wind. Oh, how she had missed being transported this way, effortlessly, in the grip of something far more powerful than herself, so powerful that it was pointless to worry about the destination or what would happen once they arrived there. The venom that had prevented her blood from clotting and closing the wound sang now in her veins, making her see colors behind her closed eyelids, making her warm inside and simultaneously relaxed and alert. No other drug could ever duplicate this ecstasy, this calm. She should know, she had had long enough to search for a substitute. Her thighs trembled, needing to be separated, and the arms around her tightened, hurt her and reassured her.

Her arms full, but under no strain, Kerry felt amazed, disgusted with herself, hopeful, but terribly afraid. She had a low tolerance for ambiguity. It slowed her down too much, made her angry. She had succumbed to temptation, and that was a dangerous weakness. She had not kept her secret, which must mean she had been careless. If one woman could ferret it out, someone else could. Furthermore, she had not slain her discoverer. This was surely stupidity. The code had been violated beyond repair. It was time for another change, another sleep, another decade, another name.

But this blood—whose? Her name was...Iduna—Iduna's blood had been very good. She had never had it offered this way, seductively, with persistence and determination, or felt it being given up with joy. But should the pleasure of feeding be mutual? It made her uneasy, no matter how many times she had imagined it and craved it. Now, of course, she wanted it again, and how she resented that! Would there be more nourishment, more pleasure from this source? Or would the woman wake up sweating with the fear of death and the devil, sick of what she had done, and repudiate it and try to make her terror public? What did it mean, to be offered blood by a mortal who claimed to know what she was doing? Could anyone who was not like herself really know what it meant? Had any of her kind ever felt this way, asked themselves these questions? Perhaps it would be better to allow her own veins to be opened, briefly become prey, and turn this taking heifer into a hated peer. That image brought too much shame, hostility, and desire (yes, desire) to be tolerated for long. What had she done?

She wrapped Iduna's cloak more snugly about her, to shut out the cold, transparent fingers of the wind, hugged her newly opened vessel to her breast, then took her deeper into darkness. The Eyrie was still far away. The slut moaned, twisted, and exposed her throat. She wanted it again. It was going to be difficult to avoid draining her completely before dawn. *What had she done?*

Safe, at home in the inhuman arms, Iduna dabbled her fingers in her still-oozing wound and thought, 'After the long hunt, the desperate search, the years of doing without, being alone and bereft, with no wings to shelter me, no sharp teeth in any of the mouths that kissed me, I have you. You are no dream, no fantasy. Finally, my treasure, my pet, my lord, I will make you my beloved. Your strength, your magic, my death and your immortality—I have it all within my reach.'

This rare and beautiful creature did not know how happy she was going to make her, how much she would change her life. Iduna assumed she would never know how Kerry really felt about her, if only because she was so ignorant about her own emotions. The first one, the almost-forgotten one, so needy and yet powerful, had been that way, and Kerry seemed younger, less experienced than it. But Kerry would always need her because her blood was so sweet. Evolutionarily speaking, it was an adaptive trait. And she knew how to make it interesting to take. She had been well schooled.

How old are you, Iduna wondered, and how old am I? Will you ever bother to ask me the kind of questions I've been asking about your kind for these countless lonely, crazy years? Is my blood, precious as it is to me, enough to pay for the wonder and contentment I feel in your presence?

She twined one arm around her captor's neck and reached with the other hand for the leather seam that accentuated, pulled up and divided Kerry's genitals. The curve was like a ripe peach pushed into her hand. It rubbed insistently against her palm. Kerry made the same noise she had made to warn the man in Purgatory to keep his distance, but Iduna only smiled. Abstinence is the mother of shameless lust.

"Sex doesn't seem to be out of the question after all, does it?" the vampire said.

O Captain, My Captain

---🦇---

KATHERINE V. FORREST

*L*IEUTENANT T. M. HARPER applied her fingertips to the print-reader at dock area 43, and boarded *Scorpio IV.* A tone sounded within the craft signifying entry; there was no other acknowledgment of her presence.

Disappointed, she realized that of course Captain Drake would be off-ship, taking advantage of the remaining hours before departure. Moon Station 13 might not be Earth, but it had Earth comforts and was staffed with bored military personnel who would welcome the august company of a civilian transport captain. And it was incomparably closer to home than either the captain or herself would be during the next four lonely months. Still, she was puzzled. Transport captains were by nature iconoclastic, and Captain Drake had earned a reputation for extreme reclusiveness.

A few of the readout screens lining the brilliantly lighted command cabin radiated data which Harper ignored, knowing it to be standard orbital information for spacecraft scheduled for departure. She glanced at the chronometer to determine what division of night and day would be operative on *Scorpio IV*: mean Greenwich time. The captain, Harper remembered, was European born. There were four command chairs, regulation for a class one transport, even though only two were needed for the voyages of this particular craft. She had not expected *Scorpio IV* to be different, and it wasn't.

Moving through the galley she looked into the computer room at the standard module and backup, then continued on toward the sleeping cubicles, directing her gear bubble in front of her. She shook her head over the unnatural brightness everywhere, knowing she would have to adjust to it. It was understandable that any transport captain spending months away from the sun's golden warmth would be greedy for bright light…

She knew the Captain's more spacious quarters would be at the end of the corridor; she would choose among the remaining three. But she halted at the first doorspace. Its portal was labeled LIEUTENANT HARPER.

Harper gazed in amusement down the corridor. She had been in-stalled the maximum distance from Captain Drake's quarters. Con-sidering all the time the captain spent trapped with unchosen company in this tiny craft, an obsession with privacy was also understandable.

Harper had good reason to doubt that she herself would retain her sanity for very long in such circumstances. She had won her officer's commission on a twelve-person battle cruiser surveillance mission to the Orion sector, had been enthralled by the challenge and adventure of those nine months, had passed the psych probes both during and after the assignment.

But back on the solid footing of Earth, for months afterward she had felt disconnected, her mind—or perhaps her soul—somehow still adrift in those spectacular reaches she had floated through like a weightless seed on alien winds. And she knew from the oblique com-ments of other members of her officer corps that her experience had not been unique.

She steered her gear into the cubicle, then programmed the door-lock to open to four rhythmic taps of her fingernail. She too would have her privacy.

She stretched tiredly, wishing she could relax on the wide, inviting bunk. Sex with Niklaus last night had been exhausting, as if the two of them had been frenziedly trying to build a storehouse against the parched months ahead. She began to stow her gear.

"Lieutenant Harper, welcome aboard." The low voice resonated like a cello.

Turning, Harper stared, transfixed.

The tall, pale figure in the doorway—dark-haired, clad in black trousers and a high-collared gray shirt—possessed a dramatic beauty so androgynous that Harper could not have guessed her sex unless she had known beforehand.

"Captain Drake," she managed to say, fascinated by the heavy-lid-ded dark eyes which seemed weary with their burden of intelligence.

"My apologies," Drake said. "I did expect you around this time; it's just that my diurnal rhythms are turned around." The smile was fleet-ing, but Harper was astonished by its magnetism. "I was resting in my quarters when you came in."

The captain crossed her arms and scrutinized Harper with open in-terest. "I trust you brought more comfortable garb. I accept your nec-essary military presence, but I detest military trappings."

Harper glanced down at her Space Service uniform to conceal her ire. The forest-green jacket had been hard won, and she was proud of it; she was proud of her Lieutenant's silver bar. But if her training and the mission to Orion had taught her nothing else…"I brought a few jumpsuits," she conceded.

"Good. I'll look forward to seeing you in them. Departure is confirmed for twenty-one hundred hours. I'll expect you on the bridge for final check at sixteen hundred."

Harper caught herself as her hand began its automatic upward flick toward salute. "Yes, Captain."

Again the brief, magnetic smile. "Call me Drake." And she vanished, moving soundlessly down the corridor.

Drake. So much warmer than Captain. Sourly, Harper pulled a green standard-issue jumpsuit out of her gear. *If she doesn't have a first name then neither do I.*

*   *   *

As *Scorpio IV* made its leap into hyperspace, Harper slumped exhaustedly in her command cabin chair.

"Get coffee, whatever you like," Drake told her in a tone of dismissal, shutting down all but a dozen of the readout screens. "You've been well trained, Harper; I'm pleased with your technological grasp of my ship."

Harper nodded, watching Drake check course trajectory, her strong, long-fingered hands moving surely over the console, entering data, changing the pattern of the templates.

For the past three hours Harper had been fully absorbed in all the readout screens, occasionally verifying and detailing a status problem for the imperious woman in the command chair beside her, observing with increasing awe Drake's total comprehension and manipulation of swiftly changing computer analyses. Well versed in the lore of civilian transport captains and their extraordinary hands-on knowledge, she had suspected the stories to be at least somewhat exaggerated—especially the claim that some of these individuals could actually direct a Robomech-four. All military spacecraft were checked and cross-checked by teams of specialists, and specialists had been involved in final systems check of this civilian craft. But Drake had ignored them. She had been as one with her ship, her glance penetrating every analysis on every readout screen simultaneously, and she had directed her own robot repairs and adjustments.

Some military craft had gone out and never returned, their final communications the stuff of legend and nightmare in the service. Harper knew that if any problem developed on *Scorpio IV*, Drake would know in an instant where it was and how to correct it.

This assignment was a prize. Other officers had been equally qualified to be the military presence on this spacecraft, but hers had been the lucky number to come up. She would be the one to reap all the tangible and intangible benefits when *Scorpio IV* returned with its priceless cargo from the Antares asteroid belt.

She rubbed her eyes; they ached and burned from staring at the readout screens in this too-bright cabin. She smiled, remembering her psych training, all those exercises in negotiating basic incompatibilities during extended space travel. There would be no negotiating with this autocratic woman. Drake possessed irreplaceable ability and the emotional components necessary for remaining sane while she expended the prime years of her life in space. *Scorpio IV* was Drake's home. Harper would be the one to adjust.

But the compensations were handsome. As each day of these next four months passed, credits would be deposited to her account, and when this tour of duty ended she would have three years' hazard pay, tax free. When her military obligation was completed she would retire and pursue an Earth-based career, perhaps settle in with the devoted, patiently waiting Niklaus.

She unfastened her restraint and got up. "May I bring you something, Cap—uh, Drake?"

Drake looked at her then, and Harper backed away in recoil from dark eyes that seemed haunted by grief, as empty and blasted as a dead star. The voice was soft, and flat: "Nothing, Harper, thank you."

* * *

Knowing better than to presume Drake would wish to share a mealtime with her, Harper assembled dinner from the autoserv, paying little attention to her selections. All food onboard a spacecraft, no matter how it tasted—and most of it tasted remarkably good—was a synthetic formulation of the same nutrients. A space crew could dine solely on chocolates and still eat a balanced diet.

Dutifully consuming her poached trout and vegetable salad, Harper concentrated on reassembling her self-assurance. Drake might know every technological configuration of her spacecraft, she reflected spitefully, but that did not mean she was a superior being. Rumor had it that transport captains were psychologically hermetic and sexually dysfunctional—major reasons why they performed so sanely and successfully in space.

And the formidable Drake did not, after all, outrank her; her captaincy was a civilian title, and civilian captains were a dying breed.

Transport craft increasingly were unmanned, guided by a network of space stations in the civilized universe. Once another method was found for either harvesting the Antares asteroid crystals or duplicating them, little work would be left for a specialist like Drake; she would be reduced to transporting conventional cargo between the few cultures who stubbornly continued to demand traditionally manned craft for commercial transactions.

Drake might be contracted to the great ExxTel Corporation, but she, Harper, represented the elite Space Service, the military arm of the most dominant coalition of corporate, military, and democratic power in the history of Earth. She had been assigned to *Scorpio IV* because she was well qualified to be military liaison on this civilian voyage to the asteroid belt girdling Antares; it was her sole responsibility to monitor the collection and transportation of the asteroid crystals to ExxTel warehousing facilities orbiting Mars.

But still...Harper suddenly pushed her food away, grimacing. She knew very well that she was a mere passenger. Only one military liaison had been assigned to this spacecraft because one person with nothing to do was sufficient. She would perform the duties for which she had been meticulously trained only if incapacitating illness or death struck the captain of *Scorpio IV.*

She would then limp this craft into the nearest Space Station—unless the illness or death occurred within the asteroid belt. Rescue within the asteroid belt, if possible at all, would have to be attempted by another transport captain because she, Harper, would be helpless to accomplish it herself. Her prime function on this voyage, she conceded darkly, was the equivalent of a hovering vulture, a cemetery watcher.

Only a transport captain with Drake's skills would dare venture into the Antares asteroid belt which had been claimed indisputably by Earth, nearby civilizations having believed it to be a mysterious, destructive wasteland of drifting rock. Nearly two centuries earlier, twelve military cruisers—nine of them investigative craft—had vanished near Antares without any visual or vocal transmission to provide the faintest clue. The sector had finally been abandoned, written off as the deep space equivalent of the Bermuda triangle, declared off limits to military patrols and transport vessels.

Then ten years ago one of those lost ships, *Pisces II ,* perhaps propelled by the effects of a solar flare from the violent Antares, had floated free from the negligible gravity of the asteroid belt, had been picked up on the scanners of civilian transport Captain Reba Morton. All controls and communication equipment in Morton's spacecraft had lost their calibration as she approached the asteroid belt and *Pisces II*, but still she had managed to dock with the dead cruiser and manually guide her craft to a Space Service monitoring station. Only a civilian transport captain like Morton could have overcome the disabling of her own basic robot repair devices and recalibrated the spacecraft's instrumentation sufficiently to accomplish such a feat.

Apparently the crew of *Pisces II*, victims of suicidal madness, had blown themselves out through a hatchlock. And Antares asteroid crystals had drifted in…Thus, by purest chance, a vital component of human life on Earth and other Earth-gravity planets had been discovered. Morton and the Space Station crew were the first to experience the wondrous property of the Antares asteroid crystals.

In direct ratio to their size and quantity, the crystals imparted weightlessness. Applications for the crystals were immediately and excitingly obvious in virtually every technological area, especially transportation and medicine. But the greatest clamor was raised by gerontologists. After a century of well-financed research, they had not been able to extend life expectancy beyond one hundred and ten years. Antares asteroid crystals were not the fountain of youth, but they represented a dramatic breakthrough, releasing individuals from the wearing, aging effects of standard Earth gravity. Use of the crystals to reduce weight to one-tenth standard gravity could add as much as thirty years to the average human life span.

The drawback was scarcity. For the first time since the twenty-first century, glaring disparity again existed between rich and poor, this time involving not the commodities affecting the quality of life, but the commodity of life itself. The crystals were costly and in continuous demand, due to the difficulty in harvesting them and their perishability: over time their power gradually faded.

Because of their priority-one military applications, the crystals had been rated as strategic materials and placed under the jurisdiction of ExxTel and the Space Service. Token patrols guarded the Antares system at a cautious half-a-light-year distance and in desultory fashion—the gates of heaven could be no less accessible.

In an age of specialization, any spacecraft large enough to transport the many technicians required for recalibrating its disabled systems would be gripped by Antares's gravity, with lethal results. And ExxTel scientists had thus far failed to provide effective shielding against the crystals' effect on a spacecraft's onboard computers and guidance systems. Nor had they made any progress toward duplicating the molecular structure of the crystals, seemingly unique in their defiance of the laws of physics, nor in recreating the environment that would allow them to self-replenish as they did within their home in the Antares asteroid belt.

Only an extraordinarily gifted civilian transport captain like Drake could venture into an asteroid system with spacecraft guidance and communication systems inoperative, and recalibrate those systems without benefit of robot repair or remote command...

Feeling a prickling between her shoulder blades, a sensation of being watched, Harper whirled. At the periphery of her vision was a tiny dark fluttering. She blinked once and the fluttering was gone. She blinked again, in annoyance. She had been in deep space a matter of mere hours; it was much too early for mind tricks to begin...

Drake walked into the room, her long lean body fluid in its movements. She drew a small tumbler of tomato juice from the autoserv and sipped it standing, her dark, unreadable gaze lingering on Harper.

"You'll have dinner now?" Harper politely inquired.

"Later," answered Drake in her cello tones. She contemplated her tomato juice and smiled, then drained it and disposed of the container. Without another word she left the galley.

Too bone-weary to further speculate about the enigmatic Captain Drake, Harper went off to her quarters, knowing the spacecraft's alarms—or Drake—would awaken her if need be, and no need would be.

*　*　*

Early the next morning Drake was absent from the command cabin. She would be in her quarters, Harper knew, although from what she now understood about the captain, those so-called unusual diurnal rhythms which required daytime sleep were undoubtedly an excuse for avoiding Harper's company.

After receiving a loving transmission from Niklaus over the privacy channel, and dispatching a message back, Harper went up to the observation deck. As she stepped off the ramp she looked around in amazement. Although equipped with the usual library and aural-visual access, the deck was definitely non-standard in its accoutrements. A huge earth-toned body-meld sofa, and two oversize chaises finished in sensuous gold fabric, faced the non-reflective windows. Harper sighed happily.

Except for her meals and an occasional mandatory status review of the spacecraft's basic systems, she spent the day on the deck curled up in the sofa, lost in spectacular coronas, shimmering veils of stardust, the blazing hues of star systems filling the windows.

Around seven o'clock that evening, as Harper finished her bouillabaisse, Drake appeared in the galley. Again Drake wore black pants and another high-collared shirt, this one scarlet. Again Harper was startled by her, unsettled by the masculine elements softened by feminine beauty. Recovering, she said wryly, "Good morning. Ready for breakfast?"

As she had last night, Drake drew a glass of tomato juice from the autoserv. "This will do," she replied expressionlessly. A pale hand resting flower-like on her hip, she sipped her juice. She studied Harper until Harper rose under the intensity of the gaze and disposed of her dinner receptacle.

"I'll be on the observation deck," she told Drake tersely. The psych probes might pronounce Drake sane, but she was *strange*.

"I'll join you shortly," Drake returned.

A tiny gesture of friendliness? Not likely. From the distance of that tone, from the look of the observation deck, Drake simply preferred to be there. Abruptly, Harper took her leave.

Several minutes later Drake entered the deck and reclined on a chaise, gracefully crossing her long legs. She had chosen the chaise across from where Harper sat on the sofa as if she meant to invite conversation, but she turned fully away to gaze out the windows. Harper looked at her with bold resentment. Drake was in her line of vision and disturbed her absorption in the spectacular vistas beyond the windows. And Drake's aloofness, her silence, disturbed for less tangible reasons. As Harper stared at her, she became gradually, unwillingly, absorbed in her.

Drake could be in her thirties or forties—perhaps even her fifties. Her skin, with its luminous, silken pallor, held no sign of age; but the dark eyes, with their weary, almost haunted intelligence, suggested that she had seen altogether too much. Drake's cap of fine dark hair, smoothed back over her ears, curled softly around the nape of her neck and over the top of her collar; a few unruly strands fell over her forehead. Her nose was thin and straight, a slight flare to the nostrils. The lips were cast delicately, the teeth interesting in their slight unevenness. Drake looked like a poetically handsome young man—or a boyish woman of intriguing beauty.

Feeling a pull on her own sexuality, stirred by the remote melancholy of Drake's face, the inviting texture of the dark hair, those strong yet fine hands, Harper reminded herself that Drake's body was the body of a woman. And she had never wished to touch or be touched by a woman. If Drake were a man...

Reminding herself of the patiently waiting Niklaus, Harper reflected that it was not much wonder Drake spent her in-port time cloistered within this spacecraft. Wherever she might venture, her striking beauty and ambiguous sexuality would arrest conversation, would compel attention no matter what the onlooker's sexual proclivities. It was also not much wonder that Drake would hold Harper herself at arm's length; Drake had been forced to endure lengthy contact with a woman in whom she had not the slightest emotional or sexual interest.

This journey, Harper groaned inwardly, would be interminable. She might as well be occupying *Scorpio IV* by herself unless she could somehow break through this woman's wall of isolation by establishing that she had no intention of making any demand of any kind.

She cleared her throat. "I can't imagine ever tiring of this." She gestured toward the windows. "I suppose you must be accustomed to it."

Drake turned to look directly at her. "The pleasure has never lessened."

The intense dark eyes compelled, and seemed suddenly dangerous, as if Harper could be drawn into their depths without possibility of release. Gathering, steeling herself against this disquieting woman, Harper offered, "I'm sure you've made great inroads in the ship's library."

Drake's face softened into a smile. "I've read everything."

Harper quickly recovered herself and smiled back, realizing that Drake was either joking or she had read only within limited fields of interest; there were half a million volumes stored in the spacecraft's memory. "How do you pass the time, then? What do you enjoy?"

"What do I enjoy," Drake repeated. She turned away again, but Harper knew she was contemplating her answer.

"I enjoy this," Drake finally responded, gesturing toward the grandeur beyond the windows. "I enjoy music." She tapped a control on the arm of her chaise, and Harper was immediately chilled by the keenly wrought grief of a solo violin. "And I enjoy...taking nourishment."

Harper gaped at her. She had yet to see Drake consume anything but tomato juice. But then in all probability she had installed an autoserv in her quarters. But still...Drake was reed slender, her flesh distributed with sparest economy over her tall frame. Autoserv controlled the balance of nutrients in the food taken from its self-replenishing banks, but did not govern the amount of intake; psych probes measured weight gain beyond the individual's established norm as an indicator of psychosis.

Drake was smiling, a maddeningly private smile. Too fascinated to feel resentment, Harper stared at her.

"Something else I enjoy," Drake said, "is learning about the individuals who join me on these voyages. I look forward to hearing about your life."

"That will take twenty minutes," Harper stated, making no pretense at modesty. Her life had taken on color and energy only since she had joined the Service.

Again Drake smiled. "We have one hundred and eighteen days before we achieve final orbit. You have twenty-seven entire years to tell me about between now and then."

"The twenty-seven years just aren't that interesting," Harper insisted, morose with her certainty.

"Perhaps not to you but they will be to me," Drake said in her low expressive tones. Again her intense gaze settled on Harper.

Whatever else Drake might be, Harper realized, she had to be very lonely. She gazed back at Drake. Her beauty seemed even more poetic than before.

* * *

For the past hour they had been sitting quietly, listening to a string quartet, watching the ever-changing spectacle transmute the view windows.

Drake broke the silence. "Tell me where you were born."

To Harper, the quiet had been companionable; and the question— this particular question—was distinctly unwelcome. "British Columbia," she answered crisply, hoping the unembellished reply would divert Drake to another topic.

Drake flicked a glance at her. "And where in British Columbia?"

Harper sighed. "New Alabama."

The fine, slightly curved brush strokes that were Drake's eyebrows moved upward. "A Trad settlement, is it not?"

"Yes. It's also the large part of my life that's not interesting."

"Your family, are they still there?"

Sighing again, Harper nodded. "They're happy to be there. I'm happy *not* being there. They're ashamed of me. I'm ashamed of them."

Drake got up from her chaise, moved to sit beside Harper. "Tell me about it. Tell me about your parents. Describe them."

She nodded again, less reluctantly. The eyes looking into hers were alert and interested. She could not shut off Drake's first attempt at communication. "My mother is a small woman, my father—"

"No. Describe them in detail. So I can *see* them. So I can see your life with them as well."

Held by Drake's dark gaze, Harper continued obediently, "My mother is fifty-three now. I have her eyes except mine are a lighter blue…"

Professing interest in the smallest detail of Harper's growing up years, Drake drew out reminiscence, her precise questions opening doors to memory Harper had closed off or forgotten existed. She had managed for the past ten years to avoid discussion and even thought of that pain-filled time when she had defied her parents, when she had scorned the Traditionalist doctrines of the militant settlements which had sprung up more than two centuries ago and to this day continued to attract colonists. The detailed recounting seemed to relieve a deep inner festering, and she spoke more and more willingly.

"It was my great-grandparents who moved there, when Montreal put in its free-trade spaceport. They packed up and left along with thousands of other Quebec families—"

Drake was nodding gravely. "And your own parents inherited all that xenophobia."

"Exactly. They thought an ancient convoluted mess like the Bible was sacred, they were afraid of the real sacredness of the entire living universe. My parents—all the Trads—have a desperate need to control some part of a world that continues to evolve all around them."

"We may dream of an unchanging present and a predictable future," Drake mused, "but real survival comes from adaptation. And the true secret is seeing the exact ways one must adapt..."

"The settlement finally judged me a non-conformist heretic," Harper continued in a rush of words, almost dizzy with the release of emotion. "But I'd been longing to escape from the time I was small..."

As she began to describe the childhood dreams of space and freedom which had been awakened by the drama and majesty of the Northern Lights, Drake interrupted her. "Enough for tonight. Tomorrow you can tell me more."

Harper looked at her chronometer in amazement. She had been talking nearly four hours. And suddenly she *was* tired. She was drained.

As she got up from the sofa she asked Drake curiously, "When do you usually turn in?"

"I always retire before six o'clock in the morning."

The next day Harper spent more than an hour in her quarters performing her entire repertoire of physical exercise, then passed the rest of the day on the observation deck, too enthralled with the brilliance beyond the windows to avail herself of the ship's library or any other distraction.

Again Drake appeared in the galley about seven o'clock, wearing a midnight blue shirt with her black pants. Harper realized that if Drake had indeed "retired" to her quarters before six this morning, she had remained there for better than half a standard day.

As Drake drew her usual beverage from the autoserv, Harper welcomed her with a smile. "You do consume something besides tomato juice?" she joked.

Drake looked at her icily. Her voice descended to an even chillier depth: "My personal habits are surely of no consequence."

Don't presume *anything*, Harper raged at herself as she shrugged mute apology. Just because she's interested in your life doesn't mean *anything* beyond that. "Perhaps I'll see you on the deck," she said evenly, and left the galley.

Moments later Drake appeared and sat beside her. Scant minutes afterward Harper was thoroughly immersed in relating memories of her Traditionalist schooling.

"Biblical voodoo," she pronounced in summary dismissal. "Ludicrous beliefs about universe creation and so many other irrationalities—you can't even imagine."

"I can indeed imagine," Drake stated in her resonant tones. "How did you come to question your indoctrination? Most people never do."

There was something besides acute perceptiveness in Drake's eyes—could it be admiration? Harper answered self-consciously, "The settlement's computers used data lockout, naturally. But anyone with half a brain could figure out how to bypass them and get into Earth's major libraries. I had half a brain."

"So you educated yourself enough to qualify for the Space Service. Amazing."

Admiration, definitely it was admiration in Drake's eyes. Warm with pleasure, Harper shrugged. "Not quite. I spent too much time indulging in novels, especially the famous ones from the nineteenth and twentieth centuries. I had to take potentiality tests and was lucky enough to finish in the top percentile for scientific aptitude. The Service's own institutions completed my education to Service specification."

"Tell me more," Drake said. "Tell me what you remember about the potentiality tests."

Why was she so interested in all this, Harper wondered. No one in her entire life had ever been interested in these nooks and crannies of her life. She said, "We've talked only about me. I'd like to know about you."

Drake shook her head, her eyes suddenly distant, shuttered.

Harper held out her hands in placating gesture. "Just a few basic questions. Like where you were born."

"In a village outside Bucharest. I want to hear the answer to my question about the tests."

"How old are you?" Harper persisted.

The slow rise and fall of Drake's shoulders clearly conveyed her inaudible sigh. She looked away, out the windows. "Eight hundred and twenty-two," she replied. "If I want to talk about myself, I will. I don't."

Then neither do I, Harper wanted to retort. But the desire was too strong to experience again what this woman had given her last night—the new and highly pleasurable sensation of someone consumingly interested in her.

She answered Drake's question. She answered many more questions about her education until late into that night, until Drake again sent her off to bed exhausted and emotionally depleted from the effort of recapturing the minutia of her life.

* * *

Over the next weeks Harper's waking hours fell into routine: the required systems monitoring and standard transmissions to Space Service Trade Liaison Headquarters; her meals and exercise regimen; exchanging communications with Niklaus; the observation deck. The hours were also spent in restless anticipation of Drake's appearance in the galley and the long, intense evening that would follow.

Drake had, Harper admitted, become an addiction. Worse than that, with each successive evening Drake's physical magnetism was pulling her ever further into its grip. The magnetizing force, she supposed, was Drake's androgynous beauty, but whatever the causative factor, what difference did it make? She was beguiled by the pale, idyllic beauty of that face, the profound intelligence of those eyes absorbing every single word she uttered.

It was absurd. And hopeless. And demeaning. Not to mention paradoxical. Drake had lavished hours of her time and the complete focus of her mind on Harper, yet had relinquished not one iota of her essential being. The spiteful speculation Harper had indulged in a month ago about Drake being sexually dysfunctional seemed only too correct: Drake's sensual response was given entirely to music and the beauty of the galaxy. Harper longed to touch that austere face, to reach some answering inner chord. But she could come no closer to Drake than she could to those stars beyond the view windows. And like those stars, Drake's hard beauty served to attract and then inflame anything venturing near...

In only these few weeks Niklaus had slipped from her thoughts, the daily message to him containing merely dutiful affection. She comforted herself that he would be there, loving and faithful, when she returned from this voyage, whereas Drake would be gone from her forever, a part of the coldly brilliant stars...

The sumptuous romanticism of a flute concerto filled the observation deck. Harper sat on the sofa, waiting, staring at Drake who reclined on her chaise, a hand on her knee, absorbed in the spectacular hues of reflection nebulae shimmering over a vast open star cluster—the same star system Harper had watched throughout her solitary afternoon. Finally Drake turned from the view windows, and Harper knew with a surge of excitement that the evening would now begin.

"Tell me about your friends," Drake said, getting up and moving toward her. "What are they like?"

"I'm pretty much a loner," Harper confessed, stirred by the litheness of the body within the white shirt and black pants. "A few people I'd term good buddies, the rest are just acquaintances."

"Sexual awareness," Drake said, sitting beside her. "When did that begin?"

It was a first venture into this subject area, and after mild surprise Harper decided that Drake was simply filling in blanks.

"Sexual awareness," she repeated, and grinned. "Probably around the age of seven. When I first understood that my gravest responsibility was preservation of my virginity. I got rid of the thing when I was twelve."

Harper was pleased; she had made Drake laugh before, but rarely.

Drake said, smiling, "You had many dreams when you were growing up. What were your sexual dreams?"

Suddenly and inexplicably uncomfortable, Harper took refuge in generality. "I dreamed mostly of sexual freedom. Of never being in a stifling relationship like my parents had. Escaping all those sexual rules assigned by the Trads..."

"Yes, but what kind of relationship, what kind of person did you dream of finding?"

Harper stiffened against discussing any of the men she'd chosen to be with, any of those emotionally sterile relationships. "I've always walked away from anyone who tried to interfere with what I wanted to do with my life."

"From what I know of you," Drake murmured, "I'd be very surprised if you didn't. When you were growing up, you surely dreamed of a sexual ideal. What was that ideal?"

Drake's dark gaze held her, pierced her. If she had ever before met someone who looked like Drake...

"I…" Harper searched for coherent thought. Her nipples tingled almost painfully into hardness, she felt heat within her thighs. "A gentle and very tender…friend."

"Who looked like…"

"Dark hair," she uttered, feeling the heat rise to her face. "Dark eyes." She tried to look away from Drake but could not, and knew that the desire closing up her throat was naked on her face.

Drake's hands taking hers—the first touch between them—unraveled her.

"What else." The eyes were mesmerizing, the voice hypnotic.

Harper swayed toward her as if bent by a wind. "A face…like yours."

Drake's hands released hers to grip her shoulders, to draw Harper to her.

Stunned, her body hammered by heartbeats, Harper slid her unbelieving arms around the slender body. Drake lowered her to the sofa, her lips a feather-light brushing of Harper's face. Harper arched as Drake's mouth came to her throat, as a velvet tongue began to stroke. She seized Drake's hair, imprisoned Drake's head between her hands and greedily absorbed with her lips the warm silk, the sculptured planes of the face so miraculously in her possession.

Drake's mouth sought hers, took hers. Harper slid her hands under Drake's shirt, then made a single sound as Drake's tongue entered her. Drake's hands momentarily held her face, then slid down to her throat, the fingertips caressing. Then Drake pulled open Harper's jumpsuit, held her bare shoulders.

Melted by the slow strokes of Drake's tongue, Harper shuddered under the hands that moved slowly down over shoulders to her breasts. The hands cupped firmly, the fingers immediately beginning a rhythmic rippling of her swollen flesh. Drake's mouth finally left hers to come again to her throat, and Drake's hands on her breasts squeezed, released, squeezed, released, until her breasts felt like bursting fruit. Drake slid her hands under her and clasped her hips. Then her nipples became a fierce sweet ache in Drake's mouth as Drake's hands on her hips squeezed, released, squeezed, released.

Drake raised her body and spread Harper's thighs fully open to kneel between them. Harper felt her wetness on Drake's palm, then writhed from the fingers that stroked her open. Overpowered by her need, she groaned as the fingers left her, watching feverishly as Drake brought those fingers to her mouth, tasted them.

"Oh so very lovely and so very wet." Drake's voice was thick, her heavy-lidded eyes an unfocused darkness of pleasure.

Then Drake was bending over her and Drake's fingers were sliding into her and filling her and Harper's hips rose as she closed rigidly around them. With a low moan Drake moved down to her. Drawing swift breaths, Harper gasped her ecstasy as the fingers stroked, the velvet tongue stroked. Stroked and stroked and stroked her to an incandescence of orgasm.

Drake eased her fingers from her. Weakly, Harper wound her fingers in Drake's hair to take her mouth away, but Drake grasped her hands, preventing her.

"I can't...again," Harper whispered, "not...after that. Not...for a while."

Drake took her mouth away. Her voice came in a murmur, from deep in her throat: "This next voyage will be as long as you could possibly wish." Her mouth came back to Harper, her tongue slid into her, began a slow circling.

Harper flung her hands up over her head, her body undulant, a rolling wave of desire spreading all the way up into her throat. She wanted the velvet tongue everywhere, endlessly.

A timeless interval later, Harper felt her body being lifted, carried, lowered into a place of blissful darkness. She was aware of a fluttering sound, a whisper of breeze. Then she became part of the darkness.

*　　*　　*

Awakening in her quarters, Harper rolled over and stretched in delicious, unthinking languor before she realized her nudity and the origin of her contentment.

It was late morning, her status confirmation report was due in shortly to Headquarters. She could not, as she usually did, wake up in leisurely fashion and use this first hour for her exercise regimen. Not that she needed exercise, she reflected wryly, not after her body had been so continuously and exquisitely wracked by sexual tension unlike anything she had ever known...

She climbed reluctantly out of bed, longing to have this time undisturbed to sort through the confusion of her thoughts.

Smoothing back the tangles of her hair, she smiled mockingly at her visage in the reflective wall of her quarters. So Drake was sexually dysfunctional, was she? If Drake had been any less dysfunctional, she, Harper, would not have survived the night.

Marveling at the euphoric lightness of her limbs, she examined herself from head to foot. She looked no different. Her body was its usual trim shape; there was no mark anywhere to signify any alteration in her. Yet there had been an alteration; she felt tangibly changed.

Cupping her breasts, she leaned closer to her reflection. The nipples were heightened in color; and they budded into hardness as she remembered how they had been savored in Drake's mouth. She inspected herself further: her vulva was an even more enhanced shade of pink. Heat flooded her along with memory, and colored all the surfaces of her skin.

Hastily she pulled on a jumpsuit, other memories of the night filtering into her. Drake had remained clothed; Harper had managed only to open her shirt. The breasts within that shirt had been small, their flesh soft and tender to her fingers, the nipples large, their firmness a constant whenever Drake's body had lain on hers. She had not been able to kiss those breasts. She had not been able to kiss or touch Drake intimately anywhere. Drake had completely overpowered her. Tonight all that would change.

*   *   *

As the morning ended and the afternoon wore on, as Drake did not appear, Harper's mood plummeted from anticipation to depression, then veered off into anger. Drake had been the initiator of last night's passion, the pure aggressor throughout. Therefore, by all logic it had been meaningful to her. And therefore she could have—should have—made an exception to her rigid routine and left her quarters to be with Harper. Harper had surrendered herself, Drake should understand that she *needed* the assurance of Drake's presence during this vulnerable aftermath…

To hell with her, Harper decided, and stalked off to her quarters. But as seven o'clock neared she could not remain there. She compromised by going up to the observation deck instead of to the galley.

Shortly afterward, when Drake entered the deck and walked to her chaise, Harper did her best to ignore her. Drake settled herself and did not speak; she did not look at Harper. Her eyes were distant and shrouded, as if their focus had turned entirely inward.

Harper looked at her in a fury of frustration. What could possibly be in this woman's unfathomable mind? What could the reason be for her unfathomable behavior? Nothing in the experience of her own life or in any fictional life she had ever read could account for this unique, inexplicable, utterly maddening woman.

She was struck by the thought that Drake was feeling her own vulnerability. Drake had no choice about who accompanied her on her voyages, but by the pitiless dictates of her lonely profession, she also had no choice—whatever her libido—about resisting a futureless emotional involvement with any of her passengers. If Drake had restrained herself behind a carefully constructed wall of self-protection, this would explain her hungered, tireless passion last night, and her withdrawal now...For that matter, it would explain *all* of Drake's behavior.

Buoyed by this possibility, Harper managed a smile and a neutral tone. "A month ago when you listed what you enjoyed, you didn't mention lovemaking."

Drake seemed to emerge from her self-absorption with effort. Her answering smile was slow and luminous. "Did I not?"

Momentarily disassembled by the renewed potency of Drake's beauty, Harper recovered herself and plunged ahead. "Last night—"

She was startled by the keening of an alarm.

"Code Two." Drake was already on her feet.

Following her from the deck, Harper was grateful that the two-note wail was not the continuously shrilling Code One signifying a major magnitude crisis. But this alarm was different from the other coded alarm signals periodically sounding throughout the craft, benign notifications of gravity force fluctuations or requests for fail-safe conformation of course changes, routine matters which Drake could and did monitor without emerging from her quarters. This alarm was ominous.

In the command cabin Drake swept a single glance over the monitor screens and announced tersely, "Breech in the aft deflection shield. It's widening."

The Code Two alarm became a Code One continuous shrill. Harper felt the hair rise on back of her neck. The shields were the vital energy force that protected the craft's surface. A breakdown could leave *Scorpio IV* exposed to a lethal bombardment of space debris...

Drake said, "Call up Robomechs AZ-niner-two and three. Robomech-four on standby."

Harper flung herself into her seat and initiated the start-up programs that would activate the robots. Drake had already cleared three screens and was leaning over the console, tapping keys. Then she stood with one hand on a hip, the other poised over the console, watching schematics flash past at split-second speed.

The hand over the console pounced, striking a key. "There, right there," she said with satisfaction. She continued to tap the key, rapidly magnifying a diagram and then freezing it on the center screen. "It's bad. The entire shield function is breaking down."

"Can it be repaired?" Harper was astonished by the calmness of her voice.

"Yes. I'll need Robomech-four."

"Right."

If the crisis had needed any further underscoring, the need for

Robomech-four had accomplished it.

Her head ringing from the Code One alarm, Harper entered the priority overrides that would channel all but basic life support computer functions into Robomech-four. Then she sat back. She had once observed in a laboratory setting the robot's dissection of the radioactive heart of a military cruiser's stardrive, three highly skilled technicians working in perfect synchrony to correlate and direct its awesome activities. There was no additional assistance she could possibly provide to Drake.

For the next hour she watched in rapt fascination as Drake, standing, her elegant body a stillness of tension, her eyes narrowed in concentration on the color changes transforming the frozen diagram on the center screen, worked the Robomech-four with nerveless surgical precision.

Finally, blessedly, the alarm cut off. Drake said distractedly, "Bring up Robomech-two for routine finish."

Minutes later, at a nod from Drake, Harper terminated all the robot programming sequences, returned the computer to its normal functioning.

She turned to Drake, words of relief and admiration on her lips. But she was unaware of the words she spoke; she was staring at the first clear, readable emotion she had seen in Drake's face: exhilaration.

"You didn't mention another item on that list of what you enjoy," Harper told her. "You love using your ability."

Drake said gravely, "It is the one acceptable power I have."

Harper watched the exhilaration fade from Drake's face. She stared into the depths of the dark eyes, chilled to see again what she had first seen weeks ago: emptiness, a haunted grief.

Drake looked away from her. "Come back to the observation deck," she said softly.

Moments later, Harper waited in indefinable, trembling expectancy as Drake sat on the sofa beside her.

Drake said, "Last night is between us now. But I want our time together to continue as before. I want you to talk to me as before."

Frustrated to the verge of tears by the riddle of this woman, Harper whispered, "I can't."

Drake sighed. "Flowers accept rain without questioning its source or meaning. Is it so difficult to simply accept what happens between us until our voyage ends?"

Harper said bitterly, "So last night you were the heaven-sent rain falling on me."

"Not heaven-sent," Drake replied evenly.

"Last night had no meaning to you?"

"To me it means that there is more between us now."

Harper said vehemently, "I need something from you. *Something.*"

"I can give only what I am able to give."

"What you're *willing* to give."

"For me it is the same."

Harper closed her eyes and turned away from her.

"Talk to me if you can," Drake said gently. "For a while. Will you, Harper?"

She thought in despair, I can either continue with her as before or try to stay away from even the sight of her for the next three and a half months. "All right," she sighed. "What do you want me to talk about tonight?"

"I think...places where you lived after you left the Trads. The houses, the cities."

She could not afterward remember what she had been saying when the pale beautiful face neared hers, filling her vision. Only that she had faltered into silence, a brushfire of desire enveloping her.

Then Drake's lips were caressing her face. But with all her strength she held Drake away, she took the gray shirt in her hands and opened it. "I want to see you."

Drake allowed her only briefly to gaze at the long sweeping lines of her body, the lean thighs, the delicate black triangle between. Then Drake's mouth came to hers and Drake took off Harper's jumpsuit. And Harper's body was covered by silk of such astonishing softness and warmth that she could scarcely breathe. Could she possibly feel like this to Drake? Could some other woman possibly feel as Drake did to her?

Drake's unhurried, exploring hands added new dimension to her desire and intensified it. Holding Harper's face, kissing her, she drew Harper's tongue into her and circled its tip. Body memory of the night before returned with such force that Harper surged into her, desire flaring into passion. She moaned her want but Drake pressed the softness of her body sinuously into her and her tongue began another slow rhythm that brought other body memory, fresh and paralyzing. Wrapping her arms and legs around Drake, fused to the nirvana of her body, Harper abandoned herself to Drake's will, to an eroticism that became the very edge of orgasm.

Sometime later Drake moved down between her legs and the edge of orgasm became its measureless fiery heart.

Harper again found herself lifted, carried, lowered.

She clung to Drake. "Stay with me," she mumbled.

"I cannot."

"Till I sleep…"
And then she was asleep.

*　*　*

In the next two weeks Harper's existence fell into a disjointed pattern. Service Headquarters had demanded extensive debriefing in order to perform their own analysis of the deflection shield failure and activation of Robomech-four; and with point-of-no-return only thirteen days hence, they had placed go-ahead for the voyage on standby.

"Cupidity, duplicity, stupidity…" Harper muttered the same litany of imprecations every morning as she pulled her unwilling body out of bed to oversee transmission of yet another mass of data on *Scorpio IV's* status. Certainly she and Drake would continue this voyage and load their precious cargo of Antares asteroid crystals—and those officious morons at Headquarters knew it. The shield failure had merely given them license to subject her to the bureaucratic minutiae that brightened their tedious, gravity-bound lives.

However unnecessary and monotonous her increased workload might be, she was grateful for its minor distractions. Her unoccupied hours without Drake stretched out blankly, interminably. She consumed her meals with indifference and because she knew she must. She passed the rest of her time meticulously grooming herself, or in dreaming contemplation of the blazing universe beyond the view windows, her mind burning with its own images, her memories of Drake.

With each successive evening, as Drake appeared on the observation deck, she seemed more dramatically beautiful, more dynamic, powerful, magnetizing. With each successive evening Harper succumbed more compliantly to the whims and dictates of Drake's mind, divulging any detail of her life that would hold Drake's complete focus—all of it a part of the waiting for the moment when Drake would reach for her, when she would slide the clothing over Harper's shoulders, when the purest part of the night would begin.

She had tried to give back some measure of her ecstasies one evening before Drake's hands and mouth once more turned her into flame. "This," Drake had told her, her eyes smoldering as she again drew Harper to her, "is everything I require."

In the small part of herself still capable of objective thought, Harper knew desperately that along with her body she was yielding her will, her identity, perhaps even her mind. She had become a voluptuary in thrall to her nightly consummations in Drake's arms, thinking of no past beyond the bliss of the night before, of no future beyond the night ahead.

It was small comfort that each night Drake's own passion did not cease until Harper lay in insensate repletion. She was Drake's sexual pawn.

On that earlier voyage to Orion she had been subtly but profoundly affected by the alien vastness of space. Could this be a different manifestation of that same neurosis? After entry into the Antares asteroid belt, when Drake was fully involved with the problems of bringing back to life a disabled *Scorpio IV*—perhaps then she could establish some sort of grip on her saner self...

* * *

As *Scorpio IV* approached within a light year of the Antares asteroid belt, Service Headquarters signaled its go-ahead just as Harper had known it would. Rendezvous would occur at twenty hundred hours.

Harper pulled on the close-fitting white coverall she would wear in zero gravity, apparel designed to adhere to any surface of the ship and prevent her from floating as helplessly as a dust mote. Like all Space Service recruits, she had undergone extensive periods of sensory deprivation, and her deep space training had also included weightlessness, a curious and amusing oddity when experienced short-term, but which had produced severe physical and psychological trauma in space-age pioneers during the first interplanetary voyages.

She moved awkwardly toward the command cabin, irrationally annoyed by the pull on the soles of her feet, the slowness of her progress. She was well aware of the source of her ill-temper: there would be no lovemaking this night—and subsequent nights as well; Drake would be fully occupied with the navigational challenges of her spacecraft.

Drake was seated in her command chair, eyes fixed on the narrow navigation windows that revealed the Antares asteroid belt, a glowing necklace illuminated by its far distant but spectacularly fiery mother star. Like Harper, Drake also wore a coverall, hers black.

"Only minutes remain for any additional transmissions," Drake stated without looking at her.

"Right," Harper acknowledged, forgiving the officious tone; Drake was immersed in computations for final approach. Before the forces in the asteroid belt could play havoc with the spacecraft's guidance systems, Drake would fully shut down its power and make use of the remaining forward thrust to drift them into a thick, crystal-rich segment of the belt. All was in readiness for the period when she and Drake would be in partial sensory deprivation and dependent on the ship's accumulated oxygen, when *Scorpio IV* would be the equivalent of a dead, drifting shell.

Having earlier completed her transmissions, including one to Niklaus, Harper now sat in quiet excitement that contained a thrill of fear. On the screens she watched each storage hatch slowly flex open in preparation for receiving the asteroid crystals; she watched through the navigation windows the unfolding drama of their approach.

Drake's calm voice penetrated the quiet: "Ten seconds to full shut down." She pulled a light mesh body restraint across herself, as did Harper.

Even though she knew, had been fully trained to expect it, Harper was stunned by the bright cabin's plunge into blackness. Then the utter silence—the silence, she thought, of the grave. Her straining eyes slowly adjusted; finally the orange-red, fluorescein-imbued room emerged into dim, eerie visibility. Drake's body in its black coverall was part of the darkness, but her face was a pale oval in the ghostly white light cast by Antares. The silence quickly became an aching in Harper's ears and she sucked in her breath to hear its sound.

A sigh of satisfaction came from Drake. "Not a trace of yaw."

"I'm glad," Harper said fervently, recoiling from the thought of *Scorpio IV* pitching continuously from side to side throughout all the hours of free fall.

"You should be," Drake said dryly. "You'd be throwing up by now."

I suppose you wouldn't, Harper thought, more amused than annoyed by Drake's arrogance. Her white-sleeved arm was floating in front of her; she steered it to the console and smiled as she tried to make her fingernails drum; the hand kept floating upward. Her preeminent physical sensation was the adhesive clothing and restraint mesh holding her body into her chair.

She stared out the navigation windows as *Scorpio IV* closed swiftly on the glowing asteroid belt. Their blind, silent spacecraft could as well be one of those aerodynamic paper airplanes she had constructed as a child and cast into the air currents. She continued to watch in speechless awe as the mysterious asteroid belt slowly gathered her and Drake into its radiance and swallowed them whole, as they became part of a thickening world of swirling blue-white crystal, brilliantly glittering jewels colliding soundlessly, harmlessly, against the surfaces of the ship.

"Drake…" Harper breathed.

"Yes. It is truly beautiful."

Drake's voice came from above her; she had risen to stand beside Harper in the spectral darkness. Drake's face seemed to float beside her as she leaned down to unfasten Harper's restraint. "For now nothing can be done for my ship. Come to me," she said softly, and took Harper's hands.

Her mouth dry, Harper allowed herself to be pulled out of her chair and into Drake's arms, against the substantiality of her body. "Some of our senses need not be deprived," Drake murmured, and her mouth came to Harper's.

She became ever weaker in Drake's arms, immobilized by the swift thrusts of Drake's tongue. Drake opened Harper's coverall, began to slide it from her. Staring into the austere, ethereally beautiful face so close to hers, her pulse pounding in her ears, Harper yielded to what she knew would be ultimate helplessness.

Naked, held to Drake only by a clasped hand, floating like an air bubble, she watched her white clothing drift away somewhere into the black.

Drake pulled Harper to her, clasped Harper's body to hers. Drake had not removed her coverall but had opened it to expose her body; and Harper felt only the exquisite surface contact of Drake's silken skin, felt her breasts only as they touched the warm softness of Drake, as they were caressingly held in Drake's hand; she felt her lips only as Drake savored them, felt her mouth only from Drake's tongue inside her. As Drake's fingers slid slowly, tantalizingly over her thighs and then between her legs, she felt her wetness on Drake's fingers, felt her weightless body swell in a ripening of desire that became a strange, new, keenly throbbing ache.

Murmuring thickly, indecipherably, Drake moved Harper's body away from her so that it again floated free. She captured Harper's hips, raised Harper to her mouth.

All feeling in her entire body was focused between her legs, fused to the slow tongue strokes, each a lightning strike of sensation. In the red-etched, black command cabin she writhed uncontrollably, helpless as a windblown flame.

"Please," she gasped, "oh please..."

But the strokes only gradually quickened. Anchored to Drake's merciless mouth, her gyrating body rose above Drake's head and then fell back down, then rotated from side to side. She felt the wetness pour from her as Drake's mouth became more avid. She approached a brilliance of orgasm as if she would fall into a star. And then the brilliance consumed her.

Harper was drawn down, into Drake's arms. "So beautifully wonderfully wet..." Drake's voice was an intoxicated whisper.

Soon afterward Drake held her against a wall, Harper's feet floating off the floor. "The human body is a miracle," Drake murmured, her warm face buried in Harper's breasts. "In new circumstances its nerve paths simply seek new connections..." Sometime later she floated

Harper free from the wall, and again lifted her. Her tongue inside the writhing, moaning Harper, Drake moaned her own joy.

Harper awakened disoriented, then quickly realized that she was still in the command cabin. Drake, she remembered, had placed her naked in a chair, lowering the chair's back. Her clothing was beside her, the restraint mesh around her. She could not see that Drake was gone, but knew infallibly that she was, that she would be in her own quarters.

She donned her coverall, made her awkward, painstaking way through the eerie fluorescence to her quarters, to the galley; then she returned to the command cabin and the chair where Drake had left her.

Cloaked by the darkness, soothed by it, she removed her coverall and again fastened herself down with the restraint mesh. She stretched sensuously. So this was sensory deprivation. If the Space Service bureaucrats could see her now...

With no sense of time passing she gazed contentedly, languorously at the jewel-laden world swirling beyond the windows, its treasures drifting unawares into the ship's storage containers. She wondered if she could have dreamed her memories, those impossible sensations of the night before.

Drake spoke her name from across the room. "How very lovely you look," she added, amusement in her soft tones.

How can she possibly see me from where she is, Harper wondered, straining to make out any image of her. And then the thought passed from her as Drake reached her, bent down to unfasten the restraint. Harper floated up and into her arms.

Drake murmured, "We have only a few more hours... Then I must take care of my ship..."

Harper learned that she had not dreamed any of the sensations of the night before.

*   *   *

Working from the lowest possible power generation, her hands translucent over the faintly illuminated, blinking console, Drake slowly built up data and set data locks, correlating larger and larger segments into the exponentially expanding design that would bring *Scorpio IV* back to life. Harper, sitting beside her in bemused incomprehension, responded to an occasional tersely worded order and performed the equivalent of handing an implement to an architect.

As the hours passed, as Drake became more immersed in the complexities of her work, her orders ceased. Harper dozed fitfully in her chair, then slept.

The leaden weight of her body and the painfully bright command cabin lights awakened her. Feeling pressed into her chair, she squeezed her watering eyes shut. When she was able to focus, the chronometer told her it was mid-morning. Beside her Drake continued to work, seemingly unaffected by the renewed gravity and light; but her face was drawn, etched in concentration and exhaustion.

Harper asked in concern, "Is there something I can—"

"Yes. Either I calibrate the major systems at one sitting or I must begin all over again. Leave the bridge immediately. Do not return unless I signal for your assistance."

Smarting with anger and humiliation, Harper made her way to her quarters. She donned normal clothing, then wrathfully stalked up to the observation deck. She watched, standing with her arms crossed, the swarming crystals. Her eyes burning from the endlessly varied bright patterns, her injured feelings unsoothed, she sat down on Drake's chaise and distracted herself with *Jane Eyre* from the ship's library.

It was late in the afternoon when a slight vibration under her feet became a hum and gathered strength; the ship's stardrive was beginning its rise to full capacity. Unwillingly, and only as a matter of what she perceived to be her military duty, she marched down the ramp and looked in unobserved on Drake. She gaped in astonishment.

Drake was slumped over her console, her feebly moving hands claw-like, her face deathly pale. Gone were all traces of her magnetism, her power, her overwhelming beauty. She looked gaunt and debilitated, as if she had aged decades.

Harper blurted her shock. "Drake—"

"Leave me." The words were hissed and vehement. "Our lives depend on it."

Harper climbed numbly up to the observation deck. Astonished and terrified, chilled to her marrow with the realization that she might actually have to fulfill her ultimate mission on this voyage, she scanned the status monitors.

All systems were approaching readiness, she saw with relief. Communications were still down, but contact with Headquarters was not essential if it fell on her shoulders to bring *Scorpio IV* out of the asteroid belt and to safety. After she cleared the danger zone she could simply trigger a signal that would pinpoint their position and effect rescue of herself and Drake.

She comforted herself with the likelihood that Drake's illness, serious as it appeared, was acute exhaustion curable by sheer release from the massive outpouring of physical and psychic energy necessary to achieve the resurrection of *Scorpio IV*. Since Drake's diurnal habits and patterns indicated her need for a lengthier restorative period than for most individuals, she had perhaps been doubly affected by this violation of her bodily needs...

As Harper sat in quiet analytical assessment of what she had just witnessed, her senses suddenly sharpened into alertness. Warily, she got up from the sofa. Later she would not be certain if she had heard a sound over the rising hum of the stardrive, or if a depth of extrasensory awareness had compelled her to the observation deck ramp.

Drake, her back to Harper, was in the corridor below. Sagging against the wall, she lurched toward her quarters, her black-clad figure doubled over by the agony of her effort, a straining hand sliding along the wall as if groping there for support.

Harper had taken several automatic steps down the ramp before the rigidity of Drake's posture, the desperate, granite determination of her struggle, told Harper that any attempt at assistance would be rebuffed with greater fury than any of her earlier offers of help. Drake had ordered her away unless signaled, and Drake had only to touch the chronometer on her wrist to summon her. But still, from the look of her...Uncertain, Harper waited at the top of the ramp, anxiously watching, poised to run.

Just before Drake reached the open portal of Harper's quarters, she paused, straightened with shuddering effort, craned to look within.

She thinks I might be in there. She doesn't want me to see her.

Then Harper saw Drake's black-clad figure crouch. Saw her body seem to contract, to dissolve into a nebulous dark bulk that shrank precipitously. Saw a small creature with sharply pointed, membranous wings gather itself and flutter weakly, erratically down the corridor.

At the portal to Drake's quarters the creature extended its wings fully, flapped once, twice, and became the crouching, collapsing Drake. The portal to Drake's quarters opened to reveal a blackness deep as liquid ink. Drake was absorbed into the blackness, the portal sealing behind her.

Her legs unable to hold her, Harper sank down onto the ramp.

If she needed clear evidence that she had lost even a tenuous grip on reality, here was the proof. Her body might survive this voyage, but her sanity had disintegrated.

Climbing shakily to her feet, Harper managed to reach the sofa where she again collapsed. She stared out into the blue-white crystals, their volatile swirling like the maelstrom within her. She focused on controlling her breathing, on reducing the rapid thudding of her heart. Then she concentrated on seeking some coherency of thought.

Whence had come such bizarre hallucinations? Perhaps she had never really recovered from a childhood filled with tales of the hell-spawned demons the Trads blamed for every evil in the universe. Or perhaps this was a manifestation of her preferred childhood reading—scary goblins and dragons and assorted ghouls.

She gazed at the library fax, still lighted from her earlier reading, a solace to her emotional tumult. There was rationality of one kind on this ship: the rigorous, unchanging printed word.

A superlatively controlled and rational woman like Drake surely would not welcome among her half million volumes any texts relating to Earth folklore. But perhaps there were general references, perhaps she could trigger some memory that would help trace the threads of this psychosis...

Harper entered:

Earth folklore

Werewolves, ghouls.

Unable to make her fingers transcribe the one word that was emblazoned in her mind, she added:

And all related entries.

The library responded:

All subject entries cross-referenced to major heading:

Vampires.

The hair rose on the back of Harper's neck. With a tremor she entered:

Display major heading.

The library responded:

Major heading: Vampires

14729 entries

Designate desired sequence.

Again Harper collapsed on the sofa. After a lengthy period of slow breathing to reduce a measure of her panic, she entered:

Vampires, classic characteristics.

Afterward she used a longer period of slow breathing, lying back on the sofa and closing her eyes to marshal all her resources. Then she sat up and considered what she had learned, and her observations of Drake and her ship.

Vampire legend held that the creatures could transform themselves into certain animal forms, most classically into bats. Aside from today's inconceivable events, she had seen a fluttering shape her first night on board, and after lovemaking with Drake had again heard fluttering and even felt the sensation of a breeze—impossibilities on a spacecraft.

Drake had been able to see her with the ship plunged into darkness. Darkness was the natural habitat of the vampire, and Drake spent better than half of each twenty-four hour period enclosed in her quarters. Drake's quarters were pitch black.

The unnatural brightness of *Scorpio IV* resulted in no shadows anywhere from any object, any individual. Masterful concealment for a vampire—because vampires did not cast a shadow.

Vampires could not be about in the daytime without severe diminishing of their powers, and they would die in direct exposure to the sun. Drake's demand for solitude as her strength and powers waned, her desperate struggle to reach the safety of her quarters—all had occurred in what would be late afternoon, Earth-time, and in proximity of a major star, Antares.

Vampires did not reflect an image in a mirrored surface. Except in Harper's own quarters, there were no reflective surfaces of any kind on the ship. Anywhere.

Vampires could be the most hypnotically erotic of creatures, but they did not require conventional sex. They did not eat conventional food; the bloodlust of feeding completely satisfied all bodily and erotic urges…

Harper sat perfectly still. *What do you enjoy,* she had asked Drake. And Drake had answered: *I enjoy…taking nourishment.*

Harper fled to her quarters, frenziedly ripping off her clothing as she ran. Again and again she scrutinized every inch of her skin in the reflective wall. There were no marks anywhere, none at all.

Her relief was only momentary. If Drake fit other classic criteria, why would she seek prolonged sexual encounters without fulfillment of her need for blood? It made no sense. Maybe, Harper thought dismally, maybe she had conjured everything—including her physical experiences, all those hours in Drake's arms. No. That was impossible. Hallucinating was one thing, but she could not possibly have imagined the ecstasies of Drake's passionate mouth on her, those very specific memories.

Wait a minute. She *had* seen Drake in the act of consuming food…

Still naked, she raced from her quarters to the galley. She drew a container of tomato juice, and with a shaking hand smelled the contents. With a relieved sigh she dipped in a finger, then stopped as the dripping finger neared her lips. Autoserv could form specific ingredients to taste and smell like any number of foods. This tomato juice might yet be...

Harper hurled the container into the decomp and fled back to her quarters.

Maybe Drake drank that so-called tomato juice, then indulged her erotic wants with Harper, thus satisfying both hungers separately but fully. Or perhaps she had simply used her sexual magnetism with cold calculation—to dull Harper's perceptions and suspicions. That would be why Drake had been the tireless aggressor in their lovemaking, and Harper its pleasure-blind recipient. Or perhaps Drake was waiting for this time when they were in the asteroid belt and cut off from all communication, perhaps this was when she would make love for the final time and in its aftermath dine lavishly on the freshly flowing blood of one supine, blissfully comatose Lieutenant T. M. Harper...

Harper leaped to her feet and resealed her door, setting in a new privacy code. Then she sat down heavily on her bed.

There was no escape. Drake would simply run computer sequences until the correct portal-opening code came up. And even if the ship's communications system was at this moment operative, what could be more ludicrous than to transmit to Headquarters a message that she was trapped in outer space with a vampire? And after they had finished laughing, after Drake had finished laughing as well, Drake would take her final satisfactions, then dump Harper's drained corpse out a hatch and report her lost in space, a victim of suicide. And heaven knew Headquarters would believe it—insanity and suicide had never been uncommon in the Service despite the psych probes...

Harper glanced at her chronometer. It was almost nineteen hundred hours, Drake's usual time to appear. In so depleted a state she surely would not be leaving her quarters tonight—not until she had recovered sufficiently to guide *Scorpio IV* from the asteroid belt.

From her bedside console Harper again called up the ship's library. Again she consulted *Vampires, characteristics,* and studied the text for some time. With a sigh she turned off the fax and lay back, hands behind her head.

Certainly there were ways to defend herself. She merely needed to plunge a wooden stake into Drake's heart, or cut off her head. Unfortunately, spacecraft were not equipped with wooden stakes or implements with which to dispatch someone's head. Drake would also have a very serious problem if Harper could figure out a way to find and destroy her coffin. Or there was the Trad religious rite—stalking a quailing Drake with a cross clutched in her hand until Drake leaped out a hatch, grateful to escape so horrifying an object. Or she could perhaps keep Drake at bay by wearing a necklace of garlic cloves—except that compatibility rules had placed garlic on the restricted list of allowable spacecraft edibles.

Harper had long since given vent to laughter which turned into wild hysteria.

She had to be crazy. Or was she crazy? She had to know. Because she had to do something.

* * *

Knowing she could not sleep, unable to bear the confinement of her quarters, Harper went up to the observation deck. She again called up the ship's library and the subject haunting her thoughts. After a time she began to pace.

"Good evening, Harper."

Whirling, she stared incredulously. She had to be hallucinating. The gaunt, desperately weak Drake of only four hours ago had vanished, to be replaced by the Drake of before, clad in her usual black pants and an emerald shirt—a beautiful, vital, regal Drake with all of her strength and magnetism restored.

Drake carried a container of tomato juice. She sipped from it, and then said quietly, "Once my work is finished I need only a few hours of rest. My recuperative powers are quite strong."

Her eyes fixing on the drink in Drake's hand, Harper thought: *Or is the real truth that it's nighttime now, and the night is your time...*

"Minimal work needs to be accomplished," Drake continued, "and we will be ready for departure."

That slightly accented voice...Drake is European, she's from a village near Bucharest...

"Are you well?" inquired Drake, her dark eyes narrowing.

"Am I well," Harper repeated. She watched Drake walk to her chaise, the strides easy and graceful.

Either I'm crazy or I'm not. And either way, at this point I have nothing to lose...

She took a deep breath. "Are you familiar with the name Bram Stoker?"

Drake did not change expression. "A nineteenth century historian."

"A nineteenth century novelist," Harper corrected her. "Author of a novel popular well into the twenty-first century."

"A historian," Drake countered with cool emphasis. "And a most limited one at that. He recorded in fictional form what glimmerings he knew of an entire species." She added, "I possess extensive knowledge in this area."

"Yes." Harper gestured to the lighted fax and then clasped her hands tightly together to prevent them from shaking. "I found thousands of references in the ship's library."

Drake studied Harper, her eyes an opaque darkness.

Harper thought of an enduring nineteenth century short story in which a man chose one of two fateful doors. In this situation it was not a matter of the lady or the tiger; it could only be both...

"I have come to believe," Harper said, her voice soft with the desperate truth of her words, "that either you are a...a member of that species Bram Stoker wrote about, or I am insane."

"I see." Drake's voice was mild. "On what do you base your...belief?"

"A lot of small things," Harper whispered. "Things about your behavior, and this ship. But mostly..." She closed her eyes for a moment. "I saw you—or I think I saw you—turn into a...bat."

Under Drake's narrowed, piercing gaze, Harper sank onto the sofa, her legs unwilling to support her.

Then Drake said, "Basic self-protection would dictate that I agree with your suggestion of insanity. But I cannot allow you to believe you have gone mad."

Able only slowly to absorb the stunning implication of Drake's words, Harper looked away from the pale face and the intense eyes. She tried to speak and failed, tried again: "How can you possibly be a...a..."

"Vampire," Drake supplied.

Harper focused on the emerald color of Drake's shirt, a jewel-like vividness against the surreal blue-white crystalline swirl in the view windows. She said, almost pleadingly, "I must be crazy. How can you be a starship captain and a...vampire?"

"I was born with considerable innate intelligence which I have sometimes been able to make use of during the eight hundred and twenty-two years of my existence."

She felt as if her mind had been set adrift, away from any mooring to coherent thought. "Uh, you mean you were born in the year...in..." Her mathematic acuity had deserted her.

"Seventeen sixty-seven," Drake said. "More than a century before Bram Stoker wrote *Dracula.*"

"How...how could..."

"How did I become as I am?"

Stricken mute, Harper nodded.

Drake shifted her gaze to the fax. Her face hardened. "Stoker painted his dark brush over all of my species, but no writer of either truth or fiction could possibly portray the vileness of the creature..."

She looked again at Harper. "In my village I lived with my husband and his niece. I was twenty-seven then. My husband was an old man, and infirm. His niece and I were lovers. It was an arrangement quite common in those times.

"Late one night Nadja and I were in the garden. Had we not been so deeply in embrace we would have heard and escaped our intruder. He bludgeoned me unconscious." The voice was expressionless. "He took the blood from Nadja right there in our garden. I later learned that she perished under his blows beforehand, and thus escaped the vampire contagion—she rests peacefully and forevermore in her grave.

"Me he carried away with him. He had bound me, and the next night, when he rose from his earthen place, he satisfied his wants in a loathsome fashion quite beyond all your imagining."

Harper, her eyes riveted on Drake, was unable to speak had she wanted to.

"He left me bound still, and barely living. The following night he came to me again and this time his appetites rendered me lifeless. But of course I later rose from the earthen mound beside him—a creature like him. He expected that I would welcome his bestowal of another existence after death. And like most men, particularly of that time, he had presumed that regardless of my screams or my struggle, in actuality I had welcomed his ravages."

Drake drew a leg up, clasped a hand over a knee. "It was only a matter of careful planning before I was able, early one morning, to drive a stake through him. I did so quite slowly—he was bound securely enough to nullify his great strength, and was as helpless to me as I had been for him. Then I dragged his disgusting remains outside to await the cleansing rays of the sun."

For some time there was silence; Drake appeared immersed in this particular memory. Then she said, "During those times existence of my species was at its most difficult. Vampire hordes lay nighttime siege to entire villages. And those villagers foolish enough to venture from their locked homes, or to give unwitting admittance to my kind, met a grisly fate that added yet more undead to our ranks. The church denied our existence as the heretical superstition of ignorant peasants, and government officials, obedient to the church, refused to send soldiers. In daytime the desperate villagers marauded the entire countryside seeking us, destroying us where we slept. At night they came out in mobs, with torches and axes and stakes, to encounter us directly—in defiance of our nighttime powers. They took terrible casualties in those battles, but they further thinned our ranks. I maintained my own existence by taking my needs from among the villagers newly dead."

She paused to study Harper. "You do not shudder at such details."

Harper, who had been shuddering internally, said with difficulty, "It seems an agonizing…It seems you…lived as you could."

Drake's faint smile instantly faded. "Always I have existed as I could. After the battles were over and the vampire hordes destroyed, I left the cave where I had concealed myself during the daylight hours. I possessed sufficient androgyny to conceal my true sex, and in those days it was essential that I do so in order to travel safely. And I soon learned to endure the excruciating pain of transforming my human body to mammalian form when necessary. It had become quite clear to me how I must live if I wished to maintain my existence."

She gazed at a point somewhere over Harper's shoulder. "I became a presence on virtually every field where men clashed in battle. There was no war whose inhuman suffering I did not witness."

In dawning understanding Harper whispered, "You mean from the eighteenth century you—"

"I witnessed carnage beyond your worst nightmares, on the soils of every land. I was present in America during the grossly inhuman slaughter of your Civil War; I was with American soldiers in all your foreign wars. I was at Verdun, Dunkirk, Hiroshima, Kuwait, Moscow…There was not a moment during those centuries when I could not find sustenance from the newly dead on some nation's battlefields."

Harper asked numbly, "You were never discovered? Suspected?"

"I was cloaked always by darkness. And for the dead in battle, no examination is ever made of them except for the obvious death-dealing wounds."

Harper uttered, "Were there…others of you?"

"Yes. There was vast provender, more than enough for us all."

Harper closed her eyes. "Then how many of you…are there?"

"I have no way of knowing." Drake shrugged. "For very good reasons I believe that only the fittest of us ever continue to survive. And we have learned there is safety in numbers—small numbers. We have also learned to be exceedingly clever at concealment—so much so that we are mostly invisible to one another as well."

Harper stared at her. "All those years, those decades, all these centuries…you've spent them…alone?"

"Not always." Drake sighed. "I met women, yes. Some I grew very close to. Some I believe loved me." She seemed to reflect over, to choose her words. "For endless years I touched none of them, allowed none to touch me. Having never forgotten the sight of others like me in their frenzied feeding upon the living, I dared not trust what the touch of living flesh might cause in me."

Harper inhaled slowly. What had the touch of her own living flesh caused in Drake?

"Then I returned to my country. I had not come back since..." After a moment Drake continued, "But in the year twenty twenty-one I had to return. And, as you know, I returned as mourner."

Harper nodded somberly at Drake's allusion to the "limited" East-West engagement waged over the hapless, innocent buffer countries of Eastern Europe, a soul-searing catastrophe which had begun to heal only a century or so ago.

"With the borders sealed, I entered from the Black Sea as a medical volunteer. Hundreds of millions were dead, but tens of thousands were still living, awaiting death from the irreversible chemicals in their bodies...

"It was in my village that I met Eva. She was but twenty-three years old, and the virulence lay gathering within her—but she was filled with the vibrant life, the innocence, the hopefulness of a child. She was to me a mirror image of my dearest Nadja, and amid all that devastation our love grew like a miraculous flower...

"The vampire legends had lingered in the villages of my country. Eva had grown up with them. Her clear, unsophisticated insight penetrated my defenses...she instinctively knew what I was. She came to me for love and would not hear of my fears, would not countenance danger. Afterward, when her illness struck, I gave her what strength I could to cushion her terrible, bewildered grief over her mortality, and when the time came I eased her path into death, having already given in to her wish for the vampire kiss, for life afterward with me."

The vampire kiss. . . Involuntarily, Harper placed a hand over her heart.

Drake looked down at her own hands, turned them over, examined them. "It is as I told you, Harper—for my species it is survival of only the very fittest. Eva could not bear the way we had to exist. Our wholly nocturnal lives, the secrecy, the hiding, the constant movement to protect ourselves, our need of that very specific sustenance, the entire dark nether world of our lives. Once, she was shut away by the authorities in Chile—she had been found wandering at night in a state of mental collapse. It was very difficult for me to obtain her release before she perished under their unwitting hands. But it was soon after that that one morning she walked out into the sunlight. I know she wished to protect me from her increasingly dangerous fragility, but I believe she had also come to need the peace of death far more than my love. We had been together nine years."

"I'm sorry," Harper murmured, "I'm truly sorry."

Drake nodded acknowledgment. "Her death drastically weakened my own emotional structure. Eventually I resumed my nomadic and solitary life, and thereafter, when I met a woman who found me desirable, I gave her nothing. Nothing. Finally she would drift away as I knew she would, leaving me again to myself."

Harper was pierced by the poignance of these revelations which served also to explain Drake's behavior with her. Never would she trade one year of her natural span for any number of years of Drake's half-life...She murmured, "I consider myself a loner, but I couldn't bear such loneliness as yours."

Drake gave her a smile of melancholy warmth. "I judge you to be independent-minded and courageous. One day an individual will love and respect that strength...You're very young, Harper, with a fierce grip on life. Tenacity kept me living too—at first. But during those terrible early years, I was certain I would simply walk into the sunlight one morning and put an end to it.

"Then I discovered something outside myself and virtually unknown to a woman born of my time: art. And with that art came maturation of my intellect. At various times throughout the centuries I have been a musician, philosopher, historian, sculptor, writer, artist— disappearing and changing my profession when too much fame or public scrutiny forced me to do so. And then late in the twenty-first century I discovered the challenges of advanced space-age technology..." Drake trailed off, lost in reflection.

Harper shook her throbbing head. The thesis that she was sane seemed to be again unraveling. She needed to know about that vampire kiss, she needed other answers as well. She asked, "Back then, was that when you laid the groundwork for becoming a starship captain?"

"It had its genesis then, yes."

Again Harper shook her head. "I can't imagine how you've accomplished any of this." She gestured with both hands to take in the spacecraft. "You're contracted to ExxTel; everyone knows about the thoroughness of their information network. I can't see how anyone could possibly slip through such a sieve."

Drake smiled. "What if I told you I have access to my records, that I can input and erase whatever data I choose?"

"I wouldn't believe you," Harper said flatly. Drake's suggestion was preposterous. "They have a standing offer of a billion credits to anyone who can break through their maze of protective programs."

"What use do I have for a billion credits? Self-protection is my single concern. Their systems were indeed interesting and ingenious— they required sixty-five years to penetrate." Drake shrugged at the gaping Harper. "I had more than enough time to devote to the challenge of the puzzle."

It was all too incredible. Too many incredible facts piling one onto the other. She was crazy; Drake was crazy; it was all crazy. Harper said sardonically, "I suppose that's how you rose to become a starship captain—falsifying records?"

"In small part. I obtained education and specific training in unconventional ways, but I advanced along traditional career paths. An enduring human instinct is to avoid nocturnal hours—and so ample opportunities exist for those willing to live and work in the darkness. Periodically I enter ExxTel's files to adjust my name and date of birth and other facts relating to me. In a monolith such as ExxTel, the personnel I interface with come and go, leaving insufficient continuity to bring suspicion."

Harper felt an icy touch of fear. "Am I the only one then who... knows about this?"

Drake studied her. "Over time, few have even remotely suspected. Since the twentieth century my greatest protection has been the refusal to believe vampire legends—especially by scientifically grounded persons such as yourself. To my knowledge, none of the women accompanying me to the Antares asteroid belt have ever added together the clues I cannot help but provide."

And it was by purest accident, Harper admitted ruefully, that she herself had. "There haven't been any men on your voyages?"

"I request only female military liaisons, and the Space Service has always acceded."

Harper blurted, "I suppose you've made love to them as you did with me."

"Yes," Drake said.

Harper forced her stunned mind into motion. If all this was actually true, then those other women who had accompanied Drake...surely she could not have managed to infect them all? Yes, she answered herself, she could have. And if she had, none of them might ever realize it until their deaths decades from now, when they tried to rise from under the straps binding them onto a conveyor feeding them into a crematorium...

"What have you done to me?" she choked. She was hurtling down a corridor of terror. "If you're really a vampire, you satisfy your sexuality only in the act of feeding. What have you done to me?"

"I have enjoyed you fully."

The hair rose on the back of Harper's neck; she rubbed a frenzied hand across it. "In the name of anything sacred," she hissed, "how did you give me your vampire kiss?"

"I have not given it to you, nor to anyone since Eva."

Harper exhaled, her limbs suddenly trembling.

"When my dying Eva wanted me to make love to her, I could not refuse. And I discovered with her the greatest ecstasy of my life. Greater even than with Nadja. Because I learned that another kind of fluid can also nourish me. It too is a vital fluid—from that place in a woman that creates life. You give it generously. You give it during that length of time when I am most fully enjoying you, and even more copiously as you approach and then experience the heights of orgasm."

Looking seriously at Harper, Drake added, "You're turning quite red."

"My Trad upbringing," Harper muttered, rubbing at her flaming face.

Drake continued, "I made love to you only because you wanted me. I come only to a woman who wants me."

Harper shook her head in bafflement. Certainly she had not invited that first approach from Drake...

"I have the capability of assuming mammal form. As a consequence I also have a highly developed olfactory sense. I knew of your desire and arousal, I could smell that nourishment I so keenly enjoy."

Again Harper felt her face flame. Mortified, feeling stripped of every defense, she lashed out, "How could you take such advantage of me? And all those other women? Don't you feel any *responsibility?*"

"Harper, have you not enjoyed what we shared together? How have I taken advantage?"

"You preyed on me. Preyed on all of us. Played with our emotions. You—"

"Harper." Drake pushed a lock of hair from her forehead, then sat up on her chaise and circled her arms around her knees. "Harper, have you at any time felt love for me?"

Harper looked at her. At the creamy smoothness of the pale face, the finely chiseled, aristocratic features, the elegant slenderness. Furious at feeling within her the edges of desire, she hurled the unvarnished, tactless truth: "No."

Drake nodded and smiled, as if Harper were a bright pupil who had found the only logical response to an illogical question. "I've given you nothing to love. Not for decades have I given anything that anyone could love."

"You think that confers some kind of nobility? You *wanted* me, you've made love to me every single night. Didn't you care anything about me at all?"

Her face closing, Drake did not respond.

It occurred to Harper that while Drake had given nothing of herself, she had opened her own self to Drake in every way. She said carefully, "Have you become attached to any of your women companions during your months alone with them in space?"

Drake looked away from her.

"Please. I need you to tell me."

Drake said tonelessly, "You've been a captivating and admirable companion; my physical gratifications have been extraordinary; this has been in all ways the loveliest of voyages. I have given as much physical pleasure as I know how to give, I have taken in return the by-product of your pleasure. Beyond that, since there is no future for us, there is nothing more to be said." She turned resolutely away from Harper.

Studying the poetic handsomeness of Drake's face in profile, she absorbed this response. Her glance fell on the drink Drake had placed on the module beside her. "Tell me," she said, deflecting the topic still vibrating between them, "when you don't have a woman to make love to, where do you get the blood you need?"

Drake turned quickly back to her. "I use existing technology to synthesize it." She seemed relieved at the new direction of Harper's questions. "But synthetic blood is not…" She searched for a term, then said with an amiable shrug, "It is lacking. For you it would be as if you were always surrounded by appetizing food yet limited to consuming only gruel. But it does sustain me, and in a manner which is ethically necessary."

Harper pointed to the tomato juice. "Is that what you…consume?"

"No." Drake smiled. "I like its smell, which seems earthy and warm, and the color, which is…" She trailed off.

"How often must you take your nourishment?"

"It's variable. I can and do frequently exist in a famished state for weeks. After I have truly feasted, as I have during this time with you, then I prefer to exist without food for a lengthy time afterward rather than return to…my gruel."

"You mean you diet between women." She could not account for her sense of betrayal, her jealousy and resentment. "For those few weeks until another woman comes on board."

Drake did not respond.

Harper's ire turned against itself. Why belabor this woman, whose singular and determined morality had redefined the compelling needs of her nature? Harper said, "And you've never told any other women on these voyages anything about this."

"Only you. Since you are the only one who has ever guessed."

Harper voiced a new apprehension: "Why tell me? Aren't you afraid I'll expose you, tear down this whole façade?"

Drake fixed weary eyes on her. "I become ever more bored with the façade. I become less and less patient with the restrictions of my existence."

Harper nodded. In Drake's place her own patience would have exhausted itself centuries ago. She said, "I saw your quarters, the blackness. Do you actually keep a coffin in there?"

Drake chuckled. "That part of the legend is somewhat exaggerated. We do need darkness during the hours of the sun, and complete darkness is most beneficial. The smallness of my quarters, this tiny ship in the vastness of space—it's equivalent enough to a coffin. In my quarters I have collected soil from many places on Earth, especially my own land, and I sleep with it gathered around me. It seems to bring me peace."

Drake smiled at her. "For your own sake I must solemnly caution you against attempting to reveal me. You are indeed sane, but others will probably not agree."

"True," Harper said, grinning at the thought of relating these astounding events to anyone—especially when she herself was convinced only intermittently that she was not hallucinating.

"In any case I am never truly safe," Drake mused. "I know that if I continue to live, one day they will come for me. With their stakes and axes, just as they came so many centuries ago in my village. Human beings always believe their own era to be more enlightened than any before, but they still avoid examination of the origin of their own food, their own blood-drenched sustenance. And of all taboos, cannibalism remains the ultimate perversion. Even those who are not affected by xenophobia would hesitate to extend tolerance to a vampire."

She gazed out at the whirling crystals. "Eva learned that immortality does not bring with it the will or the desire to live. For centuries I have held and kept the power of life. But Harper, more and more I dream about dying. I dream about journeying to a particularly gracious star system—perhaps the Pleiades—and allowing my ship to simply fall into one of its lovely stars. But mostly I dream of returning to Earth."

Drake looked at her; Harper was held unmoving by the grieving dark eyes. "I dream of the sun, Harper. I long for it. I often wonder if, when I walk out into that sun, I will know for an instant its warmth as I remember it, as I used to know it...before it begins the disintegration of my flesh..."

"You have too much to offer..." Harper faltered; there were no words to comfort the immense tragedy of Drake's existence. "You have...priceless gifts for the ages to come."

"Yes." Drake's voice held an ironic edge. "When our voyage is over,

Harper, you will walk away forever and forget. There is no choice."

"Walk away, I must," Harper said slowly. "But forget you, never."

Drake's smile bathed her in its tenderness. "That is the one immortality all of us hope for."

Harper gazed wistfully back at her. "If only I had learned about you sooner. I have two months—only two months—to hear eight centuries of eyewitness Earth history."

"Yes," Drake said, her voice suddenly eager.

Drake's beauty seemed to have acquired a youthful energy and sheen, and Harper looked at her in affection. "I still need to adjust to what you've told me," she said with a grin, "especially about my body being food for you."

"Your body is not my food," Drake gently corrected her. "Your pleasure is my food."

"I know I don't taste like gruel," Harper said, still smiling. "Do I taste like some other specific food?"

"The pleasures of you are infinitely lovely," Drake said softly. "Each night, and throughout the lovemaking of each night, there are differences, you taste differently everywhere. Your mouth is sometimes like sweet spring water, sometimes like cream. Your body varies everywhere in taste and smell, the scents are like grass and rain, sometimes like peaches or apples or berries. Your breasts taste like buttered honey; your thighs contain the most intoxicating spice..." She trailed off, looking closely at Harper.

Feeling the heat in her body rise to her face, knowing she had no defense whatever, Harper said recklessly, "And the place you've left out?"

Drake rose from her chaise, came to her. "Sweet wine that slowly intensifies into flavors I will not attempt to describe."

Taking Drake's hands, Harper murmured, "Is it possible...to return the ship to weightlessness?"

"Of course. Every night, all the way back. But later," she whispered, reaching for Harper. "At this moment I smell sweet wine..."

*　　*　　*

Harper walked down the ramp directly into the debrief section of Moon Station thirteen. She did not look back.

Sergeant Stewart saluted smartly, then commandeered her gear bubble. "Welcome back, Lieutenant." A Briton, he pronounced her ranking as Leftenant. "You look splendid. Had a bit of trouble up there, we heard."

She looked at him sharply.

"The deflection shield," he said, his thin face creasing in puzzlement.

"Oh, that," she said casually, covering her alarm. "A momentary problem for Captain Drake."

"Remarkable work, that. Can't say I know much about her, nobody ever says much. How were the four months with her?"

Harper turned then, and looked back at *Scorpio IV* where the robodrones were already assembling to unload the crystals. It was seven hundred hours, and Drake, she knew, would be in her quarters, those quarters that were as black as the grave...

"Routine," Harper answered the Sergeant. "The mission was routine."

He shrugged. "The onboard data seems fairly clear cut. Debrief shouldn't take more than half an hour, I would think."

Alone in her quarters afterward, she deposited her gear bubble. She scanned messages from Niklaus and several acquaintances she'd made here on Moon Station thirteen. The final message contained a privacy seal. Curious, she entered her I.D. code and pressed the palms of both hands on the I.D. reader.

The striking dark-eyed woman looking back at her wore her black hair cropped short, sheaves of it like petals around her face and down over her forehead. Several mission ribbons hung under the Lieutenant's silver bar on her Space Service jacket.

"Welcome back Lieutenant Harper. My name's Westra, of the Science Corps. I saw the alert come over the base intercom about your shield trouble. When I found out who your captain was, I knew you'd both make it back just fine."

The woman on the screen smiled. *"I was with Captain Drake two years ago on a similar mission to Antares. She advised me then that she could not form emotional attachments to her military passengers, and would not grant me permission to visit her should our paths again intersect—a decision I have no choice but to accept."*

Rapt, Harper stared as the woman on the screen smiled again, a slow, private smile.

"From the repros I've seen of you, you appear to be someone I would find...interesting. If I appear the same way to you, then perhaps we could meet and share a beverage together...and also share some of our memories of Captain Drake..."

The message ended with the printout of a telecode number.

Bemused, Harper played the message back. Then played it back once more, this time without the sound, freezing the frame when that slow, private smile began.

Lieutenant Westra did indeed look interesting, Harper decided. That dark hair, those intelligent dark eyes, that perfectly lovely looking mouth…Smiling, Harper reflected that along with her discovery of the pleasures to be had with a woman, she had also learned that she definitely preferred a dark woman…

What would it be like, she wondered, to share pleasure fully with a woman, to explore and experience what Drake had enjoyed in her?

Staring at the seductively smiling figure on the screen, she absently erased the other messages, including the one from Niklaus. Then she opened her private comm channel and entered the telecode for Lieutenant Westra.

𝔐inimax

❦

ANNA LIVIA

Editor's Note: After writing a fan letter to her favorite author, Natalie Barney, Minnie receives a reply: "Come. I must meet you." But there is no postmark, no return address, no clue whatsoever as how to find her. Minnie begins her search for Natalie Barney in Australia, where she is visiting her mother, Beryl, who coincidentally is employed by Natalie Barney and Renée Vivien. In this excerpt, Minnie and Natalie have just spent their first evening together. Minnie confides in her alter-ego, Milly, and the family's pet parrot, the details of her first visit with Natalie...while Natalie, in turn, confides in Minnie's mother, Beryl.

IN THE BLOOD

FOR THE NEXT few hours she sat down and stood up, lay on her bed, kicked her feet in the swimming pool, made tea, poured the boiling water into the rubbish bin, tried to fit the kettle whistle to a gooseberry fool pot and fed cauliflower cheese to the telephone. The parrot watched her progress with the omniscient benevolence of a parent.

"Natalie Clifford Barney," she declared, "I love you."

The tea and the gooseberry fools, much of which she did manage to put into her mouth and not the sugar bowl, were punctuated with little cries of, "On a park bench, Natalie, at seventy-seven! You glory."

The parrot listened to this thunderbolt and waited for the flash of light to measure the distance between Minnie's instincts and her comprehension.

"Oh!" Minnie ejaculated. "Oh, oh, oh."

For it said in the book that Natalie Barney had been taking a stroll along the Avenue des Anglais in Nice in the glorious year 1954, when she had spotted a good-looking woman and sat down upon a handy bench in order to observe her at liberty. Whereupon, the object of her interest had seated herself beside our heroine, struck up a conversation which was to lead to twenty-three years of pillow talk.

"Oh Natalie," Minnie bleated, "you must have been there all the time."

"If she was seventy-seven in 1954," chirruped the parrot, "just think how old she is today." The parrot was a long-lived old bird itself and in its revered opinion all one lost with the years were one's inhibitions. It was roused from its reverie on its own expertise (which that ungrateful prude of a water snake never got to taste; the parrot was right off reptiles) by peals of laughter.

"Imagine that," Minnie guffawed. "Just imagine that. Gertrude Stein asks Alice Toklas where Natalie gets all her women from. They are standing right in front of a whole café full of people who are hanging on their every word. So Alice says, 'From the toilets of the Louvre Department Store,' when it was benches all along."

"Benches and horse-drawn carriages, and boxes at the opera, cornfields, and the beds of her men friends..." said the parrot, wondering where its next conquest would come from.

"Naturally Natalie wanted revenge. When people began to ask what was going on between Gertrude and Alice, Natalie would say, 'Nothing. They are just good friends.' A clammy, clucking nothing. She made them sound as though they had no legs, and nothing in between. My mother would agree with Natalie. She says that in order to respect people, you must credit them with an active and exuberant sex life."

The parrot could not repress a sigh. It worked most diligently to deserve such respect; whose fault was it that success was so elusive?

"Hmm," murmured Minnie, oblivious of the parrot's psychic distress. "When Renée refused to see her, Natalie took up position beneath her balcony, accompanied by a famous opera singer, serenaded her with gusto if not passion..."

"Huh," croaked the parrot. All passion and no gusto, that was the story of its life.

"When they had done, Natalie threw Renée a bouquet of flowers arranged around a sonnet Natalie had composed."

The parrot stuck its head on one side, began its swaying little dance shuffle, and gave a convincing rendition of *"Viens poupoule."* It had nothing against lesbians and had been an admirer of Natalie Barney's ever since a migrating cuckoo told it of the time Natalie, dressed only in a white nightgown, had herself delivered to Renée in a coffin full of enormous lilies. In its decadent period, when it had insisted on dyeing its feathers black and wearing World War Two dog tags round its neck, the parrot had even fancied itself Natalie's ornithological opposite number, but John's new slide rule, whom it was courting at the time, refused to attempt a Renée Vivien impersonation. That sour, unimaginative instrument had declared it had nothing whatever in common with the young, blond-haired poet, that anyone who could discern any points of comparison between any mathematical instrument and a blond-haired poet was certainly a surrealist, if not worse. The parrot had got a lot of satisfaction the day John came home from the university and declared, "With the mass production of the pocket calculator, the slide rule is dead."

Natalie Barney had accomplished much of which a randy parrot would be proud. At the age of seventeen she had glimpsed that famous high-class prostitute Liane de Pougy riding in a carriage in the Bois de Boulogne. Natalie dressed as a page had gone on bended knee before Liane. It is said that she remained in this position beneath Liane's voluminous skirts in a box at the Paris Opera throughout the whole performance. Whatever was she doing under there? The parrot snickered like a school girl. When Renée left Natalie and surrounded herself with a bullying baroness—the parrot was not absolutely sure what a baroness was; it assumed it must be some kind of bulldog—Natalie had devised the brilliant scheme of swapping seats at the opera with a friend at the last minute so she could sit next to Renée and embrace her. All this was excellent in both conception and execution. But the parrot had a fine sense of degree, and when Natalie repeated her seat-swapping stunt at a seven-hour performance of *Die Gotterdammerung* in Bayreuth it felt its heroine was no longer gloriously immoderate but verging on vulgarity. There was very little a parrot could do in the face of such pomposity but hum *"Viens poupoule"* and change the subject. The parrot hated Wagner. No one would ever suspect that one of being a lesbian.

"They all seemed to agree that Natalie had no ear for music," Minnie mused aloud. The parrot flapped and squawked: Wagner was not music; it was early heavy metal. "But then why use *'Voi che sapete'* as a frontispiece?"

"Cognoscenti's acrostics," said Milly smugly, though if the truth be known, the natural opioids of Flanders Plain had left her with a terrible headache. It is difficult to say "cognoscenti's acrostic" in any tone other than smug. Try it. Try saying it with awe, you sound sarcastic; try it with fear, you sound sarcastic; try it with joy, you know how you sound. "It's all crashingly obvious," Milly continued. The word "crashing" came in at the last moment and had not been planned. It described the headache very well.

"Do tell," said Minnie, sounding sarcastic. She left the book open on a simply ravishing photograph of Natalie at ninety-five.

"Darling, *'Voi che sapete'* means, as you probably know…"

"You who know," said Minnie, "you know I know."

"I know you know," agreed Milly undeterred.

"You who know I know you know," parroted the parrot.

"Natalie, being unmusical," Milly ploughed on regardless, "was primarily concerned with the words. The music of Mozart was an agreeable extra."

The parrot choked on its cuttlefish.

"She used that aria at the front of her book as a secret message which only those who *did* know could decode. The song of a girl dressed as a boy, falling in love with everything in skirts, who wants the ladies already acquainted with love to look into her heart and tell her if that is the emotion which burns there. Now, Minnie, what could that possibly be about? Whose love is continually in question, continually in doubt? Renée died in 1909, Natalie in 1972, but you have recently received messages from each. How is this possible?"

"Post took a long time," suggested the parrot, ignored as usual.

"Clearly Renée knew she would live forever," Milly pursued her train of thought, forcing the headache into a corner. Whenever anyone says "clearly," it signals their intent to lecture. Minnie decided to nip it in the bud.

"*I* find this cult of nostalgia merely escapist. A desperate diversion from present political doldrums."

"I'm not talking heritage," Milly exploded, "I'm talking vampire."

IN THE BUBBLE AND SQUEAK OF LIFE

Beryl had just wiped up the last of the tortoise and thrown its remains in a body bag when the phone rang.

"It was dreadful and it was my fault. Sheer bloody-minded, insensitive boorishness. She is my perfect beautiful darling and I treated her shamefully." Beryl's cue to settle down in the winged leather armchair in Mr. Vivien's office, yearn for a hot cup of tea, and say, "Now, Natalie, bloody-minded, insensitive and boorish you may be, dear, but you usually manage to live with yourself."

"She'll never want to see me again."

"Why? Whatever have you done?"

"I can't tell you. I just called to say that I am about to do the honorable thing. I am going to open the shutters and let the hard light of day show me up and shrivel me up as the monster I truly am."

"I wouldn't do that if I were you."

"Why not?" A suspicion of hope glanced across Natalie's heart.

"Once you're gone and your body is a heap of dust on the deck you will never be able to speak to her, make amends." Beryl was still rather out of breath from the thirty-yard sprint through the Octagonal Gallery, over the marble staircase and up the vanadium spiral. She had not yet managed to convince Mr. Vivien that a telephone in the conservatory outside the 1900 Room would not be an anachronism as long as they were careful and did not abbreviate its name to "phone." Telephones, she argued, had been around since at least 1837. Whereupon Mr. Vivien would succumb to a bad dose of spleen and the matter would not be broached for another fortnight.

"I would tear the heart from my body. I would wring the blood from it and present it to her on a silver platter. I would cut it up with a knife and fork and swallow it."

The extravagance of her language was a salve in itself. The operatic bleakness a reminder of past glories.

"I don't think she'd like that very much. Come away from the shutters and sit down on your cozy old sofa. Not on the coffin, Natalie. It'll only make you morbid. Help yourself to a long cool glass of Rhesus on the rocks. Now, tell me."

"*Era per me un'angela, una creatura di sogno. Era la mia tesora.* (She was my angel, my dream, my treasure.)"

"I expect she still is."

"You're very calm."

"I think that's my role, isn't it. That's why you rang me."

Even vampires look to mothers for emotional support, and since their own have almost always died before them, and since as Natalie explained to Minnie, breeders cannot become vampires, one often finds respectable married women servicing a small coterie of the undead.

"She wrote to me, she came out of nowhere, she admired my work. I told her 'Come. I must meet you.' I begged her to hurry. She came halfway round the world to be with me. She swam out to my yacht in the high seas. She was weary, nay, exhausted. I had them run a warm bath, I spread a table before her. She ate and drank and then..."

"Yes?"

"Oh I falter, words fail me."

"Come now. I'm sure you've told me far worse about your past."

"She was sitting on the sofa, right where I am now. I still smell the essence of camellia from the bath oil. There she was, beside me, her plump soft arm almost touching mine. And I..."

"Yes?"

"I talked to her. I don't know what got into me. I talked to her for hours. I used her as a sounding board for everything that was on my mind. I meant to make love to her, you must believe me. I meant to be the best, most attentive, athletic lover she ever had. But I was so engrossed in my own thoughts that somehow I forgot the purpose of her visit."

"Natalie, you can save the situation. Genuine sentiment will win out over mere clumsiness, or the literature of the world is in jeopardy. Here is what you should do…"

"Yes?"

"Ring that poor young woman up and invite her out on a proper, old-fashioned date."

"A date?"

"Yes. Today you will send her a five-pound box of chocolates and some roses."

"A bouquet of lilies and orchids, a spray of violets, a sweet-smelling nosegay of lilies of the valley, a soprano to serenade her."

Before Natalie could orchestrate a repetition of her more famous romantic feats, Beryl cut her short.

"No. Today roses and chocolates. Tonight an invitation to go dancing. Tomorrow a corsage the color of the lady's dress. The heyday of the classic date was circa 1955. You will need a tuxedo."

Beryl set to work rethreading the crystals on the chandelier. Fortunately none were broken but it was a fiddly business. She was worried that the sharp sides might cut her fingers, but if she wore gloves she couldn't feel the little hooks and match them up with the little holes. She turned the radio on for something soothing while she worked.

"We interrupt this broadcast to announce that in a secret late night session the state legislature decided that, in line with the rest of Australia, it is no longer lawful for a local authority to intentionally promote v*****ism or to support the publication of any literature which might be considered to present the v****** lifestyle as an attractive alternative to the nuclear family. As the state premier explained, 'We in Western Australia have always prided ourselves on being geographically isolated from the worst of the corruption and vice now sweeping the Eastern states. We have until now had no v****** laws because, like Queen Victoria before us, we have not believed that v******s existed. Many people will be puzzled as to the implications of the new legislation. As a guideline to the areas affected I would like to give some prominent examples and set everybody's minds at rest. Certain films now on general release will be withdrawn forthwith: *Brides of Dr****** starring Christopher Lee, *The Hunger,* starring Catherine Deneuve and David Bowie, *Daughters of Darkness,* starring Delphine Seyrig, and

Velvet V******. All books by the author Bram Stoker will be removed from the shelves of the state libraries.'

"Glad you could join us, Premier. A report just in from London says a group of anti-v****** protesters have torn down a blue plaque commemorating Bram Stoker's Chelsea home. Meanwhile we have been asked to warn listeners that if any of you suspect that you may be living next door to a v******, please, please be careful; do not approach the suspect, do not accept any invitations from the suspect such as offers of a meal or coffee, do not lure the suspect into a deserted glade. Many people believe even in this day and age that v******s may be killed by running water, the smell of garlic, or the sight of the True Cross. This is superstitious twaddle and poppycock.

"V******s should be pulled out of their coffins and exposed to the light of day but, we repeat but, only by duly authorized personnel wearing rubber gloves, mouth-guards and dental dams, in case of accidental contact. If you see or hear anything irregular, contact the proper authorities immediately but remember: a person who sleeps all day is as likely to be an invalid as a v******, the presence of a great space between the upper median incisors, an exaggerated development of the incisors compared with the canines, and a growth of hair on the neck may all be perfectly normal signs of masculinity; sexual intercourse within the hallowed confines of the family can include some lovebites, so if you see your next-door neighbor suddenly wearing a long silk scarf round her neck to conceal those telltale hickeys, she may well have been to bed with her husband."

The rest of the broadcast gave details of the new measures in process to impound all property belonging to proven v******s. Beryl shook her head. Her dreams were so often prophetic.

FILMOGRAPHY

Because the Dawn
1988. Amy Goldstein. USA.
> A female vampire is being pursued by an aggressive female fashion photographer.

Blood and Roses (or Et Mourir de Plaisir)
1961. Roger Vadim. France.
> The vampire craves the blood of both women and men. In the American version, censors removed over ten minutes of lesbian footage.

Blood Ceremony (or Ceremonia Sangrienta)
1973. Jorge Grau. Spain.
> Set in 17th century Hungary, the Countess Elizabeth Bathory bathes in the blood of young women brought to her by her vampire husband.

Blood of Dracula
1957. Herbert L. Strock. UK.
> An unpopular female student is turned into a vampire by an attentive female chemistry teacher. Part of the "I Was A Teenage…" series.

Blood-Spattered Bride (or La Novia Ensangrentada)
1972. Vincente Aranda. Spain.
> A young bride meets an enigmatic woman vampire.

Carmilla
1990. Gabriella Beaumont. USA.
> Made for cable movie based on the novella "Carmilla," but also drawing elements from Christabel. Set on a post-civil war southern plantation.

Countess Dracula
1971. Peter Sasdy. UK.
> A psychological/horror thriller featuring Ingrid Pitt as the Countess Bathory, who accidentally discovers that bathing in the blood of virgins will keep her young.

La Danza Macabra
1963. Anthony Dawson and Antonio Margheriti. Italy.
Allegedly Poe-based, and notable for one of the first appearances
of lesbianism in the cycle of lesbian vampire movies.

Daughters of Darkness (or *Le Rouge aux Lèvres*)
1971. Harry Kumel. Belgium.
A couple on their honeymoon stop at a Belgian hotel where they
meet the Countess Bathory and her female companion. As the
young husband reveals himself to be a sado-masochist, the
Countess supports and counsels the young wife who eventually
becomes her consort and companion.

Dracula's Daughter
1936. Lambert Hillyer. USA.
The Countess Marya Zaleska, Dracula's daughter, is the unwilling
inheritor of her father's curse. One scene, in which the victim is a
female model, has strong erotic overtones.

La Filha de Dracula
1972. Jesus Franco. Portugal.
A dying woman reveals to her daughter, Maria Karnstein, that she
is a descendent of Count Dracula.

Le Frisson des Vampires
1970. Jean Rollin. France.
A honeymooning couple find themselves in a medieval castle
inhabited by two aging hippies and their vampire mistress, a
"butch" bisexual vampire in leather and chains.

The Hunger
1983. Tony Scott. USA.
The vampire, Catherine Deneuve, aware that her lover and companion is dying, pursues the female doctor he has enlisted to help
stop his aging process.

Lust for a Vampire (or *To Love A Vampire*)
1970. Jimmy Sangster. UK.
The second in the Hammer Studios "Karnstein Trilogy."
Carmilla haunts a girls' finishing school, abducting both teachers
and students.

Lust of the Vampire (or *I, Vampiri*)
1957. Riccardo Freda. Italy.
A mad doctor drains the blood from young women to maintain the youth of his beloved Duchess, a character based on the Countess Bathory.

The Mark of Lilith
1986. Isiling Mack-Nataf. UK.
Lilia, a white bisexual vampire, meets up with a black lesbian researcher whose perspectives jolt her out of a blindness caused by patriarchy.

La Noche de Walpurgis
1970. Leon Klimovsky. Spain.
The Countess Waldessa, based on the Countess Bathory, is revived by two young women, only to do battle with the werewolf in the form of Count Waldemar.

Terror in the Crypt (or *La Maldicion de los Karnsteins*)
1962. Camillo Mastrocinque. Spain.
It appears that the daughter of Count Karnstein has inherited the vampire curse.

Twins of Evil
1971. John Hough. UK.
Third in the Hammer Studios "Karnstein Trilogy." Count Karnstein battles over the fate of a set of twins, with one twin eventually becoming vampirized. The Count inadvertently resuscitates Carmilla/Mircalla in the process.

The Vampire Lovers
1970. Roy Ward Baker. UK.
First in the Hammer Studios "Karnstein Trilogy," Carmilla returns as both Marcilla and Carmilla. Carmilla's preferred victims are bitten on the breast. The others are bitten on the neck.

The Vampire of the Opera (or *Il Vampiro dell'Opera*)
1964. Renato Polselli. Italy.
A group of actors enter a deserted opera house. A mysterious woman follows a stranger into the basement, only to return as a vampire. One by one, she seduces the women, and then the men, in the acting troop.

Vampyr
1931. Carl-Theodor Dreyer. Denmark.
Although said to be inspired by Carmilla, there is no evidence of lesbianism in *Vampyr*. The vampire is an evil old woman who is vamping a young woman of the village.

Vampyres
1974. Joseph Larras. UK.
A pair of lesbian vampires lure unsuspecting men to their lair.

Vampyros Lesbos
1970. Jesus Franco. Spain.
A female descendent of Count Dracula entices young women to her lair on an isolated island.

The Velvet Vampire
1971. Stephanie Rothman. USA.
A bisexual vampire living in the desert lures a young couple to her home and seduces them both.

Le Viol du Vampire
1968. Jean Rollin. France.
Attempts are made to free two young women from a vampire curse.

SOURCES

Armstrong, Toni L. "Female Vampires in Films and on TV." *Hot Wire*. November 1987. pp. 46–47, 62.

Garber, Eric and Lyn Paleo. "Selected Films and Videos." *Uranian Worlds: A Guide to Alternative Sexuality in Science Fiction, Fantasy, and Horror*. Second Edition. G.K. Hall and Co., Boston. 1990.

Hardy, Phil. *The Encyclopedia of Horror Movies*. Harper and Row, New York. 1986.

Pattison, Barrie. "Filmography." *The Seal of Dracula*. Bounty Books, New York. 1975.

Silver, Alain and James Ursini. *The Vampire Film*. A.S. Barnes & Co., New Jersey. 1975.

Weiss, Andrea. *Vampires and Violets: Lesbians in the Cinema*. Jonathan Cape, Pub., London. 1992.

Zimmerman, Bonnie. "Daughters of Darkness: Lesbian Vampires." *Jump Cut.* Nos. 23–24. March 1981. pp. 23–24.

BIBLIOGRAPHY

POEMS AND SHORT STORIES

Califia, Pat. "The Vampire." *Macho Sluts: Erotic Fiction.* Alyson Publications, Boston. 1988.

Coleridge, Samuel. "Christabel." *The Portable Coleridge.* Viking Press, Inc., New York. 1950.

Forrest, Katharine V. "Oh Captain, My Captain." *Dreams and Swords* by Katherine V. Forrest. Naiad Press, Tallahassee. 1987.

LeFanu, J. Sheridan. "Carmilla." *Best Ghost Stories* by J. Sheridan LeFanu. Dover Pub., New York. 1964.

Lindsey, Karen. "Vampire." *The Second Wave.* V. 2, No. 2. 1972. p. 36.

Pizarnik, Alejandra. "The Bloody Countess." *Other Fires: Short Fiction by Latin American Women Writers* edited by Alberto Manguel. Clarkson N. Potter, Inc., New York. 1986.

Sommers, Robbi. "Lilith." *Pleasures.* Naiad Press, Talahassee. 1989.

Woodrow, Terry. "Dracula Retold." *Lesbian Bedtime Stories.* Tough Dove Books, Little River. 1989.

ESSAYS, FILM AND LITERARY CRITICISM

Armstrong, Toni L. "Female Vampires in Films and on TV." *Hot Wire.* November 1987. pp. 46–7, 62.

Craft, Christopher. "Kiss Me With Those Red Lips: Gender and Inversion in Bram Stoker's *Dracula.*" *Representations.* 1984, pp. 107–133.

Damon, Gene. "Lesbiana." *The Ladder*. February-March 1971, p. 36.

Faderman, Lilian. "Lesbian Evil." *Surpassing the Love of Men: Romantic Friendship and Love Between Women from the Renaissance to the Present*. William Morrow and Co., New York. 1981.

Fiedler, Leslie. *Freaks*. Simon and Schuster, New York. 1977.

Foster, David William. *Gay and Lesbian Themes in Latin American Fiction*. University of Texas Press, Austin. 1991.

Garber, Eric and Lyn Paleo. *Uranian Worlds: A Guide to Alternative Sexuality in Science Fiction, Fantasy, and Horror*. Second Edition. G.K. Hall and Co., Boston. 1990.

Gordon, Joan. "Tiny Baby Bite: Vampirism and Breastfeeding." *Hot Wire*. November 1987. pp. 44–5, 59.

Gomez, Jewelle. "Writing Vampire Fiction: Recasting the Mythology." *Hot Wire*. November 1987. pp. 42–3, 60.

Halberstam, Judith. "Sucking Blood: Why We Love Vampires." *On Our Backs*. March/April 1993. v. 9, no. 4. pp. 10, 41.

Holte, James Craig. "The Vampire." *Mythical and Fabulous Creatures: A Source Book and Resource Guide*. Greenwood Press, New York. 1987.

Kuhn, Annette with Susannah Radstone. *Women in Film: An International Guide*. Fawcett Columbine, New York. 1990.

McNally, Raymond T. *Dracula Was a Woman: In Search of the Blood Countess of Transylvania*. McGraw Hill, New York. 1983.

Pirie, David. *The Vampire Cinema*. Crescent Books, New York. 1977.

Silver, Alain, and James Ursini. "The Female Vampire." *The Vampire Film*. A.S. Barnes and Co., New Jersey. 1975.

Twitchell, James B. *The Living Dead: A Study of the Vampire in Romantic Literature*. Duke University Press. 1981.

Weiss, Andrea. "Vampire Lovers." *Vampires and Violets: Lesbians in the Cinema.* Jonathan Cape, London. 1992.

Waugh, Charles. "Introduction." *Vamps: An Anthology of Female Vampire Stories.* DAW Books. 1987.

Zimmerman, Bonnie. "Daughters of Darkness: Lesbian Vampires." *Jump Cut.* No. 23–24. March 1981, pp. 23–4.

Zimmerman, Bonnie. *The Safe Sea of Women: Lesbian Fiction 1969–1989.* Beacon Press, Boston. 1990.

NOVELS

Bergstrom, Elaine. *Daughter of the Night.* Jove Publications, Inc., New York. 1992.

Gomez, Jewelle. *The Gilda Stories.* Firebrand Books, Ithaca. 1991.

Livia, Anna. *Minimax.* Eighth Mountain. 1992.

Minns, Karen Marie Christa. *Virago.* Naiad Press, Tallahassee. 1990.

Scott, Jody. *I, Vampire.* Ace, New York. 1984.

Strieber, Whitley. *The Hunger.* Morrow Pub., New York. 1981.

About the Authors

Elaine Bergstrom is the author of four vampire novels, including *Blood Alone, Blood Rites, Shattered Glass,* and *Daughter of the Night* (The Berkeley Publishing Group, 1992).

Pat Califia's 1988 collection of short stories, *Macho Sluts* (Alyson Publications, 1988), broke new ground in lesbian erotica. She has since published a science fiction novel, *Doc and Fluff* (Alyson Publications, 1990), and a second collection of stories, *Melting Point* (Alyson Publications, 1993). She is editing a scandalous pansexual short story collection, *Doing It For Daddy,* and working on a sequel to *Coming to Power* (Alyson Publications, 1982), entitled *The Second Coming,* with her partner Robin Sweeney.

Katherine V. Forrest was born in Canada. She is the author of the novels *Curious Wine* (1983); *Daughters of a Coral Dawn* (1984); *Amateur City* (1984); *An Emergence of Green* (1986); *Murder at the Nightwood Bar* (1987); a short story collection, *Dreams and Swords* (1987); *The Beverly Malibu* (1989) winner of the Lambda Literary Award for Mystery; and *Murder by Tradition* (1991), also winner of the Lambda Literary Award for Mystery. Her novels and story collection are published by Naiad Press. Her articles and book reviews have appeared in a number of publications including *The Los Angeles Times.* She is Senior Science Fiction Editor for Naiad Press, a member of PEN International, and a jurist for the Southern California PEN fiction award.

Jewelle Gomez is an activist, teacher, arts administrator, and literary critic. A transplanted Bostonian, she has lived in New York City for twenty years, most recently in Brooklyn. *The Gilda Stories* (Firebrand Books, 1991) won two Lambda Literary Awards, for Lesbian Fiction and Science Fiction/Fantasy. She is also the author of a collection of essays, *Forty-Three Septembers* (Firebrand Books, 1993).

Joseph Sheridan LeFanu (1814–1873) was a Dubliner born to a moderately well-to-do family of Hugenot descent. His family emigrated to Ireland in the 1730s. A graduate of Trinity College in Dublin, he first studied for the bar, but soon renounced law for journalism and became the editor and publisher of several newspapers and periodicals in the Dublin area. LeFanu wrote thirty supernatural stories, including the impossibly rare *Ghost Stories and Tales of Mystery* (Dublin and London

1851) and *Chronicles of Golden Friars* (London 1871); *The Purcell Papers* (London 1880), edited by Alfred P. Graves; *Madam Crowls' Ghost and Other Stories* edited by M.R. James (London 1923); and *In a Glass Darkly* (London 1872), in which "Carmilla" first appeared.

Anna Livia is the author of four novels, two collections of short stories and an edited translation of the work of Natalie Clifford Barney. She recently completed *Bruised Fruit*, a novel about sex, secrets and sudden sympathy set in London and San Francisco. She is also translating *L'Ange et les pervers* (*The Angel and the Perverts*) for New York University Press—a novel set in 1930s Paris about a hermaphrodite who spends half her life as "Marion" in the lesbian literary salons and half his life as "Mario" in the gay opium dens of the times.

Karen Marie Christa Minns, a gemini writer (1956), believes in the absolute necessity of heroes. She also answers all of her mail. Works from Naiad Press include: *Virago* (1990), a lesbian vampire allegory nominated for two Lambda Literary awards, Debut Writer and Science Fiction/Fantasy, and *Calling Rain* (1991), an eco-feminist adventure.

Jody Scott won a Mystery Writers of America award for her novel *Cure It With Honey.* She is the author of three other novels, *Down Will Come Baby, Starmasters and I,* and *Passing for Human.*

Robbi Sommers was born in Cincinnati, Ohio in 1950. She lives in Northern California where she divides her time between dental hygiene, motherhood, and writing. The author of three collections of lesbian erotica from Naiad Press, *Pleasures* (1989), *Players* (1990), and *Uncertain Companions* (1992), her remaining free time is consumed by relentless research.

zana was bitten by the lesbian-land bug (not dracula!) thirteen years ago and has lived in community since then. She is forty-six, Jewish, disabled, from lower middle class background, and trying to unlearn patriarchy inch by inch. Working in her vegetable garden is helping her get through the ups and downs of menopause.

About the Editor

Pam Keesey is a writer, editor, and book reviewer living in Minneapolis. She received a B.A. in Latin American Studies and International Relations from Hamline University in St. Paul, Minnesota and is currently completing her thesis on lesbian vampires in literature for a Masters in Women's Studies from the University of Bradford in West Yorkshire, England. She is Head Librarian at the Resource Center of the Americas, an education and information center on issues relating to Latin America. Her articles, reviews, and bibliographies have appeared in *Hurricane Alice, off our backs, Connexions, Women's Studies International Forum,* and *Barricada Internacional.* This is her first book.

Books from Cleis Press

Lesbian Studies

Boomer: Railroad Memoirs
by Linda Niemann.
ISBN: 0-939416-55-7 12.95 paper.

The Case of the Not-So-Nice Nurse
by Mabel Maney.
ISBN: 0-939416-75-1 24.95 cloth;
ISBN: 0-939416-76-X 9.95 paper.

Daughters of Darkness: Lesbian Vampire Stories
edited by Pam Keesey.
ISBN: 0-939416-77-8 24.95 cloth;
ISBN: 0-939416-78-6 9.95 paper.

Different Daughters: A Book by Mothers of Lesbians
edited by Louise Rafkin.
ISBN: 0-939416-12-3 21.95 cloth;
ISBN: 0-939416-13-1 9.95 paper.

Different Mothers: Sons & Daughters of Lesbians Talk About Their Lives edited by Louise Rafkin.
ISBN: 0-939416-40-9 24.95 cloth;
ISBN: 0-939416-41-7 9.95 paper.

Hothead Paisan: Homicidal Lesbian Terrorist by Diane DiMassa.
ISBN: 0-939416-73-5 12.95 paper.

A Lesbian Love Advisor
by Celeste West.
ISBN: 0-939416-27-1 24.95 cloth;
ISBN: 0-939416-26-3 9.95 paper.

Long Way Home: The Odyssey of a Lesbian Mother and Her Children
by Jeanne Jullion.
ISBN: 0-939416-05-0 8.95 paper.

More Serious Pleasure: Lesbian Erotic Stories and Poetry
edited by the Sheba Collective.
ISBN: 0-939416-48-4 24.95 cloth;
ISBN: 0-939416-47-6 9.95 paper.

The Night Audrey's Vibrator Spoke: A Stonewall Riots Collection
by Andrea Natalie.
ISBN: 0-939416-64-6 8.95 paper.

Queer and Pleasant Danger: Writing Out My Life by Louise Rafkin.
ISBN: 0-939416-60-3 24.95 cloth;
ISBN: 0-939416-61-1 9.95 paper.

Rubyfruit Mountain: A Stonewall Riots Collection
by Andrea Natalie.
ISBN: 0-939416-74-3 9.95 paper.

Serious Pleasure: Lesbian Erotic Stories and Poetry
edited by the Sheba Collective.
ISBN: 0-939416-46-8 24.95 cloth;
ISBN: 0-939416-45-X 9.95 paper.

Sexual Politics

Good Sex: Real Stories from Real People by Julia Hutton.
ISBN: 0-939416-56-5 24.95 cloth;
ISBN: 0-939416-57-3 12.95 paper.

Madonnarama: Essays on Sex and Popular Culture edited by Lisa Frank and Paul Smith.
ISBN: 0-939416-72-7 24.95 cloth;
ISBN: 0-939416-71-9 9.95 paper.

Sex Work: Writings by Women in the Sex Industry
edited by Frédérique Delacoste and Priscilla Alexander.
ISBN: 0-939416-10-7 24.95 cloth;
ISBN: 0-939416-11-5 16.95 paper.

Susie Bright's Sexual Reality: A Virtual Sex World Reader
by Susie Bright.
ISBN: 0-939416-58-1 24.95 cloth;
ISBN: 0-939416-59-X 9.95 paper.

Susie Sexpert's Lesbian Sex World
by Susie Bright.
ISBN: 0-939416-34-4 24.95 cloth;
ISBN: 0-939416-35-2 9.95 paper.

POLITICS OF HEALTH

The Absence of the Dead Is Their Way of Appearing
by Mary Winfrey Trautmann.
ISBN: 0-939416-04-2 8.95 paper.

AIDS: The Women edited by Ines Rieder and Patricia Ruppelt.
ISBN: 0-939416-20-4 24.95 cloth;
ISBN: 0-939416-21-2 9.95 paper

Don't: A Woman's Word
by Elly Danica.
ISBN: 0-939416-23-9 21.95 cloth;
ISBN: 0-939416-22-0 8.95 paper

1 in 3: Women with Cancer Confront an Epidemic
edited by Judith Brady.
ISBN: 0-939416-50-6 24.95 cloth;
ISBN: 0-939416-49-2 10.95 paper.

Voices in the Night: Women Speaking About Incest
edited by Toni A. H. McNaron and Yarrow Morgan.
ISBN: 0-939416-02-6 9.95 paper.

With the Power of Each Breath: A Disabled Women's Anthology
edited by Susan Browne, Debra Connors and Nanci Stern.
ISBN: 0-939416-09-3 24.95 cloth;
ISBN: 0-939416-06-9 10.95 paper.

Woman-Centered Pregnancy and Birth
by the Federation of Feminist Women's Health Centers.
ISBN: 0-939416-03-4 11.95 paper.

FICTION

Another Love by Erzsébet Galgóczi.
ISBN: 0-939416-52-2 24.95 cloth;
ISBN: 0-939416-51-4 8.95 paper.

Cosmopolis: Urban Stories by Women edited by Ines Rieder.
ISBN: 0-939416-36-0 24.95 cloth;
ISBN: 0-939416-37-9 9.95 paper.

A Forbidden Passion
by Cristina Peri Rossi.
ISBN: 0-939416-64-0 24.95 cloth;
ISBN: 0-939416-68-9 9.95 paper.

In the Garden of Dead Cars
by Sybil Claiborne.
ISBN: 0-939416-65-4 24.95 cloth;
ISBN: 0-939416-66-2 9.95 paper.

Night Train To Mother
by Ronit Lentin.
ISBN: 0-939416-29-8 24.95 cloth;
ISBN: 0-939416-28-X 9.95 paper.

The One You Call Sister: New Women's Fiction
edited by Paula Martinac.
ISBN: 0-939416-30-1 24.95 cloth;
ISBN: 0-939416031-X 9.95 paper.

Only Lawyers Dancing
by Jan McKemmish.
ISBN: 0-939416-70-0 24.95 cloth;
ISBN: 0-939416-69-7 9.95 paper.

Unholy Alliances: New Women's Fiction edited by Louise Rafkin.
ISBN: 0-939416-14-X 21.95 cloth;
ISBN: 0-939416-15-8 9.95 paper.

The Wall by Marlen Haushofer.
ISBN: 0-939416-53-0 24.95 cloth;
ISBN: 0-939416-54-9 paper.

LATIN AMERICA

Beyond the Border: A New Age in Latin American Women's Fiction edited by Nora Erro-Peralta and Caridad Silva-Núñez.
ISBN: 0-939416-42-5 24.95 cloth;
ISBN: 0-939416-43-3 12.95 paper.

The Little School: Tales of Disappearance and Survival in Argentina by Alicia Partnoy.
ISBN: 0-939416-08-5 21.95 cloth;
ISBN: 0-939416-07-7 9.95 paper.

Revenge of the Apple by Alicia Partnoy.
ISBN: 0-939416-62-X 24.95 cloth;
ISBN: 0-939416-63-8 8.95 paper.

You Can't Drown the Fire: Latin American Women Writing in Exile edited by Alicia Partnoy.
ISBN: 0-939416-16-6 24.95 cloth;
ISBN: 0-939416-17-4 9.95 paper.

AUTOBIOGRAPHY, BIOGRAPHY, LETTERS

Peggy Deery: An Irish Family at War by Nell McCafferty.
ISBN: 0-939416-38-7 24.95 cloth;
ISBN: 0-939416-39-5 9.95 paper.

The Shape of Red: Insider/Outsider Reflections by Ruth Hubbard and Margaret Randall.
ISBN: 0-939416-19-0 24.95 cloth;
ISBN: 0-939416-18-2 9.95 paper.

Women & Honor: Some Notes on Lying by Adrienne Rich.
ISBN: 0-939416-44-1 3.95 paper.

ANIMAL RIGHTS

And a Deer's Ear, Eagle's Song and Bear's Grace: Relationships Between Animals and Women edited by Theresa Corrigan and Stephanie T. Hoppe.
ISBN: 0-939416-38-7 24.95 cloth;
ISBN: 0-939416-39-5 9.95 paper.

With a Fly's Eye, Whale's Wit and Woman's Heart: Relationships Between Animals and Women edited by Theresa Corrigan and Stephanie T. Hoppe.
ISBN: 0-939416-24-7 24.95 cloth;
ISBN: 0-939416-25-5 9.95 paper.

ORDERING BOOKS

Since 1980, Cleis Press has published progressive books by women. We welcome your order and will ship your books as quickly as possible. Individual orders must be prepaid (U.S. dollars only). Please add 15% shipping. Pennsylvania residents add 6% sales tax. Mail orders to Cleis Press, P.O. Box 8933, Pittsburgh, Pennsylvania 15221. MasterCard and Visa orders: include account number, expiration date, and signature. Fax your credit card order to (412) 937-1567. Or, telephone us Monday through Friday, 9 am–5 pm EST at (412) 937-1555.